MARIA THERESA

ASMAR

A CHALDEAN WOMAN'S STORY
DURING THE 1800s

WEAM NAMOU

HERMiZ
PUBLiSHING

Library of Congress Cataloging-in-Publication Data
2024911741

Namou, Weam

Maria Theresa Asmar
A Chaldean Woman's Story During the 1800s
(nonfiction)

ISBN: 978-1-945371-09-7

First Edition

Published in the United States of America by:
Hermiz Publishing, Inc.
Sterling Heights, MI

10 9 8 7 6 5 4 3 2 1

Books by Weam Namou

The Feminine Art

The Mismatched Braid

The Flavor of Cultures

I Am a Mute Iraqi with a Voice

The Great American Family
A Story of Political Disenchantment

Iraqi Americans: The War Generation

Iraqi Americans: Witnessing a Genocide

Iraqi Americans: The Lives of the Artists

Healing Wisdom for a Wounded World
My Life-Changing Journey Through a Shamanic School
(Book 1) (Book 2) (Book 3) (Book 4)

Mesopotamian Goddesses
Unveiling Your Feminine Power

Pomegranate

Little Baghdad
A Memoir about an Endangered People in an American City

The Onedia Man

Joseph Naayem
A Chaldean Priest's Story During the 1915 Genocide

CONTENTS

THIS BOOK IS DEDICATED TO MARIA THERESA ASMAR

PREFACE

Twelve years ago, *The Chaldean News* asked me to cover a lecture by Emily Porter, an Iraqi British professor of Art and History. She had traveled from her hometown of Great Britain to work on a project at the Metropolitan Museum of Arts in New York. Before returning home, she visited Michigan to talk about a book she had recently translated from English to Arabic and republished, called *Memoirs of a Babylonian Princess*. Porter spoke about her discovery during a lecture held on June 25, 2012, at Shenandoah Country Club, an event hosted by the Chaldean Cultural Center, a place which seven years later, became my second home.

I sat next to the parents of Dr. Mona Hanna Attisha, and chit-chatted a bit, having gotten to know them from previous interactions, before Emily stood at the podium and introduced *Memoirs of a Babylonian Princess*, written by Maria Therese Asmar. I had never heard of Maria Theresa Asmar, even though she was brought up in Telkaif, my parents' and grandparents' birthplace, and took much pride in it. During her time, and that of my ancestors, the village was inhabited mostly by Christians. That changed when ISIS invaded Telkaif in 2014.

Maria's uncle was a Chaldean priest during the Ottoman Empire rule in Iraq. She ended up traveling alone to various countries in the Middle East and Europe, met with aristocrats including the Pope and Queen Victoria, and she wrote about her experiences, which were published in Great Britain in 1844.

"The religious men of Telkaif undermined her work and

even ridiculed it while in England it was a success," Emily said. "And it's the Americans, not her own people, who brought her back to life in a book that acknowledged her as an important figure in the nineteenth century."

I imagined the influence this book could have had on me during my younger years when I thought of myself as the eccentric girl in my community. Chaldeans are an ethnic and religious minority group that trace their roots to Mesopotamia, modern-day Iraq. They belong to the Chaldean Catholic faith, an Eastern Rite of the Catholic Church. Our culture places a strong emphasis on family, community, and tradition.

Chaldean women play an important role in maintaining social cohesion, passing down culture and imparting values to younger generations. However, Chaldean women have historically had more restricted roles and opportunities compared to men. Society often expected them to marry at a young age, have children, and focus their energies on the home and family. This belief changed over the years as more Chaldean women pursued higher education, careers and financial independence. Some still face resistance and scrutiny from conservative elements within the community. The experience of immigration and adapting to Western cultures has also helped open up new opportunities for Chaldean women. But it also creates tension between traditional and modern ideals of femininity.

While going home that night, I couldn't stop thinking about the hidden gem of a memoir that had been kept from the community for over a century. I had met a woman, Maria, whom I felt I should have known long ago. The discovery made me both happy and sad. When I turned in the article to the magazine, my editor said, "I love your story! Maybe you are Maria reincarnated?"

"Maybe," I thought.

"I shall call you Weam-Maria from now on."

Thus began an inspiration that would shape the next decade of my life. Maria's story sparked in me a sense of kinship, strength, and validation for my own desires of writing, traveling, and my faith in God. Though from different eras, we shared the struggle of Chaldean women pursuing ambitions beyond the expectations of our community. Maria's long forgotten memoir had found new life, empowering another Chaldean woman nearly two centuries later.

Ten years after our initial introduction, I invited Emily Porter to give an online lecture series about Maria Theresa Asmar, again hosted by the Chaldean Cultural Center, which now housed the world's first and only Chaldean museum. By then, I'd become the executive director of this institution. This place served a multitude of meaningful purposes, including reminding me of my roots, the very roots that Maria and I share.

The Chaldeans are an ancient ethnic and religious minority group indigenous to the Mesopotamian region, the cradle of civilization that encompasses modern-day Iraq. Despite their deep roots in this historical heartland, the Chaldeans have endured centuries of persecution, displacement, and attempts to erase their distinct cultural identity.

The inhabitants of Chaldea, the Chaldeans, briefly came to rule Babylon, so its people were assimilated into Babylonia. They were the driving force behind the advancement of Babylonian astronomy and science, and their philosophers refined the already established observations and formulated sophisticated theories to describe the cosmological phenomena. Chaldea's early mathematicians devised a system dividing sunrise to sunrise into twelve equal parts. They created the sixty-minute system (i.e. 1 hour = 60 minutes) over 3,000 years ago and the time system of day, month, year as well as the Lunar and Solar Calendars. They concluded that the earth, moon, and another five planets and our sun are all part of one system, a fact that took the world two thousand years to agree with. (Roux 1993, 281).

The legendary women of ancient Mesopotamia who played a vital role in building the cradle of civilization were omitted from history until about a hundred years ago, when archaeologists dug them up and an untold story arose. Chaldea was located in the marshy land of the far southeastern corner of Mesopotamia, along the Euphrates and Tigris rivers. In 1927, Leonard Woolley excavated the site and identified it as Ur of the Chaldeans. The chief deity of the city was Nanna, the Sumerian moon-god. In the Sumerian mythology, several temples and the great ziggurat were built for him and his consort Ningal, the Great Lady. (Barrick 1979, 137). That same year, he also discovered in that region the disc of Enheduanna, a princess, priestess, and the first recorded writer in history.

Maria would have loved to witness this archeological discovery. She herself endured, leaving an indelible mark on history. Her unwavering dedication to the cause of women's rights and education paved the way for future generations to challenge societal norms and create a more equitable world. The impact of her intellectual pursuits and relentless advocacy continued to shape the course of history long after her time.

After many re-reads, I rewrote Maria's story as a single, more accessible volume. The original two-volume format, with its nineteenth century British writing style is daunting for modern audiences. Streamlining the content while preserving the core narrative and themes makes the book more engaging and easier to read. Incorporating Asmar's complete literary work *Prophecy and Lamentations* allows the reader to directly engage with her authentic voice and perspectives, providing invaluable insight into the philosophical and spiritual influences that shaped her worldview.

My aim was to preserve the essence of Maria's original

work, presenting it in a format more inviting and digestible for today's readers, especially younger generations. I also sought to safeguard the Chaldean identity she hailed and tried to preserve, which many have tried to alter to suit their own interests, to change the narrative, or out of ignorance. I maintained her direct and outspoken manner when addressing her people's persecution. In the current political climate, she would likely have been silenced.

Maria's charisma and intellect drew the attention of scholars, philosophers, and the elite, who were captivated by her ability to challenge societal norms and inspire a more egalitarian vision. Her influence expanded as she established herself as a respected voice in the pursuit of knowledge and gender equality.

Word of Maria's endeavors spread globally, as she restored Chaldean history and brought it to the attention of Europeans and Americans through her memoir, talks, and interactions, resonating with those yearning for change. Her movement gained momentum, making her a symbol of hope and empowerment for silenced, oppressed women. She became a beacon of hope.

According to a *Chaldean News* article published in 2020 and written by Dr. Adhid Miri, Maria obtained British citizenship in 1850 after a decade in the country. She then moved to France in 1853. There is little documentation until 1870 when reports state that she died in France that year, before the Franco-Prussian War. In her will, she left a portion of her wealth to restore the Church of the Apostles Peter and Paul in Telkaif. She asked for her body be buried in the churchyard of Telkaif.

MARIA THERESA

ASMAR

A CHALDEAN WOMAN'S STORY
DURING THE 1800s

SECTION I

CHAPTER 1

MARIA'S ANCESTORS

Maria's eastern family traced its origins to the Brahmins of India. Throughout generations, her ancestors had practiced Christianity in the church of Travancore, established by Saint Thomas, the apostle. According to family tradition, her ancestors left Travancore centuries ago and moved to Persia, eventually making Baghdad their home.

Maria's grandfather, Emir Abdallah, had accumulated vast riches in properties, silk production, livestock, and camels. According to her, he once possessed a staggering number of five thousand camels. Maria's father and his four brothers inherited this vast estate when her grandfather passed away.

Her father used his power and money to spread Christianity. He adhered to the Chaldaic rite, which is in communion with the Roman Catholic church. However, his home always welcomed the underprivileged, regardless of their religious background, whether Christian, Jew, or Muslim. He built a house with the sole purpose of accommodating strangers. He would go out, search for them himself, bring them back, wash their feet and serve them at the table with his own hands.

As a child, Maria vividly recalled an admirable man seeking asylum in her father's house. Gabriel Dombo, a missionary, had his tongue cut out as punishment for spreading religion. He had stayed with them for two years. Following that,

Maria's father gave him sufficient funds to set up a college for missionary training.

The plague ravaged Baghdad in 1804, causing widespread devastation. Seeking refuge from the outbreak, Maria's father brought the family to his country estate in the ruins of Nineveh. It was called Kasur El Aza, meaning Palace of Delight. Maria was born during this period, in a tent pitched near her father's house. Her mother sought solace in that place to grieve for losing multiple family members taken by the plague. She mourned the death of Maria's uncle, who suffered a fatal snakebite during a hunting trip. Before he passed away, he went through an ancient Mesopotamian therapy that involved being kept awake for five days by drumming and receiving pin pricks whenever he felt sleepy. The caregivers would continuously feed the patient milk throughout the entire time until he vomited, ejecting the venom. Maria's uncle underwent this torture for five days, but to no avail. The poison had gone too far to be remedied.

Finally, the plague ended, but not without destroying whole families and causing grief in every household. Her parents returned to Baghdad, and Maria stayed there until she was four years old. Their home was a roomy country manor on the Tigris River, just an hour away from the city. Expansive gardens filled the area, thriving with date palms, juicy lemons, and oranges, all watered by small streams from the river. Maria spent her early childhood in this delightful oasis. Amongst the many nooks and crannies, she made fond memories playing hide-and-seek with her brothers. These memories remained forever fresh in her mind.

The neighbor living next to them was Osmanli Aga, a devoted Muslim who followed all the duties outlined in the Koran and strongly disliked non-believers of all sorts. He despised

Shiites just as much as he hated infidels. Without fail, he completed the required prayers and recitations every day.

One day, at about eight years old, Maria and her brother played hide-and-seek in the garden. On a whim, she climbed a large date palm near the wall dividing their estate from the Muslim neighbor's. Maria hid herself in the leaves, thrilled by the idea of sending her brother on a wild goose chase.

Her trick worked perfectly. Peering through the fronds, she watched the little fellow scampering about, searching everywhere yet never suspecting her perch. After enjoying his confusion for some time, she pondered how to reveal her hiding spot. Seized by a mischievous impulse, she imitated the call of the muezzin that regularly sounded from the minaret, summoning the faithful to prayer. At the top of her voice, she cried in Arabic, "There is no god but God, and Muhammad is His messenger. Prayer is better than sleep."

Since it was around midday prayer, Maria's brother assumed it was the muezzin himself until her unrestrained laughter at the successful prank gave her away. He found it as amusing as she did, but he made the mistake of recounting the incident to her father when they returned home.

Maria's father was as pious and peaceful a Christian as could be, always cautiously avoiding any offense or insult to his Muslim neighbors. So instead of being amused by Maria's actions, he condemned her to three days confined to her room, subsisting only on dates and water. He impressed upon her young mind the caution, "Don't you know that the very walls have ears?"

Maria's "nimble as a kitten" childhood self did not stop her from getting involved in another naughty incident.

Enormous, sweet lemons grew over their neighbor's garden wall, which Maria had watched longingly for days as they ripened in the sun. She devised many schemes to get her hands on one. At last, unable to resist temptation any longer, she became a perfect "little thief." Several times, she was nearly caught by the unexpected appearance of her brothers or cousins.

But one day, when the coast seemed clear, she directed a servant, "Place the ladder against the wall."

Up she climbed, the forbidden fruit now within reach. Her heart pounded with anxious hope and joy as she seized the largest lemon she could find and descended with her prize. Whether the stolen fruit's exquisite flavor came from that act, she couldn't say. But it was the sweetest lemon she had ever tasted.

Her enjoyment was short-lived. She soon paid the price of guilt and remorse. Her father never failed to read the Ten Commandments to the family each day. When he got to "Thou shalt not steal," her conscience smarted afresh.

"He who is faithful in small things is faithful in large," he would preach. "To atone, one must immediately return what one has stolen."

Unable to bear her burden of guilt any longer, Maria pondered how to make amends. Since she couldn't replace the giant lemon, she tossed several smaller ones back over the wall. She thought the matter resolved, but soon her father received a complaint that fruit thrown into the neighbor's garden had hit children playing there. He gathered everyone and interrogated them one by one. All denied involvement until Maria's turn came. Her father's principle against lying, even for a good cause, sprang to mind. She fully confessed what she had done and awaited her punishment.

To her surprise, her father not only forgave her, but scolded her brothers for nicknaming her "the lemon thief." From then on, Maria resolved to never knowingly tell an untruth. This trial gave her mastery over her fears, a mastery that stayed with her in good times and bad. Her candid nature did often land her in trouble, however. She soon found that the same forthrightness that spared her punishment for stealing lemons would land her in deeper troubles throughout life. During her travels in her native country, she could never help confessing to any Bedouin she met exactly how much money she carried. If only the wandering bands of Arabia had seized the opportunity, the outcome would have been insignificant. But to her sorrow, Maria discovered that the most civilized people of Europe, who believed their knowledge had banished the mists of Eastern ignorance, exploited her guileless nature far more.

Though she wished to cling to her principles, Maria's honesty repeatedly proved her undoing. Each candid admission drew her further into an intricate web of schemes and deceits from which there seemed no escape. But she vowed to face whatever trials her truthfulness brought with the same courage that compelled her as a child to admit her crime, no matter the punishment.

Maria, as a child, preferred elders' company over peers. Her grandmother, an exceptional woman who lived to 104, brought her unparalleled happiness. Maria delighted in the stories she told of her long, eventful life. She listened with breathless interest to the tales her grandfather shared about the events he had witnessed over his even longer career. Maria never forgot the horror she felt hearing his account of the siege of Mosul by Nadir Shah in 1743 that lasted many days.

He described how the Pasha governing the town, who favored the Christians, called upon the people to pray for deliverance. The Christians tried to turn away God's wrath with charity, mortification, and penance, donning sackcloth, and ashes like the ancient Ninevites. The people valiantly defended the city. They resolved to die rather than submit. Even women and children eagerly contributed. Despite repeated breaches, the defenders constantly repulsed the attackers and repaired the breaches overnight.

Finally, Nadir Shah sent the Pasha a message threatening to detonate a mine under the wall unless they surrendered. When the Pasha refused, Nadir Shah detonated the mine, setting part of the city ablaze.

Maria's grandfather lost several brothers in the dreadful siege, along with his library, homes, and other property. The Christians fought with such gallantry they won the Turks' admiration. After Nadir Shah retreated to Baghdad, the government repaired the damaged Christian churches at its expense. Christianity's prominence in the 1800s surpassed present day, influencing culture and daily life for most people. Sunday observance, religious education, and moral codes were all central. The secularization of society has been a gradual process over the past two centuries.

Of all the family, Maria was her grandmother's favorite. When she died, she bequeathed Maria her anklets, necklace, nose jewels, and jeweled belt gifts Maria cherished until robbed of them and other valuables in later years while traveling.

Maria's mother bore eighteen children, only nine surviving—five boys and four girls. She was the second youngest daughter. Her next younger sister died at ten. Her other sisters both married. The younger one was a girl of exceptional beauty. Her skin was delicate and fair; her eyes were full and dark; and her hair was black and as soft as the finest silk. Her form embodied perfection, and she carried herself with the utmost dignity and grace. Neither were her mental endowments inferior to those of her person, though they had not had the advantage of European cultivation.

Such was the true portrait of Maria's second sister, named Ferida, meaning "the incomparable." At twelve, she was married to a wealthy sheikh of sixteen, and at thirteen she had given birth to a son.

This nephew of Maria's was the most precocious little boy she ever met. Before he was three years old, he could recite his prayers and perform the compliments that comprised early education in the East. By four, he could read perfectly.

Maria's sister lived until she was thirty-five and had several more children. But then, she and her entire family were carried off by the plague. Within days, not a soul survived in the once joyful home. The Pasha's seal affixed on the door, to prevent looting of the dead, announced the desolation now within. The tragedy was beyond words.

CHAPTER 2

LIFE IN BAGHDAD

Maria spent her time between Baghdad and Mosul from ages four to eleven, with her family choosing to spend the summer months in Mosul to escape Baghdad's sweltering heat. At the height of summer, the temperature could reach 120° Fahrenheit, so residents took refuge in the middle of the day in underground cooled by sprinkling water and large fans waved by slaves until emerging in the evenings to enjoy the breezes on their rooftops.

During the hottest months, the ladies wore only silk chemises and slippers, with no stockings. At night, everyone—men, women, children, and servants—slept on their separate terraces under the open sky. To cool down in July and August, the Baghdad women would steep their nightclothes in water stored in animal skin bags to keep them chilled. They put these on dripping wet before retiring to their palm branch beds to gain refreshing slumber. Despite this practice, people rarely heard of rheumatism there, unlike in England. In July, those who were out risked the stifling "samiel" winds that suddenly suffocated them.

Rising early was universal in Baghdad. The sun never caught a closed eye. Rich and poor alike carried their mattresses down from the roofs each morning before the heat could burn them up. The winter climate was far more pleasant. Though often rainy, the temperature was mild, with a refreshing breeze. People wore heavy wool clothing indoors because of scarce fuel and poorly heated dwellings. Ladies held braziers under their robes to keep warm.

Baghdad had gained a reputation for its indulgent ways. The inhabitants made four meals daily, starting early with coffee, followed by smoking the *nerghila*, or water pipe. At nine, they breakfasted on milky porridge with rice milk and dates cooked in butter. The dinner hour was one o'clock, with prayers performed dutifully before every meal.

The ladies of Baghdad wore a distinctive head covering—a large black and white veil called an *izar*, made of silk and cotton in Mosul, that flowed almost to the feet like a Spanish mantilla. It had a horsehair band encircling the head, concealing the face yet allowing the wearer full curiosity in the Eastern fashion. Outdoors, one could not discern rank from dress, as both rich and poor wore the same modest garb. Indoors, however, Baghdad's ladies outshone nearly all Turkish women in lavish attire—rich silks, gold ornaments, pearls and fine jewelry worn in profuse abundance.

As a girl, Maria delighted in watching the lively street scenes from the house balcony, obscured behind her izar's veil. Passing by were stately Turks on spirited Arabian steeds, humble Jews leading donkey trains, veiled women gracefully swaying, and dark-skinned slaves bearing immense loads. Strains of the merry dance rhythm sounded from taverns while street vendors sang out their wares.

Maria filled her days with play and lessons to become a proper young lady.

When Maria was eleven, her father took her on a trip to Persia. They traveled from Baghdad to Shiraz, then to Isfahan. Near Isfahan, her father showed her a famous emerald mine with an intriguing history. The mine had once yielded beautiful jewels in abundance annually. The ruling Shah, quarreling with the Ottoman Sultan, hoped to appease him with dazzling gems from this mine. He sent the Sultan gifts of immense value—a massive gold tray bristling with emeralds, twelve gem-encrusted golden cups, and a golden washing set covered in vivid green stones. Surely no anger could withstand such a peace offering!

But because of an unfortunate blunder, the Shah sent gifts via a vizier known to oppose Ottoman interests. When presented to the Sultan, he scornfully rejected the peace offerings. "What dirt is this you would have us eat? Go!" he said, turning to one of his attendants, "and see them carried to the least worthy part of our palace."

The vizier left, uncertain if his head and body would stay intact. The Shah, enraged by the humiliation, swore vengeance, and ordered the mine closed forever, as though cutting off one's nose to spite the enemy. One purpose of the Persian journey was for Maria's father to investigate reopening the legendary mine to restore his diminished fortune. But he did not live to pursue this ambition.

From Isfahan, Maria and her father continued through Tehran to Mosul. Maria later accompanied him on a trip through Mesopotamia, where he owned much land. Returning home, she spent the next three years in Mosul, immersed in religious studies and contemplation. She devoted herself almost completely to spiritual pursuits, with those peaceful days passing uneventfully.

According to the Eastern custom of betrothing children early, Maria's parents promised her at birth to a young sheikh, who was a distant relative and only three years old himself. When she turned twelve and he fifteen, her father prepared for the wedding. But Maria strongly desired to remain unmarried.

Since age six, Maria had read the lives of saints and

martyrs, dreaming of following their example. She shunned the festivities that lasted days for other family weddings, immersing herself in books on hermits and martyrs instead. The more she read, the more she yearned to share in their glory and suffering. Her father had encouraged her spiritual pursuits. Once, catching her reading Arabian Nights, he punished her with three days' confinement on just bread and water.

Because of her solitary habits, her parents nicknamed Maria "Daughter of the Desert," after the turtledove that flies to the desert to sing itself to death when it loses its young. Sensing the suffering that awaited her, Maria pleaded with her father to break off the engagement, to no avail. She confided her wish to become a nun to the young sheikh, who was similarly devout. He joined the Trappists and lived in a remote mountain hermitage barely accessible. Though parted, they hoped their sacrifice would reunite them in heaven.

Maria loved riding and often accompanied her father and brother. They would wander through tall grains that concealed them completely. One day near the village of Qaraqosh, some fifty-armed Arabs surrounded them. Though her father and brother had weapons, resistance was hopeless.

The Arab chief, struck by the beauty of Maria's dear friend Mariam traveling with them, insisted on abducting her. Their anguished pleas went unheeded. Someone seized Mariam and swiftly carried her off, while Maria watched in horror. Her brother gathered forces to pursue them, but their horses were too fast. It was impossible to overtake them.

Mariam had been staying with Maria's family and was meant to remain longer. Her parents were unaware of the peril their beloved daughter had fallen into. Trusting they could recover her, Maria's family wished to spare them the anguish such knowledge would cause.

Maria's father made inquiries everywhere and finally

located the Arabs' retreat. For a hefty ransom of fifty purses, close to six hundred English pounds, they agreed to return Mariam to her distressed friends. Maria's father gladly paid, and soon Mariam was back under their roof.

Mariam said the Arabs had treated her with utmost courtesy, lessening the horrors of captivity. Their chief had ardently pressed his suit but offered no violence or threats. She confessed to being touched by his generous conduct throughout. Both Maria and Mariam held passionate zeal for religion, each vying in devotion. Mariam's striking beauty attracted notice that she spurned, absorbed solely in piety. Together they often rose at midnight for prayer and observed Lent by meager vegetarian fasts. On Sundays they preached doctrines to crowds of women seated in fields, who listened attentively.

Like Maria, Mariam was determined to remain celibate and advance the faith, causing wonderment. Maria was the first in their region to devote herself solemnly, thus since Muslim rule, with Mariam as the second. Their unusual path was not without contention. Many pleaded with the two girls to reconsider, calling it unnatural to reject honorable marriage. But they stood firm, withdrawing more from society to avoid temptation.

Soon after her trying ordeal, Mariam's parents arranged her marriage to a prominent man in a distant town. She valiantly tried persuading them to break the engagement, but ultimately yielded to their wishes. The day before Mariam's departure, she and Maria stole away at dusk to their favorite rocky creek. There, they renewed pledges to reunite one day in a convent for prayer and service. Tearfully embracing as the stars emerged, each friend felt half her soul torn away.

The Christian Church in Mosul had enjoyed unusual freedom under the mild and tolerant reign of the Pasha. But with his death, things changed. His successor was a stern, fanatical enemy of Christianity eager to unleash vengeance.

Learning of Maria's activities, the new Pasha aimed to crush the spread of her "pestilential doctrines." He ordered all Christians to renounce their faith publicly and embrace Islam in a designated place. Otherwise, he threatened, he would take their lives. Many welcomed potential martyrdom and steadfastly held to their beliefs, like Maria, her uncle, the archbishop, her father, and Mariam. Singing hymns, they felt heaven's glory awaited, if martyred for their faith. Brought before the Pasha, they boldly professed their faith, trying to convince him of his errors. But he jailed them without debate. He locked Maria and Mariam in a room in his palace. They threw the others into a dark dungeon and subjected them to daily savage beatings. Sometimes allowed to visit, Maria wept to see her father and relatives heavily chained. They urged her to rejoice, not mourn, as she was found worthy of suffering for Christ.

They were daily brought out into a court to receive the bastinado, a torture that involved caning the soles of someone's feet. Maria, in agony, had to hear their cries and couldn't offer comfort. An uncle branded on the forehead with hot irons died. The rest finally secured their release by paying exorbitant ransoms to the rapacious Pasha. Having enriched himself and sated his religious zeal, the Pasha let Maria's family return to their former lives, at last unmolested. Maria was certain that, had it not been for her companion's charms which calmed his fury, he would have kept his word of killing them.

Maria's family lived in the town of Alqosh, about twelve hours from Mosul, near a sizable convent. With her father's permission, Maria retired to this serene refuge. A small room was prepared, furnished sparsely with a bed made of woven palm leaves, a small rug, a skull, crucifix, and some books. These included a copy of the Bible, plus lives of saints and hermits like Saint Anthony of Egypt, who devoted themselves to prayer and contemplation. In this sacred asylum, Maria's days passed quietly, if not always happily.

Her routine was deeply spiritual. Rising at six each morning, Maria kneeled for two hours, absorbed in prayer and meditation. She then took up the Holy Scripture, reading a set number of chapters. Afterward, she turned to passages from the lives of saints, concluding her devotions by chanting all fifty of the Psalms and other holy hymns. This filled her time until noon. At that hour, Maria emerged from her room to wander the convent gardens, often venturing beyond to scale the steep mountains encircling the grounds. As she climbed, stunning vistas unfolded—the Tigris River laid out below, wild and romantic scenery all around.

For hours Maria rambled the high hills, contemplating nature's grandeur. Her thoughts rose to the Divine Creator, praise songs soon flowing from her lips. The day's beauty and solitude moved her spirit profoundly. Around four o'clock, Maria returned to have a simple, light meal of bread and fruit. Every Sunday, her parents provided these provisions, sending a servant with a fresh loaf and enough dried fruits to last the week. Though meager, this diet satisfied her.

CHAPTER 3

THE PASHA'S HAREM AND OTHER ADVENTURES

Six months had passed since Maria first entered the convent. Her father, brother and two uncles then left for Baghdad, while her mother and relatives went to live near the ruins of Nineveh in a small village belonging to her father. Not wanting to leave Maria, her mother brought her along. Maria found an abandoned convent nearby and made it her retreat, continuing her life of prayer, study, and fasting. She composed several religious books during her time there. She wrote in a poetic style, addressing God, praising the divine creation, and calling for peace and prosperity.

Maria then established a place for learned women, convincing two friends to join her. The inequality between the sexes disturbed her—women treated like slaves, lacking education while men enjoyed every advantage. She was determined to provide schooling for women. One of her cousins taught in the Kurdish, Chaldean, and Turkish languages. Another, an intelligent lady friend, instructed the students in Persian. People flocked to this institution, embracing every branch of knowledge. Even ladies of rank joined them.

During this time, Maria did not neglect the poorer classes. She preached and taught them in the open air, giving them lessons of prudence and piety. She sought to better their lives and those of generations to come. A shepherd in her father's service, originally Bedouin, converted with his family to Christianity.

For Maria, a devoutly religious individual, her missionary work was a deeply spiritual endeavor. She saw it as a calling to help guide others towards a higher state of being and greater personal freedom. Through her efforts to convert and minister to those she encountered, Maria felt a profound sense of purpose, believing that she was empowering people to reach their fullest potential. Her faith provided the driving force behind this missionary work, which she viewed as a noble and transformative pursuit.

While at the convent, Maria received secret visits from local women, including the Pasha's sister, who had some education but was also a fanatic. Because of violent public prejudice against Christians, she came discreetly. Instead of the routine forty or fifty slaves accompanying a woman of her rank, she had only four attendants, two males and two females.

Their conversations dwelled on religion, the princess curious about Maria's faith and its effect on her life. Maria gave her a New Testament, which the princess eagerly studied. One discussion lasted three hours as Maria fervently expounded Christian truths and aimed to convert her guest. She presented every argument and analogy imaginable, urging the enlightenment of Christianity over human creations like Islam. She referenced her to the Bible, which the princess had gained much respect for as she studied it. Maria said, "God, the only true God, the everlasting Father, the Creator of the universe, the Giver of life, was the author of the Christian religion, not mere ambitious men or conquerors like Mohammed who borrowed much from the Bible."

"Such bold talk could cost you your life," said the princess, shocked that Maria would speak so openly about Christianity given the deadly consequences. That year alone her brother, the Pasha, executed many Christians because they would not convert to Islam. "What could make you so reckless to indulge in language, which, if carried elsewhere, might cost you your life?"

Maria declared she longed for martyrdom if God willed it, adding, "God, who does all for our good, and disposes events according to his supreme will, will not permit me to suffer, unless it seems good to his Almighty wisdom."

Surprised at this resignation to Providence reminiscent of Islam, the princess gained new respect for Maria.

After customary pleasantries, the princess returned covertly to the zenana, the part of a house in the Islamic and Hindu tradition reserved for women, particularly for princess and women associated with high-ranking figures. The Ramadan fast soon followed, where Muslims fast from sunrise to sunset. Afterwards, having first washed and scented themselves, they would make up for their past mortification by eating, drinking, and reading from the Koran all night long, with general illumination prevailing.

Maria's conversation seemed to have made a significant impression on her illustrious visitor. For at Ramadan's end, the princess sent Maria an invitation to dine with her, though she had extended such invitations repeatedly during the fast itself. But Maria's friends, concerned for her safety amid the rigors of Ramadan, would not permit her to accept then. Maria herself was reluctant to visit for many reasons. Chief among them was having to shed her usual habit of a recluse attire for one more fitting for an honored guest. As these thoughts occupied her mind, Maria's conscience advised her that the visit might reclaim sinners and spread the saving light of truth where before there was only darkness and despair. This quickly overcame all personal worries, resolving Maria to go, if by some chance she might guide lost souls to the true faith.

She would have liked to bring a beloved young friend along, but the exclusive invitation prevented it. Not daring to inconvenience the princess, Maria went alone, attended by just two slaves, her heart full of joy at the prospect of making converts. Maria dressed superbly for the occasion. Her gown was of white gold tissue, open in front in Eastern style with long billowing sleeves to the knees, cinched at the waist by an ornate gilded belt. Her trousers were of crimson silk, while chased silver anklets adorned her feet along with gold-embroidered slippers. A white muslin turban embroidered in gold and a Persian shawl at her waist completed the costume Maria wore for her first visit to the princess.

She wrote in her memoir, "Who could recognize the girl she once was in this downtrodden woman's words?" Back then, her heart overflowed with emotion and unbridled enthusiasm, breathing deeply with the hope of steering her misguided peers towards the truth."

When Maria arrived at the residence, an old eunuch greeted her and escorted her through three or four padlocked doors, which he unlocked with keys he had. He brought her into a grand courtyard paved in polished marble from Diyarbakir, gleaming like a horizontal mirror. Crossing this slippery expanse required agility, like walking on ice. As Maria entered, she saw three slave girls gathering up supplies they had used to clean the pavement.

A resplendent marble fountain with artfully arranged jets of water stood at the center of the courtyard. To the left was an open chamber, or diwan, overlooking the court. Its walls displayed vivid ornamental arabesques. A spectacular Persian carpet covered the floor, while brilliant scarlet velvet embroidered in gold draped the large central cushion.

The eunuch ushered Maria through a doorway to the left and into an immense salon even more sumptuously decorated than the apartment she had just seen, where she noticed an exquisite Persian carpet underfoot and the throne-like large center cushion swathed in red and green velvet lavishly embroidered. She thought, "This fine handiwork must have taken months of toil!"

Maria did not have the time to examine half the beauties of the salon when the Pasha's sister appeared and showed her with the utmost respect and courtesy. "You must sit on my side on the *musnud*," she said, indicating the cushion, and continued to overwhelm Maria with compliments and civility.

Three female slaves approached—all beautiful young women from Georgia, Circassia, and Kurdistan, with white moon-bright complexions contrasting dramatically with large, dark eyes and luxuriant raven locks. One kneeled and presented a round silver-gilded vessel called a *lakan*, tunnel-shaped with a perforated lid, for washing hands. A second kneeled holding an exquisite urn brimming with water, which she poured through the lakan's holes, so it trickled into the container below as Maria completed her ablutions. The third held embroidered napkins edged in gold.

With the cleansing ritual finished, two more slaves entered, each swinging incense issuing forth sweet incense perfumes that spread throughout the apartment. Next came three more slaves—one bearing a silver-gilded tray with six intricate gold cups containing sherbets in three flavors, which another handed to Maria and the princess. The third held an embroidered golden napkin.

Then three more appeared—the first holding a diamond and emerald inlaid gold tray with small painted china cups called *finjans*, and gold bejeweled saucers to protect hands from the scalding coffee within. They served this strong, unsweetened coffee boiling hot.

After the coffee came two eunuchs carrying an ornate water pipe known as a nerghila, commonly used by Mesopotamian ladies. Its soothing sound mingled with scented aloe smoke and gentle notes from a European music box, transporting Maria's senses to a dreamlike state of bliss.

As Maria enjoyed the soothing nerghila pipe, the conversation was sparse. Ten female slaves stood reverently before them with folded arms. When finished, the princess offered to show Maria her brother's harem, and, intrigued, Maria readily agreed.

They first visited the numerous lavishly carpeted bedrooms. The beds, made of branches of the palm tree and manufactured in Baghdad, were so light that one could easily lift them with one hand. The chief wife's bed had five mattresses of different colored silks, filled with peacock feathers.

After seeing some thirty such opulent sleeping chambers, they ascended to the rooftop terrace. From this vantage, Maria gazed out upon the whole town and environs, mingled with the crumbling ruins of the once mighty Nineveh. She recalled the prophet's words about its doomed riches and vanished glory: "And as for Nineveh, her waters are like a great pool, but the men flee away. They cry, 'Stand, stand,' but there is none that will return. Take the spoils of silver and gold, for the riches of precious furniture have no end. She suffered destruction and was torn apart. The heart melts and the knees fail, and all the loins lose their strength. The faces of them all are as blackness of a kettle… Behold, I come against thee, saith the Lord of Hosts, and I will burn their chariots even to smoke, and the sword shall devour thy young lions. I will remove prey from the land, silencing your messengers. Shepherds slumbered, O king of Assyria.

Maria felt these words deeply resonate, then tried to brush them aside.

On the roof were three tents of blue-green oilcloth, offering shade while admiring the spectacular view. After a short time, they descended into the immense gardens, spanning nearly a square mile. Streams of foot-wide marble-lined watercourses bordered in flowers meandered through the grounds, filling the air with fragrance from abundant rose beds.

After spending an hour in this enchanting spot, the princess then led Maria to a salon opening into the garden. Here she met the Pasha's twenty-five wives—a mix of Georgian, Circassian and Kurdish women. Despite her knowledge of Eastern customs, Maria was taken aback by the size of the harem.

Maria conversed with one wife, a beautiful eighteen-year-old Georgian with large, dark, cedar-like lashes and eyes. She shared how, at age twelve, they abducted her to Constantinople and forced her, on pain of death, to renounce her Christian faith for Islam. The Pasha's service also forced her brother, who is now a soldier, to renounce their family's religion. When Maria asked if she was happy in her current situation, the woman sadly replied that far from rejoicing, she ceaselessly mourned her cruel fate and the loss of her family and home.

When the Pasha entered, they cut their talk. The women quickly rose to greet him. The Pasha, around forty years old, had a commanding presence. His piercing dark eyes sat above a thick black beard that reached to his jewel-encrusted dagger. His luxurious garb and courteous manners inspired both confidence and respect.

The princess introduced Maria as a relative of the Pasha's lieutenant. He politely inquired about her family, especially her father, away on business. Their conversation lasted fifteen minutes until the muezzin's call to noon prayer from the minaret. The Pasha promptly departed for the adjoining mosque, leaving his harem to pray in the salon.

This summons came five times daily. At dawn, the call to

prayer urged waking believers that "prayer is better than sleep." At noon, that "prayer is better than food." The remaining alerts were at mid-afternoon, sunset, and midnight.

At the muezzin's call, the women surrendered to their devotions. Falling first to their knees, then pressing foreheads to the floor in prostration, they cried aloud, "There is no God but Allah! None but the God of Heaven, and Muhammad is His prophet. Our only hope and refuge lies with the Most High."

Throughout these rites, they kept before them a relic of the Prophet himself—purportedly a fragment of his own sister's trousers, concealed in paper and a bejeweled golden case. This precious artifact they kissed repeatedly, laying it atop their heads while praying.

Maria watched this extraordinary scene with mingled curiosity, seated upon the diwan. These pious observances lasted a quarter hour until a slave entered announcing dinner. Eagerly heeded, the group proceeded to the dining hall, one room overlooking the courtyard open wide to combat the June heat.

As Maria passed through the arched doorway, a mingling of aromas transported her senses. When she entered, she saw the dining room brimmed with Oriental delicacies. The dining room presented twenty dishes on a great copper tray six feet wide. Amongst them were two soups—one of rice and herbs, the other with green barley and chicken, a favorite of the Pasha of Egypt.

Next came a whole lamb stuffed with herbs, rice, and pistachios, its saffron dye providing both color and flavor. Roast fowl, stuffed gourds, several dishes of the vegetable *bamia*, okra. There was a veal hash wrapped in vine leaves, along with *kubba*, a pastry crust made from green barley and meat, enclosing a beef and herb mixture called "old woman's hair" despite its scrumptious taste. Maria tried kababs too, ground meat grilled on iron skewers. Many other exotic dishes followed, their names now faded from memory.

After dinner ended, desserts appeared that were no less inferior to the dinner. A snow-like substance accompanied sweetmeats in a rainbow of flavors found on leaves, deliciously sweet with a green tint, called *gasgoul* in Chaldean and *min al sama* in Arabic. Enormous six-inch figs came from Mount Sinjar, along with sweet oranges from Baghdad and Basra resembling giant shaddocks, called *laimoun halou*, sweet orange. Mesopotamia had an abundance of this fruit, selling a dozen for a penny. They also had roasted hummus kernels, harvested beans, pistachios, pomegranates, and grapes. Of course, no wine was introduced, but attendants served the women a liquor made from pomegranate juice in goblets of massive gold, which they enjoyed.

During the dinner, fifteen slaves attended to the women, some of whom fanned them continuously. They then brought them vessels to perform their ablutions, followed by pipes and nerghilas. Finally permitted to leave, they feasted on the leftovers.

After the feast, they led Maria upstairs to the *tharma*, a marble-floored sitting room overlooking the gardens. At the center lay a large yellow satin ottoman where the sultana, or the Pasha's favorite wife, reclined amidst plush cushions. Along the garden side hung cages filled with melodious songbirds chirping notes of every sort.

In this earthly paradise, Maria enjoyed the soothing nerghila pipe and sipped coffee. The Pasha's favored wife soon drifted to sleep in the Oriental fashion—a habit unlikely to find favor with ladies in colder climates, Maria mused, where napping after dinner seemed confined to elderly men who indulged in the forbidden fruit of the grape.

A fair slave stood watching over her sleeping mistress, waving a peacock-feather fan to and fro. Another rubbed the woman's dainty feet, slippers removed, while a third sang a low, melancholy tune guaranteed to promote slumber.

Maria captured the woman's attire as the sultana slept unaware, seizing this moment to later describe it to her female readers. To disclose her charms to the gaze of profane infidels! She thought wittingly, imagining how this would give her some authority to pull at the dreaded Pasha's beard, this intimidating figure whose beard only his favorite wife dared touch!

The sultana's chemise was finest gossamer silk, overlaid by a gold-embroidered white gown with crimson trousers. A bejeweled gilded belt cinched her waist, intricately embroidered by the harem's supposedly idle concubines. Bracelets with alternating pearls and diamonds adorned her arms. Around her neck was a collar of gold and precious gems. In her ears were pendants with sparkling brilliants. And in her nose—brace yourselves, daughters of Europe!—a small emerald. She wove her hair into countless small braids, binding them with chains of gold and pearls, with each lock ending in a single pearl. Two similar braids graced each cheek. A golden saucer-like ornament and bird-shaped diamond aigrette completed her elaborate coiffure.

Nearby was the sultana's treasured parrot, Dura. Dura had learned phrases from the Koran and attained such skill that it nearly matched the pious recitals of the mullah. One day, this devout fowl discovered that even faithful souls face trials. Lost in holy meditation, Dura wandered from its cage, unaware of the hawk eyeing it hungrily. With no fear of Muhammad, Maria jested in her memoir, the ominous bird—surely a heathen or heretic—swooped upon the sultana's loquacious pet.

Up it soared into the air, fully intending a hearty meal, when the parrot loudly proclaimed: "La illaha ila Allah wah Mohammed rasul Allah." There is but one God and Muhammad is his prophet. Upon hearing this, the predator grew uneasy.

As the parrot persistently declared, "All else is vanity of vanities," the hawk realized his predicament. Wasting no time disentangling from this unwelcome burden, he politely returned the talkative bird unharmed by its cage—the only amends in his power. From then on, the Pasha's servants and harem saw the parrot as the prophet's special protégé and esteemed it deeply pious.

Such was the princess's incredible tale of the parrot to Maria.

When the sultana awoke from her slumber, she strolled the fragrant garden with the princess, Maria, and others. There they chewed a pleasantly flavored greenish mineral called *ilich*, a gum found near Nineveh, which aided digestion without dissolving in the mouth.

The mullah's evening call to prayer rang out. With her hostess's permission, Maria reluctantly took her leave, though the princess was unwilling to part, and proposed an excursion to the revered tomb of Jonah. Christians and nonbelievers alike held the ancient prophet in high esteem, and his tomb sat near Mosul on the mountain Tel Nabi Yunus.

As tempting as exploring with the gracious princess sounded, Maria regretfully declined due to her ailing mother. Suffering from an affliction only relieved by the therapeutic hot springs of Ain el Kibrit near the Tigris towards Baghdad, her mother insisted Maria join her there. Still hoping to deter Maria's departure, the princess mentioned her brother had just acquired an exquisite young Kurdish slave from Sinjar with beauty beyond compare. Speaking only Kurdish, which Maria understood, the girl was sure to pique her curiosity. But deference to her mother left Maria no choice but to refuse the tempting offer.

With night falling after her long stay, Maria lodged at her married sister's home near the mosque of Nur al-Din rather than returning straightaway to the convent. The day's delights still danced in her mind as she settled in for the evening.

CHAPTER 4

MESOPOTAMIAN PEOPLE AND CUSTOMS

After her palace visit, Maria journeyed with her ailing mother to the healing baths of Ain el Kibrit. The three-hour trip passed uneventfully, without harassment from the marauding tribes who roamed these parts. To Maria's curious mind, Ain el Kibrit brimmed with fascinations. This was the source of *ilich*, that pleasant gum she had chewed at the palace. Rambling near the therapeutic springs, she often collected gum for enjoyment.

Nearby loomed the mountain Kurkur Baba, aptly named for the combustible vapors that seeped from its peaks. By digging into the ground, Maria could ignite these emissions into open flame for cooking or boiling water. Ever curious, she once ventured too close, nearly becoming a martyr to scientific inquiry! But the capricious fires could be swiftly quenched by tossing earth upon them, sealing the outlet. Naphtha springs also cascaded from Kurkur Baba into the plains below. When Maria tossed a flaming wick into these streams, thunderous explosions erupted until the fuel consumed them, breathing them in smoke. A bituminous pool also lay within the mountain, treacherous to enter. Any person reckless enough to try would likely become forever trapped in its tenacious grip.

Once her mother fully recovered from the baths, Maria and her mother embarked on a journey to Telkaif, a town approximately nine miles away from Mosul, towards Amadiya, where Maria's uncle held the position of governor. The town was pleasantly situated, as its name, which signified "the mountain of delight." It had good soil that produced nearly every sort of fruit and vegetable to be found in that latitude. The townspeople had grown carrots a yard in length and six inches in diameter there, and they were so heavy that a child could not carry one of them. They also produced turnips, sometimes two feet in diameter, which people ate both raw and cooked in various ways. The latter was most frequently seen in a horseshoe shape and was so long that when put round the neck, the two ends nearly reached the knees. It was a very common practice with the natives to pickle the turnip in vinegar; and in this state it was much used as a stimulus to languid appetites, or when the system, from heat or any other cause, had become feverish.

Besides these vegetables, the town also had *battikh*, or watermelon, which grew to an enormous size, grapes as large as walnuts, and apples in such abundance that they were almost readily available. On one occasion, the seller asked a European who wished to purchase a para's worth of apples if he had brought a basket to put them in. A para being of no more value than an English farthing, the European, when he beheld the enormous store, he had obtained for such a small investment, opened his eyes with wonder and exclaimed, "Of a truth this is the land of promise!"

The extraordinary abundance and resulting cheap prices extended beyond vegetables and fruits. In the neighborhood of Telkaif, people could purchase large sheep for three piastres, which was about two shillings English, and they could buy a chicken for three paras, which was little over three farthings. However, money seldom appeared in these transactions, which were in nearly every case carried on by simple barter, with each inhabitant devoting his land and labor to one or more kinds of produce, which he exchanged for that of his neighbor.

As for the bread made in this region, it was of excellent quality, white and highly regarded by the local Arabs. It typically sold for around four or five paras, approximately a penny farthing in English currency, per "ratel," which weighed about five pounds. Maria doubted whether European tastes would find this bread equally palatable due to its inclusion of various aromatic herbs and salt. The bread was prepared by a group of Bedouin women known as *khabazat*, who made it their profession. They would travel from village to village, staying briefly in each, and baking the dough after kneading it. They rolled it into thin, three-foot-wide rounds and baked it in ovens built with a conical shape, resembling a well. The oven's opening faced outward, and a furnace beneath the floor heated it. The khabazat would plaster the dough against the oven's side using a rush mat covered with oilcloth to prevent burning. In just two minutes, they would bake a batch and replace it with another, continuing until they achieved the desired quantity. Within an hour, this efficient process would produce an impressive mountain of bread.

When they brought the bread to the table, they placed it on a round rush mat, dampened it with water to make it pliable, and consumed it with pieces of meat, cheese, or olives wrapped inside. Women solely conducted the baking operations, and five of them worked together. These skilled itinerant bakers could produce enough bread in a single day to fill the *sella*, a large chamber with a wicker-work structure, about nine feet in diameter and four feet high. The sella served as the bread store and was crafted by the impoverished Nestorians dwelling in the desolate mountains of Zozane.

Maria's thoughts turned to Telkaif's curious method for threshing and winnowing grains—altogether different from techniques she had witnessed in Europe. The Italian approach, she noticed, seemed clumsy and laborious compared to her native country's efficient process. The method pursued in Mesopotamia, or at least those parts of it in the neighborhood of Mosul, was as follows.

Telkaif was renowned for the enormous height to which the grains growing in the surrounding fields attained. The stalk grew to such a length that a horseman could ride through a field without being seen, the point of his lance alone peering above the waving ears. The farmers cut the barley about midway between the ear and the root, leaving the stalk intact to feed the camels and other beasts of burden. Maria remembered having seen it written in some book that, in her country, people pulled wheat and barley from the root with the hand, after the manner to which referenced to in the Bible, but she could only say that she had never witnessed such a practice. The narrator had possibly been deceived by seeing the weeds plucked up in this manner.

When the barley was cut, an express law forbade the proprietor of the field from touching what remained, as the gleaning was considered sacred to the poor. So abundant was the produce, in comparison with the wants of the inhabitants, that a large measure of barley, containing from ten to fifteen ratel, or from fifty to seventy pounds, English weight, was, in good seasons, sold for three piastres.

The workers finished the harvest and collected the produce of the district in the desert. Maria observed the produce being heaped up into a vast mass, resembling a moderately sized hill. Men were placed atop this heap, constantly supplying the machine used for separating the ears from the straw and husk.

During her travels, Maria had never seen an apparatus resembling the one used in Mesopotamia and Assyria for this purpose. She attempted to describe it. A wooden cylinder, about four feet long and two feet thick, was fixed horizontally under a platform that rested on a wheeled carriage. On this revolving cylinder, at one-foot intervals, were two rows of sharp blades shaped like hatchet-heads. These blades turned within four inches of the ground. The whole machine was yoked to two or more horses, based on the quantity of barley and the district's means. It was then drawn around in a vast circular path, with the driver standing on the raised platform.

Throughout this process, the laborers on the central heap continuously threw barley into the path of the machine, and the revolving cylinder thoroughly crushed it until the entire heap had undergone the operation. Stationed around the outside of this large circle were men using an instrument resembling a rake, but with teeth arranged in circles one above another, not unlike a birch broom. They gathered the crushed barley, which was then winnowed in a simple manner by throwing it into the air and allowing the chaff to blow away. After separating the ears from the chaff, they gathered them into a large pile.

The nazur, an officer appointed by the Pasha, then imprinted his name in large characters on several parts of the heap. This action aimed to prevent any of the produce from being taken before the Pasha's share, a tenth of the total, had been claimed. These precautions, along with the threat of 500 lashes as a penalty, ensured that the government received its full due. Once the nazur had taken his share, the remaining crop became the lawful possession of the grower. Through this process, the workers threshed and winnowed a vast quantity of barley in an incredibly short time.

Each cornfield in Maria's village contained several vast wells, about twenty feet deep, with a conical form. They were about three feet in diameter at the mouth, which was level with the ground, and about ten feet in diameter at the bottom. The bottom and sides had a thick coating of the abundant bitumen in these parts, which made it impossible for moisture from the earth to penetrate. Those in the district cast the surplus produce of each year into these receptacles, to be taken out in case of need or to supply traders in barley who passed through the district in one of the many caravans. A large round stone securely covered the top, and they used ropes and a large basket to lower a man and fill it with the grain as needed when taking out the barley. It was not uncommon for vast quantities of this stored produce to be destroyed when, after a succession of favorable seasons, the supply so far outgrew demand that the article became a mere incumbrance. Maria lamented that this surplus produce could have saved many from starvation if only man would direct all his energies to the welfare of his fellow creatures.

Every owner received the amount of barley needed for the year and stored it in a specific area called the *shekliim*, located on the top floor of the house. Normally, no more than two of these available spots were used. Cloth was used to plug the hole in the wall beneath the chambers. They removed the plug when they needed barley, which cascaded out like a fountain, swiftly filling the waiting sack below.

In the town of Telkaif lived about 20,000 inhabitants, the majority of whom were Christians. The houses were built in a solid manner, using stone brought from neighboring quarries and joined by a cement made with lime, the produce of the same quarries. This cement dried quickly and became as hard as the stone itself.

Their mode of building was remarkable and surpassed anything Maria had ever seen. In the space of three or four days, workmen would contrive to finish a substantial house consisting of two or three stories. They prepared the materials beforehand, and once assembled, divided their group into two parties. One was engaged in placing the stone in layers, one above the other, while the others slacked the lime, prepared the mortar, and handed it, when prepared, to the former party. It was absolutely necessary that these operations proceeded simultaneously; otherwise, the mortar would have hardened before it could be applied to the surface of the stones.

The construction of these dwelling" did'not Involve the use of any kind of wooden beams, not even for the ceilings, which, like the rest of the building, consisted of stone held together by layers of mortar. After just thirty minutes, the entire structure turned into an almost uniform mass of remarkable solidity and strength, allowing the workmen to construct the upper level and positioning heavy stone blocks on this recently built platform.

The houses In Telkaif had a similar architectural style to those found in many parts of Assyria and Mesopotamia. They featured arcades that encircled the inner courtyard on both the ground and upper floors. A tank was typically in the center of the courtyard. Although fountains were a rare sight in the area, the Pasha's palace was an exception. The houses, constructed from stone, were often coated with the same cement used to bond them together. Once dried, the cement acquired a brilliant white color, creating a dazzling effect when viewed from a distance under the region's cloudless sky and intense sun.

Close to Telkaif, there was a fountain with tepid water that maintained the same temperature throughout the year, whether in summer or winter. The water had a pleasant taste resembling that of sweetened water. The ruins of ancient Nineveh filled the area surrounding the fountain, offering glimpses into a rich historical past.

It was in Telkaif that Maria's father established factories aimed at restoring their family's fortunes, which had suffered due to his unwavering commitment to his faith. Three factories focused on extracting oil from the seeds of a plant known as *simsim* in Arabic, sesame in English. The oil derived from sim-sim, as well as from the castor plant, was in high demand for lamps and domestic cooking among the local inhabitants.

The oil extraction process took pl"ce w'thin a factory of four spacious chambers. Three of the chambers measured approximately forty feet square, while the fourth was smaller. In the first chamber, the seeds were crushed using large wooden mallets, wielded by men standing in a row. These workers, dressed only in belts, skillfully pounded the seeds that they had previously soaked in water to soften them.

Then, they transferred the crushed seeds to the second chamber and mixed them with water while vigorously stirring. This step facilitated the separation of oil from the pulp. After allowing the mixture to settle, the oil would rise to the top, forming a distinct layer. Meticulous workers carefully skimmed off the oil, transferring it to large earthen jars, while discarding the remaining pulp.

In the third chamber, the collected oil underwent a filtration process. Within this chamber, they set up a row of porous clay pots. The first pot received the oil and acted as a filter, allowing it to slowly pass through the tiny holes and remove any remaining impurities. The filtered oil gradually flowed from one pot to the next until it reached the final pot, where it was collected in clean containers ready for storage or distribution. The smaller chamber adjacent to the others served as a storage area for the extracted oil. Here, large clay jars called amphorae were used to store the oil, protecting it from light and air, which could cause it to spoil. To ensure the oil remained fresh and of the highest quality, they tightly sealed the jars.

Beyond the oil factories, Maria's father also established a textile factory in Telkaif. Within this bustling establishment, skilled weavers operated handlooms, crafting a wide array of fabrics. The textiles produced included vibrant silk and cotton fabrics adorned with intricate patterns and designs. These sought-after fabrics not only catered to the local market but also gained popularity in neighboring regions.

Maria's father's factories became significant contributors to the local economy, providing employment opportunities and contributing to the overall growth of Telkaif. They were a source of great pride for Maria's family, as they witnessed the restoration of their fortunes through hard work and unwavering dedication.

Telkaif itself was a vibrant town with a lively marketplace. Traders from distant lands would bring their goods, creating a diverse and bustling atmosphere. The air was filled with the tantalizing aromas of exotic spices, while the vibrant colors of the market stalls captivated the senses. Telkaif served as a meeting point for different cultures, fostering an atmosphere of tolerance and cultural exchange.

Life in Telkaif revolved around a strong sense of community. Festivals and celebrations were eagerly anticipated, bringing people together in joyous gatherings. The town's Christian majority celebrated religious holidays with great fervor, attending church services and taking part in traditional rituals.

As Maria reminisced about those days, a wave of nostalgia washed over her. The bustling streets, the warm smiles of the townspeople, and the sense of unity that permeated Telkaif held a special place in her heart. It was a town where tradition and modernity coexisted harmoniously, and where the industrious spirit of its inhabitants shaped its destiny.

Throughout their labor, the workers found relief and solace by singing together in harmony. Their songs followed a repetitive and monotonous melody, accompanied by lyrics such as, "God will help us. Man is destined to earn his livelihood through hard work and perseverance." Maria loved living amidst a community deeply rooted in their Christian faith. Their devotion to their religion went beyond mere profession, as they dedicated part of each day to studying the sacred texts and strived to embody the divine precepts in their lives.

The impact of their faith on their manners and conduct was truly remarkable. Maria witnessed extraordinary examples of forgiveness, where individuals displayed an almost superhuman ability to let go of grudges and return good for evil. There was no room for dissimulation or concealed animosity among these sincere and humble-hearted people. Even those who had exchanged harsh words or insults, like calling each other *khanzir*, meaning pig, would swiftly reconcile and embrace each other in brotherhood. The fiery nature of their Eastern blood prevented them from suppressing their emotions, and thus their feelings were expressed openly. This genuine display of forgiveness and reconciliation was a testament to the profound influence of their religious beliefs.

A poignant incident that Maria recalled Involved a woman from Telkaif who had a beloved son, her source of joy and comfort in her old age. Tragically, the young man lost his life in a brawl. The perpetrator, a societal outcast without friends or protectors, found unexpected solace and support in the mother of his victim. Despite the grief he had caused her and the desolation he had brought upon her home, she forgave him. The belief motivated her act of forgiveness that, on the day of judgment, she herself would seek forgiveness from the One who, in His great humility, taught humanity the path to salvation and instructed them to forgive their enemies.

In Telkaif, the Christian community's commitment to their religious principles created an atmosphere of compassion, understanding, and a deep sense of shared humanity. Their faith not only shaped their individual lives but also influenced the way they interacted with others, fostering peace and harmony within the town. Maria cherished the example set by her fellow townspeople, as their unwavering faith and commitment to forgiveness left an indelible impression on her own character and outlook on life.

The people in this small community paid much attention to education. It was difficult to find a person, male or female, who could not read and write. Because they prioritized the useful arts and sciences, Telkaif earned the nickname "Little Athens." They strictly followed the two great commandments of loving God with all their heart, soul, strength, and mind, and loving their neighbor as themselves. Chastity held immense esteem among them.

During Lent, the inhabitants of Telkaif strictly subsisted on vegetables such as rice and truffles, which they ate either roasted or in soup. By mentioning their rigid adherence to the precepts of their religion Maria did not claim superiority for them over the Christians of Mosul and Mesopotamia in general. They were all known for the patriarchal simplicity of their lives.

Expressions like "death is certain, but the hour uncertain; for it shall come as a thief in the night! Life is even as the lightning's flash, and all the riches, pleasures, and honors of this world are but vanity of vanities!" were frequently on their lips, exerting a salutary influence over their thoughts and actions.

Their houses were plain, and they were not eager to amass wealth except for dispensing charity and providing service to their fellow human beings. Intolerance did not limit their charity towards those of different faiths. Their generosity and help knew no bounds, reaching out to all in need or tribulation, whether they were Jews, Gentiles, Muslims, or Yezidis. They believed in the principle of "casting bread upon the running waters," trusting that it would be returned to them in due time. They firmly believed that God, who feeds the birds of the air, keeps a record of all acts of charity.

Whether every dweller in Arabia considered Christian or Muslim the most sacred duty of humanity. Disputes would often arise among neighboring Christian families, each claiming the privilege of entertaining a stranger. To resolve this, they established a law that the first person to touch the stranger would become their host. They didn't view this act as an exalted virtue but as an instinct inherent in human nature, promoting their own happiness and that of their fellow human beings. They believed all people should enjoy the bountiful fruits of the earth for their comfort. Even the Bedouins, the nomadic warriors who justified their acts of robbery and killing by divine sanction, recognized the sanctity of this obligation.

No formal invitation was required to join their table; the only qualification was the need for a meal. They didn't feel obliged to inquire about a guest's background, birth, or ability to reciprocate the gesture. The stranger would enter, take a seat at the table, and partake of the abundant provisions as a matter of right. They never saved leftover food for the next day but generously gave it to the poor. The Chaldeans were unfamiliar with the sour expressions that often accompanied the unexpected arrival of a stranger or acquaintance during dinner, a common occurrence in European cultures. Only in the face of death did they display displeasure at the entrance of a friend or stranger.

Maria's father was renowned for the extent of his charitable actions. He dedicated a significant portion of his once substantial fortune to the exercise of this virtue, sometimes even bordering on enthusiasm. Not content with assisting only those who directly approached him for help, he would often venture out in search of individuals upon whom he could give his benevolence. Occasionally, he would bring these people home, seat them at his table, offer them the finest provisions, and attend to their needs. He would go so far as to wash their feet, remove their rags, and clothe them in his own garments. Maria witnessed him perform these acts repeatedly, and though her ideals were fervent and lofty, she occasionally thought he was pushing the boundaries of the virtue to its extreme.

It was not unusual for him to purchase elderly and weak slave women who were no longer capable of working. His intention was to provide them with care and protect them from neglect and mistreatment during their declining years. Maria distinctly recalls one incident that elicited amusement from a Kurdish chief, a friend of her father's from the neighboring Sinjar mountain. The chief inquired why her father would bother with such old, worn-out women. In response, her father simply stated, "Li wijih Allah," which translates to "It is all for the face of God."

The Kurdish chief, much like most of those inhabiting the mountains of Sinjar, belonged to a religious sect known as the Yezidis, who worshipped the devil. Maria recalled a severe punishment from her father when she inadvertently spat on the ground in the presence of this man. In Yezidi culture, they considered such an act as one of the gravest insults that one can offer to the evil one.

The Yezidis performed the sign of the cross and administered baptism, following the customs of Oriental Christians, eight days after a child's birth. They believed in a Supreme Being and in Jesus Christ, whom they regarded as a Savior, much like Maria and her people. They revered the rays of the rising sun, and the use of torches, candles, and any artificial means of producing light was deemed impious and strictly prohibited. It was a serious offense against their religion to spit in the fire, which they held as a sacred element.

They referred to the evil one they worshipped as Amir el Zallam, the Prince of Darkness. They made vows to him and ritual offerings, sometimes of great value, such as gold and jewels, which they cast into a deep pit in the mountains of Sinjar. Upon learning of this practice, certain Turkish authorities compelled the Yezidi high priests to disclose the location of the sacred chasm. They swiftly transferred the hoard belonging to His Satanic Majesty into their own coffers, undoubtedly utilizing it in a manner that satisfied the prince as if he himself had been solely involved in its distribution.

Maria viewed the Yazidis to be wild enthusiasts, a belief that was likely shaped by external influences such as cultural traditions and societal narratives. She had limited personal experience or interaction with them and therefore did not have first-hand knowledge. People feared the Yazidis because of their relentless cruelty towards those unfortunate enough to fall into their hands. She viewed them as notorious thieves who would not hesitate to attack caravans passing through their territory, subjecting the unfortunate travelers to extreme barbarity after robbing them. They harbored a deep hatred for the name of Muhammad, specifically targeting his followers for their refined acts of cruelty. They believed that by putting Muslims, especially a sheriff or descendant of the prophet, to death, they would secure a guaranteed passage to the realms of eternal bliss—a welcome entrance to their Jannah, or Paradise. They held the belief that anyone who died at the hands of Muslims had earned the crown of martyrdom—a sentiment that the Turks reciprocated by never missing an opportunity to execute a Yezidi. While they showed respect towards Christian churches and monasteries, Maria could never ascertain that Christians themselves escaped robbery and mistreatment when they happened to be part of a caravan targeted by these desperadoes.

When entering a monastery, the Yezidis removed their shoes and expressed their veneration by kissing the walls of the sacred structure. However, they steadfastly refused to enter a mosque. They feared offending their prince, the Great Sheikh, the Prince of Darkness, to such an extent that they expunged from their language any words bearing the faintest resemblance to the sound of his name.

The Yezidis were not devoid of scriptural texts supporting their doctrines. They placed great reliance on the account in which the devil purportedly took Jesus to the pinnacle of a high mountain, offering him dominion over the entire world if he would only worship him. Drawing from this narrative, the Yezidis argued that the government of the world must reside with Satan. Their worship of him was thought to have been driven more by a desire to appease his wrath rather than an admiration of his benevolent attributes. Maria couldn't help but wonder why they chose not to consider Jesus' response, as it might challenge their faith.

People believed the Yezidis were descendants of the Manicheans and that they had their own priests and spiritual leaders. The chief among them enjoyed the esteemed honor and privilege of direct communication with the infernal majesty himself, the Prince of Darkness. Before embarking on any significant undertaking, the Yezidis consistently sought counsel from this pontiff. Perhaps, for them, the phrase, "Go to the Devil!" would be considered an expression of good will.

Maria's knowledge of the Yazidis could have been based on her lack of understanding. She and most others could not gather further information about their beliefs, as they preferred to keep such matters extremely reserved when discussing them with outsiders. They had a designated church where they congregated, and each year they held a grand festival, drawing followers from far and wide. According to them, this sacred city was in the mountains of Kurdistan.

The Yezidis exhibited a great diversity in their complexions and hair color, suggesting a mixed heritage. They possessed tall stature and well-proportioned physiques. Those living in the mountains abstained from trimming their hair or beards, which contributed to their uncouth and ferocious appearance, aligning with their rugged way of life.

Different Pashas had made many attempts to suppress the bands, but they had all been unsuccessful. Maria's father, a devout Christian who diligently followed the ordinances of his religion, often welcomed them to his table. He believed that by doing so, he humbly emulated the example set by his heavenly teacher, who had not hesitated to share meals with tax collectors and sinners.

In her writings, Maria loved noting the details and customs of her people, such as weddings and ceremonies which were celebrated in Mesopotamian Christian communities quite different from those in Europe. Parents frequently arranged betrothals immediately after the birth of their children. The young couple was not allowed to glimpse each other until the day of their wedding. Once a woman reached the age of twenty-one, society deemed her past her prime and believed she had little chance of finding a husband.

The husband provided the dower, while the wife, even if she hailed from a noble lineage, brought nothing more than her ornaments and a few belongings. The husband had to bear the responsibility of providing presents for the bride's father, mother, relatives, and friends, besides covering all incidental expenses. However, upon the death of the wife's father, the husband would become entitled to her share of the parental property.

On the designated day of the wedding, the bridegroom, accompanied by as many friends as he could gather, made his way to the home of the bride's father early in the morning. After receiving the blessings of the officiating priest, they set out in a grand procession divided into two groups. The first group consisted of the bridegroom on horseback, his grooms- men, friends, and relatives. The second group included the bride, also on horseback and veiled, along with her own rela- tives, friends, and attendants. Alongside the specially invited participants, a large crowd of acquaintances and well-wishers joined the procession on foot.

The wedding procession made their way around the town or village where the parents of the betrothed couple lived. They filled the air with alleluias and spiritual songs, which soon gave way to the resounding clash of cymbals and the rhythmic beat of tambours. Horns and trumpets blared their triumphant melodies, piercing the atmosphere with their bra- zen sound. As they moved forward, singing and rejoicing, each person bestowed blessings upon the couple whose union was about to be sealed, their destinies intertwined for as long as their earthly lives would endure. Love and affection emanated from the hearts of all present, dispelling envy, hatred, and mal- ice from their midst.

But then, silence fell upon the jubilant crowd as they ap- proached a church. The tambour ceased its roll, the clang of the cymbal faded away, and the trumpets became as quiet as the grave. The joyous shouts that had intermittently erupted now ceased, replaced by strains of devout adoration and rev- erential awe. They left the church behind, and once more, the resounding cheers of joy and exultant hymns filled the air.

Amidst such abundant happiness, people did not forget the less fortunate. One groomsman, acting as a grateful philan- thropist, would shower coins upon the poor, distributing them from a basket attached to the saddle of his horse. The small yet appreciated coins brought smiles to the faces of the sur- rounding spectators.

Continuing their joyful caroling and hymning, the procession made its way to the bridegroom's house. As a symbolic gesture, they dashed a porcelain vessel against the door, shattering it into pieces. One of the bride's relatives, who had remained veiled throughout the festivities, gently lifted the bride from her palfrey and carried her into the reception room. Placing her on a seat, the relative joined the gathering of female friends. The room became alive with the presence of women, both married and unmarried, distinguished by their distinct headwear. Married women adorned an ornament of silver gilt, while the virgins wore white muslin turbans, occasionally embellished with printed flowers.

After the wedding festivities, the husband led his relatives and friends to another reception room in a different part of the building. These ceremonies continue for a whole week. Each day, the entire assembly, often numbering five or six hundred individuals, gathered at the bridegroom's house to eat, drink, and celebrate. Sometimes they ventured outside the town, setting up tents for a countryside feast, with the genders remaining separate throughout the ceremonial events. The bridegroom and his friends solely bore the expenses for these celebrations, as well as all the other preparations. They typically adorned the bride's tent in a light-blue color. Singing, dancing, and feasting occupied their time until the seventh day when everyone departed for their respective homes, leaving the newlyweds to enjoy their happiness undisturbed. Matrimonial disputes were rare, and the love solemnly pledged at the altar endured through good and bad times as long as life lasts.

Similarly, mourning for the loss of a relative or friend lasted for seven days. In the past, burials would take place in the morning, but due to the discovery of cases of premature burials, the period was extended to twenty-four hours. During those seven days, sorrow and lamentation filled the air. Friends and relatives of the deceased visited the grave daily, watering it with their tears and filling the air with their wailing. Mourners were sometimes hired to sing sorrowful songs and display grief. For forty days, the tomb was visited twice a week, and every Sunday for a year, for the purpose of prayer and remembrance.

Amidst the Christian communities, filial affection shined brightly, and nowhere was it more apparent than in Maria's story. In these close-knit communities, fathers remained with their children until their death, at which point the eldest son took his place, receiving the same respect and honor.

Near Telkaif, nestled within the hollow formed by three converging hills, there lied a remarkable chasm. It was believed to have been created by a thunderbolt, its depth not exceeding twenty feet. The true extent of the rift remained unknown, as its sides had never been witnessed by a mortal soul. In winter, it transformed into a lake, but during the scorching heat of summer, it lay dry. The locals held a deep fear of the chasm, deeming it infested by grotesque reptilian creatures. A woman once fell into this pit and, with difficulty, extricated by ropes.

Maria recalled an incident that occurred in this town, an event regarded by the inhabitants as a miracle, worthy of comparison to those chronicled in Scripture. The coarse marble found in the nearby mountains provided the lime used in the production of the formidable cement. The process involved burning the marble in an immense furnace, fueled solely by hay—the primary fuel source in this region of Asia.

On a particular day, a humble man known for his unwavering faith in Christianity and his virtuous life tended to one of those colossal furnaces. He had taken his position atop the furnace when, without warning, the roof that separated him from the searing inferno below gave way with a deafening crash, engulfing him in its fiery depths.

Naturally, everyone assumed he had met an immediate and tragic end, sacrificed to the burning lime. Soon after, a group of men began removing the loose stones that had fallen into the hollow chamber of the furnace. For two days, they toiled diligently, not even expecting to find the charred remains of their comrade.

However, as they neared the completion of their labor, their astonishment knew no bounds when they heard the voice of their lost companion. Instantly, their efforts redoubled, as hope replaced despair. The sounds of their axes and spades were as abundant as hail. Within moments, their joy knew no bounds as they beheld their friend, miraculously preserved. The fallen stones had formed an arch, shielding him from the flames and preventing his immediate demise.

Like Sidrach, Misach, and Abdenago, who chose to face death in the fiery furnace rather than worship the golden statue, this humble man emerged alive from the charred heap. The wonder of his rescuers was immeasurable. They, awakened to a vibrant faith akin to a conscience-stricken idolater, exclaimed with Nebuchadnezzar, "Blessed be the God of them, who hath sent his angel and delivered his servants that believed in him."

In Telkaif, the inhabitants held harmless snakes within their homes, regarding them with a veneration nearly equal to the Romans' reverence for their household deities. During Maria's stay in Telkaif, the children often engaged in the sport of catching quails, which was a favorite pastime in the area due to the incredible number of quails found there. The process involved setting up a temporary hut in the desert capable of holding a few people. From the hut, cords extended, attached to a large net that was concealed by hay, wheat, and barley. The party would hide in the hut, holding the cords connected to the net, while countless birds would gather on the net, unaware of the danger as they sought food. When enough quails had gathered, the party would suddenly pull the cords, closing the net and capturing the birds.

Maria witnessed scenes where thousands of quails were trapped in the net, desperately trying to free themselves, their cries for liberty tugging at her heart. They would often carry away several loads of quails, enough to fill multiple mules and donkeys, as the result of their day's sport.

On one occasion, while returning from a day of quail hunting, a group of wandering Arabs attacked them. Resistance of the outnumbered travelers would have been futile, so they had no choice but to surrender. The thieves quickly stripped them of everything—their quails, horses, mules, and donkeys.

However, in a moment of quick thinking, one of Maria's brothers climbed to a vantage point where the people of Telkaif could see him. He threw sand into the air, a well-known signal for help. Fortunately, the people in town noticed the signal and sprang into action. They saddled their horses, armed themselves, and galloped to the rescue.

Realizing their odds had shifted, the thieves fled the scene. The people pursued them, recovered everything that the thieves had stolen, and delivered a well-deserved beating to the cowardly marauders. Afterwards, Maria insisted on sharing most of their game with their friends and rescuers, with the rest distributed to the poor.

Maria felt obliged to share in her writings and through her talks the manners, customs, and general characteristics of the people in this small town, as she desired to garner esteem, respect, and sympathy for the followers of their holy religion among their European brethren in Christ. The virtues of these individuals deserved such recognition, and she believed that by honestly and truthfully recounting the feelings and habits of the community where she had spent several years of her life, she could most effectively achieve this goal.

CHAPTER 5

PERSECUTION OF CHRISTIANS

From Telkaif, Maria returned to Mosul, the place she had set out from, and soon after, she embarked on a journey to Alqosh, a small town located north of Mosul, said to be the burial place of the prophet Nahum. Recognizing that marauding bands occasionally plagued the road and the region, she deemed it necessary to join forces with others who were heading in the same direction for mutual safety. It didn't take long for her to learn that a caravan of approximately one hundred people was about to depart for the destination she sought. Seizing the opportunity, she eagerly joined the group, consisting of herself, her mother, one of her brothers, and a lone servant.

Setting off at sunrise, they embarked on a pleasant journey that lasted most of the day. Fortunate to have exceptionally fine weather, the members of their party were in high spirits as they passed through various villages along the way, including Telkaif, Betnaya, and several others. These villages were characterized by sturdy stone houses, as previously described.

As evening approached, they found themselves within four leagues of Alqosh, nearing the foothills of a notorious mountain range associated with many acts of pillage. With the sun having descended below the horizon, the deep shadows cast by the towering, dark masses that flanked the gorge into which they were about to enter hindered their view of any potential obstructions that might impede their passage. Sensing the need to assess the situation, Maria's brother offered to ride ahead to a vantage point atop a nearby hill, from where he could survey the surroundings and relay the information back to the group. The caravan eagerly embraced this proposal, their previous merriment giving way to uncertainty and apprehension. Without delay, the brother spurred his horse, quickly disappearing around the bend of the mountain. He was, after all, a gallant and brave young man, full of courage.

The entire caravan anxiously awaited his return, their anticipation mounting with each passing moment. However, as time wore on, and with no sign of his reappearance, they feared that some misfortune had befallen him. A startling sight interrupted their concerns—emerging from around the mountainside, Maria's brother appeared flanked by two horsemen. A single glance revealed the telltale signs of these individuals: their long beards, unkempt hair, and fierce countenances were unmistakable—they were Kurds hailing from the neighboring mountains of Sinjar, known as the most lawless desperadoes on Earth.

"Who are these?" exclaimed Maria's mother in an agony of fright. "Are you bringing a band of robbers to despoil and murder us?"

A large body of mounted bandits appeared, putting all further questions at an end. They galloped down the hill like a cloud of locusts. It was clear they were now in the hands of robbers who far outnumbered them. Maria's brother and others prepared for the resistance, determined to perish than suffer those they held most dear to become the prey of lawless rapine and violence. The parties ranged opposite to each other: the Kurds, with their long lances in their hands, reining in their pawing steeds, who, as well as their lawless riders, seemed eager for the fight, and impatient of all delay.

Maria's mother wept, she screamed, and on her knees, she implored her son to give up rather than rush to destruction. He was, however, deaf to all her entreaties. His courage roused, he was determined to yield nothing.

Maria admired her brother's noble daring and was not afraid for her own safety. She said to her mother, "What! Would you have your son act the part of a coward, by tamely submitting, with arms in his hands? If you cannot inspire them with courage, do not weaken their resolution by your womanly fears. Fear not, oh, my mother, God will not desert the righteous!"

"Your property or your heads!" exclaimed the chief, a commandment which was answered by words of defiance from Maria's brother. That was the end of their conversation. The scene that followed was chaotic, with clashes of swords and the sounds of yells and cries filling the air. The outnumbered group fought valiantly, their determination fueling their resistance against the ruthless bandits. Despite their bravery, the odds were against them.

Maria and her mother stood at the foot of the mountain, waiting with trembling hearts. They witnessed the savage yells of the Kurds, thirsting for blood; the cluttering and snorting of the horses, betokening a deadly struggle; the shouts of the living, the groans of the dying. That, along with her mother's piercing shrieks, called for Maria to gather all the strength she could to not fall apart.

On both sides, combatants fell, some struck down by a slight wound, others writhing and gasping in the agonies of death. Despite being covered with wounds, Maria's brother persevered in the contest until he was overwhelmed by numbers and compelled to surrender, with the rest of the party following suit. Their small band could not withstand the relentless assault of the Kurdish marauders.

The victors immediately began an indiscriminate and relentless pillage, sparing neither age nor sex in their unmeasured rapacity. They seized upon everything Maria and her party had—horses, camels, and baggage; and concluded by stripping all who had survived the slaughter of everything they had on. It was only by employing the most abject entreaties that Maria, at length, prevailed upon them to leave her mother, herself, and the two ladies who accompanied them, a single undergarment.

At length, sated with bloodshed and plunder, the Kurds quitted the field, having killed fifteen of their party, and wounded nearly all who remained, some of them severely; amongst whom was Maria's dear heroic brother, who lay faint and almost senseless from loss of blood. Neither could the enemy have carried off a less number of killed and wounded on their side; for their party, though small, fought like lions. During the whole of this fearful contest, which lasted about three quarters of an hour, Maria never ceased to address words of encouragement to their valiant little band.

Here, then, were they left, four leagues from the place of their destination, despoiled of every thing they had, without camels, without horses, without any means of conveyance, and nearly their whole party so badly wounded as to be almost incapable of proceeding on foot; the men stripped naked, and they with nothing on but their chemises. What was left them but to lie down and die? How could they hope to traverse with their bare feet the rough and stony mountain path that led to Alqosh?

They resolved, however, to make the effort, and summoning up all their resolution, they left the blood-stained spot, and began ascending the hill before them. Maria's mother, though not wounded, was so entirely deserted by her faculties that she had not the power to walk, and Maria had to carry her on her back; for her brother's wounds prevented him from rendering them any assistance. Indeed, poor fellow, he needed help as much as any of them.

The journey was painful and took many hours, during which they constantly had to halt. This was because of Maria being fatigued from carrying her burden, and her brother from the agony and exhaustion occasioned by his wounds. They arrived at a village near Alqosh, and the chief, who Maria's father knew well, extended to them a warm hospitality. He not only caused her brother's wounds to be bound up but fed and supplied them with clothing. Amongst all the effects of which the Kurds plundered Maria, the article she most regretted the loss of was a book of prayers on which she set a high value.

Maria and her brother had to stay detained at the village for three days because of her brother's severe wounds, which prevented him from being moved. After her brother had sufficiently recovered through their unremitting care and his excellent constitution, they wrote to Maria's aunt living in Alqosh, who promptly sent her son with horses to fetch them. They then said goodbye to their kind host and traveled to Alqosh, where they stayed for a month until Maria's brother fully recovered.

Alqosh was situated at the foot of a lofty mountain, with smaller mountains on either side. About half an hour away stood the Deir Rabban Hormuz convent, placed atop a very high mountain. The view from the convent was grand and imposing, and it was inhabited by learned men and hermits. The convent contained twelve churches, thirty-six courts, and an incalculable number of chambers, with catacombs that extended almost to Alqosh. The gates of the sanctum sanctorum in the great church were ten paces wide and elaborately carved with ivory.

The convent was home to men skilled in all branches of learning and science. Contrary to the misconception that Arabia contained only marauding idolaters and uninformed Christians, the recluses of Deir Rabban Hormuz possessed a high level of education and would have fit in perfectly in the schools of Europe. The convent served as a center for the propagation of the Christian faith throughout the East. However, lawless Kurdish bands had often attacked it, massacring its inhabitants and plundering its treasures. The convent had also been subject to the rapacity of neighboring pashas, who had robbed the sanctuary and scattered its peaceful inhabitants. Yet the monks had always reestablished themselves on their beloved mountain, supporting the institute through their frugal means.

Maria's father had supported this religious institute, providing it with resources and championing the diffusion of knowledge and science in the East, where the light of learning had once shone brightly but now lay in ignorance and barbarism. The monks cultivated the monastery's lands and yielded abundant crops, distributing the surplus produce to the surrounding poor.

Maria visited the tomb of the prophet Nahum, who was born in Alqosh. There, the local Jews had built a synagogue where they practiced their religious rituals according to the laws of Moses. Maria had once been curious enough to attend a service there, but this had earned her father's strong disapproval. The Jewish community in Alqosh was far more observant than those in Europe. They would rather die than shave their beards.

The local Christians were also devout, spending much time studying sacred texts and acknowledging the Pope as the head of the Church. In the twenty days before Lent, they performed a penitential ritual reminiscent of the ancient Ninevites, fasting rigorously and wearing sackcloth and ashes for three days—a practice that had endured since the fall of Nineveh.

The people of Alqosh were a tall, well-built, and fair-complexioned group. The women wore a distinctive headdress with a curved, silver-gilt ornament attached by a red ribbon. The men donned the traditional red tarboosh that fell to their waists.

When Maria's brother had sufficiently recovered from his injuries, they set out to return to Mosul. But there, they would face trials even more severe than the attacks by Kurdish bandits they had already endured.

The existing Christian church in Telkaif was wholly inadequate to accommodate the local Christian population. Maria's grandfather was eager to get permission from the regional pasha to build a larger church to meet the community's needs. Through extensive negotiation, he effectively addressed the concerns of the Muslim authorities by offering a substantial bribe, resulting in them granting him permission to build a new church within certain specified limits.

Maria's grandfather set about his pious task with great alacrity, and within twenty days had completed a building capable of housing all the local Christians. A single wall enclosed the old and new churches, with dwellings arranged around the inside for the officiating priests. In Eastern Christian churches, no layperson could encroach on the sacred precincts of the altar, which was separated from the main body of the church and raised three steps above the floor.

However, the architect employed by Maria's grandfather had inadvertently exceeded the prescribed limits for the new church by a mere three feet. This minor transgression might have gone unnoticed, were it not for a fanatical Turkish man who was constantly on the lookout for opportunities to accuse Christians of violating the law. This man reported the infraction to the pasha, leading to an official inquiry. The authorities took measurements and swiftly convicted Maria's grandfather of the alleged crime.

A fanatical frenzy rapidly spread through the town, following Maria's grandfather's conviction. Hordes of Muslims assembled and demolished the sacred building that he had invested so much money into constructing, shouting and cursing as they did so. They didn't stop in their frenzied fury and took twenty days to complete the work of destruction because the church had been built so substantially. They were like a pack of ravenous wolves, driven by the belief that "every Christian church is a burden upon the head of Muhammad." So, they saw the church's additional square footage as an even greater weight upon their prophet.

They imprisoned Maria's grandfather and father, along with his brothers and sons, and many other influential local Christians. The prison guards shackled them with heavy chains and subjected them to daily beatings with the bastinado.

The authorities offered them a stark choice: embrace the Islamic faith or suffer a painful and ignominious death. Undaunted by the brutal fate they knew they could expect from the Turks, they calmly but resolutely refused to renounce the faith in which they had been born and raised. They were determined to die in that faith, even if the Turks prolonged their final agonies to the absolute limit through every refinement of torture.

Maria exulted at the prospect of martyrdom, fervently hoping she could share that fate with her beloved parents. Not a sigh or lament escaped her lips—her heart was overflowing with holy fervor and pious hope. She gathered her friends around her, leading them in songs of praise and thanksgiving. She went about as though dressed for a festival, crying out, "This day shall I behold the face of the Lord! What are the treasures of this world? They are but chaff, blown away by the wind. Let us instead imitate the blessed martyrs and purchase the eternal treasures of heaven with our blood!"

But disappointment awaited Maria. The tyrannical oppressor's lust for gold outweighed his thirst for blood. They finally let go of Maria's grandfather, father, uncles, and their relations and adherents, who had suffered from the barbarous treatment. However, they only did so when her father paid a ruinous sum that compelled him to part with almost all of his lands, mills, factories, livestock, gold, silver, and jewels, reducing him from opulence to relative poverty.

Undaunted by these cruel setbacks, as soon as her father had recovered from the wounds inflicted by the merciless beatings, he set out for Baghdad, accompanied by his family. There he placed Maria and her mother in a house that he owned, at a short distance from the one which Maria had spent the happy days of her childhood. He then set out for Basra, where he had relations, hoping to repair his shattered fortune through the unremitting industry and perseverance.

CHAPTER 6

THE FAMILY'S MISFORTUNE

Two years passed, and with unwavering determination and Providence favoring his endeavors, Maria's father returned to Mosul. His goal was to re-establish his factories, regain his lost possessions, and once again become the leader of the local Christian community that had long looked to him. He undertook this task with reasonable hope, as he had been fortunate in his business dealings in Basra and saved a considerable sum of money through frugality.

During their stay near Baghdad, Maria made multiple excursions to the ruins of the Tower of Babel, about a day's journey from their home on the road to Hillah. Locals believed ancient ruins, remnants of Babylon, housed evil spirits and demons. Influenced by the prevailing superstitions, she couldn't resist the temptation to provide for herself a relic as a memento during her visits.

At sixteen, Maria and her family returned to Mosul, the site of their previous misfortunes. There, her father wasted no time rebuilding mills and establishing manufactories in the nearby town of Telkaif. For several years, they lived a tranquil and happy life, receiving visits and attention from all classes of people, including chiefs of the nomadic Bedouin and Kurdish tribes who were on close terms with Maria's father. The extended family, numbering around forty including servants, all lived together in one spacious mansion, larger even, from Maria's perspective, than the Louvre in Paris.

Maria, who preferred a solitary life, had a chamber set up for herself at the top of the house, on the terrace, where someone brought her meals daily. This allowed her to devote her time fully to study, prayer, and contemplation. Her only visitors were some local ladies who shared her religious fervor. Maria lived simply and slept little, often going out at midnight to read her favorite sacred writings by the peaceful light of the moon, sometimes kneeling for hours to recite the psalms she had committed to memory.

In the mornings, Maria would rise early and walk the half-hour to the church, often arriving an hour before it opened at seven. On one occasion, she kneeled in prayer during a hailstorm of unprecedented magnitude. Unprecedented hailstones, the size of walnuts, fell from the sky, causing the demise of numerous birds.

At another time, Maria had the misfortune of being bitten by a scorpion one summer while waiting for the church gates to open. Despite the intense pain, she persisted in her devotion. Someone eventually took her into a chamber adjoining the church and treated the wound with cauterization. She endured excruciating torment for the next twenty-four hours, and people considered it miraculous that she escaped death. Once her parents learned of the incident, they promptly arranged for her to be transported back home.

Maria experienced great happiness in those few years. Living with devoted parents, she felt blessed with all the world could offer. Her father, unhindered in his efforts to care for his family and help others, spent his free time in the company of his loved ones. Maria enjoyed close friendships with those who shared her religious devotion, leaving her ample time for prayer and contemplation.

During this time, not a day passed without Maria visiting the local poor and sick, providing what humble aid and spiritual comfort she could. Three times daily, she attended the impressive church services, which she noticed that even a visiting European gentleman had found deeply moving in their solemnity. Across Assyria and Chaldea, these services followed a format where the congregants, often numbering over a hundred per side, sang portions of the Psalms and Canticles with pious fervor, their voices trembling with ecstasy. Their European guest had never witnessed religious ceremonies so captivating.

They occasionally mixed these sacred duties with joyful rides through the surrounding countryside, where they experienced the spring landscape unveiling in a vibrant tapestry of Asiatic greenery and flowers. They saw vast fields of corn rippling in the gentle breeze like an endless sea. Maria usually selected the banks of the Tigris River or one of its tributaries as the setting for her family's excursions. One day, she was riding along the banks of the Haousera, a branch of the Tigris where many of her father's mills were located. Her brother and uncle accompanied her.

Maria's brother was riding a rare and valuable Arabian mare that belonged to their father. This mare, of the prized el kaheilani breed, was truly exceptional. Its neck was as graceful as a rainbow, its eyes like a living coal, its mane and tail cascading like a weeping willow. Its feet moved with the agility of a stag, and its gallop was as swift as an eagle in flight. Many Bedouin chiefs had tried in vain to gain this matchless mare, which was fed primarily on rice and bread. The mare's gentle nature and intelligence made it safe for children to play around its hooves.

As Maria and her companions rode along the riverbank, the urge to swim the mare across the swift-flowing stream seized her brother. The animal fearlessly entered the water, treating the strong current like a narrow canal. However, the strength of the stream proved greater than her brother expected. Despite his frantic efforts, he could not guide the mare to safety. Ultimately, he had to choose between abandoning the horse to its fate or perishing with it, as the exhausted animal had lost the ability to save itself. In the end, he disentangled himself from the mare and, through sheer determination, reached the shore.

Thus, Maria's father lost one of the finest and most beautiful Arabian steeds ever bred, a magnificent creature for which he could have commanded an extraordinary price. Yet, rather than heap reproaches on his imprudent son, the father bore this calamity with Christian forbearance and resignation, as he had with other, more significant misfortunes. They found the mare's body later and laid her heart to rest at the foot of a nearby mountain.

For some years, Maria and her family lived a life of uninterrupted happiness. Then, her father hosted an open-air celebration for his relatives and friends on the banks of the Tigris, near to Mosul. This was one way in which he enjoyed expressing his hospitality, and on this occasion, as on many similar ones, he had invited several Kurd and Bedouin tribal chiefs with whom he maintained close relationships.

The day was splendid, with nature adorned in its finest May attire. Adversity seemed to have abandoned the family, for Maria's father had once more become prosperous. Everything appeared to promise him a dignified and protracted old age until when God would call him to his ancestors.

On this spot, the family pitched their tents, and they constructed one of them to match the description of Abraham's tent in the Bible. They slaughtered bullocks, lambs, and sheep, along with an abundance of preserved quails, fowl, and every other delicacy that could contribute to the enjoyment of their guests. They then lay out their sumptuous feast.

After their substantial meal, the carousers dispersed in various directions, following their individual interests. Beyond them lay the ruins of ancient Nineveh, its grandeur evident only in the vastness of the mounds that stretched for miles. Maria, accompanied by her companions, wandered along the river, chanting spiritual songs from her ample repertoire. To respect the religious sensibilities of their Bedouin guests, she remained at a distance from them during this pious pastime.

One shepherd who had converted to the Christian faith was a Bedouin. Maria had never encountered a human being more genuinely imbued with the Christian spirit. This shepherd had converted through her efforts. She, therefore, took a great interest in his welfare and observed him with awe. Nothing could exceed his resignation to the will of Providence. He never presumed with certainty that he would find his wife and family alive upon returning from tending the horses and sheep. He was always mentally prepared for any reverses that might befall him.

When he had once suffered the misfortune of losing his son, who fell victim to the Samiri of the Desert—a fiery blast that frequently destroys those who encounter it—his only exclamation was, "The Lord gave, and the Lord hath taken away; as it hath pleased the Lord, so is it done: blessed be the name of the Lord!"

The day of celebration brought Maria the utmost happiness. She had no wish or thought beyond her blessed moment with Providence. Past cares and sorrows vanished like they never existed. Seeing her father alone at a short distance, Maria left her companions and went to his side. The recent peaceful interval marked the longest time he had ever spent with his family. Maria was never so happy as when she could enjoy his company alone. On this occasion, they wandered for hours on the banks of the Tigris, their hearts swelling with gratitude to the Almighty Disposer of events for all His mercies.

"How happy it is to spend time with those dearer to us than life itself! The voice of our enemy is silent. He no longer takes counsel for our destruction. In this world of care and misery, Maria questioned, "If happiness can be found, what can the righteous expect in a better world?"

Maria besought her father that they might again resort to this lovely spot together alone and indulge in pious musings. He agreed happily, but it didn't happen. While he imagined blissful moments together, an impending abyss threatened to swallow their happiness forever.

Information was carried to the ears of the Pasha, ever ready to entertain any charge against his Christian subjects, that treasure of immense value was discovered by Maria's father under the ruins of ancient Nineveh, and that he had appropriated it to his own use. They accused him of promoting projects to undermine the Ottoman government and Islam.

Maria's father was a prosperous businessman who owned mills and factories along the banks of the Tigris River. Despite years of cruelty, he restored his wealth and resumed providing for his community. He welcomed the hungry and destitute into his home and supported local Christian churches with his generosity.

However, his newfound success aroused the suspicion of his enemies. They couldn't understand how a man who was once almost poor could now be thriving. Desperate to find an explanation, they latched onto the idea that he must have discovered hidden treasure amidst the ruins of ancient Nineveh, where his workers toiled.

Despite the lack of any real evidence, the mere accusation was enough to justify extreme measures taken against Maria's father. They arrested him, along with his brothers, and subjected him to cruel and unrelenting torture. His captors hoped to force a confession and the disclosure of the supposed hidden treasure's location.

But Maria's father had nothing to confess. He steadfastly maintained his innocence, demonstrating the unwavering faith and calm resignation of a true Christian in the face of such suffering. All the efforts of his persecutors proved futile, only serving to further expose the injustice and fanaticism driving their actions.

Maria's family faced a tragic turn of events. Greed and brutality had once again prevailed. The authorities released her beloved father from imprisonment, but they commuted his sentence of death to the confiscation of his entire possessions. Broken in body and spirit, covered in bruises and wounds, his feet a shapeless mass of black, festering flesh from the merciless blows of the bastinado, they finally released him from his dungeon and brought him home. The change in him was horrific. Just a short month prior, they had been planning projects of future happiness and harmless enjoyment during their happy walks along the banks of the Tigris.

Despite the unwavering attention and the care of the most skilled surgeons, Maria's father's condition only worsened. Nature had been pushed beyond its limits, and his suffering had surpassed human endurance. From the moment of his release, Maria never left his bedside. As the awful moment drew near, with his soul hovering on the brink of eternity, he called Maria to his side. In faltering words, he expressed his concern for her future, urging her to preserve her strong faith and fear of the Almighty, as she would need them to withstand the assaults of their enemies. After receiving the last rites, with a countenance of heroic composure and Christian resignation, he yielded up his spirit to his Creator.

Maria was devastated. She had no tears to shed, as the fountains of her soul had dried up, and she expected her heart would burst. Overwhelmed by sorrow, grief, and wailing, she nearly lost her reason. She fell ill with fever, fervently praying it would prove fatal so she could rejoin her beloved father. But God denied her that relief, and she had to live on and endure suffering.

This last persecution led to the utter destruction of Maria's family. One of her uncles died shortly after from the treatment he had received. The Archbishop of Diyarbakir was bound to the back of a wild horse and driven into the desert, left without food for many days. He eventually freed himself and reach safety, but only after a harrowing ordeal. Maria's mother, overcome with grief, died soon after Maria's father.

The hand of Providence had weighed heavily upon Maria. Yet her cup of bitterness was not yet full. Shortly after, a pestilence swept through the land, claiming the lives of ninety-five thousand souls in Mosul and the surrounding area. All her relatives died from the plague, leaving her an orphan in the city she considered ill-omened. She longed for death, but the angel of destruction passed her by. She wandered the fields, scarcely aware of where she was or what she was doing. She moved forward, heedless of her surroundings, except when the sight of some well-known spot would lacerate her heart anew, awakening it to the bitter sense of her loss and mournful desolation.

CHAPTER 7

———— ❧ ————

ESTABLISHING A WOMEN'S EDUCATION INSTITUTION

Maria's father had entrusted her with the few possessions he had salvaged from the wreckage of their
fortune. He had placed his ring, hanjar, watches,
valuable pearls, jewels, and Persian shawls under the care of
a bishop known to him. Recognizing her destitute state, the
bishop kindly offered to accompany Maria to Baghdad for
safety. Grateful for the offer, Maria accepted, and a few months
after the devastating tragedy that had torn her world apart,
they departed from the ill-fated city, leaving behind the scenes
of her profound sorrows.

Together with a lady she knew and a Christian Kurdish
slave, Maria and the bishop embarked on their journey to
Baghdad. They traveled along the Tigris River on a kalak, a raft
constructed from inflated skins with a small cabin erected on it.

As Maria took one last look at the city she despised, she
couldn't help but proclaim, "Goodbye, you desolate place, the
grave of all I ever loved! Farewell, you accursed city, condemned
by the wrath of God for your countless sins and wrongdoings!"
Her words echoed the divine judgment that had fallen upon the
city, as if the Lord Himself had declared, "Listen, I'm coming
against you, says the Lord of Hosts; I will expose your shame
to your face, and show your nakedness to the nations, and your
disgrace to kingdoms. I will heap abominations upon you, and

humiliate you, and make an example of you. When people see you, they will flee and declare "Nineveh is destroyed! Who will mourn for you? Where can I find a comforter for you?'"

During their journey, they occasionally disembarked from the kalak and strolled along the riverbanks. Whether to navigate through rapids or simply to enjoy the beauty of a particular spot or the refreshing coolness of the air, these moments offered respite from their river voyage.

For a long time, Maria remained silent, lost in melancholic reflections of the past and plagued by grim apprehensions for the future. Her kind-hearted friend and protector attempted to engage her in conversation, using various tactics to shake her from her lethargy, but all in vain. As they passed by the spot where streams of naphtha from the nearby mountain merged with the Tigris, hoping to capture her attention with this phenomenon, he tossed lit pieces of cloth into the water, igniting the naphtha and causing the majestic river to glow with vibrant streaks of liquid fire. All these efforts were in vain. Maria was wounded to her core; her soul burdened with an unshakable heaviness. Amusement held no appeal, and even words of solace from her friend became burdensome.

Thus, the first day slipped away, with Maria consumed by the bitterest reflections. They spent the night on the kalak, and when she awoke the next morning, her mind was slightly more composed, her resolve strengthened to accept the decrees of Divine Providence without complaint. During the night, she had fervently beseeched the aid of the Almighty in her affliction, and her prayers had not gone unanswered.

As they approached the treacherous stretch of the Tigris where navigation became difficult and hazardous due to rocks jutting out from the riverbed, visible even above the water's surface, Maria and her companions faced increased risks. Accidents frequently occurred in this area, as the inflated skins comprising the kalak would burst upon contact with sharp angles of the rocks. It was customary for all passengers, regardless of their religious affiliation—whether Christian or Muslim—to offer prayers for their safety upon reaching this perilous spot.

Taking precautions, Maria and her companions disembarked just before their vessel approached the perilous area, opting to walk along the river's edge until they had safely passed it. Their prudence proved wise when, as they glanced backward, they witnessed a child struggling in the water. Despite valiant efforts to rescue the child, it tragically succumbed to the river's relentless grip before their very eyes. The child's parents, who were also traveling downstream on a kalak, had not parted ways with their little one at the right moment, mistakenly relying on their own skills to navigate the dangers. The skin of their raft burst, causing it to capsize, and the unforgiving currents plunged everyone on board, including several adults and the child. Fortunately, the Bedouin passengers, both men and women, who were adept swimmers, managed to save themselves from the watery peril.

Local inhabitants of the area shared tales of frequent sightings of enormous serpents known for their formidable size and aggression, evoking great fear among the populace. According to the accounts, these serpents would coil their bodies into a threatening vertical position, resembling massive clubs when launching their assaults.

After a five-day voyage, Maria and her companions finally arrived in Baghdad. In early spring, as northern mountain snow melted, the Tigris River flowed swiftly. Mosul to Baghdad journey took two days. However, there were no proper landing facilities, so naked porters carried both men and women ashore, save for a girdle around their waists. A comical incident occurred when one porter, carrying a lady in his arms, slipped and fell into the water along with his unfortunate passenger. The onlookers couldn't help but burst into laughter at the scene, despite Maria's long-standing solemnity. Maria, who hadn't smiled in a while, found a moment of amusement.

Maria arrived in Baghdad and stayed at a friend's house. During this time, a project entered her head, to which she directed all her energies; namely, to establish an institution for the education of women. This project held great significance for her from an early age. She was not destitute of means. With the little property that remained to her, together with the help of her friend, who was wealthy, and whose co-operation she did not despair of obtaining, Maria confidently hoped to carry her wishes into effect.

On first opening the subject to her protector, he refused to listen to it and dismissed it as a visionary scheme, believing it could only have originated from an over-confident and disordered imagination, and one that would not lead to any beneficial results. However, Maria remained determined and refused to be easily discouraged. She endeavored to raise his enthusiasm by setting before him, in as glowing colors as she could, the glory that would result from rescuing the weaker sex amongst them from the inferiority, both moral and physical, in which they had hitherto continued. She emphasized the happiness of helping them reach their intended usefulness.

Maria asked her friend how these people ended up in this state. She argued it was because of ignorance. Who let them stay ignorant, and who created the barrier blocking their minds from receiving knowledge? It was man alone who was culpable. He first denies women the means to obtain knowledge, and then uses their ignorance, a consequence of his own neglect, as justification for holding them in contempt. She declared it should no longer be said that they imitate their irreligious neighbors in the treatment of their partners.

"Our religion teaches us better," she said. "We must not merely be Christians in name."

She then asked where their church teaches that women should be slaves to men. Woman was formed to be man's companion and solace throughout his earthly existence. On what grounds, then, does man assert his privilege to tyrannize over women? Does not the female sex possess more patient endurance and tender care than the male? Like men, do they not possess immortal souls? Are a woman's sensibilities not as keen or keener than her "Lord and master's"? Yet, society often treated women as if they had neither head nor heart.

She acknowledged the weakness of the female sex yet boasted of Bedouin women who rivaled men in horsemanship and javelin-throwing, causing fear in many men. And she had never witnessed that this supposed weakness exempted women from the most laborious and fatiguing household duties. Their "indolent lords" who sat idly by, smoking, while their wives engaged in the arduous labor of setting up their tents did not consider their weakness. She claimed that the ignorance and humiliating delusions of the Christian women of the East result from neglecting the cultivation of their minds. This ignorance alone makes man the tyrant and woman the slave. Ignorance is the curse, she declared, and religious education is the cure.

Maria shared a tale she heard from her father to illustrate her point. Long ago, a nation had a tradition of yearly electing a new king to govern. To prevent jealousy and conflict, they never chose one of their own people, but sought a random stranger passing through their lands and placed him on the throne. They did this to ensure the ruler's impartiality in administering justice.

When the king's one-year term ended, they would abruptly remove him from the throne without warning and exile him to a desert island. They would take away all his honors, wealth, and means of survival, compelling him to reflect on the instability of human greatness. Others had learned this lesson, until a wise stranger arrived, cunning as a serpent. Before taking on the role of king, this stranger carefully investigated how the people typically treated their sovereigns. Upon learning of their unceremonious way of deposing them, he said to himself, "I am here only as a traveler. I must keep my mind focused on the next leg of my journey, not get entangled in the temptations of this temporary position. With divine help, I will not let this allure cause me to forget my permanent interests but will remain ready to depart at any moment. He seized the chance and prepared for future difficulties, thwarting his subjects' cruel plans.

The stranger accepted the crown and ruled with justice and mercy for his one-year term. He never lost sight of his principles, living a life of moderation and austerity even amidst the pleasures of the court. If his resolve ever wavered, he would remind himself, "Remember, my soul, you are but a traveler. Your true haven lies far ahead."

Early in his reign, the king cleverly discovered the location of his future banishment. He secretly transported cattle and treasures to that spot, and his heart was glad. "Truly," he said, "I have kept the good resolution of my heart. I have not indulged with the drunkards or revelers. Surrounded by violent men, I have kept my hands from violence. Have I not now my reward?"

Maria had completed her story and implored her kind friend and protector to emulate the example of the wise king, who, neglecting the pleasures and allurements of the present moment, made provision for the future. She told him, "Life is but a moment. Lay up the riches of virtue and good works in this world; send them to that distant land to which you know you must finally go, and assuredly your soul shall not perish."

Besides these arguments, Maria placed before him the stark contrast in the condition of women in Christian Europe versus the East, drawing on her familiarity with several languages to support her proposition.

She convinced him, and he lent his powerful aid towards the accomplishment of her project. Within a few months of arriving in Baghdad, they had established a college where young girls, both rich and poor, as well as grown women, flocked to receive instruction in reading, writing, needlework, and embroidery, with a focus on imparting the principles of the Catholic religion.

Maria and her friend worked tirelessly and with great success, driven only by the ambition of making themselves useful and redeeming the female sex from the humiliating position they occupied in the country. They neither sought celebrity nor interference, but a European missionary residing in Baghdad ultimately interrupted their efforts, frustrated their plans, and destroyed their institution through officious meddling.

This individual had got his prestigious appointment in the East through the influence of an influential and powerful person. However, he was of humble origin. His primary goal was to accumulate wealth, which he ostentatiously flaunted, rivaling even the local Pasha in the breeding of his horses and the opulence and splendor of their trappings.

Maria thought about how missionaries, who were appointed without adequately investigating their qualifications for the high and sacred office they were called to fulfill, caused truly regrettable grave harm and profound damage to the true faith in the East. She wished that those responsible for selecting individuals to inculcate the doctrines of meekness, patience, charity, and brotherly love had exercised utmost caution. These individuals were called to fulfill a high and sacred office in the East, where the people have unfortunately become all too accustomed to witness and experience the effects of the opposite qualities in their unbelieving rulers and fellow countrymen.

Maria's reflections stemmed from her years living in the East. During this time, Maria encountered many people who actively sought to convert non-believers and strengthen the faith of their fellow Christians, despite facing whippings and slavery. Only those who lived among persecuted Christians understood the value of well-trained, educated, and pious missionaries. Similarly, they could observe the consequences of choosing unsuitable people for this crucial role.

The individual to whom Maria had alluded had introduced himself into their humble establishment with the declared purpose of inculcating the principles of the Christian religion. They warmly embraced him as Christ's special messenger. They looked to Europe for deliverance and freedom. They therefore regarded and treated every Christian from Europe as a deliverer, and as such honored far beyond their Asiatic brethren.

Maria had no way to fight back, so she eventually gave in. Exhausted and disillusioned with humanity, she grew desperate. She chose to escape the cities where people gathered solely to criticize and harm one another. Instead, she would go to the desert where, "I shall at least meet with open friends and open enemies. I shall then meet no wolf in sheep's clothing, to fasten on his unsuspecting prey, who fed and protected him from the wintry blast. At least, I shall not fall by the dagger of him with whom I have broken my bread and eaten my salt."

Maria resembled Saint Teresa of Ávila, a sixteenth century Spanish Carmelite nun and mystic who is renowned for her deep spirituality, her writings on contemplative prayer and the interior life, and her role in the reformation of the Carmelite order. Like Maria, Saint Teresa experienced profound religious visions and mystical experiences that shaped her spiritual journey and teaching.

Both Maria and Saint Teresa were inspiring leaders and reformers within their respective religious traditions. They advocated for a more direct, personal relationship with the divine and challenged the status quo in their respective churches. Saint Teresa's writings, including her autobiography and *The Interior Castle*, influenced Christian mysticism. Similarly, Maria's memoirs profoundly affected history. And both women faced opposition and skepticism from the religious authorities of their time because of their unorthodox spiritual experiences and teachings. But they persevered in their callings, driven by a deep devotion to their faith and a desire to help others grow spiritually.

Of course, there are many other Christian women throughout history that one could compare Maria, such as Saint Catherine of Siena who also played a major role in the religious and political affairs of her time. She was renowned for her spiritual writings, devotion to prayer and religious reform, and advocacy for the poor and marginalized. She had a profound spiritual life and her writings on mysticism and the divine feminine have drawn parallels to Maria's teachings.

She fully intended to carry out her purpose. With a heart filled with a loathing which had well-nigh driven Christian charity from her breast, Maria addressed a letter to the chief of the Dryaah tribe, occupying the desert in the neighborhood of Babylon and Baghdad. Her father had a good acquaintance with him. The chief had many and many a time been their guest during their sojourn at Baghdad in happier days. Not in the least doubting that her letter would meet with a favorable reception, she prepared for her immediate departure, and forthwith packed up all the valuables she possessed, ready for her journey.

She was not disappointed. Shortly after she sent a letter to the chief, Dryaah Ebn Shalan sent his son and daughter to escort her, along with camels to carry her belongings and a splendid mare for her personal use. Maria felt moved to the verge of tears by this kind of display of attention from a man whom her previous oppressors would have regarded as a lawless barbarian. It felt like a divine ray of hope, shining through the darkness and providing solace for her weary pilgrimage.

Setting off with the chief's son and daughter, Maria embarked on the journey as if she were returning to her own parents. She placed unwavering trust in the tribe's hospitality, unyielding honor, and steadfast commitment to their word. Their unwavering support and kindness became a guiding light, fueling Maria's determination. Before long, they reached the tribe's encampment near the Euphrates, nestled in the vicinity of the ancient ruins of Babylon. The tribe had chosen this location for its fertile lands, abundant pastures, and the historical remnants of the once-mighty city.

Maria's reception at the encampment exceeded all expectations, with the chief warmly welcoming her into his tent and introducing her to his wife and relatives. The sight that greeted Maria as she approached the encampment was awe-inspiring. Tents covered the vast plain, as far as the eye could see in both directions. Countless flocks of sheep, camels, and horses dotted the surrounding pastures, creating a lively scene. The flat expanse of the plain was uninterrupted by mountains or trees, allowing the eye to roam freely.

It was May, and the colorful flowers that bloomed profusely made the fresh green grass of spring even more vibrant. The meandering Euphrates River enhanced the expansive verdant landscape. The gentle ripples of the river, catching the sunlight as they emerged from beneath the overhanging banks, sparkled with youthful joy. The setting felt peaceful and innocent, taking Maria back to early times. Maria pondered, where else could a wounded spirit find solace but here, in this tranquil abode? It was a sanctuary where nature thrived in its purest form, untouched by the destructive hand of mankind.

The sense of liberty and the knowledge that Maria had liberated herself from the confines of oppressive walled cities intoxicated her spirit. She hadn't felt such lightness and free-dom since the days spent with her beloved father by the banks of the Tigris. In those blissful moments, unaware of the pro-found hardships that awaited her, Maria had surrendered her-self to the joy of the present, believing it to be a prelude to a lifetime of happiness.

Maria settled into the central tent, belonging to the sheikh, which measured about seventy feet in length. Made of sturdy black camel's hair, the tent was divided into three sections. The central part was reserved for the sheikh's wife and her fe-male attendants. The tent's back was for servants, provisions, cooking, and household tasks. The front section was desig-nated for men and visiting strangers, including the reception room known as "rabka."

After the customary exchange of pleasantries, Maria and her hosts organized her accommodation within the women's area. By setting up a curtain, Maria created a semblance of privacy for herself, which was crucial to avoid offending her hostess by performing certain religious practices that might not align with their beliefs.

Maria settled into her makeshift private space, bringing her belongings with her. However, she couldn't help but shudder at the thought of sleeping directly on the bare ground, only protected by a carpet, especially considering her deep fear of harmful reptiles. Throughout her life, she had grown accus-tomed to sleeping on palm-leaf beds that rested on palm-wood frames. She recalled the mornings in Baghdad when it was not uncommon to find a scorpion speared on the sharp spines of the palm leaves, having attempted to reach the person sleeping above. But there were no scorpions to worry about here.

Once the arrangements were completed, Maria's gracious hosts quickly prepared a refreshment for everyone. They gathered around for a meal of dates fried in butter, eggs, and camel's milk—a simple but satisfying fare. Maria, fueled by her long ride and a keen appetite, indulged in the meal with gusto.

They spent the time between the midday repast and dinner taking a leisurely walk along the banks of the Euphrates, known locally as the "Nahir el Furrat." The stroll was a delightful experience for Maria, as the sky displayed a serene beauty and the air felt gentle without oppressive heat. Nature, adorned in her holiday best, enchanted her senses. At every step, they encountered vast herds of gazelles, whose sheer numbers seemed unimaginable. Maria marveled at the abundance of these graceful creatures, knowing that their flesh held high esteem among the Bedouins. Gazelle hunting parties were a common occurrence, and the flavor of their meat resembled that of goose.

As the sun neared the horizon, casting a familiar seascape-like appearance, Maria and her companions made their way back to the sheikh's tent. There, they found dinner already prepared, as the customary mealtime was sunset. Seated around the hospitable chief's table, they partook in a repast that, while lacking the refinements of culinary art, offered an abundance of hearty, substantial dishes. There were three varieties of roasted meat—sheep, lamb, and gazelle, the latter being a particular favorite of Maria's. There was also a dish that Maria could never quite reconcile herself with during her stay with the Bedouins—the roasted leg of a camel. Although she observed the Arabs relishing it daily, she found it difficult to develop a taste for it.

They were treated to a selection of fruits after finishing the main course. Maria had taken the precaution of bringing along a generous supply of lemons, dates, figs, and almonds, as well as cakes, dried fruits, and sugar-preserved fruits. She happily contributed her offerings to the feast.

The Bedouins, true to their customs, ate solely with their hands, eschewing the use of knives, forks, or spoons. They believed Allah had given humans a mouth and a pair of hands to serve one another. They saw no need to fashion strange implements out of wood or metal, considering it a mockery of the Divine. The hand of man, to them, was nature's fork, while their ancestors' success without contrivances proved their conviction. They cherished the traditions of their forefathers and found no reason to deviate from them.

Despite being accustomed to more refined dining practices, Maria respected the Bedouins' aversion to such utensils. She had brought a spoon with her, but upon learning of their horror at such contrivances, she honored their feelings. She, too, conveyed the food to her mouth using her fingers, despite the occasional scalded finger that resulted from her politeness.

After dinner, coffee was served, much to Maria's delight. Unlike the Wahabis, who abstained from this harmless stimulant due to their strict asceticism, the Dryaahs allowed its consumption. Maria was relieved that she wouldn't have to forgo the cup of coffee she had grown accustomed to. However, there was another hurdle to overcome. The Dryaah tribe abhorred tobacco, which they referred to as "the accursed weed," and prohibited its use.

Maria, who typically enjoyed a hookah after her coffee, was concerned about losing this customary indulgence. Although she had brought her own apparatus, she hesitated to use it, fearing it would offend her host and his friends. Fortunately, her considerate host understood her predicament. Having noticed her habit during a previous visit to her father, he insisted she maintain her custom and generously set aside his own reservations. His graciousness relieved Maria's distress, and she appreciated his genuine politeness, which, in her opinion, rivaled that of the most refined European gentleman.

With dinner concluded, the company followed the customary practice of forming a large circle and taking turns sharing anecdotes. Most of the stories revolved around rare horse breeds or harrowing encounters with hostile tribes. These tales were interspersed with occasional singing. Maria recalled one of the company members singing a slow, plaintive song, showcasing the musical talent that even the wandering Arab tribes possessed. The melody was short and somewhat monotonous, but had its own charm.

One story caught Maria's attention because of its moral lesson. To the best of her recollection, it unfolded: Once upon a time, there lived a Bedouin chief named Rejal el Hamed. He was fortunate enough to possess a mare of extraordinary beauty and excellence, renowned for her speed surpassing even that of the northeast wind, known as 'el shemale' in the desert. Day after day, chiefs of friendly tribes besieged Rejal el Hamed with tempting offers, all longing to gain his prized steed. However, no amount of entreaties, gold, or silver could sway him to part with his beloved mare.

Now, there was another chief named Faris el Aanta, who harbored an intense desire to possess this famous mare whose reputation had spread far and wide. No one in the south, west, north, or east had not heard of her unrivaled excellence. Faris sent numerous offers to Rejal, hoping to persuade him. But no matter how enticing the proposals, they failed to sway the firm resolve Rejal had made to keep his mare, regardless of the temptations that surrounded him.

Eventually, Faris, consumed by an ever-growing longing

for the mare, made a final desperate attempt. In a fit of despair, he dispatched a messenger to offer his entire wealth—camels, flocks, everything he owned—in exchange for the coveted mare. However, Rejal remained unyielding in his decision. He reasoned with himself, saying, "Faris el Aanta possesses camels, horses, and countless sheep, but don't others also have camels, horses, and sheep? If he lost one, would he not ask his neighbor for a camel in exchange for corn?' And in the following year, the corn he gave to his neighbor would be returned to him by the bountiful earth. But if I were to say to Faris, 'Take the mare, the sunshine of my heart, and give me what you offer in return,' will the fertile earth produce another like her, whose speed is like the wind and whose eye gleams like living fire?"

Having been foiled in his attempt and incensed by the unwavering obstinacy of his rival, Faris resolved to employ a scheme to seize the coveted treasure that had eluded him in open negotiations and despite offering all his possessions. He disguised himself, lying in wait for the unyielding Rejal, with the cunning intention of employing clever pretenses to obtain possession of his long-desired prize.

Faris changed his clothes and applied makeup to make his face appear pale and sickly, as if suffering from a deadly ailment. He lay by the roadside, knowing Rejal would pass. Patiently, he waited for his rival's arrival. It didn't take long before he spotted Rejal approaching on the coveted mare he had been yearning for.

"Help! Please, kind stranger!" Faris called out weakly, as if struck by a fatal blow. "Don't abandon a miserable soul who's on the brink of death. I see vultures circling, ready to feast on my lifeless body. I implore you, for your own sake, lend me a hand! Allah will reward you, and you'll find eternal peace. Don't turn your back on a fellow human in desperate need. I haven't eaten or drunk anything for days. Save me, or…"

Sheikhh Rejal had a compassionate nature and was always ready to assist those in distress. Faris' pitiful tale, though fabricated, tugged at his heartstrings. "You won't perish," he reassured him. "Hop on behind me! My mare is faster than the wind. We'll ride to my tent, where your health will be taken care of. We'll bond as friends and share a meal together."

"Oh, no!" cried Faris, playing his part convincingly. "How can I manage that? I'm weak, like a newborn baby. My legs tremble as if I've aged a hundred years. It's impossible!"

Moved by the well-rehearsed desperation of his deceitful rival, the kind-hearted sheikh dismounted without hesitation. He lifted the supposedly dying man from the ground. Faris, keeping up his act, allowed himself to be hoisted, appearing completely drained of strength. They placed him in the saddle after considerable effort. Just as the generous sheikh was about to mount and fulfill his promise, Faris, ungrateful to the core, seized the bridle, kicked the mare's flank, and galloped off with his long-awaited prize, leaving the astonished sheikh unable to intervene.

After a short distance, he heard the chief's voice urgently calling him to stop and make a request. With the ability to flee at any moment, he pulled the reins and paused, anticipating Rejal's words.

"It's true, you deceitful imposter!" exclaimed the sheikh. "By resorting to cunning tricks and disguising yourself in the garb of poverty and distress, you stole from me something I treasured above all the riches in the world. The deed is done, who can argue fate? But I have one request for you: please, I implore you, do not speak of what you have done to anyone. You have the mare now, and undoubtedly, you will keep her. But I ask that you refrain from revealing the way you got her."

The crafty chief inquired, "Why do you insist so earnestly that I keep this matter to myself?"

"Because," replied the noble sheikh, "if you spoke of it, charity among men will cease to exist. The hungry will go unfed, and the sick will perish on the roadside, for no one will come to their aid. Who would embrace the serpent that seeks to drain their lifeblood?"

Remorse struck the cunning Faris. He regretted his wicked intentions. He dismounted from his saddle, embraced the kind sheikh, and helped him remount his beloved mare. Bidding him farewell, he said, "You have spoken words of wisdom, O sheikh. You have awakened my soul from its darkness. Just a moment ago, I was your enemy. But now, behold, I am your friend. Take your mare. May the blessings of Heaven accompany you, and may your years be as plentiful as the sands of the desert!"

Following the feast, the joyful atmosphere continued as the evening unfolded. The guests gathered in a large tent, where lively entertainment awaited them. A talented singer took the stage, his voice carrying the enchanting melodies of a brisk and sprightly song. The lyrics playfully mocked the Turkish nobleman's fondness for fair-skinned Georgians. Although the exact lines eluded Maria's memory, she recalled the essence of the song.

Bedouin Song (Translated from Arabic)
In the Bedouin's tent, a drowsy dog is the maiden fair of skin,
The dark-skinned one, lively and rare, as if a precious gem within.
The Pasha loves his Georgian fair, a costly pleasure he pursues,
But the Bedouin cherishes his dark-eyed wife, who saves him from such dues.
The Georgian's eyes meet only stone walls, unaware of nature and men,

The Bedouin's wife, wise as her lord, no one can deceive, not even then.

The Georgian is dull, the Bedouin is gay, the Pasha an old fool, Give us the wives who share our tents, and can pull the trigger, too.

As the vocalist concluded, another storyteller stepped forward, captivating the audience with tales of daring encounters against rival tribes. The stories made their hair stand on end, relating encounters with fearsome serpents of monstrous size and hideous appearance. The night wore on, with each participant taking their turn to entertain and enthrall.

Notably, throughout the entire evening, the guests refrained from speaking any words or expressing any sentiments that could offend even the most fastidious guest. The tales shared among the Bedouins appealed to the audience due to their strong moral tone. The storytellers delivered the narratives with simplicity and earnestness, leaving a lasting impression on all who listened.

As the clock struck eleven, the festivities drew to a close. The company dispersed, each retreating to their respective accommodations. The sheikh's honored guests and his family retired to their private quarters within his tent, while the rest of the people made their way to their own tents scattered throughout the encampment. The echoes of laughter and the warmth of shared stories lingered in the air, creating a sense of camaraderie and unity among the Bedouins. It was a night to remember, filled with mirth, wisdom, and the timeless enchantment of Arabian tales woven beneath the starlit desert sky.

After bidding farewell to the lively gathering, Maria sought refuge in her designated sleeping area. However, sleep eluded her, and she found herself unable to relax in this novel and unfamiliar setting. The carpet, serving as her makeshift mattress, felt far removed from the comfort she was accustomed to. Resting on an elevated platform was replaced by the humble ground beneath her. The constant concern of venomous creatures crawling upon her body further prevented any chance of slumber, despite the exhaustion from her earlier long ride.

Her discomfort did not go unnoticed by the compassionate sheikh. Sensing her unease, he immediately acted in true Bedouin fashion. He arranged for a bed made of palm wood to be obtained from a village near Hiliah. The gesture was a testament to the hospitality and kindness that Maria had experienced since her arrival.

After performing her prayers, Maria surrendered herself to contemplation. Although her accommodations were modest, her reflections carried a sense of contentment. First, she had escaped the clutches of persecution, providing her with a reason to rejoice. The warm reception she had received from her gracious host, who treated her as a beloved daughter, was a stark contrast to the constant suspicion and mistrust she had endured. The simple bed in the open desert, surrounded by caring friends, held more appeal than a luxurious feathered mattress within the confines of a city plagued with rumors and ill will.

In this moment, Maria found solace in the company of the Bedouins, embracing their genuine goodwill and the freedom from the oppressive forces that had plagued her recent past. Desert night whispers promised peace and a new sense of belonging in this unfamiliar world. In this new environment, Maria found solace in the fact that her nights were no longer plagued by harrowing dreams of past tragedies. No longer did she awaken to the haunting images of her father and uncles, their figures mangled and bleeding. The absence of such horrors allowed her restless nights to be free from the torment that once gripped her.

The relief she felt upon waking, realizing that these terrors were mere figments of her imagination, was tempered by the painful knowledge that these scenes had tragically become a reality in the past. However, as time passed in the encampment of the Dryaah tribe, Maria experienced a transformation. Gone were the nights of tossing and turning, the throbbing heart, the aching head, and the disordered thoughts. Instead, she greeted each morning with a light heart and a calm mind, ready to embrace the day and the newfound serenity that surrounded her.

After devoting an hour to her prayers, Maria ventured outside, eager to immerse herself in the refreshing atmosphere of the early dawn. She set out on a walk that led her to the banks of the majestic Euphrates, the great river that flowed nearby. Along its shores, Maria continued her leisurely stroll, captivated by the beauty of the scenery. The sun, unobstructed by clouds, rose above the horizon, casting a radiant roseate hue over the vast encampment. Its rays illuminated the river's fast-flowing waters, making the bed of the stream appear crystal clear, as if no barrier existed between it and her vision.

In this tranquil moment, Maria felt a deep sense of peace and connectedness with her surroundings. The serene beauty of the landscape served as a balm for her soul, washing away the remnants of her turbulent past. The crystal-clear waters of the Euphrates mirrored her newfound clarity of mind, and with each step she took, she embraced the promise of a brighter future.

The atmosphere came alive with the sounds of bleating sheep and the harmonious melodies of countless living creatures, each offering their own hymns of praise and thanksgiving to the Creator. The encampment, once still, now bustled with activity as inhabitants prepared for the day. Maria's heart swelled with gratitude, and she couldn't help but express her awe in the words of the Psalmist: "O Lord, how manifold are thy works; in wisdom have, thou made them all: the earth is full of thy riches!"

Having enjoyed a delightful two-hour walk, Maria made her way back to her private quarters within the sheikh's tent. It didn't take long for her to win the affection and esteem of the sheikh's wife and his mother, who soon held her in high regard. Maria, in turn, found herself deeply impressed by the Bedouin women she encountered. They had a tanned complexion and possessed a natural beauty. They had tall and well-proportioned figures. Their slender waists, resembling the stem of a palm tree, were not achieved through artificial means but were inherent to their physical stature. Their hands and feet were delicate and finely shaped, reflecting the purity and grace of their lineage, which rivaled that of their prized and swift horses. On average, they stood at around five feet six inches tall, and their lustrous black hair cascaded in countless tresses down their shoulders, with a portion cut short to about two inches and combed straight over the forehead.

Maria admired the elegance and grace of the Bedouin women. Their natural beauty, combined with their strength and agility, formed a captivating ensemble. She couldn't help but appreciate the intricate details of their appearance, which reflected a rich heritage and a deep connection to their desert surroundings. Amid this unfamiliar land, Maria found herself drawn to the unique allure of the Bedouin women, who embodied a timeless beauty that transcended the boundaries of culture and tradition.

The prevailing nose ornament among the Bedouin women was a large gold ring that hung from the part separating their nostrils. Maria noticed a difference in the kharanfel worn by the women of Assyria, which was secured through a pierced hole in the right nostril and a round gold piece with a small jewel. She couldn't help but find the latter practice somewhat disfiguring, especially considering that many of these women possessed naturally beautiful Grecian noses that followed the perpendicular line of their foreheads. The nose ornament's deformity seemed out of place on elegant features, potentially shocking those accustomed to refined aesthetics.

Maria noticed everything about the Bedouin women, even their mouths. With typically small mouths, they possessed teeth that glowed with a dazzling whiteness. They stained their skin with the juice of the indigo plant. They would create punctures in various forms and rub the indigo into them. This resulted in a blue perpendicular line in the center of the lower lip, round marks on the center of the chin and forehead, and decorative flourishes on each cheek. They also drew the shape of a cross on the back of both hands and added a blue line from the knuckle to the nail on each finger.

As for their attire, the Bedouin women predominantly wore a blue linen chemise that extended from the shoulders to the feet. However, the wives and female relatives of the sheikhs often had this part of their dress made from red silk. They would throw a scarf over their heads, twisting the ends twice around their waist. Women of distinction would drape a "mashallah," a cloak made of Persian wool embroidered with gold, over their shoulders. Completing their ensemble, they wore yellow boots that reached up to their knees and had a top that folded over, reminiscent of the style worn by European cavalry soldiers.

Maria marveled at the intricate details of their adornments and garments, which reflected a blend of tradition, cultural expression, and personal flair. The Bedouin women's distinctive style added to their allure, enhancing the air of mystery that surrounded them. In their elegant attire, they moved with grace and confidence, embodying the essence of their nomadic heritage. Maria couldn't help but feel a deep appreciation for their unique sense of fashion and the stories that each piece of clothing and ornament told about their rich and ancient lineage.

Their moral attributes were just as remarkable as their physical perfections, and Maria couldn't help but hold the character of the Bedouin women in even higher regard than that of their male counterparts. The women's courage and endurance were remarkably impressive, surpassing the men's overall intelligence. Maria witnessed firsthand their warm-hearted kindness and generous sympathy, especially towards their fellow women, regardless of social status or religious beliefs. Her gratitude for their compassion was profound and would endure for years.

Despite being a Christian, Maria faced no harm or disrespect while living with the Bedouins. She avoided any overt display of her religious practices out of respect for the strong prejudice the Bedouin held against prescribed forms of worship. They believed in worshiping a single God, considering all humans as brothers and sisters, and meant to assist and support each other in times of need. They held contempt or even abhorrence for intricate theological debates and doctrinal intricacies, often showing their disdain to those who troubled themselves with such matters.

Once, a Muslim religious scholar, known as a mullah, visited the Dryaah tribe intending to redirect the attention of the unbelieving Arabs towards the "kaaba" (the direction of Mecca for prayer) and illuminating their souls with the light of Islam. The mullah used every means, including pomp and circumstance, to ensure the success of his pious mission. He wore a green turban, the symbol of the Prophet's descendants, signifying his lofty intellectual stature. In a display of his humility and disregard for worldly splendor, he rode into the encampment on an ass.

The mullah believed no one could resist the well-planned strategy supported by humble piety. He added, "Yet the infidel's heart remains unyielding." Neither his green turban nor his donkey was of any use. As soon as he began expounding, people assailed him with shouts of derision and cries of displeasure. Undaunted, he explained the purpose of his visit, which was nothing less than a crusade, if one may call it that, against the Christians. In forceful language and fiery denunciations, he declared them unworthy to associate even with the dogs of true believers.

"Let us," he said in a frenzy of pious zeal, "drive out the unclean infidels! Let them no longer enjoy the salt of your hospitality, nor stretch their unbelieving limbs on the carpets of your misguided charity. Expel them from your tents, if you would shield your children from the curse of illegitimacy and your wives from pollution."

He had barely finished this stirring appeal when his congregation, roused to fury by his final pronouncement, seized the flustered mullah, yanked him by the beard as a sign of derision, closely trimmed this revered appendage, and expelled him from the camp. He became a laughingstock for travelers and a warning to all mullahs ambitious enough to try propagating the true faith of the prophet among the stubborn Arabs of the Euphrates.

Similar to Native Americans, the Bedouins have a deep spiritual connection to the land and their traditional way of life, with their culture, language, and identity closely tied to the desert environment. They are an Arab ethnic group indigenous to the desert regions of the Middle East, including parts of Iraq. They have a long history as nomadic pastoralists, migrating seasonally with their herds of camels, sheep, and goats across the Iraqi desert. This semi-nomadic lifestyle has been central to Bedouin culture for centuries.

Like many indigenous groups, the Bedouins have faced challenges from encroaching modernization and settlement. As Iraq developed, the encroachment on Bedouin lands and traditional grazing routes disrupted them. Both Bedouins and Native Americans have struggled to maintain their autonomy and resist assimilation into the dominant cultures and nation-states that have surrounded them. They have faced marginalization, loss of land rights, and threats to their traditional lifeways. The Bedouins, like many Native American tribes, have a strong tradition of oral storytelling, poetry, and folklore that is central to their cultural identity and history, creating parallel experiences of cultural resistance and adaptation.

While living with them, Maria continued to immerse herself in the daily life of the Bedouin tribe, gaining a deeper understanding of their customs and traditions. She found herself captivated by the beauty and allure of the Bedouin women, particularly their striking dark eyes. Their large, brilliant eyes were accentuated by long, dark eyelashes, further enhanced by the application of kohl.

They applied kohl, a mixture of indigo and other substances, beneath the eyelashes using a small bodkin attached to a bag called a jizdana. The women believed that this practice not only enhanced their appearance but also protected their eyes from harm and disease. Maria marveled at the careful attention they gave to preserving their beauty, recognizing the universal desire to enhance one's personal charms.

As Maria spent more time with the Bedouin women, she became privy to their unique sense of sisterhood and solidarity. They supported and uplifted one another, regardless of social status or background. It provided a refreshing contrast to the religious and cultural divisions she had encountered in other parts of the world.

Maria also noticed the practicality and resourcefulness of the Bedouin women in their daily lives. They were skilled weavers and artisans, creating beautiful rugs, tapestries, and intricate embroidery. They used locally sourced materials and dyes, harnessing the natural resources of their environment to create functional and aesthetically pleasing items.

Besides their artistic endeavors, the Bedouin women played a crucial role in the tribe's survival. They were skilled in the art of herbal medicine, using their knowledge of local plants and remedies to treat various ailments and injuries. Within the tribe, they had a highly respected and sought-after expertise in healing.

Through her interactions with the Bedouin women, Maria gained a profound appreciation for their strength, resilience, and unwavering faith. They embodied a simple and genuine devotion to God, free from the trappings of doctrinal debates and religious formalities. Their spirituality was deeply rooted in their daily actions of compassion, generosity, and communal support.

Maria's time with the Bedouin tribe left an indelible mark on her heart and mind. She carried their lessons of sisterhood, resourcefulness, and unwavering faith with her as she ventured back into the world beyond the desert. The experiences she had shared with the Bedouin women would forever shape her perspective and leave her with a lasting admiration for their way of life.

As Maria delved deeper into the Bedouin way of life, she discovered that their customs and traditions extended even to their love for riddles and stories. Sheikh Ahmed, impressed by Maria's curiosity and intellect, presented her with an enigma that the Queen of Sheba to King Solomon put, when she went to hear the words of wisdom from his inspired lips. They said that the Queen of Sheba presented King Solomon with an enigma, which involved a well made of wood, but instead of water, it was filled with stones. A drawer came and let down his bucket, drew it up again, and carried the stones with which it was filled to the water, so that the water could drink from them.

The riddle intrigued Maria, and she pondered over it for hours, determined to unravel its meaning. She ransacked her brain and tried to discover the meaning of the riddle, but without success. She admitted defeat but requested, "O sheikh, grant me until tomorrow morning, and I will solve the riddle."

The sheikh laughed immoderately and granted her the delay she asked. She retreated to her dwelling, consumed by thoughts and possibilities. Sleep eluded her as she wrestled with the enigma's hidden message. At last, as the first rays of dawn broke through the darkness, clarity descended upon her. Brimming with excitement, Maria hastened to the sheikh, eager to share her revelation. She recounted the symbolism behind the riddle, explaining that the wooden well represented the "jizdana," the bucket embodied the "mil," the stones signified the kohl-making berries, and the water symbolized the captivating beauty of a woman's eyes.

The sheikh's astonishment and praise were effusive. He marveled at Maria's intellect, declaring her a witch in jest, and expressed his admiration for her ability to decipher the enigma that had confounded generations.

While Maria immersed herself in the culture of the Bedouins, she remained mindful of their aversion to books and religious formalities. She kept her modest collection of books hidden, delving into their pages only when she found solitude. One such book was "The Balance of Time," which captivated her with its moral principles and insightful examples of human virtue and folly.

One day, as Maria engrossed herself in the book's wisdom, the sheikh's wife unexpectedly entered the room before she could conceal it. Intrigued by Maria's secretive demeanor, she pressed for a glimpse of the book's contents. Knowing that its moral teachings might not align with her accustomed preferences for anecdotes and tales, Maria hesitated.

However, curiosity prevailed, and Maria relented. She flipped through the pages, searching for a passage that would both entertain and engage her hostess. She came across a story that seemed fitting—a tale of a desperate traveler pursued by a fearsome, horned monster.

A horrifying monster once pursued a lone traveler in the desert. The monster had a single, sharp horn protruding from the center of its forehead, resembling the tusk of an elephant. Driven by sheer terror, the fleeing traveler had outrun the dreaded beast, which was intent on devouring him. The traveler ran, occasionally looking back in fear to check if the creature followed. To his dismay, it remained at the same distance, no matter how hard he tried to gain ground. The scorching desert winds were no obstacle for the pursuing monster. The terrified traveler paid them no mind, as the specter of death loomed over him.

The traveler's strength was waning. It was clear he could only evade the monster's jaws for a short time longer, as it was rapidly catching up. Its gaping paw was ready to tear him apart, its eyes burning with savage delight. Just then, the traveler stumbled upon a ditch, into which he tumbled, barely clinging to life.

Beside the ditch stood a towering tree. As soon as the enraged beast spotted the wretched fugitive crouching in the ditch, it let out a thunderous roar and plunged in after him.

But the traveler had noticed the tree, and with a desperate burst of energy, he scrambled up it, placing himself beyond the reach of his attacker.

The traveler felt his heart fill with joy and gratitude to God for his miraculous escape from the monster. He felt as though death had snatched him from its very jaws. After somewhat recovering from his terror, he looked around. The exhilaration that had so quickly replaced his previous fears was, alas, soon followed by additional concerns. True, he escaped the beast, but how could he sustain his preserved life? Whenever he cast his gaze below, he beheld the monster still glaring up at him from the ditch.

Looking further around, he noticed two hideous, oversized rats—one white, the other black—busily gnawing at the roots of the tree branch he had taken refuge on. On the other side, he encountered the hateful stares of four enormous serpents, coiled up and eagerly awaiting the tree's collapse. Beyond these, he saw a terrifying dragon the size of an elephant, also seemingly poised to devour him.

"Alas, alas!" the distraught man cried, wringing his hands in anguish. "What will become of me? Woe is me, for my fate is cruel. I just thought myself saved from one horrific calamity, and now I find myself surrounded by danger on every side. Does it even matter whether I become the prey of the gaping beasts around me, or perish of hunger before their eyes? There is no escape for me! Woe is me that I was ever born!"

After exhausting himself with lamentations, the traveler's tears suddenly turned to joy as he spotted a beehive on a nearby branch. Quickly making his way to it, he restored his flagging strength with its delicious contents, the honey. His spirits lifted, he no longer focused on the perils below, only on savoring the sweet bounty that providence had so fortuitously provided. He passed time, unaware of what lay ahead, until the tree, worn by the rats' relentless efforts, suddenly fell, trapping the traveler.

This parable represents the life of man. The desert spoken of is this world. Death is the unicorn that walks constantly by man's side, from his cradle to his final hour, whether he is awake or asleep, in motion or at rest, from sunrise to sunset, and from its setting to its rising. The four serpents are the four elements—the instruments of disease and destruction that rob man of health and sweep away the young and old alike in their headlong, irresistible course. The white rat is day, the black rat is night; these silently but incessantly gnaw away at our lives from beneath our feet until the sapless trunk finally falls, delivering its occupant to the jaws of the dragon, which represents eternity.

The honey symbolizes the pleasures and seductions of this world; and woe, eternal woe, to the one who, like the careless traveler who had so recently escaped the jaws of death, recklessly devotes himself to these earthly delights, heedless of the dangers that surround him on every side.

"This is very good," exclaimed the sheikh's wife when Maria concluded the story. "These things are true, and pleasant to the ear." Then, thanking Maria with great warmth and cordiality, for the entertainment she had afforded her, she took her leave. Not long after this, she returned, bringing with her several of her female friends and acquaintances. She said, "Amira, tell these women the things you told me from the book, which is like an emerald mine full of riches, and their hearts will be filled with joy."

Maria agreed to retell the story, but only if they arrange a gazelle hunting party. She had two reasons for this stipulation—she enjoyed the sport, and she had an aversion to the taste of camel meat, which was a staple of their diet. Maria promised to recount the full story after they had spent the day hunting in the desert. The following day, they indulged in their favorite pastime, and in the evening, Maria upheld her end of the bargain, rereading the parable that had so captivated the sheikh's wife.

On returning from their daily excursions, Maria often amused herself for hours playing with the young camels, which were as playful as their elders were grave. One of these, only fifteen days old, was an especial favorite of hers. It knew Maria as well as its mother, and played with her excessively. It would take its food from her hand and show other marks of its confidence and attachment to her. On seeing Maria approach, it would leap like a kitten, and run to hide itself in sport.

The Arabs considered the camel a sacred animal, treated with great reverence. They recognized the camel's vital importance, saying, "Without our camels, we would have no food, no drink, nor any means to clothe ourselves." Camel meat provided sustenance when nothing else was available, and their milk was an endless source that prevented the Arabs from perishing of thirst in the desert.

Maria bonded with the Dryaah tribe and neighboring tribes during her stay. The Bedouin people embraced her with open arms, treating her as a cherished guest. Their hospitality knew no bounds, and Maria felt a profound gratitude for the genuine friendships she forged among these tribes which society considered lawless.

She marveled at the depth of their friendship and loyalty. Once an attachment was established, it endured for a lifetime. Bedouin willingly shared provisions with friends in need, selflessly sacrificing their own well-being. This unwavering commitment to hospitality and friendship touched Maria's heart and left an indelible impression on her.

Throughout her stay, Maria encountered numerous stories that exemplified the Bedouin people's extraordinary hospitality.

One such tale recounted an elderly widow who, despite her own destitution, generously welcomed two Indian travelers into her humble tent. With only a single sheep left, she slaughtered it and sought bread from her neighbors to feed the famished strangers. Her selflessness and trust in divine providence moved Maria deeply, serving as a testament to the Bedouin's unwavering spirit of generosity. Maria's experience with these "lawless tribes" allowed her to make more real friends in one day than one could form in a century in civilized Europe, where, according to Maria's observation, "it is possible to live for half a century without knowing your neighbor."

Inspired by the virtues she witnessed, Maria contemplated introducing her Bedouin friends to Catholicism and sharing her faith with them. She baptized a few children in secret, hoping to sow the seeds of conversion. However, her efforts to convince them to embrace the Catholic faith were met with resistance. The Bedouin held steadfast to their own traditions and were averse to established religious practices and written texts. Despite her best intentions, Maria's attempts at conversion proved unsuccessful.

She wrote the following in her book, *Prophecy and Lamentations: a Voice from the East.*

The teachings of Christ will spread the light of truth far and wide, guiding and saving more people than the sanctuary of St. Benedict ever could. In just one century, the religion of Muhammad conquered vast territories from Persia to Africa. Surely then, the boundless power of Christ's spirit, which inspires the saints with truth and hope of immortality, can reclaim the empire that succumbed to brutality.

The futile efforts of those who tried to retain Jerusalem were no match for the overwhelming tide against Judea. But a new generation now emerges, who through devotion will raise new monuments of sacred thought. Eighteen centuries have passed. Now, Christians, it is our duty to be the saviors of Asia. At this moment, Christian ships encircle her, ready to replace her shroud with the robe of righteousness and eclipse the dominion of the Saracens forever.

The progress of Christianity is quietly advancing into the Caliphate's empire, and even now finds a protector on Muhammed's very throne. May God protect the daughter of the Chaldean Patriarchs in her holy crusade.

Maria, a woman of great faith, passionately believed in Christ's teachings to enlighten and liberate all. She viewed the spread of Christianity as a sacred mission to reclaim those under Saracen rule. She recognized the oppression and lack of freedoms that many Muslim women faced and believed that by converting them to Christianity, she could help them find the pathway to the personal and spiritual freedom that she championed for women.

While living with the Bedouins, she focused on the virtues that transcended religious boundaries. She celebrated their innate goodness, their adherence to moral principles, and the profound impact their actions had on her own spiritual journey. Although she couldn't bring them to her faith, Maria found solace and inspiration in the Bedouin people's unwavering commitment to their own set of virtues and principles. As the days turned into weeks and weeks into months, Maria's bond with the Bedouin deepened. She continued to share in their daily lives, cherishing their friendship and treasuring the lessons they taught her and embracing the inherent goodness and wisdom found in every corner of the world.

CHAPTER 8

─────❧─────

LIVING AT A BEDOUIN ENCAMPMENT

After a few weeks, Maria found herself amidst a frenzy of activity in the Bedouin camp. Men and women hurried back and forth, shepherds gathered their flocks, and camels traversed the camp ceaselessly. The air was filled with the sounds of horses being saddled and tents being struck down, indicating that they were preparing to move to greener pastures.

Amidst the commotion, Maria marveled at the sight of the men tending to their spirited horses, their powerful presence filling the air with their neighs. Meanwhile, the women diligently worked on dismantling the tents and packing up their belongings, loading them onto the camels designated for the task.

It was a bustling scene, like no other Maria had ever witnessed. Everything moved in motion, and every person occupied themselves with a task. The sheer number of magnificent horses gathered in one place was awe-inspiring. They pranced and pawed the ground, their exuberance clear as they anticipated the prospect of leaving their worn-out grazing grounds behind for fresh pastures. Even the burdened camels seemed to share in the excitement, despite their heavy loads. The beasts of burden, weighed down by mountains of baggage, appeared to rejoice. Their young ones frolicked around them, bewildered by their more sedate mothers' lack of enthusiasm.

Once they securely packed the tents, gathered the flocks, and prepared everything for departure, Maria and her companions embarked on their journey in an organized formation. The men led the way on their spirited horses, an intimidating group armed with long lances held high, their gleaming points catching the sunlight. Following them were the women, with the most prominent among them riding in "maharahs," canopies with curtains, placed atop dromedaries. Their slaves and attendants accompanied them, all mounted on camels. Maria had chosen the tallest camel for herself, wanting to fully enjoy the view.

After the women and their entourage came the baggage camels, burdened with tents, provisions, and belongings of the tribe. Countless flocks trailed behind, tended by their shepherds. The journey progressed with regular halts every two hours for coffee. As they rode, men on foot approached them, carrying roasted meats, bread, and dates, calling out, "Anyone who is hungry, come forward."

By evening, they arrived at their destination on the banks of the Nahr el Kashoun, a fertile area not far from the Euphrates River. Once again, the scene was bustling, reminiscent of the morning's preparations. Everyone diligently carried out their duties, eager for the grand feast promised by their sheikh upon reaching their new quarters.

The feast was a lavish affair befitting their generous host. They slaughtered seven camels, twenty-five sheep, and countless gazelles for the occasion. After they pitched the tents, tended to the flocks, and stabled and fed the horses with camel's milk, believed by the Bedouins to provide strength and endurance, they gathered by the riverbank for dinner. They set the table on the grass, and the dishes were a sight to behold.

The dishes were filled with rice, resembling mountains, and they placed whole roasted lambs or sheep on top, requiring four men to carry them. The dishes had a shiny, silver-like appearance, but Maria was unsure of their material. There were also enormous platters containing camel's flesh joints and others filled with her favorite gazelle. They enjoyed a special dish called sambusak—a combination of burnt flour, honey, and butter encased in a thin, square crust that was baked.

Maria relished the meal, savoring every bite of the dinner provided by their sheikh on the banks of the Euphrates. She found everything delicious, except for the camel joints. The red flesh and coarse flavor were not to her liking, and she couldn't imagine ever enjoying it. Little did she know circumstances would change her perspective. Years later, living among European Christians in a civilized setting filled with wealth and abundance, she would overcome her fastidiousness.

It wasn't long after their settlement at Nahr el Kashoun that their sheikh received a wedding invitation from a neighboring tribe. The betrothed couple belonged to prominent families, so extensive preparations were made to celebrate this significant event. All surrounding chieftains, along with their relatives and friends, urging them to attend, received invitations.

The Bedouin tribes arranged marriages in a unique and amusing way. The smitten suitor, accompanied by his parents and friends, paid a visit to the tent of his beloved's father. Bedouins upheld politeness as a virtue, with courtesy and friendly gestures being strongly encouraged. Any violation of these principles was severely punished. However, when the purpose of the visit was understood to be a marriage proposal, they deliberately avoided displaying even a hint of respect or common courtesy towards their visitors. They refused to rise from their seats upon their arrival. They employed this seemingly rude behavior to demonstrate their independence and avoid appearing overly eager or desperate in such delicate circumstances.

One of the groom-to-be's friends then started the negotiation, using the following approach: "Why did you receive us so coldly? We have not taken your Nedjd marcs, nor have we shed the blood of your young men. If you have forgotten the duties of hospitality, we will immediately return to our tents."

The young lady, whose hand was being pursued in marriage, scrutinized the young man's features through a curtain hole. This curtain separated the female and male sections of the tent. If the young man didn't possess enough charm to capture the lady's interest, she gave a prearranged signal to her parents, indicating that he was not the one she chose. In such cases, the visiting party could depart with no acts of civility or apologies extended to them.

However, if the signal indicated that the lady had seen and approved the young man, the demeanor of the lady's family underwent an immediate transformation. Smiles replaced the forbidding looks, and warm expressions of friendship replaced cold indifference. The father exclaimed, "Ahalan w' sahalan," which meant "Welcome." He added, "A blessing descends upon us when you are present. Not only will we show you hospitality, but you shall have all you desire. Ask, and we will fulfill all your wishes. Our wealth is yours, and we are your servants."

In response, the friends of the young man said, "We come to ask for your daughter's hand for our friend, whom you see by our side. Therefore, tell us, O sheikh, the dowry you expect for her." They then discussed the matter seriously, settling the terms of the bride's portion with no lawyers. They determined the number of "nakas," which were riding camels, as well as the number of blood horses, sheep, male and female slaves, pairs of yellow boots, and finally, the amount of presents to be given to the bride's friends and relatives. They swiftly arranged all these important matters once the lady had given her approval.

The couple to be married were of high status. The lady had recently received the esteemed honor of being appointed as the hafta of her tribe. This appointment came after her tribe engaged in a war with a neighboring group. During war preparations, tribes selected a beautiful virgin to be their hafta. The chosen hafta had to possess exceptional courage and eloquence as her role was to inspire her followers through impassioned speeches to display acts of bravery in battle.

The hafta commanded the awe and reverence of the surrounding warriors. They regarded her as a figure of destiny, for she held the fate of their battles in her hands. Mounted atop the grandest and purest white female camel, she rode forth into the fray. They adorned the crimson-draped saddle, known as "maharah," with ornate embellishments and a deep gold fringe. Her presence on the battlefield was striking, surrounded by the tribe's most renowned warriors, whom she animated and encouraged, with her voice and gestures. She called upon the seasoned veterans to remember their past glories and motivated the young to display extraordinary valor, promising her hand to the fortunate youth who would bring the head of the enemy's general.

The tribe dedicated a significant portion of their force to safeguarding the hafta, and ambitious spirits competed for a place by her side. The warriors knew that despair would grip their ranks, and defeat would be inevitable if she fell into the enemy's clutches. Prior to the commencement of the conflict, each warrior approached her individually, seeking her inspiration, courage, and enthusiasm. They implored, "O most beautiful among the beautiful! I go to battle for you. My life is yours. Let me behold the radiance of your countenance, that your slave's heart may be filled with valor. May my voice roar like a lion's in the enemy's ears, and may my lance be like the angel of destruction." To which the hafta replied, "Go, brave youth! May your heart be as fierce as a lion, and may your lance be like a deadly plague. I am the hafta, the reward for the bravest of the brave, and my price is the head of the enemy's chief."

During a recent war, the chief's daughter, Hafta, lived near Maria's encampment. A relative of a neighboring sheikh had presented the severed head of the opposing chief at the hafta's feet, claiming his right to the privilege. They wasted no time in making preparations to celebrate the marriage of the young hero and the sheikh's daughter, honoring their noble lineage and remarkable achievements. Maria and her Bedouin friends were fortunate to receive an invitation to this splendid wedding ceremony.

Typically known for their modest attire, the Bedouins adopted a remarkably different approach for marriage ceremonies. The Bedouins adorned themselves in garments of exceptional splendor, which Maria suspected they had plundered from unsuspecting merchants who never imagined their wares would be used in such a manner.

Maria faced a slight predicament. Her own wardrobe, consisting solely of garments she had worn in Baghdad, was not suitable for such festive occasions. Driven by her intense desire to witness a Bedouin wedding and a wish to divert her thoughts from melancholic reflections, Maria had a dress tailored for the occasion. Thus, attired as a Bedouin woman, she eagerly made her way to the celebration.

They saddled the sheikh's finest mares for their use, and at daybreak, the party, which included around twenty individuals, including slaves, set off towards the encampment of the bridegroom's father, who was a relative of their sheikh. After riding for approximately three hours, they reached the Dryaah camp. Upon arrival, Maria marveled at the picturesque scene that unfolded before her. The encampment was in a location teeming with lush pastures, where countless flocks, horses, and camels roamed freely—a testament to the owner's wealth. The sprawling peaks of the tents, crafted from camel's hair, stretched as far as the eye could see, resembling a bustling city. As Maria approached the encampment, she took it upon herself to count the tents, and to her amazement, their number surpassed a thousand.

They rode straight into the heart of the encampment, where Faris el Hamadan, the bridegroom's father, had pitched his tent. A multitude of women emerged to greet them, extending warm hospitality and respect. Their hostess guided them into the sheikh's tent, uttering the customary compliment, "Anastuna sharaftuna," which expressed their gratitude for the honor of their visitor's presence. Coffee was promptly served, a gesture of kindness facilitated by Maria's friends, who secured her permission to indulge in her beloved nerghila, despite the Bedouin taboo against tobacco.

Following a delightful dinner, the evening unfolded in a lively atmosphere of dancing, singing, and storytelling that carried on until midnight. At daybreak the next morning, they rose and prepared to visit the encampment of the bride's father, which was located just a short distance away. Before sunrise, everything was in readiness, and the procession began in the following order:

Leading the way was a lone horseman mounted on a splendidly adorned mare, wielding a byrakh—a massive flagpole stretching at least fifteen or sixteen feet in height. At its summit fluttered a white flag, and as the procession advanced, the standard-bearer periodically proclaimed, "We go to seek honor without blemish." Behind them came the camels, bearing the bride's dowry, adorned with garlands and branches collected from the banks of the Euphrates. Their handlers guided them, followed by a resplendently attired black slave, also part of the dowry, who rode on horseback. Men on foot surrounded him, joyfully singing and chanting. Next in line were a troop of fully armed mounted warriors, their steeds prancing proudly as they discharged their muskets into the air from time to time.

After the warriors, a group of women appeared, carrying censers filled with sweet incense, casting fragrant clouds into the atmosphere. Vast flocks of sheep followed them, forming part of the bride's dowry, tended by their shepherds. The shepherds cheerfully marched alongside their charges, singing a song that began with the words, "Thus did Chibouk, the brother of Antar, two thousand years ago," proudly affirming the Bedouin's adherence to ancestral customs.

Soon after, Maria and her companions ventured into the desert, dividing into two groups—the bride's friends forming one and the bridegroom's friends the other. They reached the designated spot, where the young men from each side separated and arranged themselves in battle formation, while the elders positioned themselves to observe the proceedings. A playful mock battle ensued, to capture the hafta, a symbol of victory.

Eventually, the bridegroom's party emerged triumphant, carrying her away in celebration. They entrusted her to the care of the bridegroom's female relatives and friends. A joyful gathering of young maidens surrounded her to the entrance of her tent, where her splendidly adorned camel awaited her, its back draped with a large scarlet saddlecloth, fringed with colorful threads. Ostrich feathers adorned its head, and her headband sparkled with embroidered glass and a variety of colors. Small mirrors, strategically placed on the camel's body, reflected the brilliance of the scene, casting shimmering flashes of light as they caught the sun's rays.

The camel's maharah, a decorative pavilion, was adorned

with a luxurious Persian carpet and silk-covered cushions. With the help of the bridegroom's female companions, the hafta entered the maharah, and they arranged themselves for the procession. Some rode on camels, while others walked, harmoniously singing as they traveled, accompanying the hafta to her husband's tent.

While these preparations were underway, a group of the bridegroom's friends galloped ahead to announce the imminent arrival of the bride at the bridegroom's tribe's tent. The bridal procession continued its journey towards the final destination, accompanied by songs of triumph and jubilation. Some particularly enthusiastic well-wishers even sacrificed sheep at the feet of the camel carrying the hafta as a symbolic offering of goodwill.

After the camel carrying the bride's maharah, two others followed. One carried her tent and furnishings, while the other bore the Persian carpet and kitchen utensils. In this orderly procession, they arrived at the bridegroom's tent, where they escorted the hafta inside. The entire ceremony concluded with a grand dinner, unlike anything Maria had witnessed before.

The next morning, the couple exchanged presents, and the husband covered most of the expenses. So as not to disappoint her generous friends, Maria presented the bride with a jisdana and a golden mil, tools used to enhance the appearance of eyelashes, as previously described. She gifted the bride a necklace and bracelets made of amber. In return, the bride presented Maria with a sizable and valuable emerald set in a ring. She also received a generous Persian shawl, crafted from the finest cashmere wool, extending from the shoulders to the feet. Despite its size, it fit in one's hand. Later, when faced with dire circumstances, Maria sold the shawl in Rome for two hundred scudi. The bride gave her a valuable necklace composed of three rows of exquisite pearls. Maria found it interesting that the Bedouins were unaware of the items' true worth. They would readily exchange diamonds worth thousands of francs for a sack of dates worth a mere five francs, or beautiful and valuable Persian shawls for a bag of rice.

While deeply grateful for the kind gesture behind the sumptuous gift, Maria couldn't help but feel apprehensive about accepting such treasures. She feared offending those who had shown her such kindness. She also suspected that the items were stolen from a caravan. It seemed likely that the tribe had attacked a caravan on its annual journey from Basra to Damascus, passing through Baghdad not long ago. As Maria contemplated these thoughts, she realized that her own uncle had lost some valuable jewels that were part of the very caravan she suspected the tribe had plundered. Determined to restore the precious gifts to their rightful owners if fate ever allowed her the opportunity, she managed to quiet her conscience, albeit with a somewhat equivocal sense of morality.

They spent three days with the tribe, during which time the focus was on indulging in food, drink, dancing, and singing. The tribe gathered around a large fire, forming a circle of about fifty people, dancing hand-in-hand. The musicians, positioned in the center, played tambours and pipes, creating a lively atmosphere. It was a gathering of pure joy. All were resolute in seizing the moment, disregarding the future. The Bedouins regaled each other with stories and performed amusing antics that could cause even the sternest individual to burst with laughter. But Maria, lacking the spirit for such revelry, often found herself mortified by her own solemn countenance among the sea of joyful faces. In moments of frustration, she would retreat from the merry crowd, seeking solace in solitude.

After the festivities ended, they bid farewell to their new-found friends. Wishing happiness upon the newlyweds, Maria and her companions embarked on their journey back to their own encampment. Once settled, Maria resumed her previous routine. She would rise early each morning and venture alone into the desert, seeking solace and performing her devotions in the tranquil solitude, hidden from the sight of all but the divine Being to whom she humbly offered her praise and adoration. One morning, she wandered along the bank of a canal that flowed into the Euphrates. Engrossed in reading her favorite book, she was deeply moved by its powerful messages, which appealed to the nobler aspects of human nature. Lost in words, she was oblivious to the world around her. She refrained from kneeling to pray, respecting her hosts' customs.

The chapter she was reading vividly depicted the beauty of God's benevolence toward humanity and the lamentable ingratitude that often-marked human behavior. The poignant portrayal overwhelmed Maria and moved her to tears. She fell to her knees and, lifting her eyes heavenward, she implored the Holy Ghost for strength to recognize and fully appreciate God's goodness in her life. Youthful and brimming with enthusiasm, Maria possessed a fervent imagination and an open heart. As she raised her eyes to the heavens, a dazzling light seemed to emanate, leaving her transfixed in that very spot. She remained lost in her reverie, unaware of her surroundings. It was the voices of her Bedouin female friends that eventually broke the spell. From a distance, they had observed her sudden descent to her knees and rushed to her aid, their faces marked with concern and alarm.

"What happened?" they asked anxiously. "Did something befall you?"

"It is nothing," Maria replied, reassured by their presence. "I am well now."

"But how is it," one of her friends inquired, "that we saw you fall as if overcome by some mystical force? These occurrences are strange to us; we cannot comprehend them."

What was Maria to do now? She was discovered, and she found the idea of lying or deceiving repulsive. She couldn't help but feel remorse for the dissimulation she had already engaged in, as if she had denied her Creator and been ashamed of her devotion.

"Oh, if only I could be an instrument, a humble vessel, to guide these simple-hearted children of nature toward the true worship of You, my God!" Maria silently prayed. "May they perform these acts, which they now do instinctively by the goodness You have bestowed upon them, for the glory and honor of Your holy name! Your commandments are written in the hearts of all people, though sometimes obscured by the stains of ignorance and debasing superstition! I will proclaim my heavenly Father to these children of error. Perhaps I can be instrumental in turning their hearts toward a just understanding of Your mercy and teach their voices to sing the praises of Your holy name."

Turning to her friends, Maria spoke with conviction, "My friends, it was not sickness that brought me to my knees, nor was it the influence of any malevolent force. The cause of what you witnessed lies within the pages of this small book."

"What do you mean?" the women exclaimed. "Who has ever seen someone struck down by a mere book? We do not understand, unless this book contains some kind of talisman."

"It is not a talisman," Maria clarified. "The power within this book lies in the truth it conveys. There is no magic here, only the power of truth. You can judge for yourselves, for I will read to you from its pages."

Intrigued, the women gathered around Maria with eager curiosity written on their faces. Opening the book at a random page, Maria read aloud the following legend. Once, a hermit spent sixty years in the desert, accompanying St. Anthony of Egypt in contemplation of the divine Creator. The world and all its treasures meant nothing to him, for his focus was solely on the afterlife.

For sixty years, this devout man faithfully observed his religious duties, engaging in strict fasting and unwavering prayer. But then Providence tested his faith by subjecting him to a powerful temptation. One day, as he roamed the desert, an evil spirit attacked him, seizing him in its clutches and subjecting him to relentless torment and anguish day and night. In his desperate search for relief, he questioned the demon about its motives and actions, including why it and its kind were constantly seeking to torment and harm humanity.

"Our motive," the fiend replied, "is jealousy; our motive is envy. Haven't we fallen irreversibly? Who shall save us from our eternal damnation? To humanity, the Almighty has granted the power to secure their own salvation. The unspeakable blessings of heaven are within reach of every child of Adam, if they only strive to obtain them. Therefore, we desire to make mankind like ourselves. Therefore, we seize every opportunity to torture them, to push them toward abandoning their faith, so that they may curse God and perish."

The hermit, intrigued by the fiend's description of the heavenly abode, pressed further, asking about the effect it had on the demon. The foul spirit replied, "No description, no words, can adequately convey even the faintest notion of the glories I witnessed there. The most intense sensory pleasures, both spiritual and worldly, pale compared to the sensations experienced in that blessed realm. The greatest beauty of this world becomes hideous deformity, and its sweetness turns into bitterness and sorrow."

Eager to explore the demon's longing for his former state of happiness, the hermit inquired what the fiend would give to return to that state. The demon answered he would willingly endure all the torments inflicted upon humanity since the beginning of time and suffer the pains of the damned if it meant being able to revisit those glorious regions. The paths in that realm were gold, and the walls shone with emeralds and diamonds greater than those of Golconda. The brightness there outshone the noonday sun, moon, and stars, rendering them mere shadows of death. In that realm, weariness and tribulation were absent, and hunger and thirst were unknown.

Upon hearing this, the virtuous hermit cast off the evil spirit, shaking it away from him. "Why worry about life's pains and troubles when the reward is what I just heard?" he declared. "Who wouldn't face worldly ills for heavenly acceptance? My soul is adorned with the armor of faith, and I shall no longer fear the assaults of my enemies." With newfound courage, the hermit continued on his way.

The women, captivated by the legend, listened with wonder and profound attention. The story had sparked something within them, and some seemed moved, expressing a desire to follow the example of the virtuous hermit. One woman, with charming simplicity, asked Maria if there were camels in the realms she described. She remarked, "How could we live without camel's milk? Yet, didn't you say there is no thirst there?" This question momentarily perplexed Maria, but she assured the woman that since everything the heart desired would be found in that realm, they would undoubtedly have camel's milk available too.

Seeing their receptive mood, Maria then read them a chapter from the Gospel, and they paid keen attention. She hoped that through her humble efforts, she could turn their souls toward the worship of the one true God.

CHAPTER 9

Pilgrimage to the Holy Land

Maria had long dreamed of visiting the biblical sites she had read about since childhood. The idea of climbing the mountains where God had revealed himself had captivated her, seeing the desert where the Savior had fed thousands, and witnessing the scene of his passion and crucifixion. This obsession had consumed her, leaving little room for anything else.

Although Maria had lived contentedly among her gracious hosts, she felt constrained to conform to their beliefs and customs. Later in life, she sometimes wondered if she would have been better off remaining with these untaught but kind people, rather than seeking virtue in the Christian European civilizations she had encountered. Only God knew the troubles she could have avoided.

Maria had often begged her dear father to undertake this pious pilgrimage with her, and she believed he would have agreed, had religious fanaticism not taken him from her. Since she could not make the journey with him, she resolved to fulfill her long-held dream alone, leaving behind the land of her ancestors—a land stained with the blood of one she held dearer than life, where the rulers had made her family home a desolation and she herself a wretched outcast.

Before departing her kind hosts, Maria wandered once

more among the crumbling ruins of mighty Babylon, "Glorious among Kingdoms, the pride of the Chaldeans," as she and her people referred to it. Retracing her steps through the shapeless mounds and broken pottery, she decided to leave the tent of the Sheikh Dryaah Ebn Shalan and make her way as best she could towards Palestine, trusting in the Great Spirit who had so often preserved her in peril.

Eager to leave the Bedouin camp as soon as she could, Maria went straight to the chief's tent to tell him her plans. The sheikh was sad to hear of her departure but said that if fate demanded it, there was no use fighting it. It was even harder for Maria to leave her Bedouin female friends. Their genuine and simple kindness had won her heart. Leaving them was almost as tough as parting with close friends and family.

After many goodbyes, tears, and hopeful wishes to meet again, Maria left the Bedouins after six months. She headed to Baghdad, looking for the next caravan to Damascus. The chief kindly offered her an escort to Baghdad, but Maria didn't feel right to accept it.

As she said farewell to what she considered the "simple-hearted children of the desert," Maria thought about the virtues she was leaving behind—virtues she feared she might not find among more "civilized" people, like hospitality, charity, and steadfast friendship. Though the Bedouins robbed and killed, Maria imagined that if they could mix their courage, endurance, and other good traits with Christian piety, they would surpass all others.

Maria discovered a gathering of travelers in Baghdad, preparing to depart for Damascus in March due to unsafe roads in the past seven to eight months. She joined this caravan to continue her journey to Palestine. Among those waiting for the caravan was a Christian bishop named Deir Stefan, an old friend of Maria's father, who was also making the pilgrimage.

Maria joined the bishop and a lady from Basra with her children, forming a friendly little travel group since the lady was also a Chaldean Christian. The bishop's piety and learning reminded Maria of her own father.

The caravan, camped in a vast plain about an hour and a half from Baghdad, had about 15,000 camels and horses, based on Maria's estimation, and included a huge number of travelers and pilgrims of both Muslim and Christian faiths. Daily, the caravan welcomed fresh arrivals. People came from all directions—sometimes whole families of pilgrims joined at once. The caravan also grew with traders heading to Damascus and other parts of Syria; Persians, Osmanli Turks, and merchants from Basra.

For ten days, the arrivals were nonstop. Maria found it fascinating to see diverse people, with different languages, manners, and dress, gathered. She witnessed many heart-touching scenes: parents saying goodbye to children, and children to parents; wives tearfully bidding farewell to husbands about to face the dangers of the desert, perhaps never to return. Sadly, there was no one to weep for Maria. She was alone, with no one to bless her. She felt her loneliness deeply. Her comings and goings went unnoticed, like a wind-blown date leaf in the desert. Her soul felt dried up, her heart empty.

Maria turned to Heaven, praying to God to protect her, His unhappy daughter without friend or protector, from the dangers of the desert—the deadly simoom wind, the attacks of robbers and murderers. She also prayed to her dear father, asking him to intercede for her at the throne of grace, that she might escape those dangers and find forgiveness for her sins.

The caravan had many camels, but the travelers were less than five thousand. Maria and the bishop had five camels each for personal use and their attendants. The woman from Basrah had at least fifteen for herself, children, and servants.

The camels were not owned by the travelers but rented for the journey. The proprietor had to load, unload, and feed them during the whole time, as well as provide drivers to attend them. Maria paid about three hundred piastres for each camel, which included everything, so that she didn't have to trouble herself with further details. She also brought along a horse for an occasional gallop over the desert.

Camel load after camel load poured into the camp, providing three to four months of supplies for the journey; flour biscuit, rice, basterma, which is beef sausage dried and kept well for a considerable length of time, kaourma, hashed beef or mutton, cooked in grease and crammed into skins, halawah, a sweet solid substance composed of sesame puree. In addition to these, they placed piles of carpets, cushions, and bedclothes on every side, along with an enormous quantity of kitchen utensils of every description.

Maria and her companions shared a tent divided by a curtain, with men on one side and ladies on the other.

The caravan finally moved forward. Maria watched the camels, with a solemn demeanor, march in perfect formation like disciplined soldiers. They had colorful saddles on their backs—vibrant reds, deep purples, emerald greens, and rich blues. Each saddle could hold six people, making the caravan look like a moving city of brilliantly colored houses. Maria thought that this file of animated beings, struggling along with a tardy pace, looked like a gigantic snake writhing its way over the wide stretching plain before it.

The caravan was escorted by Georgian cavalry from the Pasha of Baghdad. The cavalry riders had fair skin, which contrasted with the darker complexions of the caravan members they protected. The caravan included a variety of animals—camels carrying baggage, supplies, and passengers, as well as horses, sheep, and cattle. It also included both wealthy and poor pilgrims, some riding and others walking. As the large caravan moved across the plain, it startled herds of gazelles, causing them to flee in panic.

The speed with which the camels were unloaded, and the tents erected was astonishing. In less than half an hour, a sprawling tent city materialized, as if by magic. The inexperienced traveler admired the square's construction, only to discover a lane of tents appeared out of nowhere, like magic. After building the "city," they rapidly constructed a rampart around it using camels' feeding troughs and pack saddles placed in a perimeter. They took precautions to guard against a sudden attack, and the travelers then turned their attention to supper.

The traveling butchers sprang into action, and people made purchases throughout the camp. They slaughtered sheep, and everyone bought according to their needs, paying about five or six paras per ratel, roughly five pounds for five farthings. The meat was quickly prepared, the cooks matching the tent-builders in speed and expertise. Ground fires filled the air with sizzling sounds, sweeter than a lover's voice, softening even the sternest faces.

Before each tent, Maria observed slaves busily spreading large white cloths on the bare ground. It wasn't long before groups surrounded every cloth, clearly eager to dive into their meal. In under half an hour, they made whole sheep disappear and ate towering piles of rice. After the group finished, the servants enjoyed the plentiful leftovers. Maria's party consisted of twelve, and each member seemed determined to contribute to the communal comfort. After supper, they conversed until eleven o'clock, by which time it was pointless to try to sleep given the incessant loud laughter, shouts and clamor of the Georgian guards calling to each other across the encampment.

At eleven, however, they rolled out their carpets and lay down to sleep. Maria, now accustomed to resting on the ground, slept soundly through the night. Her six-month apprenticeship with the Bedouins had indeed prepared her well for caravan travel, and she found herself more comfortable in these conditions than those who had lived only in cities.

They woke up early and departed in the same order as before, skipping breakfast. Each traveler ate at their own pace, the food and water they carried suspended from their camels. In this way, they would dine and even sleep, rarely dismounting until they reached the day's stopping point. They continued their journey for ten days, skirting the lush, winding banks of the Euphrates, enjoying the fresh greenery and gentle spring breezes. Each night they built a temporary camp, only to dismantle it again the next morning, leaving no trace beyond the cold ashes and scraps from their meals.

After ten days, their route turned westward, forcing them to cross the river and trade its pleasant shores for the salt, arid desert beyond. At Hid, they crossed the Euphrates. Moving people, animals, and baggage across the wide stream was a huge task. For two days, ferries worked constantly to shuttle the crowd, though many were also employed in the effort. To prevent the camels from struggling and capsizing the boats, the animals were secured by their right forelegs. Drivers sang a calming song, "Shekh shillunu" or "Lend a hand to the old," which had a surprising effect on camels' behavior.

The boat that carried Maria and her companions across the river was in danger of capsizing. Maria, accompanied by friends, servants, camels, and baggage, packed into an insufficiently sized vessel. The gunwale sat mere inches above the water as the boat swayed and eddied in the current. Maria feared the water rushing in at any moment. Alarm was etched on every face when one of the more frightened camels managed to free its leg from the tether, its uneasy movements greatly increasing the peril. The terrified cries of the animals only added to the terrors of their situation.

Maria felt genuine alarm as she watched their craft drifting far downstream, seemingly beyond the boatmen's ability to steer it back to the intended landing. She resigned herself to at least a thorough soaking, when suddenly, more by the direction of a cross-current than any skill of the crew, the boat drove ashore about half an hour's walk from where they were meant to disembark. As soon as Maria's feet touched the ground in the small town of Hid, she gave thanks to God, convinced this was nothing short of a miraculous deliverance.

Weary from fatigue and anxiety, the exhausted travelers set about preparing their evening meal. They happily retired and rested after the day's toils and perils. The next morning, Maria and the others rose at daybreak as usual, preparing to depart the Euphrates. She felt a twinge of regret, as she would be leaving behind the river's smiling face, which had cheered and beguiled them on their arduous journey.

They were now about to cross a vast salt desert. The ground was white with saline particles, and the whole prospect before them was as dreary and desolate as one could imagine. Since there would be no opportunity to resupply for some time, the caravan spent the two days of the crossing constantly working to provision themselves, filling their water skins from the Euphrates. Maria was quite fortunate in her foraging efforts, to the astonishment of her fellow travelers—she had managed to purchase a good quantity of chickens, eggs, and other provisions in the town of Hid.

Across the featureless desert, hour after hour, no patch of green could be found. The tired eye searched for something to break the monotonous plain but found nothing. Relief came when a wild animal galloped in the distance, startled by the approaching caravan. Maria heard they might be lions but couldn't see their shapes clearly. There was no discernible path, and they kept their course by compass and stars.

On journeys like this, each person's camel served as their well-stocked "ship." The saddles were quite comfortable, both for sitting and reclining. Two daily meals were taken on the camels during the caravan's early morning start. It wasn't as inconvenient as expected. The gentle rocking of the camels was like a cradle. The necessity of taking these meals in relative solitude only made the social gatherings at the evening's halt all the sweeter.

Maria spent most of her time reading during the journey. But as the day wore on, the heat combined with the gentle swaying motion of the camel's gait often proved too much, and sleep would overcome her. One day, she dozed off while reading, and the book slipped from her hand to the ground. The perceptive camel immediately stopped and refused to continue until Maria had retrieved the book. This exemplified the intelligence of this humble creature. The camel obeyed the slightest gesture from its master, gracefully kneeling at a moment's notice, as if intuitively divining its human's wishes.

On the third day after leaving Hid, Maria was idly riding along when she noticed a commotion up ahead in the caravan. Intrigued by the strange commotion, she questioned a concerned passerby about the incident. "The simoom! The simoom is approaching!" he cried. Maria was perplexed—the sky was clear and cloudless, with not a breath of wind stirring. How could the dreaded desert scourge be on its way?

She quickly discovered that the leading camels in the caravan had stopped, a clear indication of the approaching simoom. Camels sensed its arrival hours in advance, becoming even more stubborn than donkeys or mules. They would bury their heads in the sand and refuse to budge until the torment had passed. The Creator bestowed upon the animals this remarkable instinct, which not only protected themselves but also saved the lives of countless travelers who would have been overwhelmed and suffocated by the simoom before they could react.

Realizing the imminent danger, the caravan immediately halted. The tent camels were quickly unloaded, and the tents were pitched with haste fueled by fear and dread. The horses were secured, their heads covered, and their ears filled with cotton. The camels, heralds of the simoom, relied on instincts.

The travelers now sought refuge in their tents, casting themselves on the ground and covering their heads with the "mashallah." A profound silence descended upon the vast caravan, as if everyone was hoping to escape the fury of the wind by concealing their very existence.

Yet, the simoom did not arrive. An hour passed, and the sky remained serene, the air tranquil. During this time, Maria encountered a Turkish lady who seemed inclined to laugh at the fears expressed by the more experienced travelers. The lady asked Maria to join her for coffee and a chibouk, confident the simoom would be delayed. Faced with the continued fine weather and stillness of the atmosphere, Maria was tempted to share the lady's optimism and accepted her invitation, hoping to pass the time pleasantly until the wind's arrival.

Maria lifted the curtain and noticed a slight motion in the air, but she didn't pay it much attention. Instead, she sat comfortably with the Turkish acquaintance, sipping excellent coffee and enjoying a chibouk. As they conversed, she noticed the sides of the tent begin to rustle, gradually increasing in violence. Quickly rising from her cushion, Maria parted the curtain and looked out upon the desert. To her horror, she witnessed a vast, lurid column reaching from earth to heaven, slowly but steadily approaching the encampment. The gusts of wind became more sudden and violent, chilling her blood one moment and scorching her the next.

Overcome with a sense of terror, Maria felt her strength abandon her limbs. Knowing the simoom was near, she accepted the futility of returning to her tent. She hastily closed the curtain and stretched herself on the ground, covering her head and face with her "mashallah", as did her companion. The tent sides shook violently; Maria feared it would be lifted by the blast, exposing them to destructive fury. The tent became like a hot bath, and the women struggled to breathe. In that moment of terror, Maria admitted in her memoir contemplating having to die in the company of an unbeliever. Over the years, she got over herself.

The storm lasted for seven or eight hours. When it finally subsided, the travelers emerged from their tents, shaken but unharmed, and thanked God for their preservation. Maria checked on her friends and saw others doing the same, all appearing risen from the dead. As the tents were taken down and the camels loaded, the caravan resumed its journey. Along the way, they were horrified by the scorched bodies of several Arabs who had fallen victim to the storm's devastation.

For several days, the caravan continued without incident, though the travelers had not seen water for eight days, and their camels were growing increasingly thirsty. On the ninth day, the camels suddenly became agitated, pricking up their ears and sniffing the air. Out of nowhere, they surged ahead, leaving the travelers struggling to keep pace. Maria, riding a tall camel for a better view, unexpectedly took the lead in the camel race. To her surprise, the camels led the caravan to a nearby stream, where her camel plunged in up to its middle and began to drink eagerly, forgetting its usual polite behavior.

Maria had difficulty maintaining her seat when only the animal and herself had the water to themselves. But now, it was next to impossible, as camel after camel dashed in, plunging and jostling. She considered it a miracle that she escaped drowning in desperate extremity. She called out the driver, who stood at the bank, with utter indifference. "Come and save me," she said. "If you do not, I and your camel will both sink."

"Fear nothing," he replied, "the camel is wise; Allah has given him knowledge that he may not perish in the water."

"That may be true, but how is it possible that he can know the depth of this stream, in which he most probably never was before?"

"By the beard of my father, by the light of my eyes, you are safe," insisted the driver. "Which of the dangers of the desert has Providence hidden from the holy animal?"

Maria understood the calm surrender to destiny when it didn't threaten her. But despite his assurances, she felt great alarm at her perilous position, from which she saw no means of rescuing herself. But as the driver refused to lend her any assistance and seemed resolved to leave the result to Providence, she could only resign her fate into his hands.

When the camels had drunk their fill, they walked out in the calmest manner imaginable, with their bellies swelling to the size of mountains. They then proceeded to unload the beasts and pitch their tents, as they had determined to spend the night at this refreshing spot. Here, Maria enjoyed a delightful walk along the banks of the stream before supper.

The next day, they unfortunately fell in with a predatory tribe, whose name Maria did not learn, though she had reason to believe they were part of the great Anazi family. Resistance would have been foolish, so they immediately showed the chiefs the greatest courtesy and respect, living by the saying that "If you cannot cut their throats, you must all but lick the dust off their shoes."

Maria observed the unwelcome visitors to be more just

than others in the same profession. They assessed how much each individual should pay based on their income. Of course, this wasn't a simple matter. Many who had boasted just hours prior of their wealth now suddenly claimed impoverishment. Maria's share amounted to about one hundred and fifty piastres, which she did not consider outrageous, as she had a bag of pearls and jewels hanging at her saddle, which she was carrying to a merchant in Damascus.

The Bedouins held real power in these regions. The sultan's authority couldn't reach there due to the Wahabis, who had previously looted his caravan. After completing their business, the plunderers and the plundered enjoyed a feast that lasted until late.

Up to this point, Maria had enjoyed excellent health, but a few days after the encounter with the wandering tribe, she fell ill. A derangement of the stomach gradually increased in violence, and she began to fear she might perish in the desert without reaching the holy places she had so ardently longed to see. She believed her illness was caused by drinking the long-stored, slightly rotten water in the skins. Those skins were generally prepared for use by leaving inside them, for a few days, bits of pomegranate skin steeped in water. The pomegranate seeds were supposed to counteract the disagreeable flavor that would otherwise be communicated by the bladder. On this occasion, the skins she received were not properly prepared, causing the water to decompose.

Maria's illness rapidly increased and her strength failed her. She was tormented by a violent headache and consumed by fever. She couldn't get off her camel all day and had to go to bed when they stopped for the night. As she became weaker and weaker, she gradually abandoned all hopes of recovery, she resigned her soul to the will of her Creator; for where else could her hope be? She sent for her kind friend, the bishop, and besought him to administer to her the Catholic sacraments and consolations. He responded to her call with Christian zeal, and, with the tenderness of a father, prepared to watch the flight of her departing spirit. She confessed, and made her will, giving whatever she possessed to the poor, and appointing him her executor.

They were now drawing near to Tadmor, the ancient Palmyra, and Maria requested her friend, in case she should be overtaken by death before she reached that place, to see her buried there, at the foot of a mountain which she indicated to him. She besought him likewise to place over her grave a monumental stone, with these words, "Here lies the Daughter of Misfortune." She made him promise to pray for her soul, and think of her, in his wanderings amongst those holy precincts where she had fervently hoped to accompany him.

Many days passed before Maria could quit the back of her camel. At length, the disorder having reached its crisis, she mended by slow degrees, and by the time they reached Tadmor, she was sufficiently recovered to mount on horseback, and pass the day following their arrival in riding, with her friends, round the widely extended ruins of this relic of departed grandeur, where Zenobia, the proud Queen of the East, once flourished, guarded by her warriors, and counseled by her wise men. Her thoughts reflected upon the futile efforts of valor and wisdom to save her city from destruction or herself from the conqueror's chains. Her glory had faded, like that of the wisest kings who built Palmyra in the desert and other strong cities in Emath.

As they rode along, Maria and her friends beheld endless rows of Corinthian columns, of which all the buildings seemed to have been, except for one, the Temple of the Sun. Maria estimated this row of pillars extended for at least a mile. She saw a couple of unfinished items, in good condition, just as the workmen had left them. Street widths and directions were indicated by house foundations in many places. All was silence and desolation. The palm trees, which gave the city its name, were nowhere in sight. The few inhabitants who still haunted the desolate city had taken up their quarters in miserable huts, built within the enclosure of the once renowned Temple of the Sun, which they called "elkhala," the castle.

Maria spent some time amidst the forest of columns in the ancient city. The columns were extremely white, preserved by the purity of the climate, offering a pleasing contrast with the sandy waste that formed the background. Maria visited the Valley of the Tombs, located beyond the city's limits. This was perhaps the most interesting part of her excursion. The tombs, square buildings of two or three stories, held niches for dead bodies. Some contained mummies resembling those found in Egyptian pyramids. Many chamber ceilings showcased visible paintings, predominantly diamond-shaped compartments with painted heads.

Maria was shown a fountain, surrounded by a pile of huge stones, which she was told had been constructed by Aurelian, the Roman emperor who reigned from 270 to 275 during the Crisis of the Third Century. Arabs called it Ain Ornus. The inhabitants of Tadmor did not occupy themselves with labor of any kind. They neither sowed nor tilled but depended for their small supplies on the sale of salt and soda, the latter of which they supplied to the soap-makers of Damascus.

The tract Maria had to pass on her way to Damascus was dreary and desolate, similar to the one she had already traversed from Hid to Tadmor. After two days of travel, a far-off mountain was pointed out to her, thought to be Sodom and Gomorrah. The mountain had streams that caused harm to humans, believed by Arabs to be a divine curse.

Maria noticed a fog over the mountain, but the sky around

her was clear and bright. She learned that the fog never left the cursed area, a perpetual symbol of divine wrath. There were claims that the pillar of salt, where Lot's wife turned, can still be found here. Maria received this information with the most solemn assurances of its truth, but without feeling any irresistible desire to verify it by actual investigation.

CHAPTER 10

―⦾―

TURKISH BATHS AND THE LADIES OF DAMASCUS

T he caravans traveling from Baghdad to Damascus did not usually exceed forty days. Despite their large numbers and the extensive merchandise they carried, the loading and unloading consumed significant time. Consequently, they spent almost two months on the road and remained in the desert. After leaving the hills that bordered Palmyra to the northwest, they emerged into an open sandy plain without trees, greenery, or hills. Continuing in a northwestern direction, they could now clearly see in the far distance a tall range of mountains that grew in height and grandeur as they approached.

Eventually, on the fourth or fifth day after their departure from Tadmor, as they rose with the early dawn and prepared to set out on their daily march, the domes and minarets of Damascus appeared in the distance. The glittering tops of the city stood out boldly against the massive Anti-Lebanon mountain range, which the rising sun had just adorned with a beautiful rose-tinted hue. This captivating color, whose beauty is difficult to imagine for those who have not witnessed it rise in a mountainous region, filled their hearts with joyful anticipation. The entire caravan seemed to undergo a transformation. Instead of plodding forward wearily and listlessly, exhausted in body and dispirited by the monotony of the endless desert, cheerful conversations resumed, and an air of liveliness replaced the previous drowsy emptiness that had been etched on every face.

All eyes were focused in one direction, eagerly fixed on the long-awaited city. With each step, the city lost some of its enchanting and dreamlike quality, revealing the sober reality of a human dwelling place, the backdrop for everyday needs, and the stage for commonplace actions and occupations.

When they arrived at the spot where their caravan would make its final stop, about half an hour's distance from the eastern gate of the city, it was three o'clock in the afternoon. To their left, in the far south, rose the gently swelling heights of Harran, surrounded by the green abundance of the surrounding valleys. The rising crops in these valleys fully supported the claim that this fertile region was known as the "granary of Damascus." The contrast between the dreary and barren region they had left behind and the sight of flourishing fertility before them was striking.

The Christian burial ground stood between them and the city, which sprawled out before them amid a vast plain, surrounded by mountains of various shapes and characters, ranging from gently sloping hills to bare and rugged granite peaks covered in eternal snow. The irregular masses of white houses, which were quite dazzling under the scorching sun and cloudless sky, were adorned with numerous domes and cupolas belonging to mosques, churches, and convents. At intervals, graceful and exquisitely beautiful minarets towered above everything else and traced their elegant forms against the backdrop of the majestic Lebanon Mountains.

On their right, they could clearly see the source of the Barada River, known in ancient times as Abana and Pharphar. In the Bible, Naaman exclaimed that the Abana and Pharpar are greater than all the waters of Israel (2 Kings 5:12). The river's seven channels greatly contributed to the fertility of this

fortunate place, and its course was distinctly visible beyond
the city, marked by the deep fringe of trees lining its banks.
Gardens, orchards, or rather forests, of olive, palm, fig, apri-
cot, pomegranate, and orange trees surrounded the city from
every side, enveloping the "mole of beauty" and covering the
vast plain. From here, they could also discern the line of the
street referred to as the "strait" in the Acts of the Apostles.
The prominent public buildings lining its course, such as the
castle, palace, main inn, and the grand mosque, which was
once the Christian church of St. John, made it easily recognizable. The Christian quarter lay between them and the "strait
street," distinguished by the tops of its churches and the towers of its convents.

Upon arriving at their campsite, they found a multitude
of expectant friends and relatives who had set up their colorful tents near the designated area. They anxiously awaited the
caravan's arrival, creating a scene of bustling activity and confusion. Questions were asked and answered rapidly, with everyone talking simultaneously and filled with enthusiastic delight.
Some were overjoyed to find their friends safe, having experienced considerable anxiety and alarm on their behalf. Others
were equally pleased to discover that their merchandise had
escaped the clutches of Bedouin thieves. Fresh arrivals joined
the encampment every hour, further intensifying the cacophony of conversation in which everyone was eager to speak,
and no one wanted to listen.

The travelers now had an important task to complete: settling their accounts with the owners of the camels provided
for their journey. Once this matter was resolved, Maria's group
prepared for a grand celebratory feast. Maria was then met
by a wealthy merchant of Damascus named El Hawaja Yusuf
Hanhowri, to whom she had brought letters of recommendation. He brought his children and his brother with him, and

after offering his services, politely insisted that Maria and her companions use his home as their own until they could settle in Damascus. Maria and the others gratefully accepted his proposition.

That night, they slept in their tents for the last time. The next morning, Maria left the encampment with her traveling companion the bishop, the woman from Basra and her family, and Yusuf Hanhowri to the various gates. Upon reaching the eastern gate, they encountered a problem. In Damascus, like in many other Middle Eastern cities, Christians were forbidden from entering the city on horseback. Maria, who was feeling unwell, was riding a mare she had brought with her. The guards at the gate, recognizing them as Christians by their attire, refused to let them pass unless Maria dismounted.

A heated argument ensued. Yusuf Hanhowri, a highly respected and influential man, was outraged by the notion of detaining and insulting anyone under his protection. He engaged in a heated altercation with the guards. Yusuf's message to the troop commander quickly obtained permission for Maria to pass through the gate. They all took up residence in Yusuf's hospitable home until they could find a suitable dwelling, and during their stay, they were constantly shown kindness and genuine goodness of heart.

The day after her arrival, Yusuf's wife proposed that they all go together to the public bath. Maria gratefully accepted the offer, as she had grown accustomed to this luxury twice a week. Her two-month deprivation posed a significant challenge. They were a group of ten, accompanied by ten slaves. Maria's traveling companion from Basra and her daughter joined them as well.

The bathhouse's main hall was a sight to behold, adorned with polished marble walls and intricately designed mosaic floors that shimmered like mirrors. The ceiling, in the form of a dome, dazzled with glazed tiles of vibrant glass in a multitude of colors. While the establishment had several bathing rooms, they chose the largest.

Upon entering, they encountered around two hundred women, each clad in a white silk apron with colorful stripes, reaching down to their knees. Some were engaged in the bathing process, while others relaxed on divans, enjoying refreshments and smoking hookahs. Laughter echoed throughout as groups of beautiful individuals engaged in lively conversations.

The bathing procedure followed the typical practice in many Eastern cities. Incline-shaped fixtures lined the walls at regular intervals, providing a continuous supply of warm and cold water. Each pair of fixtures was accompanied by a marble basin mounted on a pedestal, exquisitely crafted and about two feet tall and wide.

The bathers sat on low wooden stools, elevated about a foot from the ground. The bathing attendants stood in front, pouring warm water over the bather's head and body. Another attendant stationed behind the bather used a special earth from Aleppo called "gil," mixed with fragrant herbs, to rub the head and skin gently. This cleansing earth was kept in a basin, and warm water was poured into it before use. It had the remarkable ability to purify and soften the skin, leaving it smooth and silky.

Another attendant supplied warm water to wash off the earth after vigorous rubbing. Vase after vase of warm water cascaded over the bather, followed by a lathering of scented soap. A final rinse with warm water concluded the bathing process. The bather's skin was then dried and gently rubbed with a bag made from the fibers of a plant called "leef," which provided a pleasant tingling sensation and increased blood circulation. The soles of the feet were polished with a smooth pumice stone attached to a handle, often made of metal, gold, or silver.

This invigorating procedure, though at times intense, lasted for about an hour. Afterward, some of the bathers reclined on the divans in the antechamber, while others lounged on the polished marble floor. They indulged in sherbet, coffee, and hookahs, while their slaves and attendants pampered them with an array of exquisite and fragrant perfumes sourced from the region's abundant floral landscapes.

The cacophony of chatter overwhelmed Maria's senses, a level of noise she had never experienced before. It was enough to bewilder anyone's mind, for the public baths of Damascus were notorious as the scandalous markets of the bustling city. This was where the beautiful people of Damascus settled rivalries, spread their elegant slanders, and whiled away the hours indulging in bathing, eating, drinking sherbet, smoking hookahs, and engaging in lively conversations and even dancing. The employed female slaves, who tirelessly kept the movement alive maintained the constant rhythm of the dance. Each woman took her turn, standing and joining the dance until feeling tired and resting.

As a stranger among them, Maria naturally piqued their curiosity, and she found herself immediately surrounded by a throng of her fellow bathers, bombarding her with countless questions. It would have taken her a week to answer them all truthfully and satisfactorily. She informed them that she hailed from Baghdad, which only fueled their curiosity further. They bombarded her with inquiries about the ladies of her city—how they dressed, how they looked, their amusements, their height, complexion, and body type. They wanted to know every detail about their habits, appearance, and how they were treated by their husbands. Maria did her best to answer their queries as succinctly as possible.

Among the crowd, there was one woman who stood out, fairer than the rest. Maria noticed a change in her countenance when she mentioned Baghdad. The woman's cheeks flushed immediately, her lips trembled, and Maria thought she saw a tear welling up in her eye. After Maria had somewhat quenched the thirst for information burning in the hearts of the Damascus belles, she turned her head and noticed the lady who had been so visibly affected by her mention of Baghdad had positioned herself by her side. The woman gazed at Maria with intense attention and obvious concern.

"You're from Baghdad," she whispered into Maria's ear.

"Yes, I am," Maria replied, curious about what would follow.

"Alas!" the woman exclaimed, growing visibly more agitated. "I, too, am from that city. May I request a moment to talk?"

"Of course," Maria answered, and the woman led her to an adjacent room, away from prying stares. As they walked, she playfully invited Maria to challenge her to a swimming race in the adjacent pool, ensuring their departure wouldn't attract attention.

Once alone, the woman burst into tears, taking some time to regain her composure before speaking. Maria did her best to console her, offering gentle words of comfort and encouraging her to share the cause of her profound grief, assuring her that Maria would share the burden.

"You have no idea, my lady, the emotions that single word you uttered evoked in me," she sobbed. "How could you possibly understand the mixed feelings of past happiness and bitter regret that name has stirred within me?"

The woman's father held a position of influence and respect in Baghdad, despite his Christian faith. He provided her with a nurturing upbringing and education, as her mother had passed away during childbirth. Tragedy struck again at the age of thirteen when her father died, leaving her without any family or protector.

During her father's life, they often received visits from a wealthy Turkish Aga who displayed friendly sentiments toward him and treated his daughter with special attention and respect. Once the customary period of mourning had passed, the Aga's visits became more frequent, and she couldn't ignore the growing realization that his extraordinary attentions were driven by a romantic interest in her.

The Aga soon confirmed her suspicions by declaring that his sole desire In life was to possess her. He tirelessly praised her virtues, claiming they surpassed the number of stars in the sky. He made lavish offers and promised her extravagant gifts, hoping to sway her with his generosity. However, she was resolute in her refusal. She couldn't fathom spending her life with a man who denied the truth of her religion and regarded its followers with disdain. She would rather face a thousand deaths than abandon the faith of her ancestors.

Enraged by her unwavering rejection of an offer he believed to be irresistible, the Aga resorted to forcefully abducting her a few days later. She was powerless to resist, and her struggles proved futile. Overwhelmed, she fell unconscious and awoke to find herself in the Aga's zenana, the women's quarters of his residence. The Aga persisted in expressing his love and presented her with priceless and rare gifts, but her determination remained unyielding. Frustrated and desperate, the Aga found himself at a loss. The strict laws of Islam forbade violence against women and mandated severe punishments for those who violated this prohibition.

In his desperation, the Aga turned to a potion called "zuhor," reputed to awaken feelings of love in the hearts of the previously indifferent or hostile. He secretly drugged her coffee with this potent charm, rendering her unaware of her actions. In her stupor, she unwittingly consented to their union, and their marriage was promptly arranged. The woman's heart sank as she recounted these events to Maria, particularly the moment she renounced her religion.

"All of this happened within the span of forty hours, during which the deadly drug I had swallowed maintained its power," she said. "When my senses returned, it felt as if I had been awakened from a horrific dream, and I was about to offer a fervent prayer to Providence, when the dreadful truth dawned on me—that I could not retrace my steps. For who has ever known the stern, relentless follower of Muhammad to release their grip on a victim once trapped? I was devoted to the prophet, and instant death stared me in the face if I refused to obey his law. What was left for me but to vent the grief consuming my heart in fruitless tears and lamentations? Heaven knows that, while my tongue took part in their impious rituals, Christianity remained in my heart; my conscience never ceased to torment me for my outward hypocrisy.

They soon departed from Baghdad and settled in Damascus, where they remained ever since. The woman's mind was burdened with grief, and the Aga made constant efforts to alleviate her suffering. She reigned supreme in his zenana, and her desires were treated as law. However, nothing could compensate her for the degrading apostasy she had been forced into.

When she was done relaying the story, Maria tried to console her, telling her to take heart, and that Providence would eventually remove the sinful burden from her shoulders, urging her to openly profess the faith she cherished in her heart.

"Imagine," she continued, "the emotions that took hold of me when I heard, just a while ago, that you were from Baghdad—the very place where I said goodbye to happiness forever! You must have noticed my agitation, a sign that my mind was elsewhere, away from the oblivious, joyful beings in the adjacent room."

To avoid arousing suspicion, they rejoined the crowd in the grand saloon. But the woman extracted a promise from Maria to visit her, despite Maria making excuses of ill-health. She even offered to send her a tahterawan, a sedan chair with curtains, to facilitate the visit. Aware of the deep-seated animosity that Damascenes held towards Christians, especially those from Baghdad, Maria protested, citing her objection to visiting the homes of Muslims. Yet, the woman fervently assured her that her husband was free from bigotry and harbored a particular fondness for followers of her faith. Furthermore, she wielded great authority within her own domain, and no one would dare to challenge her or oppose her wishes.

Unable to resist her pleas, Maria reluctantly agreed to pay her a visit. With a serene countenance that reflected the relief of sharing her sorrowful tale, the woman bid Maria farewell. She departed in her tahterawan, accompanied by an entourage of attendants, mamelukes, and eunuchs, heading towards her palace.

Returning to the large saloon, Maria found the ladies thoroughly enjoying themselves. Some were engaged in spirited and lively dancing. When they caught sight of her approaching, one of them called out, "Mashallah! Here comes our friend from Baghdad! Let's see the Baghdad step! We're tired of our old routine." The others joined in, eagerly requesting a demonstration of the renowned dance from Baghdad, invoking the names of prophets in anticipation.

Maria reassured them that she had no dancing skills whatsoever, old or new. She was content sitting on the marble floor, enjoying her shisha pipe, with a firm determination not to engage in such absurd entertainment. She explained her fatigue, attributing it to being out of practice and her long journey to Damascus. And she mentioned being weakened by a fever during the trip. She added that a series of misfortunes had left her spirit broken, and she couldn't, in short, succumb to their pleas.

However, these good-natured, and in Maria's opinion, thoughtless individuals remained convinced that she possessed hidden talents and attributed her reluctance to excessive self-doubt. One of them approached and placed a garland of flowers on her head, while others showered her with delightful perfumes. Two of them, more persistent than the rest, grasped her arms and lifted her off the ground.

It became clear that Maria couldn't escape their insistence, and realizing the futility of resisting, she decided to satisfy them as best she could. She attempted to recall the long-forgotten dance steps she had learned in her childhood, but her mind wandered, and her body had forgotten its grace. The marble floor was as slippery as ice, and as she turned, she lost her balance and fell backward, striking her head violently against the floor.

The women's mirth instantly transformed into sorrow and sympathy. Maria fell and blood pooled around her, flowing from a wound at the back of her head. The remorseful crowd, considering themselves responsible for her misfortune, competed in showing their compassion. They wasted no time in sending a messenger to the nearby apothecary, who promptly provided the necessary treatments. It was strictly forbidden for men to enter the bathing area while females were present, and any violation of this rule was punishable by immediate death.

For a long time, despite their best efforts, they couldn't stop the bleeding. It seemed as though Maria might bleed to death. Eventually, they applied a burnt camel's hair to the wound, which miraculously stemmed the hemorrhage. They carried her to another room and laid her in bed.

When Maria regained consciousness, her mind was in a whirl. She had no memory of the recent events and the role she had played in them. But gradually, the facts returned to her, and she realized she was in an unfamiliar room. Looking up, she felt relief as she saw her newfound acquaintance's face. They had shared secrets at the bathing area. The woman, as fair as the moon, leaned over her with affectionate concern, as if they had been close friends since childhood. Grateful for the circumstance, Maria appreciated the tender and caring heart she encountered, even among strangers. She later learned that people like that were rare in big cities.

Once Maria was safe, the woman made her promise to visit as soon as she could go out. She arranged for her own tahterawan—a carriage-like conveyance—to transport Maria to Yusuf's house. With that, she departed. A few days later, a sedan chair carried by four strong black men arrived and carried Maria to the house of Yusuf Hanhowri. Maria remained confined to her bed there for ten days. During this time, the Aga's wife sent her slaves to make daily inquiries about Maria's progress towards recovery.

Once she felt strong enough to venture outside, Maria decided to fulfill her pledge and express her gratitude to her new friend. On a beautiful day in May, accompanied by Yusuf Hanhowri's wife and her traveling companion, Maria left Yusuf's house in the Greek quarter of Damascus and made her way towards the Aga's residence. Unlike the plain exterior of many distinguished houses in Damascus, the Aga's dwelling presented a different sight. The street front appeared as a black wall, resembling a European convent, with only a low entrance portal and a small shibbak, or grating, above it, breaking the plainness.

However, once inside the gate, Maria discovered a vastly different scene. She found herself in a spacious courtyard paved with marble and shaded by tall sycamore and Persian willow trees. Numerous fountains adorned the courtyard, sending forth water in beautiful, intricate patterns that cooled the air and counteracted the sun's scorching rays. The walls were covered with vines, forming trellis-like patterns. Maria paused to admire the beautiful courtyard, causing slight impatience among the attendants waiting to guide her.

Eventually, Maria was led into a lavishly furnished saloon, surpassing anything she had ever seen before in terms of opulence. There she found her beautiful friend, who greeted her with overwhelming joy at her recovery and showered her with kindness. The friend mentioned that the furniture and decorations in the room they were in alone cost 150,000 piastres, and there were ten or twelve other equally splendid rooms in the Aga's palace. Despite her apparent luxury and control over her surroundings, Maria's friend was troubled deep down. Being a Christian at heart, she felt her body and soul enslaved amidst such splendor. When Maria entered, there were several of the Aga's wives and slaves present, all of them varying degrees of beauty and wearing cheerful expressions that contrasted starkly with the melancholy and pensiveness etched on her fair friend's face.

Maria found it truly remarkable how long the wives and slaves of the wealthier Turks were able to preserve their good looks and youthful appearance. Often, the mother and daughter were hard to tell apart due to their close ages. Taking on significant life responsibilities at a young age did not result in premature aging, unlike in other nations. The life they led largely contributed to this result.

From birth to death, these women were largely exempt from any kind of worry. They passed their days peacefully, untroubled by the passionate concerns that plagued even the highest echelons of civilized society. Their time was spent either in idleness or in pursuing accomplishments like music, dance, and embroidery. They had little knowledge of or interest in the go-ings-on of the outside world. Few could read, and Turkish men disdained discussing business or serious matters with women, reasoning details were not their concern. They question why she should bother with the road she will never travel. Besides this, a feeling of jealousy furnished an additional motive for keeping them in ignorance. The zenana, where all that they could desire was administered to them without stint, and the hammam, where they met their female acquaintances, and enjoyed a healthy luxury of bathing, were the whole world to them.

Women in Damascus dressed elegantly, surpassing those in other Eastern cities. They wore their hair in long braids adorned with gold, pearls, and diamonds that sometimes reached the ground. Maria found them to be amiable and kind-hearted, with a natural, unaffected demeanor full of genuine warmth. In later years, when she reflected on the serenity and tranquility that characterized these uneducated Orientals and compared it to the company she had kept in European cities, she often wondered whether the former did not have a more privileged state.

Maria was captivated by the grandeur and opulence of the house and its surroundings. It was a stark contrast to her pre-vious experiences, and she couldn't help but reflect on the true meaning of happiness and contentment amidst such luxury.

After the customary offering of coffee and nargilehs, the Aga's wife pressed Maria to stay for dinner, but she had to de-cline, having already accepted an invitation to visit a wealthy Christian friend of Yusuf Hanhowri who lived in a beautiful country house north of the city, surrounded by extensive, fruit-laden gardens. Though prosperous, this friend prudently kept his wealth hidden from the government, a discreet precaution that Christians under Muslim rule found highly convenient. Bidding her fair hostess farewell, Maria promised to return at the earliest opportunity.

The host was of the Greek church and lived in a house situated a few miles away from Damascus, in a picturesque area near the Barrada River. As they arrived at the gate, Maria couldn't help but admire the extensive and fertile grounds surrounding the house. Fruit trees grew abundantly, creating a forest-like atmosphere, and the pastures were dotted with camels basking in the sun. Inside the house, the same sense of wealth and order prevailed. The dining table was set in a large, beautifully decorated saloon adorned with two exquisite marble fountains, emitting fragrant scents from the garden. The air was filled with the gentle breeze created by the fountains' sprinkling water.

The dining party consisted of around forty people, seated in a circle around a large salver placed on a luxurious Persian carpet. The stand supporting the salver was a remarkable piece, made of cedarwood from Mount Lebanon and intricately inlaid with mother-of-pearl from the Red Sea. Men and women sat on opposite sides of the table, unlike in Mosul and Baghdad. Behind the guests stood a group of slaves, their hands crossed.

The dinner was excellent, featuring a variety of dishes such as roasts, pillaws, kababs, and sambousack, commonly found in Eastern cuisine. Maria also had the opportunity to taste a specialty called "jild el faras," which translates horse's skin, a delicacy made from Damascus apricots known for their flavor and size. They boiled down the apricots to a thick marmalade, rolled it out into a large sheet, and cut it into wafer-like pieces. The dish had a delightful taste and in modern times it's called "Qamar al Deen," which means "Moon of the Religion."

Wine was served during the dinner, including a particular variety called ebi del Asfar, which Maria found particularly enjoyable. She learned that Italians imported a significant quantity of it. The atmosphere was festive and filled with the chatter and laughter of the guests, creating a vibrant ambiance. Musicians played their instruments, adding to the festivities. Maria, not a singer, solved it by persuading her fellow traveler's daughter to sing instead. The young woman's beautiful voice was liked by the company.

After dinner, the guests moved to a separate chamber to enjoy fruits, like the European custom. This was followed by serving coffee and smoking pipes filled with aloe wood. It was believed that this interval helped with digestion, as it was a prevalent notion in these countries that consuming fruits immediately after a heavy meal could be detrimental to digestion.

During the meal, a Turkish Aga, just returned from a pilgrimage to Mecca, took it upon himself to regale the company with tales of his journey. Maria became the target of his attention, as he shared stories of the wonders he had witnessed, both real and imagined, at the miraculous "Beyt Allah," the house of God, which he claimed was built by the Almighty Himself.

Once the prophet had a look at the celestial realms, the story goes that he spotted a temple that caught his fancy. He couldn't resist putting in a request to use it for the faithful down on Earth. And wouldn't you know it? The temple was sent down to Mecca where it still stands, bringing great comfort to devout Muslims and causing utter confusion to any unbelievers, assuming there are any of those filthy dogs lurking around the sanctuary, claimed the devout Muslim. He then went on to assure Maria that the temple was guarded day and night by angels. It was called the Kaaba, and every true believer turned their face towards it when they prayed. They also sent gifts to the Kaaba every year if their conscience was bothering them, and it was considered a religious duty for every believer, regardless of their circumstances, to make a pilgrimage to the Kaaba at least once in their lifetime. It was a way to cleanse themselves of their sins and purify themselves before the holy prophet.

After Ramadan, three massive caravans set off for Mecca from Baghdad, Damascus, and Egypt. These caravans usually consisted of no less than a hundred thousand pilgrims and two hundred thousand camels. Once they arrived in Mecca, they circled the mosque known as Beyt Ibrahim seven times. They also believed it was "wajib," or necessary for their purification, to kiss a peculiar black stone found in Mecca. Legend had it that the stone descended from heaven pure white and later turned black.

The man continued his tales, this time about the wonders of Koum town, where the prophet's daughter was buried. He claimed three holy tombs existed in Koum, with the most magnificent belonging to Fatima, daughter of the prophet and wife of Ali, revered by the Shia sect. His daughter's name, wrote Maria, "is scarcely less sacred to the sons of Irak, than that of Muhammad himself."

The man described the tomb as a marvel, standing at a height of about twelve feet with seven steps of solid silver surrounding it. The steps were adorned with the most luxurious fabrics, embroidered with gold and studded with precious stones. That's the kind of honor they bestowed upon the divine Fatima, whom faithful believers regarded as the pure and immaculate virgin, the chaste mother of the twelve illustrious vicars of Allah. However, the man clarified that Fatima's body wasn't actually in the tomb since she had been lifted to heaven by the Almighty. He mentioned two other tombs in Koum, which he deemed less splendid than Fatima's, but still remarkable in terms of structure and decoration.

Maria was often taken aback by the reverence Turks and Persians held for the Blessed Virgin Mary and Jesus. The talkative Hadji, who shared these details with her, always spoke of these sacred figures with utmost respect. Yet, she couldn't help but notice that Hadji was deeply entrenched in fanaticism, completely swayed by credulity, and harbored a strong hatred for all Christians, regardless of their denomination.

As the sun began to set, Maria and her companions embarked on their journey back to Damascus. They enjoyed a pleasant ride by the Barrada, made delightful by the cool twilight and westerly breeze from the sea, carrying a touch of chill from the Lebanon peaks. By the time they arrived home, darkness had descended, and they promptly retired to rest, contented with their day's excursion.

The following morning, after breakfast around nine o'clock, Maria ventured out with her two travel companions for a shopping expedition in the bustling bazaar adjacent to Khan Assad Pasha. The bazaar stretched so long that it took a good half-hour to traverse. Outside, an eerie silence prevailed, with no sound of horses or carriages to betray the presence of life behind the monotonous walls lining the narrow streets. Upon entering the bazaar, they were overwhelmed by the myriad of conversations in diverse languages.

There, in the vast throng, one could spot the robust figure of a Turk, his vibrant garments a striking contrast to the modest clothing of a Bedouin wrapped in a coarse and ample aaba. Occasionally, a wealthy Aga would pass by, resplendent in luxurious fabrics and furs, his girdle adorned with a jewel-hilted hanjar, his sword trailing along the ground. Accompanied by ten or fifteen slaves, some of whom carried his nerghila and smoking paraphernalia, the Aga moved with a slow and dignified stride. His smoking apparatus consisted of an intricately embroidered cloth bag, so richly adorned with gold that it almost concealed the fabric itself. The bag contained tobacco and a pair of gold pincers used to fill the pipe.

Maria marveled at the intricate patterns and stunning

variety of silk fabrics displayed by the dealers. The traders of Damascus impressed her with their courteousness and unwavering dedication to assisting customers. They'd go out of their way to help find specific items, even if not in their own stalls.

Maria and her companions were captivated by the array of Indian textiles available. They purchased several pieces of gold and silver tissue at remarkably low prices compared to what she had encountered before. The quality and brilliance of the satin fabrics also caught their attention, surpassing anything they had seen in European markets while being surprisingly affordable.

After completing their purchases, they ventured into the renowned Khan Assad Pasha, a magnificent complex adjacent to the bazaar. Its grand cupola left a lasting impression on Maria, reminiscent of the splendor of St. Peter's in Rome. They later sought respite by the banks of the nearby stream, where they observed groups of people enjoying coffee and tobacco in the shade of the trees.

As they rested and admired the scenery, their attendant, burdened with their purchases, also sought a moment of reprieve. However, a mishap occurred when their load accidentally tumbled down the bank and into the water, leaving them in shock. The poor attendant, visibly distressed by the accident, stood helplessly as their precious fabrics sank beneath the surface. Recognizing his genuine concern, Maria and her companions refrained from scolding him and watched as he hurriedly rushed back to the bazaar, likely in search of a solution to salvage their lost goods.

Maria was taken aback by the extraordinary events that had unfolded. At first, she thought the attendant had run off, fearing punishment for his actions. However, he soon returned, bringing with him a professional diver, known as a "rhathas," who frequently lingered around the bazaar in search of employment. The driver immediately plunged into the river, remaining underwater for an unusually long time, but ultimately returned empty-handed. He descended multiple times, but the rapid current had likely swept their lost package far away from the initial spot where it had fallen into the water. Exhausted, they eventually returned home, leaving the slave and the diver to continue the search, with little hope of ever recovering their lost treasure.

To Maria's surprise, the next day, the package was brought to the house of Yusuf Hanhowri, though in a completely ruined state. Despite their disappointment, Maria and her family embraced the principles of their Christian faith, accepting the loss with resignation and fortitude.

The house of Yusuf Hanhowri was a magnificent structure, comparable to the homes of the most distinguished Turks. It was remarkably spacious, with separate quarters for the men and women. One of the saloons was particularly grand, with a beautifully decorated ceiling, gilded grilles, and two fountains in the center. The room also housed an aviary filled with a variety of colorful and melodious birds. It was said that these birds were sometimes utilized by lovelorn individuals to deliver secret messages, using the doves as clandestine letter carriers.

The room's floor held exquisite Persian carpets. At one end, a raised dais stood about a foot above the rest of the floor, draped in the finest carpet. This was where the host would traditionally receive his most distinguished guests. The walls were adorned with intricate arabesque designs, accented with gleaming gold.

Amidst such lavish splendor, it was not uncommon to see a baby's cradle placed on a simple wooden board atop the carpet, rocked gently by the mother as she and her female relatives worked on their ornate needlework and embroidery, a craft they had mastered. Maria saw the remarkably skilled embroidery they produced, decorating napkins and handkerchiefs.

In this culture, it was seen as almost a moral failing for a woman to refuse nursing her own child, unless illness prevented it, a view shared by the nomadic tribes as well. The Christian women Maria associated with in Damascus displayed great intelligence and purity of thought in their conversations. Great care was taken to shield young girls from any corrupting influences or inappropriate ideas.

In the presence of strangers, Christian families maintained customs as rigid as those of the Turks. Husbands and wives acted as complete strangers, refraining even from the slightest touch or greeting. Saturdays were devoted entirely to bathing, with Fridays spent preparing. Maria observed the Christian women's unwavering devotion to their religious duties, sometimes even skipping meals to attend mass or vespers.

The male head of the household spent much of his day in his private quarters, rarely without his ever-present pipe, with a servant bringing him coffee every quarter-hour. Considerable wealth was lavished on elaborately decorated pipes, some with amber mouthpieces adorned in gold and precious gems. Both Turkish and Christian men also occupied themselves by running amber beads through their fingers, reciting prayers on their rosaries.

CHAPTER 11

VISITING A MOSQUE

E veryday the Aga's wife sent Maria a message, urging her to fulfill her promise and visit her soon. Despite not desiring the meeting, Maria felt compelled to go. This time, she went alone. Upon reaching the Aga's residence, she was immediately ushered into the salon where the women of the household spent their time embroidering and making silk shirts and muslin headscarves adorned with lace for their lord.

Their needlework displayed remarkable skill and precision, a testament to their long and devoted dedication to the craft. The women rarely ventured outside, except on bathing days, and when they did, they were always accompanied by slaves in a curtained sedan chair, shielding them from the gaze of strangers, which was considered impure according to Islamic beliefs.

The restrictions imposed on them and the inconveniences of going out dampened their desire for outdoor activities and limited their enjoyment. Most of the women, except Maria's friend, couldn't read or write. Having been purchased at a young age, their needlework became their primary occupation. Despite their conversion to Islam at a young age, many of these Georgian women, born Christians, still longed to return to the faith of their ancestors. They showed Maria, an open Christian, more respect than they would have shown the Sultan himself. When they learned that Maria planned to travel from Damascus to Jerusalem, they exclaimed, "Blessings upon you, oh pilgrim! What happiness you have!" and asked her to remember them in her prayers.

After going through the customary ritual of washing and refreshing themselves with coffee, sherbet, hookahs, and perfumes, they engaged in conversation until it was time for dinner, which was usually served between midday and one o'clock. The Aga's feast was grand, and the attendants seemed more numerous than Maria had ever seen before, often getting in each other's way.

Shortly after dinner, Maria rose to take her leave, but her enthusiastic friend insisted that she stay the night. A messenger was dispatched to Maria's host's house to inform her friends of her decision to remain at the Aga's residence. In the afternoon, they went to the magnificent terrace on the rooftop to enjoy the evening breeze and admire the breathtaking view. The surrounding landscape was indescribably beautiful. Fruit trees stretched for miles, undulating like waves in the breeze, while the gleaming minarets, adorned with polished tiles resembling burnished gold, and the elegant cupolas and majestic domes encircled them. In the distance, the ancient Anti-Lebanon range stood, its weathered slopes turning deep purple as twilight descended. They could also see the generous Barrada River flowing abundantly, nourishing and embellishing the splendid city.

While the other women left the terrace as the evening grew darker, Maria remained captivated by the scene, her eyes fixed upon it. Her charming friend joined her, and they requested that the dessert be served on the terrace, so they could savor the view as long as possible.

As twilight approached, their conversation naturally turned to religious matters. Maria exclaimed with wonder, "Imagine the joys that await a true Christian when, at the end of their earthly journey, the Almighty calls them to eternal happiness in the realms of bliss! If we mortals are privileged to witness a scene as magnificent as this, let us learn to elevate our thoughts from these beautiful creations to their all-bountiful Creator, who has even greater blessings in store for us."

The Aga's wife couldn't contain her emotions and burst into tears. "How can I speak of such things?" she sobbed, wringing her hands. "I am an outcast, with no inheritance in Heaven. I have lost my birthright. My soul is in bondage."

"Take comfort!" Maria exclaimed. "Who can say what trials the Almighty Father may decree for His children to test their faith? Do not surrender to despair. Have faith in God, and He won't forsake you in need."

Without replying, the Aga's wife fell on her knees, and she pleaded, clasped her hands, and looked up to heaven. "Please, merciful Father, release me from the shackles of the infidel. The burden is heavy, and I am powerless to free myself. Bring me back to your holy communion, lest I perish in my sin!" The outpouring of remorse provided some solace for the woman, and she regained enough composure to descend to the salon as darkness fell.

When she and Maria entered the room, they found the other ladies gathered, their faces concealed behind veils except for their eyes. To pass the time, they engaged in various games, including "fanagin," where cups and a ring were used, and chess. Amidst the conversations and games, the evening passed relatively pleasantly, and even Maria's sorrowful friend seemed to regain some of her spirits.

At eleven o'clock, Maria was shown to her chamber, situated in a secluded corner of the harem. She slept soundly and rose early the next morning, engaging in her customary devotions undisturbed in the privacy of her room. As soon as the Aga departed, his wife managed to slip away from the others and join Maria in her chamber. She was determined to devise a plan for her escape from the grip of Islam, disregarding the immense dangers and severe consequences that awaited her. She had already accepted the possibility of a cruel death and braced herself for the worst.

Aware that Maria would soon embark on a journey to the Lebanon, she implored her to take her along. Maria was taken aback by the request. She fully understood the dire consequences they both would face if their secret were discovered. While Maria had long contemplated martyrdom for her faith, she couldn't bear the thought of condemning such a beautiful soul to a gruesome fate.

"Consider the dangers that surround us from all sides," Maria exclaimed, her voice filled with concern.

"I have, I have," the woman replied. "But what are they to block my path to the mansions of the true God?"

"The Aga is powerful," Maria emphasized, "his slaves are told by hundreds; he speaks the word, and his horsemen cover the desert. Are we foxes, that we should escape his vigilance? Here you have riches and plenty; your wishes are laws; the Aga is himself your slave. Consider carefully before trading these pleasures for poverty, punishment, and a shameful death."

"I know that the Aga is powerful. I know that certain death will be my lot, if my evil destiny should frustrate my attempt to escape. I have pondered on this over and over again; but neither poverty, nor punishment, nor the dread of death itself have power to change my resolution. If God wills it, I am prepared to sacrifice my life for his holy faith. You, who have urged me to remain steadfast and cling to the Rock of Salvation, why do you now suggest that I pursue wealth and status instead of focusing on heaven and sacrificing everything for the love of God?"

True, Maria had many times and often so exhorted her, and her pupil was now in her turn become her instructress.

She felt quite ashamed of the truckling, time-serving counsel which her anxiety for her personal safety had but just now
prompted her to offer. Her fears, however, soon vanished; she
became as enthusiastic as herself. She determined to unite her
fate with her friend's, for good or for ill. She entered at once
warmly and heartily into her scheme. She fell upon her neck,
and they shed warm tears of joy, not unmingled with fear and
sad forebodings.

Maria and her companion proceeded together to the
salon where the Aga's wife typically spent most of her time.
Fortunately, they found the room empty, giving them the opportunity to formulate their plans and arrange the details of
their future operations. Adorning the walls of this salon were
various pipes and hookahs, all extravagant in their fittings.
Among them was one of superb craftsmanship and rare materials, which the Aga had recently presented to his favorite as
a gift worthy of her acceptance, professing his deep affection
for her. The mouthpiece was made of silver gilt, inlaid with
precious stones of considerable value. The Aga's wife pressed
Maria to accept this as a testament to her unwavering esteem.
Knowing the circumstances under which it had been gifted,
Maria was quite reluctant to take advantage of her friend's
generosity. But the more she persisted in declining the offered
gift, the more determined and insistent the Aga's wife became
in her pleas.

While they were deeply engaged in this friendly dispute,
the Aga himself entered the room. Upon learning the cause
of their discussion, he, to Maria's slight surprise, joined his entreaties to those of his wife, urging Maria to accept the present that she was so eager to bestow. It was sufficient that his
wife desired it; had the gift been ten times more valuable, he
would have insisted that Maria take it. After such ardent pleas
from a dear friend, seconded by the man whose wealth had

purchased the ornament, Maria would have had to be made of stone to refuse this exquisite hookah, upon whose beauties even the greatest poets would not have disdained to lavish their sweetest verses. Maria accepted the gift.

After some conversation on inconsequential matters, the Aga took his leave, and it was not long before Maria followed suit. However, not before she had given his wife a pledge that she would be tireless in her efforts to bring about the objective most dear to her heart. Accordingly, upon returning home, Maria sought out the good bishop, who had been her traveling companion from Baghdad, to consult him on the best course of action in this delicate matter. She had no doubt that his age and experience would be able to suggest a better plan than the rash and untrained intellects of herself and her friend could devise, fully expecting to find in him a zealous and eager collaborator in this pious endeavor.

To Maria's grief and surprise, even to her indignation, she found the worthy man indifferent to the point of coldness. He magnified the dangers to be feared and appeared, to Maria's perhaps overly enthusiastic mind, to greatly underestimate the immense importance of the objective at hand. Although grieved and mortified beyond measure by this unexpected apathy from one on whom she had so confidently counted for sage counsel and prompt assistance in furthering her goal, Maria nevertheless did not succumb to despair. She was determined to redeem, if possible, the pledge she had given to her unfortunate friend, alone and unaided, save by Him who is ever present to support the friendless.

Maria scarcely went a day without spending time with her new friend. Together, they visited the Pasha's harem. The courtyards and apartments were like other wealthy Turkish households, but more spacious and lavishly adorned than any Maria had encountered. Silks, velvets, and gold embroidery adorned every surface, almost overwhelming the eye with the sheer opulence. The ornate cushions were the most luxurious she had ever encountered, covered in rich fabrics and intricate needlework. The gardens, almost as big as Regent's Park, aimed to bring joy to the inhabitants. They lacked freedom, education, and inner peace, which money alone couldn't offer. In almost every harem room, mournful turtle doves cooed, lulling the mind into a pensive melancholy, while vibrant parrots squawked and chattered, lively distractions for the female residents.

One day, the Aga's wife invited Maria to accompany her to the grand mosque. This was a risky proposition, as an unbeliever caught polluting the sacred space could be met with instant death. Her marriage to a powerful man in Damascus would not offer any protection. Yet she was insistent, assuring Maria that she could effectively disguise her so that even the most vigilant Muslims would not detect the deception. Curious to witness their religious rituals, Maria's scruples were soothed, and they set out one Friday morning. Dressed head-to-toe in Turkish attire and closely veiled, preceded and followed by six slaves, they soon reached the mosque.

They entered the foreboding precincts, doubly daunting for a Christian in fanatical Damascus. Ascending to the women's gallery, they found several others already assembled. Below, the male congregation sat on the marble floor covered in plush Persian carpets. The mullah climbed onto his pulpit, situated among them, and commenced his sermon, which lasted about half an hour and proved quite entertaining.

The mullah began by expounding on matters of faith and concluded with exhortations. Maria found great amusement in his explanation for the Muslim prohibition against eating pork. He said, "When Noah brought a male and female of every creature into the ark, he declared, 'The pig was not created but was engendered later by the enormous mass of excrement accumulated by the elephant.'" In another part of his sermon, while referring to the failure of Mohammed when he struck the bare rock, imitating Moses in front of a multitude of disciples, expecting water to gush forth at his command, the mullah claimed that the disaster occurred not due to any lack of supernatural power in the holy prophet or any unwillingness on the part of the water to obey his inspired command. The well collapsed due to pigs digging it up, causing the water to escape.

Maria's companion informed her that the same learned preacher had previously described, in vivid detail, how the faithful would be transported to the realms of eternal bliss after a life spent in virtuous and holy deeds. "The prophet," he said, "will appear in the form of a lamb, and the multitude of true believers will gather in the form of vermin within the lamb's abundant fleece. So, when the sacred animal ascends to the heavens, the chosen ones will be shaken out into boundless happiness."

With the doctrinal aspects covered, the preacher proceeded to deliver a fervent exhortation, urging the cultivation and propagation of the true faith without hesitation regarding the means employed, sparing neither fire nor sword, persecution nor extortion, chains nor slavery, all for the sake of accomplishing this sacred goal.

Having successfully roused his audience to the necessity of following in the footsteps of their faith's founder, the mullah descended from his pulpit and stood amid the congregation, calling upon everyone present to join in prayer. Responding to his call, the men below rose from the carpet and gathered around their priest in an attitude of reverence. "La haoul wala kouat ila b' Allah," the mullah exclaimed loudly, which meant "There is neither aid nor strength save in God." With reverence, the congregation repeated the words, turning their heads right and left.

The mullah proceeded to recite various other passages from the Koran, with the people repeating and adjusting their postures according to the prayer's meaning—bowing their heads, sitting on their heels, and prostrating themselves in the name of Allah and the prophet. The women in the gallery also participated in the ceremony, their veils remaining almost as tightly wrapped as when they walked in public streets.

Everything had gone smoothly so far. Maria had ample time to observe the ceremony, and her disguise seemed to have effectively concealed her true identity. As they were preparing to leave, Maria noticed a few women in the gallery staring intently at her face. She felt a surge of alarm and urged her friend to hasten their departure.

"Let's get out of here quickly," Maria whispered anxiously. "Those women are looking at me suspiciously."

Whispers and furtive glances spread among the other women, and hostile murmurs filled the air.

"Look, there's an outsider defiling the sanctuary!" one woman shouted. "I recognize her—I saw her at the bathhouse!"

Another woman countered, "No, you must be mistaken. It can't be."

The first woman insisted, "I swear, I'm certain it's her!"

Disturbed by the hostile comments that reached her ears, Maria pleaded with her friend to leave immediately.

"Don't worry," her friend reassured her. "I'll protect you. Let's show them what happens when they offend the friend of the Aga's wife."

Encouraged by these words, Maria followed her companion with a steady and fearless pace, doing her best to conceal any signs of anxiety or fear. Once they were outside the sanctuary, they hurried back to the Aga's house, reaching it in less time than it had taken them to reach the mosque earlier. Every moment during the journey was filled with terror and alarm for Maria, and she didn't feel truly safe until she was inside the palace.

Now they had to consider the best course of action under such critical circumstances. It was evident that Maria, as a Christian, had been discovered defying the strict Turkish law that prohibited non-Muslims from entering the holy precincts, under penalty of death. She knew those who exposed her would quickly report to authorities, eager to please the prophet and his followers. Her only hope of survival lay in hiding.

Returning to the house of her host, himself a Christian and already suspected of being wealthy, would be like walking into a trap. It would not only endanger Maria's life but also put her generous host and his kind family at risk of oppression or worse. Yielding to their pleas, Maria agreed to remain under the Aga's roof for at least a few days, awaiting the outcome of her unfortunate adventure.

Every passing day increased Maria's and her friend's anxiety as they waited for the officers of justice to visit, fearing each new arrival might be the khadi. Maria entertained faint hopes of ultimately escaping detection in a place like Damascus, where most of the population were inflamed by intolerant bigotry. She tried to resign herself to the idea of martyrdom.

Amidst the painful suspense, Maria heard a stir in the house, as if an important visitor had arrived. She was breathless with expectation but dared not emerge from her place of concealment. Soon, her friend rushed into the room with terror on her pale face.

"Hurry! Hurry!" she cried. "Hide yourself in the most secluded part of the harem. The khadi is here—I saw him myself.

Don't waste a moment! I'll do everything I can to thwart their search."

Maria, full of fear, hurriedly left the room and went to a secluded lumber room in the harem. The question now, how to conceal herself. Looking around, Maria spotted a large roll of matting in a corner. It had been recently moved from one of the lower rooms for cleaning. She immediately got down on her knees and crept cautiously into the huge roll, patiently and resignedly awaiting the outcome. She knew she had taken every precaution possible to preserve her life. For at least half an hour, the house fell into a deathly silence. Maria couldn't hear a sound of what was happening outside her hiding place. The initial flurry and excitement caused by her friend's announcement had subsided, replaced by a calm and almost serene state of mind. If it weren't for the inconvenient and confined situation she was in, Maria could have allowed herself to indulge in a pleasant daydream.

"But wait!" she thought, hearing a sound in the distance. "They're searching the rooms below." Her reverie was abruptly cut short, and her heart started pounding with anxiety. It was the sound of footsteps, not just one, but several individuals. The noise grew louder and clearer with each passing moment. Now she could hear them on the landing, directly below the room where she lay concealed. "Sadly," Maria cried. "My dear, kind-hearted friend, your efforts have been in vain! I am discovered, and we will both pay the price for our recklessness."

They were now right at the door! Large beads of sweat formed on Maria's forehead. She struggled to suppress the sound of her breathing, nearly choking in the effort. As far as she could tell from the noise, there appeared to be only two people, but she couldn't see them. They approached the roll of matting where she lay concealed. Maria almost surrendered until she thought of spying on the intruders through a hole.

Maria's immense joy came when she realized that the much-dreaded individuals were actually ten female servants of the household who came to deliver additional furniture. She was delighted and silently thanked Providence for her continued safety, when suddenly a heavy load was thrown atop the roll of matting where she lay, nearly making her cry out from the sudden impact. Load after load came, almost burying her alive, as she fought to stay silent in her plea for mercy.

Realizing this had become a serious matter, a question of life or death, Maria made one desperate effort to extricate herself, thrusting the roll of matting forward with such suddenness and force that the servants shrieked in terror and rushed out of the room, crying "A genie! A genie!" leaving Maria to free herself as best she could. It was undoubtedly an amusing scene, one that Maria might have greatly enjoyed had she not been in imminent danger of suffocation.

Maria made several attempts to free herself, but without success. She was beginning to think the servants' efforts would have rendered the actions of the khadi unnecessary, when she heard the light, cheerful footsteps of the Aga's wife, familiar to her ear, coming up the stairs. The woman rushed into the room, glanced around, and called for Maria. However, Maria could barely make herself heard, muffled by the thick matting and nearly suffocating.

Finally, the woman heard Maria's voice and, after considerable effort, managed to remove the pile of matting that covered her. Maria emerged at last, a picture of dishevelment—her hair disheveled around her face, her countenance smeared with dirt. She rushed into her friend's arms, and the Aga's wife told her it had indeed been the judge who had come, but his visit was on official business with the Aga. Maria had risked suffocation needlessly.

Once they had exchanged mutual congratulations, they

began to perceive the ludicrous nature of the situation and descended to the woman's room, laughing until tears streamed down their cheeks.

Day after day passed without further alarm, and Maria eventually resolved to return to her friends, to plan for their swift departure to the Lebanon, confident her imprudent escapade had not come to the authorities' attention. However, before leaving, she carefully outlined her planned route to her warm-hearted friend and provided her with the name of the convent where they were to reunite. With an affectionate embrace, Maria bid her friend farewell and set off on her journey.

CHAPTER 12

―――――∽―――――

LIFE IN A CONVENT

D ays later, Maria departed Damascus with her companion. They proceeded to Zahle and pitched their tents on the side of a mountain overlooking the town, where they remained for ten days. Then they headed to Baalbek. On their road, they met women with remarkable headdresses. A twelve-inch round shield was attached on the right side of their head. The sight of them alarmed Maria. She mistook them for armed brigands and thought the headdresses a complete disfigurement. As they came closer, they saluted the travelers in a friendly manner and Maria realized they were women.

After visiting Baalbek, Maria and her companion returned to Zahle to stock up on provisions. They then traveled to a mountain, where they set up camp near a convent on the Anti-Lebanon range. The Aga's wife joined Maria the day after their arrival. Disguised in male attire, she had escaped from the Aga's house before daybreak. Once she reached the open country, she quickly found a guide. With him by her side, she faced the dangers of the road and evaded her pursuers.

Upon seeing her, Maria felt joy and immediately introduced her to the superior of the convent as her relative. She shared her story and the risks she had taken to return to her faith. The superior offered to help the new guest, including a permanent asylum in the convent. The convent stood secluded, high in the mountains, surrounded by rugged scenery. Its expansive gardens that were ornamented by fig trees provided for the needs of the fifty nuns who lived there, along with the superior, a confessor, and workers. Most of the nuns came from Christian families in places like Baghdad, Mosul, and Persia, where convents were scarce.

Maria stayed with her friend for two days before continuing her journey through the Holy Land with her companions. She promised to return and stay with her friend permanently once the trip was over, and paid her friend's entrance fee, urging her to be cautious. The next day, she and her group set out westward towards the sea. The rugged terrain made travel difficult, with constant steep ascents and descents. After a day's journey, they reached a small Maronite village at the bottom of the Wadi el Salib. The welcoming villagers hosted them warmly.

A young man in elaborate dress then entered, his somber expression and the family's mixed emotions suggesting something amiss. Maria learned that the previous day, the man had been escorting his sister to her Maronite wedding in Zahle when they were ambushed by a band of Motowlies. The sheikh leading them ordered his followers to abduct the bride-to-be and carry her off by force. The distraught brother, fully armed, saw his sister's abduction as inevitable and shot her dead. He then rushed the Motowlies, killing them all before staggering back to his village, devastated by his drastic actions taken to prevent his sister's dishonor. The villagers wept for the tragic fate of the young woman but viewed her brother's desperate deed as heroic. Maria observed it as a remarkable self-sacrificing affection between siblings. The sheikh even gifted him his own pelisse.

After resting, Maria and her group continued their journey. The steep, rugged terrain made riding treacherous, so they proceeded on foot, leading their horses. Suddenly, Maria's horse stumbled, causing them to fall. She remained seated, but her left arm broke, and the horse suffered severe injuries. Maria's friend carried her to the nearest village, and crudely bandaged her arm since no surgeon was available, leaving her in great pain. They then moved on for about three days without further incident, until they reached a convent dedicated to St. Anthony, situated atop a mountain in the western Lebanon range. Maria resolved to spend some time there recovering her health.

The convent housed sixty nuns who primarily engaged in silk spinning, which provided substantial revenue. Like the previous convent, it had an abundant garden with a variety of vegetables and fruits. The mountainsides had mulberry trees that fed the convent's silkworms. The weather was pleasant during Maria's twenty-day stay, which she was told was typical for the location.

The convent was a hub of activity, with the nuns cultivating numerous practical skills, though silk production remained their principal occupation. They descended daily into the surrounding valleys to collect mulberry leaves for the silkworms, which inhabited large chambers within the convent. Besides the productive facilities, the convent boasted a spacious church, a large refectory, and an airy recreation room.

Maria found their society so agreeable, and the situation so delightful, that she had serious thoughts of proposing to the Aga's wife that they should make this convent their settled home. She was worried that her retreat might be discovered and expected to hear from her daily. The thought of what would happen horrified her. However, she received a letter from her friend before her departure, assuring her that all was right. This gave Maria inexpressible relief.

Maria's life at the convent perfectly suited her taste and disposition. She went to prayer seven times a day, and she frequently remained for a couple of hours with two or three sisters singing psalms and canticles. Her enthusiasm returned in full force, now that her mind was undisturbed by the worldly anxieties which were inseparable from travel and beyond the reach of external influences. One night, the moon was unusually brilliant. After her midnight prayers, she walked out to enjoy the cool night air and engage in solitary meditation, which she always liked. She strolled into a field that adjoined the convent and found herself only separated from the valley, which lay far below, buried in impenetrable darkness, by a low wall.

Lost in a pleasing reverie, Maria walked on, contemplating her future wanderings in the Holy Land. Without realizing it, she found herself close to the wall. She leaned over, peering into the darkness with idle curiosity, hoping to spot an object on the mountain's side. Everything was a black void—no objects or sounds. For minutes, she stood, gazing into the infinite abyss, contemplating eternity. She imagined hearing a noise, like something creeping outside the wall. It ceased; and she thought it must have been her imagination. It returned. She heard rustling and saw fiery eyes glaring from the grass.

Mistaking it for a tiger, Maria ran away in fear and heard a high-pitched cry, similar to a child's. In an instant, the animal bounded over the wall and pursued her. Escape was impossible, she saw. She heard the footsteps with increased distinctness every moment. Courageous by nature, she turned round and faced her pursuer, which she found to be a wawia.

This somewhat calmed her terror. Putting her trust in God, she made a desperate effort and grabbed the creature by the throat. It was about to spring on her. Summoning all her strength, she dragged the animal to the wall and repeatedly dashed it against it until it grew weaker. She cast it over the precipice, then rushed back to the convent, where she hurried to her chamber and fell to her knees, giving thanks to Almighty God for her deliverance.

In the morning, Maria recounted her adventure to the nuns. They congratulated her on her escape and set out to see if they could find the animal's body. After some search, they discovered it in a hollow near the bottom of the valley, nearly dashed to pieces by coming in contact with the sharp-pointed crags in its fall. Having thus verified the truth of her tale, they surnamed Maria, "The Heroine."

Maria was impressed by the nuns' devout, regimented lifestyle. Their unwavering commitment to their spiritual devotion and disciplined routine struck Maria as a powerful rejection of worldly concerns. Their singular focus on worship and self-denial demonstrated an almost inhuman level of indifference to earthly pleasures and vanities.

The nuns wore simple woolen clothes and sandals made of goatskin, with shaved heads and crosses on their breasts. Round their waist they wore a cord, to which was suspended in front their rosary. At all hours, they engaged in communal prayer, chanting hymns and Bible readings with fervor. After prayers, they carried out their assigned duties—teaching, sewing, tending to the convent. They forbade idle moments and used every minute productively. Those who broke convent rules performed public penance during mealtimes. At midnight, the bell rang for prayers. At its last sound, for they slept in their clothes, every sister straightway quit her cell and went to church.

Mealtime at the convent was spartan. Two nuns brought in a large cauldron of simple vegetable stew, which they ladled into plain earthenware plates. As one nun read aloud from saints' stories, the sisters ate in total silence, sipping water from small, awkwardly shaped jugs meant to discourage excess. After the meal, fruit was served, and the nuns had a brief period of recreation, sometimes performing religious plays. Visitors were rare and strictly segregated by screens.

Each Friday, the nuns would flagellate themselves with knotted cords while chanting the "miserere" in a darkened chamber. Some even bound their waists with thorns, drawing blood. On a nearby mountain peak stood a platform with a large cross, the "place of crucifixion." The nuns raced to reach it first every Sunday. Sadly, an elderly sister had fallen to her death on the path.

Maria found the mountain view breathtaking—the towering Lebanon range, sparkling sea, and distant Cyprus—and would often kneel in ecstatic prayer, tears of joy streaming down her face. After their devotions, the nuns would enjoy a simple picnic of fruits and coffee. Nearby, a building housed older adults, convent confessor, gardeners, and visiting clergy, including the bishop who had traveled with Maria from Baghdad. Adjoining it was a paddock for the convent's animals—cows, donkeys, mules, and over 500 fowl, who dutifully retired to roost with the evening "Ave Maria" bells.

Maria's fervent Christian faith and innate optimism about human nature initially shielded her from the bitter trials she had endured. She attributed her calamities to divine providence rather than the malice of others. Suspicious hypocrisy and deceit were foreign to her idealized worldview. Over time, however, this vision of human perfection faded. Spurned, deceived, and abandoned by all but a precious few, Maria grew disillusioned, questioning the inherent goodness of mankind. Trust seemed impossible amidst the deception and hollowness.

She observed with dismay how those who preached faith often concealed worldly greed and malice. The Muslim "strikes his foe with the sword," but the faithless Christian "wounds his brother with a poisonous tongue." Only the souls in the convent remained untouched by the world's falsehoods and iniquities.

Reluctantly, Maria prepared to depart the convent, whose simple kindness and safety had won her over, save for one incident. A young, beautiful Druze had embraced Christianity and became an inmate of the convent. A Druze chieftain, who had been confident about obtaining her hand in marriage, became furious when he learned of her step. He rode to the convent, attended by a considerable number of horsemen belonging to his clan, fully armed, and used every argument he could to convince the girl to leave the convent. He threatened he would sack the convent and massacre its inhabitants if she didn't obey. In desperation, he stuck the musket through the gate bars and fired at the terrified nun. She stooped down, and the ball hit the wall. The chieftain fled.

Maria wished to visit more convents, but the bishop she traveled with needed to reach Beirut urgently. Wolves devoured his valuable mare from Baghdad after it escaped the convent's paddock, and the bishop had received an urgent letter from his jeweler brother, who had recently returned from India.

The convent superior provided Maria a letter of introduction to an Amira, a distant relative of the Emir Bashir, who lived in an elegant palace near Beirut. Their three-to-four-hour journey began at eight in the morning in May, a later start than Maria would have preferred.

They reached Amira Haidar's palace at noon, Maria relieved to be out of the scorching sun. The Amira, having expected their arrival, sent retinues to greet them. After Maria presented her letter of introduction, the Amira expressed sympathy for her misfortunes, assuring Maria the house was hers. The Emir, around seventy, held an impressive bearing despite his age. His bright, benevolent eyes and healthy complexion conveyed cheerfulness, he and his wife adorned in great splendor befitting their noble abode. They had one married daughter.

Before retiring, Maria took in the palace terrace's stunning view. Gazing northwest, she beheld a mountainous chain stretching for leagues, crowned with convents and overlooking the town of Beirut, its tall minarets silhouetted against the brilliant sky. Olive and mulberry forests filled the steps between the town and Mount Shimlan.

The next morning, they descended to Beirut. The bishop first purchased a fine white Hauran mare from the city's horse market. He then located his merchant brother, who had just arrived by ship from Egypt and was anchored offshore. They boarded the vessel, which Maria found astonishingly massive. The delighted brothers caught up after their long separation. When business matters were settled, the ship's captain insisted on inviting them to dine on board before they returned to shore in the evening. Late that night back in Shimlan, they received an invitation to a grand party at Beirut's principal bath, hosted by the wife of the Pasha of Acre's secretary. The celebration was in honor of the secretary's sister's impending nuptial the following day.

The all-day bath party resembled a grand European ball, lasting from eight in the morning to dusk. Invitations were sent fifteen days in advance, with significant preparation and expense. The bride and female guests alternated bathing, dancing, singing, eating, drinking, and smoking, often with professional performers. Government-operated public baths were open to women from 8 am to 4 pm and later to men. Guards prevented improper visitors. For notable occasions like this, they would reserve a bath solely for the bride and her friends for the full day, implementing measures to exclude strangers.

The bath hosting the bridal celebration left a lasting impression on Maria. It was divided into three chambers, the first at ambient temperature, the second slightly warmed for disrobing, with beds for rest. The bathing chamber was magnificent: fifty feet long, forty wide, and twenty high, with a domed, stained-glass ceiling casting a soft light on the polished marble. Arabesque ornamentation adorned the walls, with strategically placed hot and cold water taps and attentive bathing attendants.

Maria arrived at two o'clock in the afternoon to find over 350 ladies already there since eight in the morning, some bathing, lounging, eating sweets, smoking, singing, dancing, and socializing. The visitors included prominent ladies from the area, some with as many as ten slaves and white attendants.

For eastern ladies, the bath was a rare place of relaxation, where they could freely socialize, vent, and share joys with friends. Maria wrote in her memoir that only there, an eastern woman was free from her lord's jealous espionage, which stopped at the hammam's threshold. Free to all but for a small fee, the baths were lavishly maintained public establishments, providing amenities like sherbet, coffee, and pipes.

After a day of festivities, exhausted, Maria returned home. The next day, the Emir Bashir's widowed stepdaughter Sitte Hadouch visited, arriving in a caravan of servants and attendants adorned in flowing white veils. The Amira and Maria watched the procession approach their palace before greeting the illustrious guest. When Sitte Hadouch removed her veil, Maria observed her striking appearance, with a tall, golden, jewel-encrusted headdress and elegant drapery.

Sitte Hadouch, a nearly sixty-year-old widow, had led a solitary life for years. She engaged Maria in discussions about her country and customs, displaying intelligence. She showed deep sympathy for the cruelties and oppressions suffered by Christians in Maria's birth land, contrasting with Sitte's own favored abode. Maria shared her sorrow and misfortune, including her planned pilgrimage to the Holy Land and her intention to return to Lebanon to live in peace, devoted to her Creator. Sitte Hadouch, herself a lifelong recluse, assured Maria of the greater satisfaction in such a life. Before departing, she secured a promise from Maria to visit her the next day, and said she would write to her stepfather, the Emir Bashir, to advocate on Maria's behalf.

Maria spent the next day at Sitte Hadouch's palace on Mount Mansouria near Shimlan. It was a large, elegant residence with abundant fountains and comforts. Sitte Hadouch had extensive grounds, gardens, and livestock, and generously provided free accommodation for any visitors. She was the daughter of the late Emir's wife, celebrated in her youth for her beauty and known as Sitte Shams, "the Sun." The Emir had been a devoted husband to her.

Sitte Hadouch lived a life of charitable good deeds, impressing Maria with her hospitality during the five-to-six-day visit. She slept little, often only three to four hours per night. To pass the time, she kept a skilled female Arab storyteller in her household, who was of noble family but had fallen from affluence to poverty. Maria departed Sitte Hadouch's with regret, promising to visit again after Jerusalem. Sitte Hadouch provided Maria a letter of introduction to Emir Abdallah, nephew of Emir Bashir, who governed Kasrawan, Maria's next destination. Accompanied by her companions, Maria traveled to Razir to meet Emir Abdallah. He welcomed her with the generous hospitality characteristic of the Shehab family and arranged an escort to show them the local sites.

They visited Deir el-Harisa, a seaside convent atop a high crag with sweeping views. A valley of olive groves and picturesque homes lay below, along with the beach where Jonah was cast ashore. To the left were the sparkling port of Beirut and the magnificent Italian fir forest planted by Fakr el Din. The bishop was moved to exclaim, "The earth is filled with Thy glory." Departing Harisa, they returned to Razir before setting out for the famed Cedars of Lebanon, about forty miles distant. After a treacherous two-day ascent, they reached the high-altitude summer village of Eden, just below the snow line—the highest human habitation in Lebanon, abandoned for the plains in winter.

The Maronite sheikh of this village, to whom they had a letter of introduction, received them with great hospitality in his castle—a handsome structure, of considerable size and strength, in the Arabic style of architecture—and furnished them with guides to the Cedars; for which they started, after staying to refresh themselves a few hours at Eden. They went to a ridge that overlooked the steep-walled Wadi el Kadisha valley, where a waterfall thundered over a hundred feet. Descending by a perilous rock-cut path, they reached the village of Bashirai and finally the famed Cedars of Lebanon—just sin even ancient giants, remnants of the once-glorious forests.

Reflecting on these timeless witnesses, Maria pondered the rise and fall of nations they had seen. She recalled the Biblical analogy of the Assyrian empire as a great cedar, nourished and elevated, until felled by God's judgment and cast away. These survivors had endured both time and man's ravages. Yet they remained, a link to the past—to the Temple of Solomon, and the exiled children of its worshippers now scattered across Frangistan and the Muhammadan lands. How many empires came and went under the Cedars' shadow?

This passage from Ezekiel compares the king of Egypt to a majestic cedar of Lebanon—lofty, thick-branched, and providing shelter for multitudes. Due to the king's pride, God would deliver him to a mighty nation to be conquered. The once-great cedar would be cast away, its branches broken on every rock. This allegory warned the Egyptian king of the dangers of arrogance, cautioning that even the mightiest can be toppled by divine judgment for their exalted, self-aggrandizing ways. The Cedars of Lebanon themselves stood as ancient witnesses to the rise and fall of empires, a sobering reminder of humanity's transience before the eternal.

From the village of Eden, Maria went to the renowned Deir Marantonias Kashaia convent near the cedars, revered by Christians, Druze, and Motowlies alike. During the three days Maria remained there, she met a childless Druze Amira who, together with her husband and many attendants, had taken up her abode in the pilgrim's quarter. She was seeking prayers for divine blessing. The two women became fast friends, sharing their sorrows and Maria's plan to make a pilgrimage to the Holy Land. Amira asked Maria to pray for her at the shrines, and Maria promised it would not be in vain.

From her infancy, Maria associated with the pensive and melancholic rather than the joyous and light-hearted. She preferred solitude to society and longed to lead the life of a lone bird on the mountain, communing with nature and nature's all-beneficent Creator. This longing had only increased after seeing the wickedness, fickleness, and perfidy of corrupted human nature. The Amira's situation touched Maria, and her faith in the efficacy of prayer charmed her.

CHAPTER 13

A VISIT TO JERUSALEM

Maria proceeded straight to Beirut with the bishop. There, they stayed three days with the bishop's brother, waiting a ship to Jaffa. Maria disguised herself as a man to visit the Holy Land with more freedom. She did not get the customary pilgrimage tattoo symbols related to Jesus' life on their arms, which served as a permanent record of peoples' pilgrimage.

Assuming the name "el Hawajah Amin" (the Faithful), Maria set sail from Beirut with a letter of recommendation to the Russian consul in Jaffa. Aboard the "shaktura" were other pilgrims, including a Greek family who provided entertainment during the voyage. Sleeping on deck, Maria awoke to see Caesarea and felt a sense of reverence approaching Mount Carmel. In the evening, they anchored at Jaffa, also known as Joppe, the biblical site of Noah's ark construction and the landing point for cedar wood sent for the Temple.

They stayed at the home of a respected silk and fabric merchant, Yusuf el Mosali, who showed them his out-of-town garden. Maria watched how, during dinner, his two children stood behind their parents, ensuring their needs were met. After dinner, they went to the terrace to enjoy the view. They could see vessels from Gaza, nearly fifty miles away.

The following day, they went to the Russian Consul's

house, which was crowded due to the assistance provided to pilgrims by the Russian government. Before leaving Jaffa, Maria took a stroll through the streets and admired the town's beauty. Despite some areas' ruined past sieges by Djezzar Pasha, fine marble fountains and lush gardens of pomegranate, apples, lemons, and other trees adorned Jaffa.

Their journey from Jaffa took them across the once-fertile plain of Saron to Ramallah. Although the plain no longer bloomed with flowers and lush vegetation, it still provided pasture for cattle, flocks, and goats. According to tradition, it was near Ramallah that the biblical figure Samson burned the Philistines' cornfields in retaliation for the Thamnathite taking away his wife. Samson, an Israelite hero and judge, lived during the rule of the Philistines in the Book of Judges. Story has it that Samson married a Philistine woman from Timnah, and when her people took her away and gave her to another man, he set fire to their crops by using torches tied to the tails of foxes. Consequently, the Philistines burned the woman and her father. Foxes still abound in the area, as the legend goes.

Before Ramallah, Maria visited a tank rumored to be built by Saint Helen, then went to a nearby Tower of the Forty Martyrs, once a convent steeple now a mosque minaret where the Holy Family was said to have rested during their flight into Egypt. In Ramallah, they stayed at the Kanisat Mar Nicodemus convent, believed to stand on Nicodemus' house, and inhabited by two elderly Spanish monks. En route, they passed through Jeremias village, home to the influential Abu Ghousta tribe who demanded tribute. As they approached Jerusalem, Maria's anticipation grew. Seeing the Mount of Olives filled her with emotion. They entered through the Gate of the Beloved to stay with a prominent Aleppo Christian who had promised them refuge during their stay in Jerusalem.

The next day, Maria visited the Church of the Holy

Sepulchre, unexpectedly encountering a priest she had known from Alqosh. He had a peculiar story. He had decided to leave his wife and children and enter a monastery. His wife resisted at first, but eventually consented when she saw his resolve. For eighteen months, he lived in seclusion, but then yearned to return to his family. His wife was hesitant, fearing he would be unfaithful to his vow, but eventually allowed him to come back. Troubled by his wavering, the priest was now on a pilgrimage to atone for his actions.

After briefly seeing the main sites of the church, Maria planned to revisit the next day. But a plague outbreak prompted their immediate departure from Jerusalem. They sailed from Jaffa to Alexandria, then on to Grand Cairo and Mount Sinai. After several weeks, Maria continued to Smyrna and Constantinople for nearly twelve months. To avoid a tedious catalog of accounts which were covered already by other travelers, Maria summarized this period briefly. She noted in her memoir, "My object being merely to give to the British public a plain and unpretending narrative of my misfortunes."

Maria returned to Jerusalem just before Holy Week in 1826. On the day before Palm Sunday, she eagerly participated in cleaning the church in preparation for the upcoming festival. She was assigned the task of sweeping the dust from Calvary and the Sepulchre itself, a sacred duty that filled her with joy and profound emotion.

Entering the church left Maria in awe and reverence. The dim interior encouraged deep contemplation on the solemn events that unfolded within its walls. The very name "Holy Sepulchre" carried weight for her, as it was one of the first words her father had taught her.

The sight that greeted Maria upon entering was the stone of Jesus' anointment. Covered with a marble slab and protected by corner knobs, the stone measured nearly eight feet long and two feet wide. All denominations—Catholics, Greeks, Armenians, Nestorians, Copts, and others—took turns ceremoniously perfuming the stone daily.

Thirty paces from the anointing stone, beneath the central dome, lay Golgotha—the tomb of Christ, a small rock-carved cell possessed by the Latins. Upon the slab where Christ's body was laid, with His head west and feet east, Mass was celebrated. Kneeling there, Maria experienced ecstatic devotion. Her lips glued to the cold marble, tears streamed down her face.

Within the Holy Sepulchre, forty-four lamps burned perpetually, with three roof openings for smoke. A domed chapel enclosed the tomb, adorned in exquisite marble. In the antechamber stood a stone marking where the angel had rolled away the tomb's sealing stone, addressing the three biblical Marys. The inscription tells of the women who found the empty tomb and were told by angels that Jesus had risen, as predicted. They then returned to tell the disciples what they had witnessed.

In her memoir, Maria recorded every detail of the church and her steps inside it, that she ascended to the summit of Mount Calvary, where they had constructed a chapel on the bare rock after removing the soil. The east-west running arcade divided the chapel into two parts, with the northern Latin section enclosing where Christ was bound to the cross, its mosaic floor in red marble. The southern section held the hole where Christ's cross was planted, flanked by the thieves' crosses, with over thirty lamps on the north and fifty on the south. Nearby was the Chapel of the Mater Dolorosa, commemorating where the Blessed Virgin stood during Christ's crucifixion.

Nearby was a chapel housing a half-column of gray marble with black spots, where Christ was believed to have been bound during his scourging and crowning with thorns. The other half was in Rome's Basilica of Saint Praxedes. In the Greek choir's center was a marble circle believed to mark the earth's center and Adam's burial place. This site witnessed humanity's fall and the Savior's crucifixion, granting redemption to all.

To the right, Maria encountered a thirty-step staircase to the Grotto of St. Helen, where she had prayed while the true cross was discovered below. Armenians owned St. Helen's Chapel above, Latins owned the chapel with hidden relics for 300 years. Maria recalled receiving a fragment of the true cross as a child, a gift from a Roman legate to her father. In exchange for this precious relic, he gave valuable gifts, including a magnificent horse.

Maria noticed a mysterious hole on the wall as she descended. It echoed the sound of a rushing river below, its source and destination unknown, like a curse on the parched city. She then reached a chapel marking where Jesus was stripped of his garments before crucifixion, fulfilling scripture. Nearby were two chapels—one where Christ first appeared to the Blessed Virgin after resurrection, the other where he appeared to Mary Magdalene as a gardener. The first belonged to the Latins, the second to the Nestorians.

Maria's most unforgettable experience was the Easter Sunday festival at Jesus' tomb, with devout pilgrims from around the world gathered in ecstatic prayer. As she stood with fellow Chaldeans, she felt a deep connection with the immense crowd, from mothers carrying children to the Schismatic Greeks' midnight procession seeking the paschal light. This day was the pinnacle of Maria's life, a moment she held dear, filled with joy, prayers, and surrender to the sacred.

Inside the sanctuary, the patriarch and two priests stayed while outside, the anxious and credulous crowd awaited in breathless anticipation. Finally, the patriarch emerged from the sepulchre's door, proclaiming that their prayers had been

heard. In an instant, the lamps around the sanctuary were ig-
nited, and the patriarch and his attendants emerged, holding
lit tapers. The cry of "A miracle! A miracle!" filled the air, and
everyone rushed forward eagerly to light their own tapers.

Even the Turkish governor of Jerusalem, accompanied
by his officers and sometimes even members of his harem, attended this ceremony. His presence was deemed crucial to ensure the manifestation of the divine blessing, but Maria viewed
it as a vain and unworthy charade, a gross deception played
upon a gullible people. She thought, "As if the Almighty would
patiently wait for an unbeliever's convenience to display His
grace and perform miracles!"

The ceremony took place at midnight, and the Greeks
made great efforts to secure a spot near the entrance of the
tomb, hoping to embrace the sacred light believed to possess
extraordinary powers. Maria positioned herself to witness the
spectacle, only to discover that the supposed "divine" light was
man-made, not supernatural.

One elderly man with a long white beard rushed forward
eagerly to embrace the "divine lights." But the flames burst
forth at that very moment, and his beard caught fire and nearly
burned away. He cried out in pain, and his wife, standing beside him, screamed in terror. She sent one of her slaves to fetch
water, which helped soothe his pain.

On Easter Sunday, the grand structure was brightly illuminated by countless wax tapers, the heat almost unbearable in
the crowded church. Yet the fervor of Christ's followers could
not be extinguished, as they processed through the church,
thousands of lights flickering below the galleries filled with
pilgrims, predominantly women, dressed in their finest attire
and holding their own tapers. A joyous "Alleluia!" erupted, the
walls trembling, as the procession was led by priests, youths,
and standard-bearers. As an act of grace, the usual fee imposed

by the Turkish government on Christian pilgrims during Holy Week was waived.

The following day, Maria descended to the valley of Josaphat through St. Stephen's Gate, Maria recounted the martyr's biblical account. She passed the Turkish tombs, situated beneath the wall that bordered Mount Moria, which once was the site of Solomon's temple. Now it was occupied by the Mosque of Omar. Crossing the Kedron, she visited sites like the tombs of Zacharias and Absalom, the grotto where the apostles proclaimed the creed, and the place Jesus taught the Lord's Prayer. Kneeling beneath ancient olive trees, believed to have witnessed Jesus' anguish, Maria prayed fervently, gathering olives to make chaplets for herself and friends as reminders of her Savior's sufferings.

A few ancient olive trees, said to have existed during the time of Jesus' earthly sojourn, still stood. Their roots appeared gnarled and twisted into peculiar shapes. Maria knelt and fervently prayed for some time beneath one of these trees, believing it to have been nourished by Jesus' tears. \Before leaving the garden, she gathered a large quantity of olives and had them made into chaplets, which she presented to her friends in various places. She kept one for herself, using each stone as a reminder to offer prayers and reflect on the sufferings of her Savior.

They left the garden and, descending to the subterranean church, they visited the tombs of the Blessed Virgin, St. Thomas, St. Joachim, St. Anne, and St. Joseph, before standing before the Virgin Mary's tomb. From the Holy Mount, they gazed into the solemn valley and reflected. All would be summoned for judgment, filled with awe and trepidation. Lies, hypocrisy, and the revelation of the righteous would be exposed.

There, the bishop passionately implored the Lord, lamenting the desolation and wickedness plaguing their souls, and begging to hasten the day when their groans would turn to joyful hymns and their sins to acts of grace. He prayed for the wicked to be banished and the righteous to dwell eternally in the blessed realm, where the radiant Son of Man would welcome the chosen ones who had followed in His footsteps through darkness and trial. With a heart full of longing and hope, the bishop cried out to the Lord, seeking an end to their earthly exile and the eternal reward awaiting the faithful.

They then visited the Siloam Fountain, where Jesus healed the blind, and the Bir Nami cistern, where Nehemiah hid the sacred fire. Encountering crippled souls seeking healing, they continued to the village of Siloam, named for Solomon's idolatrous practices. After filling their containers with water from the sacred fountain, they departed and retraced their steps toward the north. They visited the grotto of Jeremiah, the Tomb of the Kings, and the tombs of the prophets, before returning through the Bab Daoud gate, weary from their journey. Exploring the Via Dolorosa, they paused at each significant spot along Jesus' path from Pilate's house to Calvary.

CHAPTER 14

THE JORDAN RIVER AND JERICHO

Maria decided to join the annual pilgrimage to the Jordan. She set out from Jerusalem with a group of around ten thousand people, led by the governor and his guards. The journey through the wild and desolate terrain posed various risks, but they eventually reached Rihhah, a village near the site where Christ had spent forty days fasting and praying.

At their campsite, a Bedouin sheikh, who was part of the governor's escort, pitched his tent nearby. Maria quickly established a friendly rapport with him. The warmth and kind treatment she had experienced from the Dryaah tribe had left a deep and lasting impression on her. It also helped her become proficient in their Arabic dialect.

The sheikh extended an invitation to a fellow Bedouin who appeared to be in need, offering him a share of his dinner. As they were about to finish their meal, another equally destitute Bedouin passed by. The sheikh kindly invited him to partake of the remaining food. "Eat," said the sheikh, "until you are satisfied, for it is God's will."

Maria fostered a favorable opinion of these generous and uncomplicated "children of nature." The Bedouin man hailed from the Hauran region. He was strong and sturdy, wearing a white aaba with blue stripes and carrying weapons like matchlocks and lances. His wife was strikingly beautiful, with jet-black eyes and long, lustrous braids. This hairstyle was common among the local Bedouin girls. The Hauran Arabs, known for their gentle and courteous nature, were in contrast to the ferocious Jericho Arabs who had long inhabited the region.

The sheikh hosted an elaborate dinner for Maria, slaughtering more animals than they could consume. After the feast, they relaxed on Persian carpets, enjoying hookahs—a contrast to the ascetic Bedouins Maria knew from the Euphrates. Maria didn't dwell too much on how he acquired the fine rugs.

While Maria indulged in her hookah, her mind drifted back to the stories recounted in the Old Testament. She imagined the Jews, led by their priests, each carrying a lamp, and could almost hear the thunderous collapse of the walls of Jericho. Amidst her musings, a Bedouin woman approached their camp, clutching something wrapped in her apron. To Maria's surprise, the woman unveiled a newborn baby. The woman went into labor while working in the fields. Without any assistance, she had given birth and, after performing a quick washing in the Jordan River, she was hurrying home to present the child to her husband.

Maria marveled at how differently mothers in so-called civilized cities might have reacted in such a frightening situation. Intrigued, she struck up a conversation with the Bedouin woman to learn more about their child-rearing practices. The woman explained that they washed their infants every day in cold water and, for the first month, bound their arms across their chests to prevent them from accidentally harming themselves. They applied a fragrant earth called "akhmar" mixed with powdered herb called "as" to their armpits and joints, believing that this concoction would protect their delicate skin from the harsh effects of the scorching climate. They dipped their infants in the river every morning for forty days to strengthen their bodies. They believed that, thanks to these rituals, Bedouin children could often start walking before they reached eight months of age.

The locals were so kind, they brought them an abundance of poultry, eggs, and fruits. When Maria expressed her desire for some flowers, they presented her with a bouquet of the most exquisite roses she had ever seen.

The group later journeyed from Jericho to the banks of the Jordan River. Maria watched the sacred, swiftly flowing stream, winding through lush green banks dotted with graceful willow groves. As soon as their tent was set up, Maria changed into her bathing costume and rushed to the riverbank. An experienced swimmer, she underestimated the river's strong current, which challenged her to reach the opposite shore through a vigorous struggle.

Throughout her eventful life, Maria had experienced numerous near-death encounters—falling from trees, horses stumbling down cliffs, being thrown from a camel into the Euphrates, and violently unseated by a galloping dromedary. Though often dazed and injured, with scars to show, Maria had miraculously survived each perilous situation, as if Providence had always safeguarded her well-being.

Death had stared at her more than once, wielding its sword. Only Heaven knew why she had survived through countless perils, enduring numerous sorrows and afflictions. For what destiny was she reserved? This world proved to be a tearful and desolate place. Maria shares the sentiment of Petrarch, an Italian scholar and poet. He expressed his life as a constant suffering, seeking different places since he was born by the Arno River.

Undaunted, Maria crossed the estimated 120-foot-wide Jordan River. She reached the opposite bank, triumphantly cut a cane and gathered pebbles as relics to her friends, before returning to her tent.

Among the pilgrims, a Greek man and his wife from Constantinople attempted to cross the Jordan River. Maria took the plunge when she and the woman entered the Jordan River. Observing that the strong and rapid current frightened the woman, Maria volunteered to carry her a certain distance into the river in her arms, and the woman accepted. While Maria was busy assisting the wife, the husband swam out and made his way towards the opposite shore. He seemed to be an experienced swimmer. However, shortly after reaching the other side, he cried out for help and vanished before anyone could swim to his aid. His distraught wife let out heart-wrenching cries upon witnessing his desperate situation. She wanted to rush to his aid but knew it would only result in another life being lost. So, she carried the grief-stricken woman to shore as she succumbed to violent hysterics.

People rushed to the spot where the husband was last seen, and they searched for two hours, but their efforts proved fruitless until they finally discovered his lifeless body. The tragic incident cast a somber shadow over what would have otherwise been a joyous occasion. Some of their fellow pilgrims shared with Maria that the Greek man, despite being a competent swimmer, had indulged a bit too much in either wine or spirits, impairing his skills and rendering him heedless of the consequences.

At sunrise, the pilgrims mounted their horses, water containers filled from the Jordan. Before departing, Maria separated herself on the riverbank, kneeling in prayer and contemplation. Reflecting on God's words at Jesus' baptism, she renewed her baptismal vows to renounce Satan and walk in God's path for the rest of her life.

Traveling south, the pilgrims reached the desolate Dead Sea, its salt-coated ground causing their horses to sink. To their right, peculiar hills resembled pyramids and fortified towers. The soldiers bathed in the lifeless waters, but Maria declined, unwilling to defile her recently baptized body. Retracing their treacherous path, the pilgrims navigated jagged ridges and dry streambeds amidst the desolation, encountering only hungry eagles soaring overhead.

Some of the eroded rocks took on the most bizarre and fantastical shapes. One cluster, on the dry side of which a few feeble flowers struggled to eke out a brief existence, remained vivid in Maria's memory. Later in life, she would reflect on certain scenes she had witnessed in bustling European cities, where women, at an age when their hearts should be occupied with weightier matters, focused solely on adorning their bodies. They still harbored the delusion that they could elicit admiration from the opposite sex and stir envy among their peers, oblivious to the fact that their efforts went unnoticed by the former and served as fodder for mockery or perhaps even intensified the malice of the latter.

The scenes of the flowers struggling to burst forth into life, for such a brief existence, brought Maria's thoughts to the women of her own country. In their youth, they took pride in their beauty and competed with each other in dazzling displays of ornamentation. However, even at that stage of life, their adornments were reserved for their husbands, their families, not for the immodest scrutiny of prying crowds. Yet, as the sun of their days began to set, they discarded all thoughts of outward show, focusing only on what was necessary for cleanliness and comfort. They turned their minds to solemn contemplation, preparing their souls for the peaceful departure of their earthly existence and the ultimate encounter with their eternal Judge. Maria pondered the comparison between the so-called civilized daughters of Europe, who clung to vanity and pride even in old age, and the humble matrons of oppressed and declining Christians in the East, who dedicated themselves to acts of kindness towards the sick, the poor, and the distressed, wherever they may be found.

At the same time, in later years, Maria gained a sense of gratitude that prevented her from indiscriminately criticizing the inhabitants of European cities. Among them were individuals who she could not disclose, though her Eastern frankness tempted her to do so, whose generosity, or rather, whose princely nobility, surpassed all expectations, while their eagerness to remain anonymous only amplified their noble deeds. Maria had received favors from them that she could never hope to repay, and their memory would endure until her last breath, even if it spanned a thousand years.

Maria and her caravan reached Jerusalem around one o'clock in the afternoon, greeted by a bustling crowd that filled the roads. The multitude hailed their return with joyful shouts and songs of welcome. Upon her return, Maria discovered a letter waiting for her, bearing the seal of Emir Bashir, the revered Prince of Lebanon, known for his unwavering support of Christianity in the East. The letter was prompted by correspondence from Bashir's daughter and the Armenian Patriarchate, informing him of the unfortunate tribulations that had befallen Maria and her family, particularly her uncle, Mar Basilius Asmar, the distinguished Archbishop of Diyarbakir.

To the Esteemed and Honorable Lady Maria Teresa Asmar,

May God watch over you with special care! We have longed to see your esteemed presence in good health and happiness. May God's abundant grace descend upon you.

We received news of your arrival in our lands, as well as the misfortunes and persecutions that have beset your family and your uncle, the illustrious and noble Mar Basilius Asmar, Archbishop of Diyarbakir. We learned that you intend to seek refuge in a convent nestled in our mountains and spend your days in seclusion within our domain. We desire to extend our utmost hospitality to you, firstly within the confines of our palace, and then to make the necessary arrangements to fulfill your wishes.

In any case, we implore you not to delay and make your way directly to our palace, for our daughter, Sitte Hadouch, who currently resides in our harem, eagerly yearns to meet you. She has fervently beseeched us to extend this invitation to you, and we hope that you will not hesitate to accept.

May you be blessed with a long life!

Signed,
Bashir El Shihab

Overwhelmed with gratitude, Maria composed a response, graciously accepting the prince's invitation to visit his palace once she had completed her pilgrimage.

CHAPTER 15

OTHER HOLY PILGRIMAGES IN JERUSALEM

On the following day, Maria departed from Jerusalem through the Bethlehem gate, joining a caravan of approximately two or three hundred pilgrims headed for Bethlehem. She exchanged her spirited horse for a leisurely donkey to better appreciate her approach to the Blessed Virgin's birthplace. Reaching the Mar Elias convent, they viewed Elijah's stone bed, then crossed the plains of Rephaim before glimpsing Rachel's tomb.

In Bethlehem, they entered the fortified convent's splendid church with towering marble pillars, descending to the grotto where St. Jerome had lived and taught, his self-flagellation and influence lingering in the sanctified space. From St. Jerome's grotto, they proceeded to the Innocents' grotto, adorned with reverential paintings. Descending to the Nativity grotto, a small cavern meticulously covered in marble and decorated with sculptures and paintings, thirty-two ornate silver lamps burned perpetually. A white marble slab, inlaid with a radiant silver star, marked the exact birthplace, inscribed "Here Jesus Christ was born of the Virgin Mary" and illuminated by ten lamps.

According to tradition, the star that guided the wise men to the birthplace of Jesus was said to have remained stationary directly above this revered spot. Adjacent, the recessed marble manger where Christ was laid featured an altar marking where Mary cradled the infant Jesus. Maria prostrated herself in reverence and poured out gratitude, contemplating Mary's lament over cradling the Creator of all, then a child.

They spent three days in Bethlehem, exploring sites like the impressive cisterns of Solomon. Then they continued to the tombs of the prophet Amos and the convent of the Holy Cross, where Maria reflected on Christ's sacrifice. They toured the church at Zacharias' house, adorned with bas-reliefs commemorating John the Baptist's birth and Jesus' baptism. Exploring Bethlehem's historical and spiritual sites, they visited the valley of Terebintha, a fertile land abundant with olives, pomegranates, and figs, where David had slain Goliath. The fleeting nature of human endeavors resonated deeply within her as they continued their exploration.

At Bethlehem, Maria and her companions were shown a bank where the Blessed Virgin and St. Elisabeth were said to have rested. Locals gave them olives from the abundant trees near St. John of the Desert, which Maria found delicious. This was believed to be the site of Blessed Mary's "Magnificat."

Maria noticed the women of Bethlehem wore dresses of red and blue, similar to depictions in sacred Italian paintings. The local shepherds still dressed as their ancestors. Bethlehem customs, such as early betrothals and adultery punishments, reminded her of Assyria and Chaldea.

After exploring Bethlehem, Maria returned to Jerusalem to prepare for a visit to the Prince of Lebanon. There, they dined with the hospitable Hawajah of Aleppo, who shared a story about two brothers who owned a field on Mount Moria, prior to the Temple of Soloman's construction. They cultivated and shared the produce equally. One brother was married with many children, while the other lived alone. Every harvest, they would stack their crops separately, but the unmarried brother felt it unfair for him to take an equal share when his brother had a family to support. So each night, he would secretly move forty sheaves from his stack to his brother's.

The married brother, moved by compassion and concern for his brother's solidarity, would do the same. At dawn, the brothers were astonished to find the stacks unchanged from the day before. They pondered the mystery behind this miracle, their hearts troubled yet determined to fulfill the desires of their own hearts. Night after night, they continued to add forty sheaves to each other's stack. Eventually, they resolved to keep watch throughout the night, eager to unravel the mystery. Thus, they discovered the truth. Witnessing the profound love they harbored for one another, they embraced tightly and gave thanks to God for the bond they shared.

As the conversation shifted, the group discussed the structure that now occupied the site of the former Temple. A Christian member of the party recounted how he had disguised himself as a Turk to enter the Mosque of Omar, where he claimed to have seen remnants of the ancient Jewish temple. He promised to arrange a visit to a Muslim acquaintance's home, which would offer a view of the mosque's interior and its elaborate marble courtyard.

It was well-known that severe consequences awaited any Christian who dared enter the area surrounding the mosque. Death or conversion to Islam were the penalties, supposedly based on a Muslim belief that any Christian prayer within the sacred temple would be granted, potentially leading to the downfall of Islam.

A Christian once obtained a decree from the Sultan granting access to the forbidden sanctuary. When he presented the decree to the Pasha in Jerusalem, the Pasha acknowledged its legitimacy but pointed out that it lacked any provision for the Christian's departure. The Pasha warned that if the Christian insisted on entering, he would never leave the mosque. The Christian entered and was never seen again.

According to the Turks, the Mosque of Omar housed a miraculously suspended stone, defying gravity. The group spent time gazing at the mosque and its beautiful surrounding enclosure. Afterwards, they strolled into the Valley of Josephat. There, they witnessed Muslim women in a Turkish cemetery at the base of Mount Moria, grieving over the graves of their loved ones. The women had set up tents near the graves, bringing flowers and incense to honor the departed souls.

Mesmerized by the women's actions, the group sat captivated until sunset. As the moon rose, illuminating the scene, the whiteness of the mourners' veils and the gleaming tiles of the Mosque of Omar created an enchanting atmosphere. Suddenly, a piercing cry shattered the stillness. Maria's companions assured her that the cries came from the graves of unrepentant usurers, their spirits unable to find peace. Yet, Maria identified the sound as a jackal, the same creature she had encountered at the Lebanese monastery.

The following day, Maria joined a group of around twenty friends of the Howajah. They gathered on the Mount of Olives, setting up a tent for the day. The Howajah's servants prepared their meal. After eating, Maria found a spot slightly higher up the mountain, offering a magnificent view of the holy city. Inspired by the sight of sacred Zion, she began singing, pouring out her heart until evening approached and she had to stop due to exhaustion and thirst. When they returned to the tent, Maria requested water, but found the vessels had been emptied. Desperate, she went to a nearby Turkish house and pleaded for water. The homeowner kindly offered her coffee, sherbet, and a pipe, which she gratefully accepted before rejoining her companions. This was likely her last visit to the place of Jesus' ascension.

The following day, she obtained permission to spend her final night in Jerusalem at the Holy Sepulchre. Kneeling beside the stone where Christ's body had been laid, she became overwhelmed by profound ecstasy, almost believing she could see the Savior again. She wept for her past transgressions and prayed for forgiveness, desiring to walk with a pure soul before the Lord. Maria offered a heartfelt prayer for her deceased parents and the faithful in the land of Christ's ministry, even wishing to lay down her life beside the sacred tomb. However, she surrendered to the divine plan, accepting God's will.

Before leaving Jerusalem, Maria visited the city's main synagogue, renowned as a significant Jewish place of worship. In fact, it seemed even poorer and more unassuming than any synagogue she had seen in Chaldea. While disappointed by its modest appearance, she was impressed by the fervent, devout spirit of the congregation. She noted the reverence shown towards the sacred Pentateuch, with a multitude of lamps hung in front of it which never extinguished, symbolizing the eternal flame of faith. Her father, after reading a portion of the Bible, used to devoutly kiss the book and carefully place it in a safeguarded place. It was considered sacrilegious and impious to place any other book, especially one dealing with worldly matters, upon it.

Maria was, therefore, appalled by the disrespect and desecration she witnessed toward the sacred scriptures in European society. She observed the holy book being carelessly tossed amidst frivolous novels and works that mocked the religion it supported. On one occasion in France, she expressed her indignation at this treatment in mixed company. Her outrage was met with laughter and dismissal. A reputed philosopher argued that the Bible was mere fiction, created by those seeking to exploit human gullibility. He claimed the biblical account of creation had been proven false, asserting the world predated the timeline described in the book of Moses. The philosopher dismissed this knowledge as a "vain philosophy" that would not prolong his life or save him from the grave, where his pride and worldly wisdom would be meaningless.

Maria couldn't help but remember Cicero's observation about philosophers saying absurd things. She was dismayed by the cavalier attitude toward the sacred text, a stark contrast to the reverence she had witnessed in Eastern Christian and Jewish communities.

Equipped with numerous rosaries and crosses as gifts, Maria and her companions bid farewell to their hospitable hosts, Howajah and Susan Khatoon, who had accompanied her from Baghdad and decided to remain in Jerusalem. The Howajah gave them recommendation letters for the Haznadar, the Pasha of Acre's treasurer, and for contacts in Nazareth and Saida. The bishop, Deir Stefan, joined Maria as they set out with a caravan of about 300 people, traveling to Nazareth and Mount Carmel en route to Lebanon. They secured two horses and two mules to carry their belongings, hiring muleteers to manage the animals, tents, and water supplies. They also had personal servants to cook their provisions, which included dried sausage, rice, dates, and other dry goods, supplemented by local lamb and poultry.

As they approached Jaffa, rumors of a plague outbreak led them to bypass the town and camp in the surrounding fields. Their friends in Jaffa, which produced no fewer than thirty-two different kind of figs, came bearing gifts of lambs, fowl, and local fruits and vegetables such as okra, artichokes, and pumpkin. They demonstrated a remarkable sense of fellowship, while the Turks isolated themselves, their doors and windows shut so tightly that it was impossible even for a cat to enter.

During dinner, they were joined by Howajah Yusuf and his entourage. They slaughtered sheep and poultry to host their guests appropriately. Maria was delighted when Howajah Yusuf presented her with a box of authentic manna, a delicacy from her homeland. The leftover food was given to nearby Bedouins, and the guests departed with blessings for the travelers' safe journey.

Before sunrise, the caravan bustled with activity as they prepared to depart for Mount Carmel. After a ten-hour journey, they set up camp near Mukhallid, exhausted. As night fell, the group gathered, smoking nerghilas and conversing lively. The Bedouin muleteers entertained with tales, jokes, dancing, and Antar's love ballads. Maria sat alone in her tent, lost in the melancholy music. A Bedouin from Damietta sang an Antar love song that stirred deep emotions in her, reminding her of lost loved ones and separation. Overwhelmed, she wept, contemplating love and absence.

Continuing their journey, they found themselves in a lush, verdant plain with white camels, cows, goats, and sheep. They left the pastoral scene, crossed the desert to reach the ruins of ancient Caesarea, now inhabited only by migrating Arabs. Without lingering, they pressed on to the village of Sakhra Maktouah, named for nearby ancient rock dwellings, believed Canaanite homes.

The village women of the tribe were striking figures, tall, and well-proportioned, with long black hair cascading down to their knees. But they marred their appearance by wearing a large ring that hung from their noses, passing through a pierced hole in the cartilage. They bared their breasts and wore blue khamis, a type of dress, cinched at the waist with a broad black leather belt.

Their sheikh warmly welcomed the travelers, offering hospitality in the Arab fashion; a pipe and a dish made of flour, butter, and honey. In conversation, they discovered shared interests. The sheikh, from the Baghdad desert, provided valuable insights and told them of interesting ruins to be seen at a short distance from the village. Maria's companions proposed exploring the nearby ruins while their meal was prepared.

With the sheikh's permission, they ventured to the ruins and found themselves amongst broken architectural fragments. The sheikh had guided them to a towering structure, believed to be an ancient temple converted to a Christian church during the Crusades. Upon entering, they were startled by a number of birds with beautiful plumage, some with breasts of brilliant red and others of a deep blue. Maria figured these were the temple's only inhabitants when, to their astonishment, they found young women weaving carpets within the courtyards.

They were about to return when suddenly, a menacing group of nine or ten armed ferocious bandits blocked their exit. The sheikh had assured Maria and her companions that visiting the temple held no danger, so they had ventured forth without extensive weaponry or reinforcements, only a hanjar and pipe. The bandit leader demanded their money and valuables, threatening death if they refused. Maria's companion stubbornly resisted, against her vehement protests. Several of the attackers advanced with daggers, prompting her companion to draw his hanjar and prepare for a defense. However, they were quickly outnumbered and overpowered. Witnessing this, Maria also drew her hanjar but suffered the same fate, swiftly disarmed and left at the mercy of their assailants. They robbed Maria of her money, gold, and her hanjar, which had a beautifully ornamented silver handle.

With the bandits gone, Maria and her companion painfully made their way back to the village, their bare feet bruised by the large, rolling stones that littered the path. The scorching heat of the sun seared their heads, for they lacked turbans to shield themselves. Upon learning of their misfortune, the sheikh was consumed by rage. He swiftly had his own horse and two others saddled for Maria and her unfortunate companion. Then, summoning as many tribesmen as he could, he commanded them to mount their horses and hasten after them. Together, they galloped to the site of the robbery.

At the temple, they found it deserted, devoid of any signs of life within its ruined courtyards. They decided to survey the exterior, circling the outer wall. It didn't take them long to stumble upon the bandits, sitting in a circle on the ground, busy dividing their ill-gotten gains. Seeing Maria's party, the bandits sprang up in disarray, feigning resistance. However, upon recognizing their chief among the newcomers, they relinquished their weapons and paid him the expected respect.

All of Maria and her companion's belongings were promptly returned, except for her twenty silver coins. Maria insisted the men keep it, and together with the sheikh, they returned to the camp. Deeply grateful for the sheikh's intervention, Maria expressed her regrets for not having a proper gift to offer him but promised to send him a suitable present upon reaching her friends' residence in the Lebanon. However, the sheikh declined her offer, swearing by his beard that he had only fulfilled his duty in assisting friends with whom he had shared bread and salt.

Upon reaching their tents, Maria and her companion discovered their friends in a state of great concern due to their prolonged absence. They reassured their worried companions and proceeded to recount the harrowing details of their encounter with the bandits. Grateful for their deliverance, they offered heartfelt thanks to Providence for their safety. Exhausted from the day's events, they sat down to supper, recounting their experiences once more while nourishing their bodies. The weariness finally overcame them, and they retired to their tents, seeking much-needed rest and respite from the fatigue that had accumulated throughout the day.

CHAPTER 16

MEETING AN EASTERN PRINCESS

Maria and her companions continued their journey, passing through ruins, mountains, caves, and grottos that indicated that the Canaanites had once inhabited this region in significant numbers. Upon reaching the convent situated at Mount Camel's highest point, they were greeted by a friar whose face radiated serene cheerfulness and benevolence. Filled with kindness, he warmly welcomed them and offered refreshments. Maria was struck by his countenance, which harmoniously combined contentment, benevolence, courage, and resignation. Having spent forty-one years as a resident of the convent, he embodied a remarkable presence.

They began their exploration by touring the large and comfortable convent, which, at that time, housed only three priests. Subsequently, they sat down to a delicious meal of fish, birds, and vegetables cultivated by the friars on the mountainside. As they concluded their meal, they proceeded to an adjacent fountain, where they were served coffee and pipes.

They then ventured to the expansive grotto of Elias, a cavern hewn into rock with a towering height and breathtaking coastal views. A dervish resided here, the place where the inspired prophet had imparted sacred mysteries and foretold divine vengeance. Maria contemplated the prophesied retribution for the hypocrisy and iniquity of those who sacrificed companions for personal gain. The tale was told, yet rebellious humanity remained mired in blasphemy, rendering the Redeemer's sacrifice in vain.

The next day, they journeyed nine hours to Nazareth, which was hidden until they ascended a hill and saw the city nestled below—white houses, churches, and a central mosque amid fertile lands, a refreshing contrast to the barren landscapes. Beholding the city where her Savior lived, Maria dismounted, reciting the Ave Maria with deep reverence. Remounting, she wept with joy, penitence, and hope, unable to sleep that night, consumed by thoughts of the sacred sites she would visit.

They stayed with a Maronite family and visited the Church of the Annunciation, with its grotto believed to be the site of the Annunciation. Nearby were the Madonna's former kitchen and cellar, as well as Joseph's workshop chapel. Exploring Nazareth's vibrant streets, they went to the Mount of Precipitation, where Jesus was nearly thrown off a cliff. In Cana, they visited the church commemorating Jesus's first miracle. In Nain, they recalled his raising a widow's son from the dead.

Returning to Nazareth, they cherished memories before continuing their pilgrimage to the mountain where men would have cast Jesus, and the synagogue where he learned the law. From the summit, they saw Hermon, the Galilee plain, and the Sea of Galilee. At the summit of Mount Thabor, they found a small Christian church amid the ruins of ancient buildings. Descending, they crossed the Jordan River and visited nearby baths with reputed healing properties, where the local sheikh greeted them. In Nazareth, they saw the site of St. Peter's house near the Sea of Galilee, as well as the tomb of the "Arabian Nights" author Ibn Lakman. They also visited the location of the wedding feast where Jesus turned water into wine.

Returning to Acre, Maria declined the Pasha's offer to visit his harem, as it would delay her departure. She then joined a group of merchants traveling to Deir Elkamar, accompanied by a bishop. Maria was captivated by the regal appearance of Emir Bashir's palace in Beteddin, with grand terraces and palm-like arcades.

As Maria gazed at the picturesque landscape before her, a group of horsemen arrived, led by their leader who informed them that he had been sent to escort them to the palace. Riding in what seemed like the opposite direction, they circled around the base of the mountain where the Emir's palace stood, eventually reaching the secret gate.

Palace guards admitted Maria, who was then guided through a courtyard by an old Mameluke that knocked on a door. It swung open, revealing a room where two white female slaves awaited her. They led her through a magnificent court adorned with cages filled with singing birds. In the center, a beautiful marble fountain with two majestic lion heads spouted crystal-clear water. At the end of the court, a large balcony offered a stunning view of the road they had traveled. Fragrant flowers adorned the balcony, and a Persian carpet covered the floor of the iwan, a grand hall. On the carpet sat a musnud, a thick mattress covered in scarlet silk and embroidered. The ceiling boasted intricately carved and gilded lozenge-shaped ornaments, while the walls displayed exquisite paintings of flowers in arabesque patterns, likely the work of artists from Damascus.

Adjacent to the iwan, a door led to a vast saloon adorned with silk hangings and a diwan draped in yellow silk. On the right, a charming little chamber provided delightful views of the breathtaking scenery of the Lebanon mountains. Maria was ushered into this room, where numerous white slaves attended to her needs. They presented her with water for washing and napkins made of the finest material with gold embroidery along the edges.

After washing, the diligent attendants brought incense in a silver sensor and rose-water in a silver vessel equipped with a mechanism similar to that used in churches for sprinkling holy water. Two slaves held a large napkin over Maria's head to ensure the incense fumes dissipated gradually, while another swung the sensor back and forth. A fourth slave sprinkled her with the fragrant rosewater from the vessel.

Once the ritual was complete, Maria was served coffee and a nerghila. The bowl of the pipe contained aloe-wood, filling the chamber with a pleasant aroma. Left alone for two hours, Maria savored the tranquility. The refreshing ablution, the attentive care of the servants, and the fragrant scents that filled the room offered respite from the hardships and fatigue of her journey. The peacefulness, interrupted only by the songs of birds and the gentle murmur of the fountain, contrasted with the earlier tumultuous sounds of horses' hooves and shouts. Knowing she was under the protection of a Prince who upheld the dignity of Christianity in the East, Maria felt a sense of serenity and gratitude, offering thanks to God for guiding her to this safe haven.

After an hour had passed, Maria took a leisurely stroll around the cool and shaded marble court. Eventually, she returned to the boudoir and found Emir Bashir and his Amira waiting for her, having come to seek her presence. Maria felt a sense of awe as she approached the venerable Emir. His appearance embodied her ideal image of the patriarch Abraham. Kindness and sympathy emanated from him as he greeted her and exchanged customary compliments. They all took their seats. The Prince expressed his condolences for the misfortunes that had befallen Maria and her family and inquired about her future plans and prospects.

Expressing her gratitude for his sympathy, Maria shared her long-standing desire to withdraw from the world and seek solace in a convent. She acknowledged that fate had brought her under the protection of a Prince who upheld Christianity in the East. Recognizing the Emir as a beacon of faith amidst the challenges of fanaticism, Maria saw an opportunity to find peace and hoped to spend her days in a convent in the safety of his patronage. The Emir, however, dissuaded her from this path and generously offered her asylum in his palace as a companion to the Amira. He assured her that she would have ample opportunity to cultivate and practice Christian virtues within his household. Convinced by the sincerity of the Prince and his venerable presence, Maria accepted his offer.

She soon settled into her new role as the Amira's first lady of honor, with her own quarters in the harem adjacent to the Princess's chambers. The palace's layout included a grand hall, the tharma, which opened onto a wide terrace where the Emir and Amira often spent their afternoons. Amira's apartments were left of the tharma, an apartment on the first floor, with a Christian chapel on the right where the Prince and Princess prayed daily. Maria was entrusted with the key to the chapel and instructed to keep it hidden during visits from Druze and Turkish ladies to the harem. These visitors, sometimes numbering a dozen, stayed for extended periods, and Maria would show them around the palace, avoiding the room containing the Emir's arms and treasure.

After a short time at Beteddin, Maria was entrusted with the keys to the rooms housing the Emir's treasures and would send him supplies during his expeditions. When esteemed guests, including members of the Shehab family, Druze and Maronite chiefs, Greeks, and influential Turks from Acre, Beirut, and Damascus, visited the palace, the days were spent strolling in the garden, dining, drinking, and alternating between conversation and smoking. Twice a week, they would enjoy the hammam or bath.

Maria noticed that the Druze ladies never ate the food sent from the Emir's kitchen during their communal meals. Instead, they were served by their own attendants, who brought baskets filled with various provisions. Curious about this custom, Maria asked one of the ladies about it. She explained that their religion forbade them from consuming food prepared by unfamiliar hands. Maria found this surprising, as she had seen the same lady eat at a Christian Aga's house during their mountain journey. The lady confessed secretly that her people viewed Emir Bashir as an usurper, rejecting anything he offered without rightful authority.

Maria was taken aback by the unjust and baseless opinions that had taken hold among some of the Emir's subjects. Determined to dispel such absurd notions, she engaged in a conversation with her companion, aiming to change her perspective. "Shouldn't the lord of the mountain collect taxes? How else can he reward the just, assist the poor, and punish the unjust and violent? All his actions serve the well-being and happiness of those under his rule. For eight centuries, the Shehab dynasty has governed Lebanon with justice and mercy. Can the Druze label him as an usurper? Remove him from his throne, and who will provide clothing for the destitute, whom the merchants of Deir el Kamar clothe at the Emir's expense? Who will feed the hungry, for whom the Emir's ovens tirelessly produce sustenance every day? Who will slaughter the fat sheep for them, and ensure they are not left empty-handed? The naked and the hungry, the widows and the orphans, whom his generosity alone shields from ruin, will deeply regret the day that strips him of power."

Maria also reminded her friend of the Emir's acts of kindness, such as purchasing slaves at great expense to set them free and send them back to their families—a fact known to all the inhabitants of the region. "All this is true," her friend conceded.

"The Emir is just and merciful. May God grant him a long and prosperous reign over us. But who am I to disregard the decrees of the Akhals?"

Maria's arguments were compelling, yet her companion continued to exclusively consume Druze poultry.

After their meals, they would often gather in the tharma to enjoy pipes and coffee. They found amusement in the performances of some African women serving the Amira, who engaged in various dances, some of which were so comical and eccentric that they elicited smiles from the company (as hearty laughter was considered impolite among the Eastern ladies). Meanwhile, other African women sprinkled water on the marble floor of the tharma to cool the air.

To introduce some novelty to their entertainment, Maria once devised a prank with the princess that nearly had serious consequences for herself. During one of their gatherings, while the ladies were indulging in their hookahs after dinner, Maria discreetly left the room. She quickly adorned herself in one of the Emir's magnificent outfits, featuring a golden-tissue jacket, rose-colored trousers, a muslin turban adorned with intricately embroidered flowers, a precious Persian shawl, and a splendidly jeweled dagger. With a hint of masculine swagger, she reentered the room, masquerading as a man.

Upon seeing what they believed to be a man audaciously intruding into their presence, the ladies, Druze, Turks, and all, leaped to their feet in great alarm, uttering piercing screams and calling for help. Little did they know, the Amira was in on the prank. She found immense amusement in their reaction. The situation could have had serious consequences for Maria, but luckily, it ended in laughter and mirth.

Maria's presence caused a stir among the ladies, but she remained unfazed and approached a Shehab family member, embracing her. The lady, blushing and alarmed, hurriedly left the room, followed by the startled African women. As Maria reveled in the success of her prank, the harem guardian, a tall and formidable man, burst into the room wielding a sword. He seized Maria by the collar, berating her as an unwelcome intruder. The Princess, unable to contain her laughter, eventually explained the situation and ordered the guardian to stand down. The ladies, once recovered from the fright, joined in the amusement, though Maria, still feeling the guardian's grip, silently vowed to avoid such tricks in the future.

In the evenings, they entertained themselves with plays, and Maria always took an active role. One play she devised was based on the visit of the Queen of Sheba to King Solomon. Maria portrayed Solomon, donning a magnificent ceremonial outfit provided by the Princess. Precautions were taken to inform the guardian not to intervene, regardless of the sounds or cries from the African women. The Princess, exuding charm, assumed the role of the Queen, adorned in a resplendent costume and sparkling jewels.

They chose a spacious salon within the harem for their theater. Maria sat on a throne, elevated by six steps and adorned with luxurious fabrics. The Amira, accompanied by a procession of beautifully dressed attendants bearing gifts, approached the regal presence. The scene was a spectacle of grandeur, with the opulent decorations of the salon, the exquisite attire of the Amira and her entourage, and the picturesque costumes of the Druze ladies wearing their jeweled horns on their heads. The remaining guests of the Princess sat at the other end of the room, smoking their ornate hookahs, forming a mesmerizing audience. The entire tableau presented a display of magnificence that was hard to surpass.

Gifts included a dove and a monkey, with the monkey receiving the loudest applause. The monkey approached the throne, kneeling and kissing the ground. Then, rising to his feet, he placed his hand on his mouth, forehead, and heart, adhering to the Eastern customs. The audience cheered in response, but the actor remained composed, maintaining his dignified demeanor.

With such enjoyable pastimes, everyone participated with enthusiasm and good humor. They occasionally engaged in chess or played fanagin, a game where a ring is hidden under one of ten cups, and the blindfolded player must find it. These activities filled our evenings with pleasant entertainment.

In addition, they took leisurely walks in the gardens and enjoyed the hammam (bath). Following Eastern customs, their departing guests received presents according to their rank and status. Ladies of distinction received bouquets of diamonds and valuable rings, while those of lower rank received about fifteen draa of gold tissue to make a dress, and the attendants received a similar amount of inferior fabric. Thus, these visits to Beteddin required more than mere inexpensive courtesy from the Prince and Princess. Their farewells were filled with warmth and heartfelt emotions.

The Emir Bashir maintained a group of musicians in his palace, who entertained him during his leisure hours and provided solace when the burdens and exhaustion of governing weighed heavily on his mind. On grand feasts, these minstrels stood behind the Prince's throne, singing songs that praised and extolled the virtues of the Emir himself or honored esteemed visitors in attendance.

CHAPTER 17

THE PRINCE OF LEBANON AND HIS WIVES

The Beteddin palace often welcomed visits from the Druze, Motowlies and Anzaries chiefs and their families. The Motowlies were followers of the Ali or Shiah sect of Islam and strongly disliked their rivals. They avoided dining with people of different faiths and feared physical contact with non-believers. Despite their aversion to dining with infidels, they were remarkably hospitable to strangers of all backgrounds, although they would destroy any utensils used by such guests. The Motowlies were generally looked down upon by the mountain inhabitants. The Anzaries, like the Druze, hid their beliefs and rituals from outsiders. People thought they were idolaters like the Druze, worshipping dogs. They revered the Dog River as a sacred stream, and their ancestors had practiced this form of worship for centuries.

The Druze woman with whom Maria had engaged in a previous argument extended a heartfelt invitation for her to visit. Maria declined, citing her duties in the palace as an excuse. To demonstrate her high regard of her, the woman sent Maria two large baskets of fruit. Unfortunately, the servant tasked with delivering the fruit couldn't resist indulging himself along the way and arrived at Beteddin with empty baskets. He was in such a terrible condition that he could barely move. Maria had to arrange for him to receive medical care from the Emir's doctor for ten days before he could return home.

If Maria had known that she would one day publish her memoirs, she might have recorded more intriguing details about these unique people, particularly the women, with whom she associated frequently during her time at Beteddin. However, no one can predict the fate that lies ahead. As the Arab proverb aptly states, "This world is a wheel that constantly turns; joy does not last, nor does sorrow. You have knowledge of your birth, but you cannot predict how you will live or where you will die."

It was well known that the Emir Bashir descended from Mohammad, and his family had held the governance of the Lebanon for over seven centuries. For a century and a half, the head of the family had secretly embraced the practices of the Christian church, although many mountain residents still believed he adhered to Islamic doctrines. The Emir's outward conformity to certain Turkish customs only reinforced this impression.

When Maria was a guest in the Emir's palace, he had ruled for forty years. Through his firm and inclusive policies, he had managed to unite the diverse and conflicting factions under his authority, fostering a sense of unity among Maronites, Motowlies, Muslims, and Druze. Peace reigned in the mountain, and religious differences no longer fueled animosity. They regarded each other as brethren.

The Emir's palace housed a spacious harem, which some assumed was similar to other vice-regal establishments found in the palaces of powerful governors appointed by the Ottoman Empire. However, this assumption couldn't be further from the truth. Maria lived in the Emir's palace for years and proclaimed the zenana of the Prince of Lebanon as a school of Christian virtue, not a den of self-indulgence.

During the early years of his reign, the Emir was forced to pardon numerous acts of treason and insubordination committed by two of his nephews. However, when they became deeply involved in a conspiracy to overthrow him, he had no choice but to execute them to protect himself, his people, and the region from anarchy and devastation. The act affected him deeply, leading to a commitment of redemption through kindness and grace. He established two ovens that operated daily, solely dedicated to feeding the poor and hungry wanderers from all corners of the world. He dispatched emissaries to the valleys surrounding his palace to identify those deserving of his benevolence.

The harem had young slaves, both Georgians and Circassians, some of whom possessed great beauty. He had purchased them at a significant cost with the intention of setting them free. The homesick were assisted to return, while those remaining with the Emir were often paired with compatible partners. The Princess supported those who chose to remain single. Those who chose solitude were sent to convents in Lebanon. The Emir also liberated many Mamelukes whom he had purchased, allowing them to reunite with their loved ones. A lot of them chose to serve him faithfully, to defend him with their lives if necessary.

His wife, whom Maria served, was his second wife. The Emir had acquired her, along with several others, at a substantial price in Constantinople, intending to select a worthy partner after the passing of his first wife, El Sitte Shams. He had been married to El Sitte Shams for forty years, demonstrating an unwavering and tender love, even during her prolonged battle with dropsy. He chose his present Sultana from among the others, captivated not only by her beauty but also by her amiable nature and purity of heart. Before their union, she willingly embraced Christianity and was baptized, a decision she made independently. The Emir would never resort to leveraging his power or rank to coerce a hypocritical conversion, as such methods contradicted the spirit and principles of his faith. Maria often heard the Amira express gratitude to Providence for guiding her towards the worship of the true God.

The Amira had received an education following the customary Eastern traditions. Though her education had its limitations, she possessed remarkable intelligence that compensated for any deficiencies. She couldn't read or write, so Maria managed her correspondence. She spoke both Circassian and Turkish fluently but wasn't conversant in Arabic. Her amiable temperament and affectionate heart made Maria willing to do anything for her, even to the point of sacrificing her life.

The Princess loved the Emir unconditionally, despite their significant age gap. When Emir Bashir was away leading his troops to quell an insurrection, the Princess was consumed with worry for his safety. She couldn't sleep at night and went days without eating. One winter night, Maria was in bed, unable to sleep, and heard the Princess's door open. Maria got up and dressed. It was bitterly cold with snow lying on the ground and covering the terrace. A chilly gust rushed to the first floor. Groping her way, and aided by the light that the snow provided, Maria followed the Amira's footsteps to the terrace. She found her kneeling in prayer inside the church, her face wet with tears. Maria joined her and tried to convince her to return to her chamber to escape the cold, but the Princess refused, continuing to pray fervently for her beloved's safety. Unable to persuade her, Maria decided to stay by her side, offering comfort and spending the night together in conversation and music.

The small oblong church, hidden from Muslims, had the capacity for about forty people. It was richly adorned with variegated marble, painting, gilding, silver gilt candelabra, and Persian carpets. It served as a place of solace and private prayer for the Emir and Amira, with the Emir visiting every morning after he dressed. On special occasions, a priest would celebrate mass, but otherwise Maria would lead private Arabic prayers.

Within the harem, some of the slave women had converted to Christianity, thanks to the Emir's benevolence. However, two of them harbored resentment towards the Emir and his household. Not content with not converting, they wanted vengeance. Maria overheard them plotting to denounce the Emir to the Mufti for introducing a priest into the zenana during a recent saint's day, violating the rites of Islam. They also planned to escape over the palace walls using a ladder, which Maria promptly removed to thwart their plan. Despite her precautions, the two women managed to escape using makeshift tools. Eventually, they were captured and sent as a gift to a Christian in Damascus.

The Emir had a habit of visiting the harem in the afternoon, accompanied by the Amira, to enjoy his pipe on the terrace after the evening prayer. On one occasion, Maria recalled a significant moment when the Prince sat on the terrace, overlooking the breathtaking view while communicating with the Princess's apartments. The terrace was adorned with beautiful vines and housed a large aviary filled with colorful birds. The surrounding landscape showcased the magnificent ridges of the Lebanon mountains, with steep ravines leading towards the coast. The Emir, dressed in regal attire, sat on an exquisite English chair gifted by Lady Hester

Stanhope. His turban was intricately adorned with flowers, and his garments were of luxurious materials, such as a golden jacket and scarlet trousers. He exuded a commanding presence with his tall stature, penetrating dark eyes, and a flowing silver beard that reached his waist. His voice possessed a deep resonance, capable of both rallying cries on the battlefield and tenderly winning hearts.

Despite his advanced age, the Emir commanded respect and ruled over the diverse population of the Lebanon with a blend of firmness and paternal care. He maintained order, ensuring that the lawless were swiftly punished and the hardworking were rewarded. Under his reign, farmers could rely on reaping the fruits of their labor, while bandits faced quick justice.

The Emir became conscious of Maria's presence and commanded two of his beautiful Georgian slaves to bring her coffee and a pipe. As Maria joined the Emir and the Princess on the terrace, they sat in contemplative silence, savoring the beauty of their surroundings. It was customary in the East to continue smoking during conversations, occasionally acknowledging each other's presence with a slight inclination of the body. Eventually, the Emir turned to Maria and began discussing the abundant mercy and compassion of the Almighty. He cited the example of King David, whose grave transgressions were forgiven when he repented and resolved to walk in righteousness. The Emir's thoughts were likely triggered by his own remorse over the tragic events Maria had previously recounted. Despite his remorse, he had attempted to make amends by showing kindness and providing support to the wives and families of those involved in the unfortunate incident.

The Emir asked Maria to tell him a story to pass the time. Without hesitation, she shared a tale she had heard from her grandmother in Chaldea when she was a child. There was once a pious hermit who lived alone, dedicated to fasting, prayer, and the pursuit of truth. One day, he wept for the wickedness in a distant city. An angel approached him and offered to show him the most sinful and most virtuous person in the city.

The angel instructed the hermit to position himself near the city gate at sunrise. The first person to come out is the biggest sinner, and the last person to enter at sunset is the most righteous. The hermit obeyed and saw the man depart at sunrise with skins, then come back at sunset, the final one to enter the city. Questioning the man, the hermit learned that during the day, the man had been confronted by a child's questions about God, leading him to repent of his former wicked life.

Deeply moved, the hermit reflected on how wisdom can come from the most unexpected sources. He had witnessed the remarkable transformation of the city's "greatest sinner" into its most virtuous resident, all through the simple inquiries of a child.

The Emir attentively listened to Maria's tale and expressed his satisfaction, remarking that it had provided him with entertainment. And so, their conversation continued, filled with similar stories, interrupted only by breaks for coffee served in small golden cups and the enjoyment of pipes. They carried on until eleven o'clock when they finally parted ways for the night.

As Maria made her way to her chamber, she came across a group of Georgian slaves who served the Amira. Some appeared to grieve over a misfortune. Curious about their distress, Maria asked them the reason for their unhappiness. "Why are you weeping?" she inquired.

"We weep," cried one of them, "because we are far from our homes and loved ones."

Maria replied, "My dear friends, your lamentation lacks reason and is senseless. Isn't it better that you've ended up with a virtuous Christian prince, just and devout? Imagine if you had been forcibly taken into the harem of a Muslim, where you would have been treated no differently than a slave. Here, you can freely practice the faith of your ancestors in peace and security. There, you would have been forced to conform to a worship that you abhor."

Moved by Maria's words, the slaves expressed their gratitude for the comfort she had tried to offer them and bid her good night. "O beloved one, you have spoken the truth," they said. "The Almighty has sent you to bring us solace." With these words, they retired for the night, grouping themselves in pairs or threes, as they were afraid to sleep alone, each group occupying a separate chamber.

CHAPTER 18

———— ✤ ————

Visit to a Druze Priestess and Astrologer

The Emir was an early riser, waking soon after sunrise. The entire harem was quickly bustling. After morning prayers, the Prince and Princess enjoyed coffee on the terrace while reclining on a diwan. A Mamaluke brought the Emir's ralioun to the porter, who passed it to a black slave. She delivered it to a kneeling Georgian slave, who presented it to the Prince. The Amira sometimes performed these tasks herself, despite the Emir's protests.

The Emir then proceeded to the council-chamber, where he diligently attended to the tasks of governance, accompanied by his Mamelukes and surrounded by Maronites, Druze, Turks, Motowlies, and Greeks. The Emir dispensed fair justice to all. The Princess had breakfast in her room, enjoying sherbet, chicken soup, ricc milk, cream cheese, kharisha, dried fruits, and sweets.

One day, Maria visited her Druze acquaintance, who lived two hours away in a splendid mountain-side building near a Druze temple. She was led into a well-furnished room with a garden view. In the center, on a Persian carpet, sat a venerable Druze with a long white beard and turban. Beside him, reclining on the carpet, was a tall, saffron-robed figure. Despite a pale appearance, the figure exuded dignity and majesty. She held a nerghila and an amber rosary.

Upon Maria's entrance, the venerable akal and the lady, whose extraordinary height became apparent, stood up to greet her. After pleasantries, Maria was invited to sit beside them, and a conversation soon ensued. Throughout, Maria felt the lady's intense scrutiny, though she couldn't pinpoint why. In fluent Arabic, the lady addressed Maria courteously, "You are from the land of the wise. It was in Chaldea that science first dawned; it was there that astronomy, astrology, and magic attained their highest perfection." She inquired if Maria possessed astrological knowledge.

Maria replied that her father, not being a strong believer, discouraged her from studying astrology. Instead, he urged her to focus on the Word of God and Christian virtues, as the future in the stars was beyond mortal comprehension. This response visibly disappointed the lady, who likely expected profound mysteries. Undeterred, she expressed how she had devoted time to studying the stars and claimed to discern Maria's birth star as Mercury.

"That is quite true," said Maria. "An astrologer in Chaldean told me the same, and also the great Suleiman el Hakim in Damascus."

"I knew him well," said the woman, her countenance brightening. "There lives not a man more deeply skilled in the divine art." She continued, "We are all born under celestial bodies, and our destiny is settled by the character of our natal star. This is our fate, and it is useless to struggle against its power. Whence comes a mortal antipathy between men born under opposing stars?"

Though she did not place great faith in science and astrology, Maria did not dispute the lady's belief that everyone is born under celestial influences that shape their destiny. It was their fate, futile to resist. That instant antipathy between individuals often stemmed from opposing birth stars. Yet, Maria maintained that while one's nature may lean towards virtue or vice, Heaven furnishes sufficient power to overcome evil.

After discussing astrology, Maria spoke of her plan to visit Europe, expressing delight at witnessing Christian virtues and learning, protected by an enlightened government. The lady laughed and said Maria had been misled—Europe's sun has set, and its sons have lost the virtues of old. Piety and learning have been replaced by cunning, intrigue, and hypocrisy. "Stay where you are, and you will see religion untainted by self-interest," the lady warned, having experienced Europe's degeneracy firsthand.

Years later, Maria, tossed by misfortune, saw the lady's words as those of a true prophetess. Maria realized the lady was no mere astrology pretender. How often she regretted her rash resolve, wishing she had heeded the wise caution that could have spared her years of sorrow. But who can avoid their destiny? As the Arab proverb says, "All reverence to the Almighty. Seek not to know the past nor divine the future, for all is ruled by Providence."

A Druze sheikh claimed the power to divine hidden treasures. Maria questioned why he didn't use this to improve his own circumstances. "The reason is plain," he said. "If a magician uses their art for personal gain, their power is lost forever."

Maria found this dubious, but her hostess's astrological friend supported the sheikh's explanation: magicians are forbidden to use their arts for self-benefit. Afterward, the woman rose, and bidding everyone farewell, she departed. A spirited charger stood at the gate, awaiting her. She put her foot in the stirrup and started off at a rapid pace, galloping over rock and mountain ahead of her large entourage, with a fearless skill like a Mameluke.

Curious to know the name of this eccentric lady, Maria

asked her hostess about her. "That is Lady Hester Stanhope," she said.

Maria was delighted to learn she had been conversing with someone she had heard so much about. They later became close, and Maria spent wonderful hours in the woman's company.

After discussing the departed personage, the hostess proposed visiting a nearby Druze priestess, a relative of hers. They reached the priestess's well-built, spacious home, shaded by wide-spreading trees. Under one of the trees, the priestess sat on a carpet, enjoying the breeze. A sleeping child rested in a suspended cradle, and fattened sheep grazed in the field, some so heavy-tailed they could barely walk. The Druze would attach small carriages to the sheep when moving them, to relieve the burden of their prodigious tails.

As Maria and her hostess approached, the priestess rose and greeted them with kind words, saying, "May this day be one of happiness for you, O lady." She invited Maria to sit by her side. They soon engaged in conversation, during which the priestess displayed intelligence and courtesy. Maria noted that the Druze were remarkably amiable and free from prejudice, treating people of various religions with respect. They even sent their children to be educated by Christians, sometimes leading to conversions. If a child insisted on remaining Christian and declined initiation into the Druze religion, there was no persecution or estrangement—a display of charity and tolerance worthy of emulation.

Education was highly valued among the Druze, and many of their learned men, known as akhals, were renowned for their wisdom and knowledge. The priestesses, in particular, were esteemed, and they occasionally preached from a pulpit in the Halouah, a Druze temple. During their conversation, the priestess expressed great curiosity about Maria's homeland, its customs, and its beliefs. She asked numerous insightful questions, demonstrating her keen intellect.

Eventually, the priestess called upon her friends to join them, excitedly introducing Maria as an accomplished stranger from the East. The friends gathered, offering warm welcomes and showering Maria with kindness and appreciation. They made her feel deeply welcomed and valued, their genuine care evident in their actions. The flattery was almost embarrassing.

As it happened to be a day for their religious gathering, the group soon departed to participate in their sacred rituals at a nearby Halouah, leaving Maria alone with the sleeping infant in the cradle. While the Druze were known for their religious tolerance, they strictly prohibited outsiders from entering their sanctuaries. Sentinels guarded the approaches to the Halouah, ensuring that no one intruded. Trespassers who persisted faced severe consequences, even death.

With the company gone, Maria seized a narrow-mouthed vessel, used for drinking, and filled it with water from a nearby stream. She decided to baptize the infant in the cradle, a two-year-old boy, naming him Paul in the name of the Father, Son, and Holy Ghost. Maria took such opportunities whenever she could, hoping that her humble and earnest actions would sow the seeds of faith.

The Druze were believed descended from an Arab tribe that refused Mohammed's faith, seeking refuge in Lebanon's mountains, where they've practiced their own religion in secrecy. Some theorized they descended from Jews who abandoned worship of the true God for a golden calf. The Druze kept their practices hidden from outsiders, effectively maintaining this secrecy.

Maria had a chance to explore Druze religion when Emir Bashir, quelling a Druze rebellion, acquired golden calves and Druze prayer books. Though she held the key to the locked chamber, her religious upbringing deterred her from reading the forbidden texts, fearing it a grave sin. Later, Maria realized the Catholic Church's position was more nuanced—it cautioned, but also encouraged facing challenges directly. Reading the Druze books wouldn't have threatened her faith.

The Druze seemed to worship the golden calf, like Baal's ancient followers. Their elite, the akhals, practiced rites differently from the common djahels. They venerated Moses, Christ, and Muhammad, holding weekly gatherings of men and women, led by a sovereign pontiff in Mouta.

When a Druze man wished to divorce his wife, he simply posted a brief written declaration of his intention on the wall of his room, without any prior notice. If the wife saw this paper, her fate was sealed. The husband would declare, "You have read your fate," and the wife must immediately cover her face with a veil and leave her husband's home, returning to her parents' house and leaving behind all of her children.

At a Druze's burial, attendees testified to the deceased's conduct. Favorable testimony prompted the akhal's call for divine mercy, which the crowd repeated. Unfavorable testimony yielded solemn silence.

The Druze believed souls transmigrate, inhabiting virtuous men or animals based on one's life. The Druze often attended services in Maronite churches and were quite familiar with Christian doctrine, often displaying a good understanding of the Bible. Their women covered their entire face except for one eye when meeting a stranger. A Druze person is as hospitable as any desert Arab, offering shelter and food to Christians, Muslims, and others without distinction or hesitation. Europeans in particular were held in high regard by the Druze, which led some to speculate that they may be descended from Crusaders.

CHAPTER 19

∽

Daily Life at the Prince's Palace

One of Maria's favorite pastimes during her stay in Beteddin was waking up before dawn to visit a garden owned by the Emir, located just a short distance from the palace. The garden encompassed a magnificent palace, where the Emir often went for leisure. The palace there was exquisitely furnished, with luxurious balconies and splendid iwans, filled with Baghdad and Damascus's finest.

The vast garden overflowed with diverse fruits and flowers, enticing the senses. Flowing streams divided it into sections. In solitude, Maria would witness the morning star fade as the sun rose, accompanied by birds' joyful melodies celebrating their Creator. The songbirds flitted among the flowers, their delightful songs mingling with the scent on the air. During these magical moments, Maria would join the birds in praising and thanking God, her love surpassing a lover's for their beloved.

The Emir's elderly relative, driven by religious zeal, often debated Maria about converting to Islam in the garden. The man would loudly perform prayers, hoping to capture Maria's attention. When Maria objected, the man insisted he would eventually convert her with the prophet's blessing.

"Why do you persist in pestering me with endless rituals which you know I abhor?" Maria retorted, snatching his prayer carpet. "This garden is large enough for us to pray in peace. Why then this unceasing persecution? Have I offended you that you've singled to annoy me?"

The stunned Emir replied, "The day will come when you see the truth of the prophet's religion. I will not cease to impress it upon you until this happy moment arrives."

"That day will never come," Maria shot back, "even if you live a thousand years. Sooner could I convert the whole Muslim population to Christianity."

"The time will come, the time will come," he said, shaking his head. "The prophet will aid me to enlighten your understanding."

The two debated further, with the Old Emir warning Maria about obstinacy and the fate of unbelievers riding on a Jew in the last days. Muslims believed that on the last days, Jews would turn into donkeys and serve to convey the Christians to hell. Maria accused him and other Muslims of turning away from Christianity's salvation and wandering in the darkness of the shadow of death.

"Mashallah! Though art, I see, an astrologer, like the Queen of Tadmor," he replied, and wishing her good day, departed to seek his lost carpet.

Though the Old Emir remained convinced he would convert her, Maria steadfastly kept her own beliefs, finding solace in the garden. Eventually, she even succeeded in turning the tables, convincing him to convert to Christianity. Upon reflection, she decided he was a good, sincere man, motivated by concern for her soul.

Lady Hester Stanhope, known as the "Queen of Tadmor," had a close relationship with Emir Bashir and his family. A frequent visitor to their garden, they became intimate acquaintances. She had abandoned European comforts to live among the generous, brave desert people, held in high regard by the

Druze, Maronite, and other tribes. Passing Bedouin sheikhs would visit, bringing valuable gifts.

She had no regrets about her voluntary exile, preferring the simple character of her chosen people over the perceived cold-heartedness and lack of hospitality in Europe. Maria recounted an incident where a French traveler, hosted by Emir Bashir, was provided ample provisions on departure. When the traveler tried to tip the servant, the servant refused, explaining it would endanger his life. Lady Hester remarked the servant's conduct was wise and humane, as in Europe, no one would offer even bread without demanding payment.

She was highly esteemed by Jews for her perceived sympathy towards their religious sentiments. Their bankers and merchants willingly assisted her. She had faith in a future savior, a second Messiah, who would cleanse the world, a belief founded upon her interpretation of the passage in the gospel where Christ declares that although the truths of his religion are conveyed in parables, the day shall come when they shall be proclaimed openly.

In a paddock in the garden, Maria often visited the noble-bred horses of Emir Bashir. Their lineages were zealously preserved, tracing back to King Solomon's stables. The Arab horse of noble blood is distinct from the common horses, excelling in intelligence, courage, endurance, symmetry, and proud spirit. Even wounded in battle, the noble steed will charge on, its haughty crest only bowed by death.

Lady Hester was one of the boldest horsewomen Maria had seen, exciting the highest admiration even among the Arabs, who were themselves the best horsemen in the world. She often rode fearlessly along ridges, and up the steep and rocky sides of mounts, where every step seemed to threaten destruction. Spending hours smoking her nerghila, she would admire the beautiful steeds which stood, no less than fifty in number, with their fore legs chained to spikes driven into the ground as they grazed before her.

Among them was a mare of extraordinary beauty, which the Prince had purchased from a sheikh at a hefty price. He himself rode a remarkably swift and smooth-gaited mare, once demonstrating his skill by drinking coffee without spilling a drop while at full gallop. Seeing that Lady Hester had taken a particular fancy to this mare, he made her a present of the horse. The certificate of the mare's nobility mentioned that she was noble from both the father's and mother's side. It also possessed the qualities of the mares spoken of by the prophet.

The Prince also gave Lady Lester a female ass, believed to be a descended from the one Jesus rode on his entry into Jerusalem. The idea was to provide her with donkey's milk for her ailments. Months later, Lady Hester's mare gave birth to a foal with a back that resembled a natural Turkish saddle. Considering this miraculous, she kept the foal for the Regenerator, whose coming she awaited with steady faith. The Emir, amused, laughed outright. Easterners believed that the Messiah would come riding on a horse that had a natural saddle.

Emir Bashir had three sons, each living in magnificent palaces near their father's residence. They would together hunt gazelle, partridges, and other game across the Beteddin plains. Kassim, the eldest son, was a serious, fifty-year-old man who avoided political turmoil. He exhibited resignation to God's will, quickly making amends for any unintended offenses. Kassim constantly sought to improve his virtue, asking friends like Maria to point out his faults. Kassim's wife was an amiable, well-educated woman skilled in reading, writing, and poetry—an impressive accomplishment for an Oriental woman. She and Maria shared a close friendship, exploring the mountains and valleys together while engaging in charitable acts.

Kassim, once a parolee, was imprisoned in Acre's palace under Djezzar Pasha. During his captivity, Kassim observed the cruel ruler's character and eccentricities, recounting stories of Djezzar's brutal conduct. As Djezzar neared death, he planned to have several noble Syrian prisoners he had stripped of power and wealth executed, fearing they would seek to regain influence after his demise, leading to anarchy. Fortunately, Djezzar died before carrying out this plan, and the intended victims obtained their freedom. Djezzar was infamous for his barbarity, personally executing victims and leaving a legacy of abominable cruelty across Syria.

However, Djezzar occasionally displayed moments of justice and humanity. Kassim told Maria about a Christian merchant in Acre and his son. The son had requested to switch the damp lower rooms for the more pleasant upper ones to accommodate an upcoming marriage. The father agreed, but the son failed to return the rooms as promised. The father's health deteriorated in the dampness, but he patiently waited, trusting his son would switch rooms with him. When the deadline expired, the son callously refused to honor his word, devastating the father.

Informed of the situation, the ever-vigilant Djezzar summoned the young man before him, surrounded by officers and executioners. Trembling, the young man stammered his Christian faith, believing it to be his final testament.

"You claim to be a Christian," said the Pasha, "then show me the sign that Christians make."

The young man crossed himself. But Djezzar demanded to hear the words that accompanied the gesture, his hand on his dagger.

"In the name of the Father, the Son, and the Holy Ghost," the young man cried, half-dead with fright, while repeating the sign of the cross, touching his head, heart, and shoulders.

"So, it seems your religion teaches that the Father should be above and the Son beneath," the Pasha remarked. "Therefore, you cursed creature of injustice, prove that you have adhered to the rules of your faith if you wish to keep your head on your shoulders."

It didn't take long for the father to receive his just rights.

These occasional displays of justice were like fleeting rays of light, barely illuminating the constant darkness of Djezzar's cruelty. The Emir Kassim once witnessed one of the Pasha's enemies carried in a sack to be burned in a lime kiln. The cause, as always, was jealousy. It was even rumored that if Djezzar caught sight of someone he found displeasing, he would send his executioners to strangle the person, claiming, "Such an ugly fellow is unworthy of life; surely he must be one of the devil's offspring."

The wife of Emir Kassim, a devout woman, would gather her household for prayers every morning and evening. She often read passages from the Bible. A deep bond formed between her and Maria, but it was tragically cut short when she passed away prematurely during childbirth. Following the customary Eastern practice, she was buried seven hours after her death, and Maria was haunted by the terrible thought that her dear friend may have been buried alive.

Emir Kassim mourned for a long time, consumed by grief. As his sorrow began to wane, he found himself burdened by loneliness and yearned to find a worthy successor to his departed wife. Recognizing the affection that existed between his late wife and Maria, he sought her guidance in choosing a new spouse. She recommended a beautiful young Georgian woman recently acquired by Emir Bashir. The Georgian possessed not only physical beauty but also a kind and loving nature.

Emir Kassim embraced Maria's suggestion and pleaded with Maria to facilitate the marriage. So, Maria approached the

Amira and presented the proposal. It was difficult for even the noblest of women to resist the pangs of jealousy when faced with the prospect of elevating someone of lower status to her own level. The amiable Amira favored the Georgian woman, currently one of her attendants in the harem. Yet, despite this, she vehemently opposed the idea of such a union and did everything in her power to prevent it.

Maria found herself in a delicate and challenging position. Advancing the marriage between Emir Kassim and the deserving Christian woman, knowing it would elevate her to a position equal to the Amira's, risked alienating the very woman she loved and respected. However, determined to follow the path of righteousness regardless of personal consequences, she persisted in her efforts, even accusing the Amira of injustice and oppression unworthy of a heathen, let alone a Christian.

Despite her persuasion and reproach proving fruitless in changing the Princess's mind, Maria put her trust in God and disclosed the matter to Emir Kassim, who ultimately agreed to the marriage. For a while, Maria sensed a slight coolness in the Amira's demeanor towards her. Yet, her good heart quickly let go of any resentment, and they resumed their old intimacy.

Amira Kassim, overflowing with gratitude, considered Maria her guardian angel and the orchestrator of her happiness. She wanted to shower her with valuable gifts, but Maria refused, explaining that her actions were driven by a sense of justice and the glory of God, who would surely reward her for fulfilling an obvious duty. Nevertheless, she insisted that Maria accept a beautiful European watch adorned with diamonds as a token of her affection and esteem.

The Prince's second son was named Khalil, meaning "the beloved." He was a Christian, between forty and fifty years old, and regarded as the hero of the Shehab family because he was renowned for his enterprise, his courage and skills in the art of war. He was married and the father of two daughters and eight sons, born in eight successive years, all of them young giants. The eldest was a special favorite of Ibrahim Pasha, so he presented the youth with a magnificent sword.

The third son, Emir Amin, was known for his intelligence and learning. He was a celebrated poet in Lebanon and had a reputation for his wit and brilliance in conversation. His father regarded him as his right-hand man and entrusted him with important governmental matters. Emir Amin was tall and handsome, with a dignified expression on his face. His true nobility emanated from his soul, reflected in his intellectual and moral excellence.

Despite his exceptional qualities, Emir Amin lacked haughtiness and treated everyone with equal respect. Whether it was the most powerful Emir or the poorest shepherd, he spoke to them in the same tone, demonstrating a liberal and egalitarian conduct uncommon in the East. He would even engage in hunting with common shepherds, who saw no presumption in joining the sport alongside the ruler's favorite son. The interactions were marked by the customary salutations of the East, filled with cordiality and goodwill.

Emir Amin's superiority over his elder brothers, both in talent and his father's favor, never bred jealousy among them. On the contrary, they expressed satisfaction that Providence had blessed him with abilities that would bring stability to their father's government, rejoicing in the honors bestowed upon him.

He was married but had no children, which caused him great sorrow and his wife immense distress. She fervently prayed day and night, seeking divine intervention to remove the curse of barrenness and the resulting social stigma. She visited various churches and convents, hoping for the intercession of patron saints, but her efforts remained unsuccessful. She often found solace in reading the story of Sarah, Abraham's wife, shedding tears as she empathized with her plight. The Amira had a deep love for flowers and spent much of her time arranging beautiful bouquets, adorning her room with vases filled with blooms and even placing a flower on her nerghila pipe.

As Emir Amin's presence was required in Beteddin, the Amira became a constant resident of the harem, allowing Maria to enjoy her company and spend hours with her, especially on bathing days. The baths in Beteddin were grand, featuring six different chambers. One notable addition was a glass pavilion constructed at considerable cost by architects from Damascus. The pavilion housed a stunning fountain at its center, which spouted clear streams of water into a basin filled with gold and silver fish. Surrounding the basin, statues emitted soft musical sounds created by a mechanical apparatus activated by the water's motion. Diwans covered in luxurious fabrics lined the outer edge of the pavilion, where people sat and enjoyed coffee and nerghilas after bathing.

Maria spent many delightful hours in the charming baths where she experienced true enjoyment, pure innocent pleasures, unbought by others' woe or others' shame, uninfluenced and unswayed alike by the laws of opinion or the wanton caprice of fashion. Here, the warm affections of the unfettered heart, for husband, parent, child, flowed unchecked, as nature prompted them, unchilled by dread of sneering ridicule. The benign instincts of her nature, planted in her heart to bless her brief journey through this valley of tears, preserved in all their native glow of energy the warm and virtuous feelings of her heart.

CHAPTER 20

A STORMY SEA VOYAGE

Maria enjoyed the Emir's unwavering respect and trust. She held a special place in his confidence, and he willingly granted any favor she sought. One instance stands out among many. One day, Maria's fellow countryman arrived at Beteddin in a state of distress and urgency. He pleaded for an audience with Maria, recognizing that she was the only connection he had to reach the esteemed Prince.

The man had incurred the wrath of the Pasha of Damascus, who had imprisoned him along with his entire family in a dark dungeon. Somehow, he managed to escape, but his son was still in captivity, enduring horrific tortures. The Pasha believed that the man was hiding a certain treasure to evade confiscation, and he subjected the son to unspeakable agony in an attempt to extract the information.

Maria recognized this man as an old and inveterate enemy of her family at Mosul, where he had used every art to bring ruin on their heads. His former haughty look was changed into an expression of deep dejection and sorrow. Seeing this, Maria put aside their past enmity. She immediately wrote a letter to Emir Bashir, explaining the situation and pleading for his intervention with the enraged Pasha on behalf of both the father and the son. Maria was compelled to help, as if saving her own father or dear brother. She handed the letter to the man and said, "Go, it will secure you an audience with the Great Prince. I have no doubt that he will do everything in his power to save your son's life. Our Redeemer has said, 'Do good to them that hate you. Forgive, and you shall be forgiven.'"

The Emir promptly granted the man an audience and, upon learning the dire circumstances, immediately dispatched a messenger with a letter to the Pasha of Damascus. Three days later, the messenger returned bearing a letter from the Pasha. It stated that the son had been released, all seized property restored, and the father was now free to return without fear. Overwhelmed with joy upon hearing the news, the old man could hardly believe it at first. When the reality sank in, he threw himself at Maria's feet, tears streaming down his face, expressing his profound gratitude. He declared that he and his family would forever consider themselves Maria's slaves. Maria humbly replied that her reward was in her heart, for everything she had done was for the glory of God. She sincerely wished she could spend the rest of her life performing similar acts of duty.

For a long time, Maria had harbored a fervent desire to visit Europe. She believed that Christianity shone there with unobstructed glory, free from the shadows of tyranny and unbelief. Moreover, she had heard of the holiness attained by some European priests, and her yearning to set foot on that blessed land, where Providence had bestowed such regenerative influence, surpassed any restraint. Over the years, Maria had occasionally shared her aspirations with her kind friend and protector, the Prince of Lebanon. However, he always staunchly opposed her decision. He assured her that her idealized notions of Europe were exaggerated and likely to lead to bitter disappointment.

"Piety and virtue are not confined to this or that country," he said. "They are to be attained in all corners of the earth, if we will but diligently seek them."

Besides this, he always vowed that she should on no account leave the Amira. He brought forth so many friendly arguments for her not to leave Beteddin that her resolution to pursue her dreams wavered time and again.

The palace of Beteddin stood on a mountain surrounded by other picturesque mountains, each with its distinct character. Among them, Mount Mahsaf boasted an enchanting view, capturing the beauty of land and sea that the mind could conceive. It was a favorite gathering place for the Amira and her companions. From its summit, one could behold the entirety of the mountain on which Emir's palace stood, its terraced structure rising like steps built by daring giants seeking to reach the heavens. The Emir had undertaken the construction of a splendid summer palace on this mountain, which was nearing completion when Maria left Syria. In the valley below, countless rivulets sparkled, spreading fertility across the landscape with lavish generosity. These rivulets were lined with groves of mulberry and other trees, brought at great expense from the river Aasi by Emir Bashir.

After many years as a resident in the Emir's palace, Maria accompanied the Amira and her friends one beautiful afternoon to Mahsaf, where they customarily enjoyed their pipes and coffee. Suddenly, an overwhelming desire for solitude overcame Maria. She left her companions behind and wandered to an elevation that provided a vantage point over the plateau where they reclined, offering an even more extensive view. Here, she began plucking fragrant herbs and surrendered herself to a delightful reverie, surrounded by nature's resplendence. Her gaze turned toward the deep blue Mediterranean, calm and serene like the cloudless sky. As she gazed, lost in her reverie, the awareness of her surroundings gradually faded, until her entire being was immersed in an ecstatic vision. In that vision, Maria saw herself standing on the shores of a distant land, surrounded by magnificent cathedrals and devout worshippers. She fancied herself transported to the land of promise in the West, where she hoped to perfect the work of her salvation.

She had just finished reading a book written by Saint Alphonsus of Liquari, who had recently been canonized in Rome. The book emphasized the vanity of worldly things and the extraordinary beauty of Christian virtue and spiritual works. In a moment of deep contemplation, Maria felt as though she saw the newly canonized saint himself, radiating heavenly benevolence and illuminated by the light of holiness. It was as if he extended his hand, beckoning her to embark on a journey to the blessed land where true and vibrant faith thrived.

As Maria emerged from her reverie, the vision remained etched in her heart, compelling her to sever the ties of friendship and affection, relinquish honors, riches, and pleasures, and heed what she perceived as a divine sign. Determined to follow what she considered a special calling from Providence, she sought an audience with the Prince to share her unwavering decision to journey to Rome. Despite the Prince's repeated arguments against her departure, Maria remained resolute, firmly convinced that neglecting her vocation would be sinful. Eventually, the Prince relented and granted his consent, recognizing the depth of her conviction. With the Prince's blessing, Maria set about making preparations for her imminent departure.

Amidst her flurry of arrangements, Maria received a letter from an old friend of her father, Jebrail Khan, who had traveled from Mardin to Damascus, intending to embark for Europe. A man of around fifty-five years old, he owned vast tracts of land which he leased to various tenants. In adherence to the customary practice of the region, the tenants shared half the produce as their contribution. This arrangement fostered a relationship of equality and mutual obligation between the landlord and tenants. Jebrail was renowned for his wealth, which he dedicated primarily to charitable causes. He established schools to educate the youth in various fields of useful knowledge and had even set up printing presses in his hometown to promote the revival of learning and science in the East. Maria's late father held Jebrail in high regard, and the two families had a longstanding friendship.

Jebrail's purpose in traveling to Rome was noble and praiseworthy. Accompanied by four young students, he aimed to enroll them in the College of the Propaganda, where they would receive an education to become teachers for their compatriots in the arts and sciences. It was a remarkable endeavor, far superior to relying on ineffectual adventurers whose sole motivation was personal gain. Jebrail's dedication to advancing the intellectual and moral welfare of his fellow countrymen through education resonated deeply with Maria.

The letter from Jebrail presented Maria with an opportunity. She saw it as a fortuitous alignment of their paths and a chance to travel in the company of someone she deeply respected. Not only could she embark on her spiritual journey to Rome, but she could also contribute to Jebrail's mission of nurturing knowledge and enlightenment in the East. With renewed determination and a sense of purpose, Maria eagerly prepared herself to join Jebrail and his group on their journey to Rome, where she hoped to find spiritual fulfillment and share her experiences with others.

The allure of Europe and the spiritual enlightenment it held called to Maria. Her departure from her familiar surroundings at Beteddin would be bittersweet, as she left behind cherished friends and a life of comfort. However, the prospect of embarking on a transformative quest, guided by her unwavering faith and fueled by the desire to deepen her understanding and connection with God, filled her with anticipation and resolve. With the blessings and support of those she held dear, Maria embarked on her journey to Rome, ready to embrace the challenges and discoveries that lay ahead.

Maria thought, "If only we had the resolve to rise again, confident in our own resources! Why must we now wait for mental sustenance, when the light of religion and science once diffused from the East? Our people must arise once more! Let our dissension be silenced and let us unite for the regeneration of our fallen race. We must brush the dust of ages from the books of our sages—the fountainheads of knowledge that has made Westerners so wise, that they now scorn their forefathers in the land of the rising sun. We should no longer fear to see, in the words of our ancestors' wisdom, the evidence of our own degeneracy. There we shall find abundant stores of all that the human mind hungers and thirsts for—good measure, pressed down and shaken together, overflowing to spread light and plenty where now all is darkness."

Maria's father had told her the story of her ancestor, Mor Yusuf, the first patriarch of the Chaldean Catholics. Mor Yusuf had discovered a vast library in the catacombs of Deir Raban Hormiz, built by another ancestor, Chaldean Patriarch Tomarso. The library contained thousands of volumes in various languages like Chaldean, Stangheli, ancient Syriac, Arabic, and others, covering art and science. The tomb of a Persian prince, a Christian martyr, was also held in high regard in the catacombs. The library moved to Diarbekir and was passed down through generations, preserved and never sold. The last patriarch, Mar Augustinus, had instructed the current Archbishop of Diarbekir, Maria's uncle Mar Basilius Asmar, to never allow any part of the library to leave the Patriarchate, no matter the persecution it might bring.

Maria did not have the opportunity to examine the library. But given what she'd heard, she had no doubt that some of its volumes threw considerable light on the condition of the early Christians in the East.

In Baghdad, the first mechanical watch was created. And didn't one of their cities support six hundred skilled doctors to treat the poor and afflicted? Sadly, in these days of darkness and ignorance, European charlatans, pretending medical knowledge, often deceive gullible Orientals based solely on their name and origin. They hail from a land and speak the language of people whose talents and benevolence have earned their country reverence in the East as healers of humanity's ailments.

The venerable Jebrail had another purpose for visiting the eternal city—to settle a dispute with a Roman legate. In a letter, he informed Maria of his plan to leave Damascus soon, heading to the coast where he would find a ship to Italy. Along the way, he planned to visit Suida and Deir el Kamar, and he mentioned that he would take the opportunity to pay Maria a visit.

This was a fortunate turn of events. Maria's doubts were dispelled, and she joyfully wrote a reply to Jebrail, expressing her delight at the prospect of seeing her old and valued friend. She informed him of her intention to visit Europe and asked him to postpone his departure for a month or six weeks, allowing her time to make the necessary arrangements. Jebrail's quick response fully supported Maria's plans and expressed his satisfaction in providing her with protection and companionship during the long journey.

The most difficult part was breaking the news to the Amira, whom Maria loved dearly and who had treated her with sisterly affection. The Amira was deeply saddened by Maria's decision and tried every argument to dissuade her, but Maria's mind was made up, as if destiny was urging her forward. Maria often wonders at her own callousness when she thinks back to the heartfelt and poignant pleas of her dear friends, whom she rashly and thoughtlessly left behind. She paid a high price for her indifference in the privations and hardships she faced since leaving the kind home where she received daily displays of affection and esteem.

Finally, the day of departure drew near, and Maria's chosen companion for the adventurous journey, Jebrail Khan, arrived in Beteddin. He was warmly welcomed by Emir Bashir, who hosted him in a princely manner for several days. Jebrail, a practical man, proved invaluable in finalizing Maria's arrangements. With his assistance, she converted her Turkish currency into gold and silver ingots, which he believed would be more useful in Europe. In addition to the precious metals, Maria brought valuable jewels and trinkets. Her wealth upon leaving Beteddin amounted to nearly eight thousand ghazi, a coin with a value ranging from fifteen to twenty shillings in English money. With everything in order, Maria bid farewell to the Princess, the Amira Amin, and all her female friends, with mutual tears of regret. She then sought an audience of the Prince and told him the hour had come when her destiny bade her leave his hospitable roof.

The venerable Emir was moved, and after gently chiding her for her obstinacy, invoked blessings on her head, saying, as she kissed his hand at parting, "May God protect thee against all perils of land and sea, and may'st thou, under his protection, reach the land of the West in peace and safety! May his mercy and grace be showered upon thy head! May his holy will be fulfilled in thee, to the glory of his name! Remember, in leaving Lebanon, you leave a loyal friend and protector. Rest assured, you'll always find the same friendship and esteem you left behind. May God be thy guide!"

Maria had no words to express the tumult of feelings that

arose in her breast when her noble protector concluded his benediction. Fervently kissing his hand, which she bathed with warm tears of gratitude, she hastened to her room. There, she remained sobbing and agitated by a conflicting mix of emotions, before summoning enough resolution to depart. It was the most acute anguish she had felt since the day she lost her father and kindred at the hands of a ruthless oppressor, finding herself a lone outcast in the wide world. Despite the pain of parting from such sincere friends, she found consolation in the fact that she was about to embark on a holy pilgrimage to fulfill the long-cherished desires of her heart. She had the firm assurance that she had a warm, kind-hearted, generous, and above all, powerful protector whose door was always open to receive her.

The instability of earthly things troubled Maria's thoughts. Those once hospitable doors were now closed to the noble and magnanimous Prince who had kindly offered her his protection. If the Prophet Jeremiah could visit the earth again, he would surely lament the woes that had befallen the daughter of Zion. He would shed bitter tears at witnessing the wrongs and humiliations inflicted upon her. The Assyrian was no more. Haughty Babylon, with her hundred gates of brass, where was she? The proud king, the Lord's chastiser for his people, where was he? They were gone, and their graves were forgotten. But they had found successors just as terrible in the rulers whose yoke now pressed heavily on the necks of God's people, especially since their civilized brethren in Europe had interfered with their devastating policies.

In the midst of this sorrowful situation, Maria's heart burned with a determination to fulfill her sacred mission. With a heavy heart, she made her way to the harbor where a ship awaited her. Towards the end of September 1832, Maria bid farewell to the East, perhaps for the last time. She remained overwhelmed with grief for the first half hour. After the preparations were done and she was alone, she thought of her dear friends and cried. Her mental anguish was soon replaced by severe physical suffering, as the weather was so tempestuous that she had barely been on board for half an hour before becoming seasick. She remained in this state the entire voyage to Cyprus, spending most of the time in a semi-conscious state from exhaustion due to constant retching. She ate and drank nothing and believed she would have died had they not make port into Cyprus.

They spent twenty days in Cyprus, during which time Maria fully recovered. Before embarking again, she purchased several casks of sweet red and dry white Cyprus wine to bring as gifts to Europe. She also had four of the finest large-tailed sheep from the Druze loaded onto the ship, intending them as a gift for the Pope, as well as a small case containing some of the true mau-el-lamma sent from Diarbekir.

The weather remained stormy when they left Cyprus, with adverse winds and towering waves. Maria soon found herself in a miserable state again, utterly unable to leave her berth. Luckily, she had a cabin all to herself, or her situation would've been worse.

After several days at sea, one of the Druze sheep had gorged itself on biscuit and died, unable to move on the deck due to the rough weather. The captain ordered it thrown overboard. Days later, another sheep suffered the same fate. However, the sailors, tired of salt provisions, resisted the captain's order to discard the carcass and wished to divide it among the crew. This led to a quarrel between the sailors and the captain.

Below in her cabin, Maria lay sick and miserable on her bed when she suddenly heard the sound of many voices on the deck, evidently in anger. The noise grew, nearly drowning the roar of the elements. Eventually, she heard the stomping of feet and other sounds of a deadly struggle, accompanied by loud curses and cries of pain.

Ill as she was, Maria managed to climb the ladder to the deck and was met with a horrifying sight. The deck was spattered with blood. The captain and supporters fought fiercely with crew members who wanted the dead sheep. Knives were brandished on all sides, and many were bleeding from frightful gashes inflicted by their enraged shipmates.

Maria called on them in God's name to cease their inhumane fighting. She attempted, despite having difficulty making herself understood in their language, to learn the cause of the quarrel. Upon discovering that the carcass of her sheep had sparked all this bloodshed, she pleaded with them, for the love of heaven, to take one of the remaining live sheep to divide among them and throw the dead one overboard as the captain had ordered. This compromise seemed to satisfy both sides, and the struggle soon ceased. Relieved that she had intervened so timely and sacrificed one of her sheep to likely save many of her fellow travelers, Maria retired to her cabin.

Shortly after, the weather abated, the sea became calm, and the sky bright and clear. As a result, Maria's health improved rapidly, and she was soon able to enjoy the fresh air on the deck. She was in awe at the sight of the sun sinking beneath the waves, painting the vast expanse of the sea with a fiery glow. And to see the same sun rising in the morning, accompanied by a gentle breeze, casting a golden hue upon the countless waves. It was a breathtaking spectacle.

Maria cherished the privilege of witnessing these sights daily, weather permitting. During that period, she spent most of her time on deck, sometimes leaning over the edge and gazing at the gently swelling waves as they passed by the ship. Other times, she observed the various groups on the deck—a young man engrossed in reading, a sailor diligently mending a sail with a needle as sharp as a stiletto while humming a cheerful tune. Everyone seemed content and happy, indulging in activities of their choice. The ship sailed smoothly, seemingly requiring no guiding hand. Even the helmsman's face, usually marked by care and anxiety, now displayed a serene countenance, reflecting pleasant thoughts.

Every evening, as the sun neared the western horizon, the captain called the crew for vespers. The crew member with the best reading ability and voice would take the Prayer Book and lead the singing of "Ave Maris Stella" and recite the Litany of the Blessed Virgin, followed by the rest of the crew. Maria fervently participated in these vespers, which evoked deep devotion within her, mingled with awe and reverence. The wrath of the Lord upon the vast and untamed ocean appeared truly terrifying. She wondered, who could guarantee seeing the sun rise the next day after closing their eyes to the watery wilderness? The Arab saying held true, "He who fears not the ocean fears not God."

The period of calm weather was short-lived due to the winter season. The wind soon picked up again, strong and opposing, diverting the ship far from its intended course and shattering their comfort. It then escalated into a full-blown storm. The waves grew to towering heights, showering the deck with foam and spray. The sun disappeared from view, both at sunrise and sunset, and the sky transformed into a gloomy expanse covered with dark, ominous clouds. The storm raged relentlessly for two days and nights, leaving the crew exhausted from constant vigilance and tireless work since the storm's inception.

On the evening of the second day, the storm transformed into a fierce hurricane. Every sail was furled, and the ship tossed and pitched like a log amidst the churning waves. As night approached, the leaden hue of the sky gave way to utter darkness. The wind howled, mimicking the sounds of distressing groans, shrieks, or the cry of a frightened camel, or even the roar of countless wild beasts hungry for prey. Amidst the chaos, snippets of instructions and the captain's firm voice issuing orders could be heard, conveying composure and resolution, providing solace to the fearful and instilling courage in the wavering.

The night dragged on, the wind intensified, and torrential rain mixed with hail began to fall. The masts bent like slender reeds before the fury of the gale. It seemed impossible for the ship to withstand such a tempest. The darkness added uncertainty to the already horrifying situation. Occasional flashes of lightning illuminated the terrifying scene, unveiling its horrors to the terrified crew, while thunderous peals drowned their shouts and cries of terror. Despair filled the air, and the captain finally declared the situation as dire.

Jebrail gathered his young men, and together they knelt on the cabin floor, expressing calm resignation to the will of Providence. Radiating serenity, he fervently prayed to the throne of Divine grace, beseeching the Almighty to intervene with His all-powerful arm—their only hope for escaping instant destruction.

Maria's courage remained steadfast during emergencies. She was one of the few women resistant to fear. She had experienced danger multiple times, witnessing bloodshed in ferocious battles, seeing men fall beside her, gasping their last breaths, with whom she had engaged in cheerful conversations mere hours before. She had seen her dearest friends perish in the cruelest of tortures, and her own life had teetered on the brink of death numerous times due to violence and accidents. Yet, her heart had never been so pale with fear as on that night. There was no distraction from the impending danger, and all human efforts seemed futile in averting it.

Hearing the confusion and cries of terror on deck, Maria could no longer restrain herself. She made her way up the ladder as best she could and beheld the crew in despair, clinging to ropes or anything within their reach, abandoning all efforts to ensure their safety. Sunk in utter and complete despair, some offered fervent prayers to Heaven, while others uttered piercing cries of terror, answered only by the roar of the thunder and the crash of the elements.

Maria, breathless with terror, retreated to her cabin and joined her prayers with those of the devout Jebrail and his pupils, preparing to die. In this somber mood, she retired to her bed, now her grave. She surrendered to prayer, not to rise again in this world. At first, the thoughts of the dear friends she had abandoned rushed upon her mind, and she shed a flood of tears—tears of bitter regret and remorse. Her mind later became more composed, as she thought, "Of what importance is it whether my bones rest beneath the ground or are scattered on the bottom of the boundless deep? Shall not the All-seeing eye discover them in the day of judgment? God's will be done!"

Full of hope in the goodness of the Almighty and resigning herself humbly to His will, with crossed arms and a tranquil mind, Maria awaited the flight of her soul into eternity.

CHAPTER 21

ARRIVAL TO ITALY

I t was late on the following morning when Maria awoke. The cabin was filled with bright, comforting light, and a sense of tranquility permeated the air. The ship no longer jolted and groaned like a wounded horse; instead, there was a gentle undulating motion that almost made her believe she was safe on land, no longer at the mercy of the furious waves. She rubbed her eyes, looking around in disbelief. Everything was peaceful. The only sound was the steady, unhurried footsteps of a seaman pacing the deck above her. The previous night's horrors faded like a fevered nightmare.

Her first instinct was to offer fervent thanks to God for her preservation. Then she dressed hastily, eager to join her fellow survivors in expressing their gratitude to the Higher Power for their miraculous escape from destruction. Maria recalled the wise words of Sindabad El Bahri El Baghdadi, "Suffer destiny to roll on in her course, and sleep with a mind at ease; for between sleeping and waking, the current of events is often completely reversed."

The first person she encountered upon reaching the deck was the captain. "Praised be God," he exclaimed, "the storm is over, and a fair wind has sprung up."

Maria stepped onto the deck, greeted by a cloudless sky and brilliant sunlight. Passengers and crew crowded the deck, exchanging congratulations for their providential escape from the clutches of death. The entire day was dedicated to festivity and rejoicing. Fowl from the hencoop were slaughtered and consumed, and copious amounts of wine were drunk in celebration of their deliverance. Maria felt like she had been given another chance at life, as if she had come back from the dead.

Unfortunately, the nice weather didn't last. After a couple of clear days, storm clouds gathered once again, fulfilling their expectations and ending their celebrations. They were confined below deck, but the storms that followed were far less threatening. Though insignificant, they still brought back waves of nausea and robbed Maria of her appetite for the remainder of the journey.

Maria had never been as weary of anything in her life as she was of that voyage. Her yearning to glimpse land was akin to a baby's longing for its mother's embrace. The captain, aware of this sentiment, since she promised a handsome present to whoever should first show her land, and being a bit of a prankster, came to the door of her cabin one morning in a frenzy. "Come up, Signora," he said, "and I will show you part of the Montenero."

Maria hurriedly ascended to the deck, scanning the horizon for any sign of land, but her eyes found nothing. "Where is this rock you promised to show me?" she asked the captain, who casually leaned against the railing.

"Come this way, Signora," he chuckled, leading her to the galley. He produced a small piece of stone, claiming it had been chipped off from the Montenero. Despite her usual humor, Maria's weariness and sickness left her unable to find any amusement in the prank. Disappointed, she retreated to her cabin, feeling a twinge of chagrin.

Finally, after three months of navigating the seas, often pushed back by contrary winds, they arrived at Leghorn and dropped anchor. The passengers were immediately taken to the lazaretto, where they were sentenced to forty days of strict surveillance. Each person had their own room and could only leave during a designated time for a short walk on the strip of land near the lazaretto, closely monitored by guards. The regulations were enforced rigorously. If someone who had completed thirty-nine days of quarantine so much as touched another person who had arrived more recently from suspicious countries, their quarantine period would reset.

The sight that greeted Maria's eyes as their vessel anchored was unlike anything she had ever seen in the eastern cities. The bustling quays were filled with lively and animated people engaged in earnest conversations, devoid of any visible worries. The attire of the crowd, though sober and dull, stood in sharp contrast to their vivacious demeanor. Gone were the flowing garments and dazzling turbans, replaced by a more somber, yet animated, scene. The sense of equality was palpable, as every person regarded their neighbor as a brother. The women, young and unveiled, displayed their charms without fear or shame, a sight that initially shook Maria's sensibilities but eventually made her contemplate the freedom enjoyed by females in this land.

The houses stood tall and imposing, with numerous large windows on each floor, revealing a lack of concealment and a willingness to share the inner lives of their inhabitants. Maria wondered about the designated areas for females within these houses, marveling at the openness and seemingly happy nature of the country. She couldn't help but exclaim, "Happy country! This is indeed the land of promise. I would have braved any danger to set foot on your favored shores!"

However, Maria's longing to mingle with the joyful throng on the quays was curtailed by the reality of their situation. They were taken to the lazaretto and given individual rooms for quarantine. The confinement was dreary, and Maria's health, already shattered from the sickness endured during the voyage, continued to deteriorate throughout the quarantine period. When they were finally released, Maria was so weak that she had to be taken to an inn in Leghorn, where she remained bedridden for three months, battling her debilitating condition.

Upon unloading her belongings from the ship, Maria discovered that the wine casks had been nearly emptied by the sailors, who cleverly drained the contents through a reed inserted into the partition of her cabin. Her precious Cyprus wine, intended as a gift for those she had letters of recommendation for, was rendered valueless. Despite this loss, she accepted it with resignation, recognizing its irreparable nature.

Jebrail, who had urgent business in Rome, stayed with Maria in Leghorn for two months, witnessing her helpless state. Seeing no immediate prospect of her being able to accompany him, he reluctantly departed with his students. He urged Maria to join him as soon as her health permitted. Little did they know that their misfortunes in Europe were just beginning. Destiny seemed to lay its heavy hand upon them both, as Jebrail faced relentless persecution, ruinous exactions, and tyrannical interference upon his return to his homeland. His noble efforts to regenerate his country were thwarted, his property confiscated, and he met an ignominious death.

It was clear that Jebrail's untimely demise had cut short his potential for success in realizing his cherished goals. He possessed learning, virtue, courage, resolution, and sufficient wealth to support his noble endeavors. Yet fate had different plans, and he became a martyr defending greatness and goodness in human nature. His name was honored and revered.

Since that period, Maria's life became a continuous succession of care, vexation, and bitter disappointment. Her experiences in Europe had been unfortunate, as she found herself surrounded by deceitful individuals. Sometime after Jebrail's departure for Rome, she found herself in need of money to pay for her board and lodging during her prolonged illness. She had been given a letter of introduction to a businessman in Leghorn, who had been recommended as a trustworthy person who could assist her in arranging her financial affairs. Wishing to convert some of the silver ingots she had brought from the East into local currency, Maria summoned this man, who came and received several bars from her to exchange into cash. When he returned with the money, the small amount surprised her, as it seemed disproportionately low. However, the man assured her that he had provided her the full value and that it would be impossible to get more, claiming he had sent the bars to Florence to secure the best price. Maria, trusting in his honesty, was unaware that she had been grossly cheated. She later learned he had given her only about one-tenth of what her ingots were worth.

After six months, Maria had recovered enough to continue her journey. She joined a respectable party traveling to Rome via Civita Vecchia. On the journey from Civita Vecchia to Rome, an amusing incident occurred. The passengers were a wealthy and distinguished Roman gentleman, a poor Capuchin friar, Maria, and another individual. The rich man was carrying valuable gold trinkets that he had brought from somewhere, intending to present them as a surprise to his wife awaiting him in Rome. This precious cargo caused him great unease, as he feared having to pay heavy duties on it when entering the city. He racked his brain to devise a scheme to evade the vigilance of the Roman customs officials and smuggle his wife's trinkets in duty-free.

Eventually, he hit upon an expedient. Addressing the Capuchin friar, he earnestly beseeched the simple man to oblige him by concealing the treasure under his capacious tunic, knowing friars were seldom searched by customs as they were not expected to carry worldly possessions. The good-natured friar agreed to help pass the jewelry through. Upon reaching customs, each person was asked if they had anything to declare. The stranger and Maria had nothing. When it was the friar's turn, he shook his tunic and said he had valuable jewelry and gold articles intended as a gift "per la signora." The officers, seeing the Capuchin as a jokester, heartily laughed at the idea of a mendicant friar carrying such valuables, and allowed them all to pass without further delay.

Once beyond customs, the owner of the jewelry complained to the friar, saying that but for a lucky accident, he may have lost the whole lot due to his foolish candor. "Had you told me that you meant to betray me to the Customs," he said, "I would have taken the risk myself."

"I don't understand your suffering, or by what right you make this charge against me," replied the friar. "For here is your wife's present duty-free," he said, handing him the packet, "and I have not stained my conscience with a lie."

After this, Maria went first to a hotel in the Piazza di Spagna, from where she dispatched the letters of recommendation she had brought for Cardinal Odescalchi, the Pope's Vicar-General, Cardinal Prefet of Propaganda, Cardinal Weld, and other church dignitaries. She received much friendship and assistance from many of them, especially the first two eminent individuals, during her four-year stay in Rome.

Shortly after her arrival in Rome, Maria was presented to the Pope, who received her graciously and expressed sympathy for the calamities that had befallen her family, of which he was well aware. As her family was long known to him, the Pope directed his Vicar-General to place Maria in the best convent, where she remained for some time. Finding her health declining and being recommended to change her residence, the Pope permitted Maria to enter another convent. However, she failed to derive any benefit and continued growing weaker, suffering severe headaches. Ultimately, she was advised to give up the idea of remaining in Rome.

During her stay, Maria was robbed again. The previous loss in Livorno had been minor, but this second misfortune almost reduced her to beggary. A box containing her family's valuable pearls, jewels, and a considerable amount of money was broken into and looted while she was visiting a Roman noblewoman. Discovering the theft, Maria was driven to despair, feeling her misfortune would never end. She immediately sought advice from friends, who recommended she report the crime to the police without delay.

Maria promptly did so, and the matter was thoroughly investigated. Suspicion fell on a certain individual who had fled immediately after the robbery, but despite the police's utmost efforts, he was never found. It was likely he had planned the scheme and crossed the border as soon as he committed the theft.

This circumstance, combined with embarrassments, Maria became the victim of from speaking her mind with perhaps imprudent frankness, a frankness natural to her and common to those born and raised in her homeland, as well as her constantly declining health, ultimately determined her to quit Rome after a four-year residence. Maria now longed earnestly to return to her beloved friends in Lebanon and would have immediately gone to Livorno to seek passage on a ship for that purpose. But her health and fear of the sea prevented her from fulfilling her yearnings. To her, it felt like casting herself headlong into the way of death. Staying in Rome had become impossible, so acting on medical advice and with the full approbation of the Pope and her principal friends in the city, Maria determined to try the atmosphere of France.

CHAPTER 22

―――――❧―――――

THE DOWNFALL OF THE PRINCE OF LEBANON

In the spring of 1837, Maria left Rome and embarked on a journey to Paris, accompanied by the Marquis de Montblanc, whom she had met in Rome. They made several stops along the way, including Marseille, Lyon, and Dijon. Her travel companion, known for his piety and virtues, introduced her to the Archbishop of Paris and the heads of various convents. Additionally, the letters of recommendation she carried opened doors for her to meet prominent figures in the French capital. Maria was grateful for the kindness and protection extended to her by a wise and influential man who held a prominent position in the French government. The Queen graciously received her and showed genuine interest in her well-being.

Maria stayed in Paris from 1837 until 1841, during which time she had the opportunity to associate with the city's most distinguished individuals. However, her world was shattered when she received the devastating news that her noble and generous protector, the Prince of the Lebanon, had been overthrown and forced into exile. This news deeply saddened Maria, as she believed the fall of the prince, a staunch defender of Christianity in the East, was partly due to the actions of a nation that he had favored and embraced.

Maria questioned the motives behind this injustice and expressed her hope that justice, morality, and Christian principles would prevail over narrow-minded state policies. She fervently wished for the return of the prince to his rightful throne and implored the nation responsible for his exile to rectify the situation and restore peace and stability to the land.

Although Maria acknowledged her limited understanding of diplomacy and state policies, she maintained confidence in the strength of a righteous cause and the good faith of at least one of the nations involved. She believed that, despite political complexities, reparation would eventually be granted, and the Prince of the Lebanon would be reunited with his loyal subjects.

Maria longed to end the discord and violence plaguing the holy mountain's valleys. She recalled the 1840 military operations on the Syrian coast, where the Sultan and European allies sought to subdue the rebellious Pasha of Egypt. The Emir Bashir played a significant role.

In Beirut, four British ships arrived to support the Sultan's forces and summoned the Emir Bashir and Egyptian troops to obey promptly. Soliman Pasha, leading Mehemet Ali's forces, tried to prevent communication between the British squadron and local leaders. Despite this, the Emir, after much effort, sent a reply to the British commander, who acknowledged the Emir's circumstances and promised protection once the Sultan's troops arrived.

After this assurance, the Emir prepared to fulfill his promise. But Ibrahim Pasha, learning of the British squadron, swiftly gathered his forces and dispersed the Emir's family to ensure compliance. Turkish troops and the fleet, commanded by Azza Pasha and Admiral Stopford, arrived off Djouni. The admiral sent a clergyman to remind the Emir of his commitment. The Emir expressed willingness but requested time to rescue his family and remove Ibrahim Pasha. The commanders accepted the delay.

Finally, the Emir convinced Ibrahim Pasha to depart. Before the deadline, another priest arrived with a letter from the Ottoman and British commanders. It assured the Emir of safety, protection, and assistance, as long as he remained obedient. The document, dated October 5, 1840, was signed by Admiral Stopford and Commander Aza Pasha.

Two days after the communication, Ibrahim Pasha's forces withdrew seven hours from Beteddin. Free of Ibrahim, the Emir secretly told his family to escape to Saida, where he planned to gather Lebanon's leaders before surrendering. The Emir informed the British admiral of the situation and requested transport to the fleet. The admiral sent a ship to Saida to pick them up. In Beirut, the Emir was told he couldn't disembark but would be received on the admiral's ship. The admiral said the Lebanon governorship firman had been given to someone else and the Emir must go to Malta until Ibrahim left Syria.

Provided a document guaranteeing his property's safety, the Emir returned to Saida, reunited his family, and they all went to Malta. For nearly a year, the Emir remained there at his own expense, supporting around 150 loyal followers. A firman from the Sultan later granted the Emir freedom to travel Ottoman territories except Syria/Damascus. The Grand Vizier then urged the Emir to come to Constantinople, assuring him of the Sultan's hospitality. Trusting British advice, the Emir boarded an English frigate with his family and followers and set sail for Constantinople.

Upon arriving in the city, the Emir was disappointed to find a small house prepared for him and his family, unable to accommodate everyone, forcing him to rent additional houses at his own expense. The situation worsened when the government ordered him to find alternative accommodations. The once-great Prince of the Lebanon had been deposed from his government and exiled from his homeland, reduced from princely affluence to destitute poverty. His houses, lands, and inheritance had been destroyed or given to strangers. Relying on the British government's pledge to restore him after Ibrahim Pasha's evacuation of Syria, the Emir endured these reverses with serenity and resignation, buoyed by the hope of reparations through the justice of his cause.

Maria trusted the British government had the power and responsibility to rectify the injustice suffered by the Emir and his family, whose sole dependence lay in the justice and honor of the British court under whose protection they had been compelled to place their fortunes. Though state policy may have necessitated temporary delay, Maria hoped the Emir would not be allowed to die as a beggar and outcast, his virtuous governance and unhesitating submission to the sovereign's commands unrecognized.

As her resources dwindled, Maria gradually reduced her food intake, eventually allowing herself only one meal per day—a little semolina boiled in water on a spirit lamp, as she could not afford fuel, and a small portion of bread. Her situation became desperate, as she had to pay twenty shillings per month for her lodging, while her income did not exceed five shillings per week from the two lessons she gave every Tuesday and Friday.

Maria's situation continued to deteriorate after the Emir's fall from power and her uncle's imprisonment. Facing poverty and despair, she gave language lessons to make a living, but struggled to secure enough pupils to sustain herself. Tragically, she was deceived and robbed, losing her remaining funds. The bitter experience taught Maria that true character is revealed not in social settings, but in the crucible of circumstances, as people's intentions can be veiled.

Living in one of Europe's largest capitals, Maria resided in a humble apartment belonging to a noble lady. She had lost everything and was reduced to bitter poverty, her only means of subsistence coming from teaching Arabic to a pupil recommended by the late, kind-hearted Duke of Orleans. This meager income of three francs per lesson was her sole means of survival, as she could teach several Oriental languages.

One bitterly cold winter day, when the snow was thick on the ground and the river frozen, Maria set out, barely able to walk, to give her pupil a lesson. She had not eaten for thirty hours, having nothing left to purchase even a morsel of bread. Yet, she went in the full confidence of receiving the payment for her labor, with which she intended to buy food to save herself from starvation.

Maria arrived at her pupil's residence, only to find out he couldn't have a lesson that evening due to accepting a ball invitation. He apologized profusely for the trouble, and Maria had no doubt he was sincere in his protestations. However, these words struck fear into her heart, as her livelihood depended on the meager payment she expected to receive from the lesson. Her heart sank, and the pupil's voice sounded like a death knell to her. She did not know what she said, but she left him and found herself trudging through the deep snow, each icy blast seeming to freeze her blood and chill her bones.

In this dreadful predicament, Maria's pride gave way. She determined to try and borrow a small amount from her friends. The first one she approached dismissed her politely, and the others were reportedly not home. Defeated and heartbroken, Maria returned, committing herself to God as she had no other refuge. She reached her cheerless apartment, weaving through the servants of the wealthy individual she lodged with, who were bustling between the kitchen and their master's apartment for a grand feast.

Alone in her room, she threw herself on the bed, praying for death as the pangs of hunger and humiliation racked her body and soul. She thought longingly of the bountiful meals she had once enjoyed at her father's table. Recalling the words of Dante, she lamented the sorrow of remembering happier times in her misery.

Maria yearned for the scraps she had often seen given to the poor and destitute. She now longed for the camel's flesh, despite previously finding it repulsive with the kind Bedouins. After a torturous night, at first light Maria wrote letters to two friends, one of whom had professed eternal friendship, hoping for aid. When neither reply came, she was forced to sell a precious relic, a purported piece of the true cross, in order to pay a messenger and buy herself a meager meal.

Consumed by bitterness, Maria wandered one day into the Jardin des Plantes, and climbed the mound upon which the famous cedar, brought from Lebanon, was planted. She sat down under the shade of its wide-spreading branches. The recollection of the joyful hours she had spent amidst the eternal mountains where its roots were nourished flooded her mind. She gazed upon the sturdy tree, like herself a stranger from a land warmed by a more temperate sun and blessed with purer skies; its trunk was firm, and its robust branches extended in every direction, adorned with lush, verdant foliage. In every aspect, it displayed signs of health, strength and prosperity, and seemed destined to follow its gradual path to maturity and old age through the centuries to come, disdaining in its robust vitality the paltry influences of climate. The fate of the previous ruler of the ancient giants, from whom this sapling came, was vastly changed. The solitary tree flourished like its forebears of old in the lofty Lebanon; but the unfortunate princess was cast in her decline to wither, seared and sapless, in a foreign land.

Stung by these bitter reflections, Maria broke down in tears and gave herself over to sadness and lamentation. Eventually, as her grief found expression, it began to subside, giving way to her returning resolve. She fervently prayed to the Almighty to grant her the strength he had so often bestowed during her previous calamities and placing her full trust and confidence in his mercy, she dried her tears and hastily departed the gardens, going to the home of a student to give a lesson.

In Paris, Maria had the good fortune of meeting English nobility and gentry, either visiting for pleasure or connected to the British embassy. She had the honor of being introduced to Lady Granville, Lady Cowley, Lady Bentinck, Bishop Luscombe, Sir George Denys, and many other distinguished individuals, from whom she received numerous courtesies and expressions of consideration. Through these connections, Maria eventually became acquainted with the late, lamented Earl of Munster, who was the President of the Royal Asiatic Society of London. Learning that Maria hailed from the East, the Earl took a keen interest in her welfare.

Upon being informed of the unfortunate circumstances that had so suddenly and unexpectedly reduced Maria to destitution, resulting in the total loss of all her property, the Earl took great pains to devise a plan that might alleviate her present needs and provide for her future wellbeing. The enlightened Prime Minister of France, who had long been Maria's steadfast friend, had advised her to travel to England, where he anticipated she might find ample opportunity to utilize her native language skills given the country's vast Eastern holdings. The Earl of Munster strongly concurred with M. Guizot's recommendation, promising Maria every assistance in his power. He offered to present her at the Court of Queen Victoria and to use his influence to try and secure a pension or compensation from the Ottoman government for the losses she had sustained due to the Syrian expedition, which had ruined a Beirut merchant holding a substantial portion of her assets. Failing that, the Earl said he would endeavor to obtain a grant from the British government, whose military operations had precipitated these heavy losses.

Lifted by this renewed glimmer of hope amidst the gloom of her darkened fortunes, Maria promptly determined to heed their advice. Soon after, she left Paris for London, well-prepared with recommendation letters to esteemed individuals in Great Britain.

Maria first arrived in London in May 1840. There, a certain duchess, whose name Maria chose not to divulge, professed the strongest attachment to her. The duchess showered Maria with affection, referring to her as a sister and daughter. The lady had shining talents and was once married to a wealthy man, but they lived apart. The duchess also possessed substantial independent property.

During a long and severe illness, the duchess was incessant in her visits and attentions to Maria, earning her deep gratitude. One day, the duchess visited Maria and narrated a tale of financial troubles. She spoke of the large sums she had lost during the French Revolution and asked to borrow 4,000 francs from Maria. Overjoyed at the opportunity to prove her gratitude, Maria readily agreed, considering the money as safe as if it had remained in her own possession.

Soon after, the duchess visited Maria again, sharing her misfortunes and subtly suggesting another loan. When she asked for a loan, Maria admitted that she had no money to spare. She instead offered her valuable diamonds to the duchess, which were eagerly accepted.

Unfortunately, the duchess deceived Maria. She sold the jewels and squandered the proceeds at the gaming table. Unsatisfied with despoiling Maria of nearly all she possessed, the duchess went on to solicit money from a princess of Maria's acquaintance. She falsely claimed that Maria was in great need and too ill to visit the princess herself. This caused the princess and some of Maria's friends to go against her.

The duchess had frequently hinted that she intended to leave her property to Maria upon her death, but it was later discovered that the property was so heavily mortgaged that the duchess could not claim ownership of a single para. Maria's trusting nature had led her to fall victim to the duchess's schemes. From an early age, she had been taught not to judge others, and she found it highly criminal to think ill of a cherished friend. The striking difference between this principle and the maxim she later heard in Rome—"Trust no one."

Maria's friends advised her to institute legal proceedings to recover the property, and the judge praised her conduct in the transaction. Yet, when the moment arrived to enjoy the ruling's rewards, Maria was disheartened. The duchess had transferred her entire property to someone else and vanished, leaving Maria with no compensation.

After spending several months there, Maria was advised by the Earl of Munster to return to Paris, settle her debts, and then move to London. She said her farewells to friends in Paris and returned to London in March 1841. She landed at the Tower stairs and proceeded, in the company of Colonel Boyd, gentleman who had accompanied her on the journey from France and shown her the utmost attention and courtesy, to a nearby hotel where they ordered breakfast.

As they awaited their meal, the waiter brought the morning newspaper and handed it to Maria's fellow-traveler. After some time, Colonel Boyd's countenance suddenly changed, as though he had received some distressing news. Maria was devastated to learn that the Earl of Munster had taken his own life the day before due to insanity. Maria was overwhelmed with grief, feeling as though she was irrevocably doomed to misfortune.

For the next three years, Maria existed in this great modern Babylon in solitude. In the midst of millions, she remained isolated and silent, having once dreamed of the sweet spiritual seclusion she had known in her hermitage at Mar Jirgis, a preference borne of her ardent, youthful enthusiasm, only to find herself now reduced to a seclusion of a very different kind, out of dire and inescapable necessity. However, Maria would forever cherish as one of the most pleasurable events of her life the introduction, facilitated through the kindness of M. Guizot, to the amiable nobleman who represented the French nation at the Court of London. From his gracious and accomplished countess, Maria had always received the affectionate treatment of a sister.

Those to whom Maria had brought letters of introduction received her with the utmost courtesy and continued to treat her with unwavering kindness. Still, she pondered how it could be possible, within the highly civilized and artificial community of England, for a poor, unfortunate stranger without fortune or status to maintain intimacy with the rich and powerful. She thought it would be easier for a camel to pass through a needle's eye. The education Maria had received in the primitive society of the East proved but a poor preparation for the polished salons of Europe. Amongst her own people, the virtues of friendship and hospitality existed in perfection, but alas, the artificial accomplishments that adorned Western society were unknown to them.

One small solace Maria occasionally indulged in to break the monotony of her existence was a visit to the Zoological Gardens in Regent's Park, where she had the privilege of entering on Sundays thanks to the kindness of a subscriber to the society. The lonely, exiled condition of many of the poor, confined animals touched Maria's heart, and she felt a deep sympathy for their plight. Similar to her, numerous animals hailed from warm Asian regions and became isolated in an unfamiliar place. The situation of the lion, above all, painfully mirrored the feelings of Maria's own mind, as it hung its majestic head and passed its narrow cage, pining for the liberty and freedom of its native forests. She expressed these sentiments aloud, "Noble descendant of the lord of the forest! Like you, I live isolated, friendless, and in a foreign land."

The sight of the camel, Maria's childhood playmate and trusted companion, deeply affected her. The sight of that animal evoked a long train of cherished recollections from the happy hours of her earlier life. "Alas, poor beasts!" she said as she watched the camel and dromedary move slowly and sadly from one side of their enclosure to the other. "How different the chill, damp atmosphere in which you now live, compared to the brilliant skies and scorching sun that shone upon the plains of Asia! Here, it is true, you are spared the parching deserts and heavy burdens, the extremity of thirst. But how greatly you must prefer those hardships in your native clime to lingering out a useless, captive existence under these blighting, ungenial skies, your energies untasked and your sagacity untried!"

As Maria uttered these words aloud in Arabic, the camel turned its grave eye upon her with such a melancholy expression that she believed the creature understood her.

Maria's expectations of deriving an income by teaching her native language and translating Oriental works and manuscripts had not been realized. The situation would have been different if the nobleman who cared for her had not died. Maria had also suffered greatly in health since her stay in England, where her formidable enemy, the 'tic douloureux', had returned with a vengeance, occasionally subjecting her to such violent paroxysms that they nearly deprived her of reason.

Maria's sensitive mind suffered cold indifference in the West. For her, remaining calm and strong in the face of pain and calamity was considered heroic, but when applied to injuries caused by false friends, it became a cold, uncaring egoism that dulled her emotions and resulted in indifference towards all that was virtuous and good.

Maria's humble abode bordered a Roman Catholic chapel, and it was a sweet solace to her, when lying exhausted on her bed, to catch the pious strains of prayer and thanksgiving from the assembled congregation. She hoped those she knew would practice the lessons they heard and visit the poor and sick, but she waited in vain.

The efforts of her friends to recover some of her lost property and secure her a pension had, thus far, proved unsuccessful. Kindness and generosity from a noble person and a noble-hearted friend saved Maria from dire circumstances.

During her stay in London, Maria had been deeply indebted to the kindness of the noble and high-minded Chevalier Bunsen, whose talents and efforts were always at the service of those he could benefit, as well as the considerate attentions of his amiable lady. She had also been fortunate to become acquainted, through the kind introduction of Sir Robert Inglis, with the widow of the late Mr. Rich, the former British Consul at Baghdad, who had been a comforter in Maria's sickness and a consolation in her adversity.

As Maria reflected on her circumstances, she could not help but feel a sense of hope. Providence had, at last, cast her upon a shore whose inhabitants were renowned the world over for their noble institutions that provided relief for every ill to which humanity was subject. Here, the hungry were fed, the naked were clothed, and the destitute and homeless never failed to find shelter.

Filled with renewed courage, Maria resolved to await the

unfolding of events with patience and resignation. In the last page of her memoir, Maria earnestly prayed that no one reading the book's pages would ever endure such calamities. She then respectfully bids the British public farewell, for now, and ended her story.

In the appendix of her memoir were many letters written to Maria, two of which were the following:

Bishop of Alkoush's letter to Maria, written shortly after her father's death and translated from Chaldean. The Bishop explains that he has been in communication with an old friend, El Sheikh Abd El Ahad, regarding Maria's brother. Sadly, the Bishop must deliver the tragic news that Maria's brother has also been killed, meeting a similar fate as her father and the rest of the family. The Bishop acknowledges this is difficult news to share, but expresses confidence in Maria's strength and faith. He invites her to visit him if she is able. The letter is signed by the "humble Girgis, Bishop of Alkoush".

The second letter is from the Great Amira Hasni Jehan, the wife of Emir Beschir, writing from Beteddin to Maria in Rome, dated April 15, 1834. The Amira expresses deep sadness over Maria's absence, missing her gentle and pensive presence. She hopes they will be able to see each other again before the Amira passes away, if not on earth then in heaven. The Amira states she has understood everything in Maria's previous letter and that she is currently well in body and mind. She asks Maria to write to her as often as possible and prays that God will preserve her.

SECTION II

PROPHECY AND LAMENTATION:
OR, A VOICE FROM THE EAST.

An
Appeal to the Women of England,
on the Regeneration of the East, and the Elevation of Their
Sex to the Rights and Dignities, of Which They Have Been
so Long Deprived by Their Mohammedan Masters

By
The Babylonian Princess
Maria Theresa Asmar

London:
John Hatchard and Son, Publishers
187, Piccadilly
1845

Dedication

TO HER MOST GRACIOUS MAJESTY
VICTORIA,
QUEEN OF ENGLAND AND THE INDIES

The profound emotion that vibrates in my heart for the gracious protection afforded me by Your Majesty is much easier to feel than to express.

Had any doubts existed in my mind as to the success of the sacred task I have undertaken, "The Emancipation of the Women of the East," the sympathy of so great a Queen would have dissipated them.

In the glorious cause of Asia—my beloved country!—the voice of truth and enthusiasm speaks thoughts that burn and sink into the soul!

Oh, may the cry of liberty be heard from Albion's shores, to rend the chains that bind my father-land!—where all the jarring interests of contending states, lawless ambition, the avarice of individuals, a false prophet, and a false faith, have blasted the blossoms of domestic joy.

Where the sword of despotism ever thirsts for the blood of the innocent—and where the name of "Christian" is a byword and a reproach!

Oh—sacred land, once loveliest of all! may Albion's Queen thy just rights restore, and pluck the wild flowers from thy roofless homes!

May the voice of the lone orphan of the Emir, who is come from the ruined halls of her fathers, now silent and deserted, sink deep into the hearts of the women of the West!

Let but Albion's Queen, and the fair daughters of her sea-girt Isle be with me, and the cry of liberty shall yet be heard to arouse each noble impulse of the heart;—let them come, with the sacred fire of true religion, to give strength and virtue to the freedom of the East, and despotism will hide its hydra head. The daughters of the harem will cease to weep, and the light of gladness and joy will shine from soul to soul!

Civilization, commerce, liberty, and the arts, flow like a mighty ocean from Great Britain to the shores of my native country.

It was Your Majesty's subjects who first opened the port of Suez to the commerce of the Indies—it is Your Majesty's citizens who daily pass Mount Lebanon;—wherever we roam, the pilgrims of Albion are to be met with, diffusing benefits around by their example and industry!

Your Majesty's steamers were the first to float over the Euphrates and Tigris—proudly to brave the main from the borders of the Mediterranean to the Gulf of Persia. The flag of famed Britannia waves in every breeze, and by her powerful sway Asia shall be restored to liberty and happiness, for the intrepid energy, undismayed perseverance, holy enthusiasm, and moral force of the British character, surmount all difficulties!

The inspiring hope that your Majesty has kindled in my heart, affords a sweet consolation to my wounded spirit; and assures me, that the tree of life—of true religion, and of freedom, will, under the aid and wisdom of Divine Providence, be planted by your Majesty in my country,—that it will take root—flourish—and shelter beneath its wide-spread branches the lovely flowers of the East!

Ah! how many millions of Asiatic women are plunged in the depths of darkness—shrouded in ignorance by the customs of their country—bought and sold, as a mere article of furniture! Alas! what degradation of the Almighty's fairest gifts!—what strange perversion of pure Nature's laws! Knowledge can ne'er reach them, for their dark rulers are jealous even of the day which lights them.

Come, then, ye highly flavoured daughters of the West, and pluck the wreaths of ignorance from their brows, and the thorns of sorrow from their feet. Let the voice of the Great Spirit of British Freedom be heard in the Land,, and the fields of verdant hues, the groves, the valleys, the hills, and rocks sublime will echo the joyful sound.

Oh! thou mighty Queen that reigneth in glad palaces, ever surrounded by love and joy, remember, oh, remember the wronged women of the East—shut up within their living tombs, the Harems! hitherto surrounded by an impenetrable barrier raised by the united force of pride—vain ignorance—and selfishness—the absolute despotism of the master, over his slave!

The mind left fallow—and the soul untaught, they suffer wrongs as deadly as humanity can inflict—wrongs which blight the mind, and wither the soul's energies. Within their living tombs the blessed light of Christianity ne'er penetrates—the sacred volume of the Gospel never glads the heart, there all the divine laws of equality—pure love—and mental wisdom are cast into the devouring furnace of despotic power.

Albion, blest land of Liberty! long may the sacred fire of wedded love burn brightly in thy palaces and cottages! Where e'er that holy flame burns pure, content and true affection dwell—it is the cheering light that alike illumines the splendid hall and humble cottage—it is the bright meteor of heaven that sheds the atmosphere of Paradise around where e'er it beams.

Mysterious Providence! that hath so long permitted to my sisters so sad a fate! Oh, let Albion's Queen and daughters be the divine instruments in thy hands to raise the fallen sisterhood of Asia.

Alone have I quitted the land of the Patriarchs.—Alone,

have I abandoned the tombs of my martyred sires.—Alone have I come to implore the protection of the first Queen in the world—the Queen of Liberty and Justice!—the Queen of England, in favour of a once noble and free people!

In the blessed name of true Religion—the Holy Religion of Christ—in the name of Nature's dearest, tenderest sympathies,—in the name of all that gives life a charm, and age a hope, to ask, implore, to urge your gracious Majesty to succour, and befriend my sisters of the East.

The generous sympathy I have hitherto received from your Majesty, assures me of the future—and thus protected beneath the shadow of Britannia's sceptre I fear no evil. Gratitude now occupies my heart—and the lone daughter of the Patriarchs of Chaldea now joyfully and confidingly resigns herself and noble cause at the feet of the illustrious Queen of England,— who has so graciously deigned to accept this tribute of the gratitude, and high consideration felt in the heart of her most admiring and devoted Servant,

Maria Theresa Asmar,
Daughter of the Emir Abdallah

Prophecy and Lamentation, or A Voice from the East

Or,

A Voice From the East

Invocation

God, the Almighty Sovereign of the universe! who hath given me a heart to love Thee—a mind to contemplate and adore the wonders of thy mighty creation, and the celestial glory of thy majesty—all hail!—My heart and mind are all thine!

Glory to Thee—wisdom supreme and infinite! that made light to spring from the bosom of darkness! that made the firmament, and the waves of the ocean beneath, to reflect the stars on high! that made the night! and suspended in the blue vault of heaven the silvery moon, whose pale and melancholy light softens the gloom of darkness!

All hail! Divine Creator of the universe! that hath launched me into the eternity of life with a ray of thine intelligence! Divine Creator! who for impenetrable and mysterious reasons, hath permitted the monster of ignorance and fanaticism to extinguish the light of the East—my Country!

Hail glorious God! thou who keepeth the universe in harmony; thou, who from the heaven of heavens ordains that each celestial orb revolve in glorious and magnificent order around thy throne; oh! render tranquillity to my Country—to the Land of the Patriarchs!

Fill up the measure of thy beneficence—reunite her divided and unhappy people. Cast down the sword of the homicide from out the hands of her warriors! Give peace to Asia! Asia now barren, deserted, and weighed down beneath the scourge of despotism. Give unto her new life, and with that life, restore her ancient and once flourishing fertility! And we, Almighty Benefactor, we will aid thy bounteous designs by cultivating peace and civilization. We will not cease to observe and obey thy holy word, and daily to offer up new tribute of gratitude and praise!—Hail! hail! all hail!

I have traversed the vast deserts,—I have traversed the regions of Lebanon,—I have passed the stormy and tumultuous seas,—I have traversed Europe to call the women of the West to succour their sisters of the East; for at the voice of the women of the West the spirit of the ancient warriors of my country will revive, as when resplendent with purple and fine gold— yea! and if need be, at their voice, the swords and lances of the avengers of the Son of God, will shine as the stars of heaven; will rise, numerous as the white waves of the ocean which roll on the far-stretched shores of the grand Atlantic! The children of the destroying prophet shall fall like the dead leaves in autumn,— and, at the rising of the sun, their vanquished leaders be no more!

Arise, then, women of Nineveh,— of Babylon and Palmyra— yea, ye who added lustre to the fame of Ninus, Odemath, and Niacon, hover around the champions of our liberties, and restore us the honour due to our injured sex! Come ye shades of departed greatness, reanimate our fallen energies, to rebuild the ruined altars of our fathers!

Compatriots! abjure your errors, give the true hand of amity to the fair daughters of Albion, and God will be with you—will blot out your iniquities from beneath his malediction!

Women of the East and of the West, the oppressors will

tremble at your approach, as did Belshazzar in the presence of the Prophet of Chaldea, and of the wise and learned men of Babylon, when he saw the mysterious and prophetic hand-writing on the walls of the Hall of Festivity!

Yes! there are still happy days in store for my beloved Asia! The venomous poison of the serpent which stung her is well nigh exhausted. Arise, then, my sisters, achieve the conquest of our rights, broken and trampled down in our vast and extensive portion of the world! if an arrow pierce our bosoms, glorious will be our death,—for the Parthian who shall hurl the dart, will do so in his flight!

'Tis ours—the privilege to guide the armies of the powerful Christian who will upraise the broken walls of our palaces,—rebuild our fire-consumed cities, and wash out the life-blood stains which flowed from the devoted hearts of our young warriors, when the victorious infidel mowed them down as the wild grass!

Barbarians! they proclaimed to all the earth, perpetual desolation unto Asia! as if our sacred temples could be doomed by mortal, to be o'er-grown by noxious plants and briars throughout eternity? To be the dark retreat of serpents and hyaenas? as if the hungry vulture, and low eagle, should alone be seen to perch upon our battlements, and hover o'er the summit of our pyramids?

No—no! after the bloody mission of the sword, that sword so long unsheathed, the holy men of religion will come to unshackle the slaves attached to the chariots of the conquerors.

Religion! holy flame of heaven! that giveth true and steadfast principles of action—that cometh with sweet healing on its wings,—inspiring sentiments of peaceful harmony and love! Yes! 'tis religion must regenerate those sweet and lovely flowers of humanity, which then, like the stars in the firmament of night, shall shed a heavenly influence over the darkness of the Harem.

The sacred word of Christ shall upraise the sublime column of Truth in the face of day, to enlighten, to guide, to save, more glorious and universal far, than the vast asylum of St. Benedict for those suffering souls, who hope thereby to be restored unto the realms of light. In one century, Mahomet overspread and subdued even fair Persia inaccessible to the Roman Legions, as well as Palestine, Egypt, the Libyan Desert, Africa, and even a part of Europe.

Will not, then, the spirit of Christ, which sheddeth the perfect principle of harmony and of order, which animated and inspired the holy saints of old to teach us the pure light of truth and hope of immortality—yea, will not His unbounded power reconquer, and make fair an empire which succumbed to brutal force? Futile, indeed, were the vain efforts of the combatants to retain possession of the Holy City—alas! no human power was able to resist the fatal and overwhelming tide which flowed against Judea! But a new era, a new-born generation appeared in the land—illustrious—edifying—who in the silent study of religion will raise new and sublime monuments of sacred thought.

Eighteen centuries have passed—what hath man done? Henceforth, fair Christians, 'tis for us to be the saviours of Asia—at this moment she is encircled by a thousand Christian vessels, ready to change her dying winding sheet for the bright robe of righteousness, and to eclipse for ever the dominion of the Saracens. The first step is already made—the progress of Christianity is silently gliding into the empire of the Caliph, and it finds even now a Protector seated on the very throne of Mahomet.

God of Heaven! protect the unfortunate daughter of the Patriarchy of Chaldea in this her holy crusade! Oh! give her but one atom of that sacred, powerful persuasion which in former ages staggered the unbeliever,—staggered even those, who in the first ebullition of their frenzy caused the downfall of Syria, and laid Palestine at the feet of the conqueror! Oh! give her but a spark of that Divine eloquence to agitate the soul, but not overthrow it—to alarm, but not to wither!—to penetrate, but not to lacerate! Her mission is not to condemn, to lacerate, or to wither. No! but to dive into the hidden recesses of the heart, and to unroll the secret folds wherein the passions lie concealed; to the end of obtaining new and eternal life!

Father of Mercies! Graciously direct my energies to expose the evils and calamities which have laid waste my unhappy country, and accord me the power to make known the remedy to heal and save her! What country ever had so many disasters to repair? So many wounds to heal? Hatreds to extinguish? And divided interests to conciliate?

What though the study of modern constitutions may show us that those who liberally occupy themselves in morals, literature, and the sciences, are for the most part excluded from the government of public affairs, does that prevent exalted spirits from devoting their time, influence, and wealth, to philosophy, religion, science, and to the noble cause of ameliorating the condition of their fellow creatures? No! And the words, writings, and example of such men are productive of the most important and durable influence.

The fruit of study, the results of observation—are they lost because woman hath no voice in the tribune of her country? No! Doth she not possess the power to concentrate all the divine energies of the soul for the advancement and happiness of mankind, by giving her support and influence to the precious light of truth alone?

Revolutions! Grand, gigantic! Whose resistless sway hath changed the whole face of the globe; to whom are we indebted for these changes? To woman! To her unseen, often unknown, but deep and certain influence. Let woman, then, implore the light of heaven to guide her silent bias.

Hath not the Almighty ruler of events, ordained in his unerring wisdom, that the illustrious sceptre of great and powerful Britain, with India, and her countless millions,—the sceptres, too, of bright Hispania and of Lusitania,—should at this eventful period of the world be centered in the hands of three young Queens? O! Like the radiant day-star of the East, which guided the watchful shepherds to Messiah's birth-place, may they illumine the benighted people of my unhappy country, by rendering assistance to one of their own sex in so glorious a cause!

The Almighty, in his heavenly munificence, was pleased to create a world surpassing other worlds, more lovely and superb than those revolving mid the vast infinity of space! One chosen land therein he blessed beyond all others, on which the heavenly treasures of his grace he shed. This favoured region, blessed land, is Asia—Asia, in which he who dispersed the bright worlds in space, who groups the stars in heaven, hath suspended his golden and eternal lamp of light!

The East, fair country of fertility, of innumerable souls, phenomenon of greatness, is the birthplace of science, arts, literature, and commerce. From this all-creating region of vitality, where the Supreme Intelligence hath everywhere engraved his magnificent and gorgeous emblems, emanated the effulgent and immortal light of truth that burst forth to illumine and dispel the mists of ignorance which for so many ages had been coiling round the fane of pure religion.

Oh my country, never, perhaps, shall I see thee more! Can I abandon the blessed hope of rescuing Chaldea and Jerusalem?

Can Memphis have disappeared forever? Proud Babylon? Incomparable Palmyra? And all those mighty cities which, alas, consumed each other by the strife for power? Even here, reposed within the bosom of proud Europe, surrounded by the alluring charms of high refinement and politeness, can memory forget the heavenly gifts which the Creator in his munificence bestowed upon the children of the Sun? Can memory forget those children's woes?

But how, alas! shall I, lone daughter of the Desert, resist the mandate of omnipotent displeasure, which, like an avalanche, hath fallen on the erring cities of my nation, and left them desolate?

I look around; the sublime and solitary ruins alone remain of all those vast and splendid temples, noble palaces, and glorious works of art, no longer recognizable! But still, they are the wonder, pride, and admiration of the world.

Alas! When art or science now appears within our smitten land, it is as the rose which blossoms 'mid the tombs.

I have contemplated those lovely palms which still wave their lofty and majestic heads on the mountains of fair Eden, but the daughters of Tudor are no more; the Sacred harmony of the Prince of Song hath ceased to be heard in the land. Sweet poesy and the celestial harmony of past ages have fled to the palace whence they came, to heaven! In vain your thirsty soul will ask, in vain implore; the harps have ceased their melody!

All, all, alas! hath disappeared, and soon none will remain to weep or rejoice in the valleys of Syria!

My eyes are veiled by the mist of tears, for the barbarians have covered the country of the Lord with mourning, and the trembling light of the lamp of Jerusalem will soon cease to illumine the Christian of the Desert, unless some mighty power stretch forth its hand to feed the source!

Ask for Jesus of Nazareth? Alas! No voice replieth unto

your voice, save that of the lone echo 'mid the ruins of his Temples. Oh, my sacred Country! Thou art indeed but as a tomb! Thy glory—once encircled by the halo of righteousness—hath fled far from thee. 'Tis the thunder of Mahomed which now roars around the hill of Sion, where kneeling may be seen the false ministers of God! The scattered Christians can no longer meet to hear the Word within their sacred precincts, for the Rock of Sinai is now invoked by the adorers of Baal!

The virgins of Salem can no longer sing or weep at liberty; their brilliant tears suspended 'neath the silken lashes of their eyes, hang as the glittering dew-drops on the petals of the lily! But, courage, O lone daughter of the Desert! If the harp of David is no more, the soul-inspiring spirit of his muse still lives—will live for ever!

Then string your golden harps, fair daughters of the East, and sing your plaintive strains in presence of the world! Recount the frightful sufferings and calamities of thy oppressed and wandering people, less favored than the wolves—deprived as they have often been of a wild cave for shelter!

Awake, Great Women of the East, awake! O, come forth from your tombs, Zenobia! Semiramis! Esther! and Cleopatra! Yea, all ye noble and illustrious spirits of the past; the time hath come when Asia shall withdraw the veil that hath hidden her face for ages; as the young daughter of the East, when she enters into the Zezena of the harem!

Arise, then, ye Niobes of the Desert! Ye have sufficiently wept over the ruins of Asia, Assyria, and Mesopotamia! The prophecies of Isaiah, the son of Amos, are fulfilled. The desolation of Babylon—the confusion of Egypt—of her ancient Princes of Tyre—Jerusalem—and of Nineveh, have been accomplished!

The once magnificent city lay in ruins, its high, gigantic walls and proud, countless towers now barely recognizable.

The lovely hanging gardens, once a paradise, had vanished without a trace. The destroying angel had passed over, leaving only desolation in its wake.

Yet, the prophet's words foretold a joyful future for Christ's kingdom. It would blossom abundantly, adorned with the glory of Lebanon, Carmel, and Sharon. The blind would see, the deaf would hear, and the ransomed would return to Zion with songs of everlasting joy, their sorrow and sighing fleeing away.

The time of rejoicing was at hand, as the eyes of the infidels within the walls of Constantinople were opened to the light of God and the truth of Christianity. The lone exiles would soon return to their beloved homeland, singing praises to the Lord who had orchestrated the resurrection of the East.

Isaiah's prophecy spoke of the Egyptians turning against one another, their spirit failing, and a cruel lord ruling over them. The waters would fail, the rivers would dry up, and Babylon—the glory of the kingdom—would be laid waste, becoming like Sodom and Gomorrah, never to be inhabited again.

The denunciations of the immortal Prophet have been fulfilled. As the Lord has proclaimed, "from one moon to another, and from one Sabbath to another, all flesh shall come to worship before me." Egypt, under the protection of the Pasha's scepter, has been revived. Science and art have raised their heads, and their benign influence and sympathy are felt across the land of Miasraim, the son of Ham and the grandson of Noah.

The curse and scourge of war has been broken, fallen, and forever gone. Fathers will no longer draw swords against their children, nor children against their fathers. Neighbors will no longer wage war, for the entire nation feels the genial influence of a rising empire. Each day, the arbitrary rule of despotism, which once governed every aspect of social order, is weakened.

The profound wisdom of the mighty men who built

Alexandria, the Catacombs, the Labyrinth, the Obelisks, and the Pyramids, now eloquent in their ruins, will soon awaken in the souls of their descendants. The fair land of the East shall laugh in the renovated fertility of its natural luxuriance.

The King, the herald of this resurrection, has spread his firm, just, and protective scepter over the land where he has broken the iron rule of despotism. Instead of raising the hideous giant that has long oppressed and crushed the country, the admiring world sees Ali Pasha opening the portals of his empire to admit the rush of vast intelligence and knowledge that now overspreads the globe. Rapidly, his empire's barks ply the seas from the Persian Gulf to India, and the ancient names of the oppressors of the East adorn the prows of his huge steamers as they pass along the Tigris, Nile, Euphrates, the Levant, and the Mediterranean, to the wide oceans of the world.

In half a century more, the caravans of pilgrims will glide like the Sirocco over the gloomy sea of sand from Jerusalem to Diabekir, from Constantinople to the Gulf of Persia. Chariots, urged along by the impetus of fire, will traverse the Isthmus, astonishing the wondering population of the East. Asia, in a few short years, will possess a communication as rapid as the fire of heaven with Africa and Europe.

The time is quickly approaching when the religion of the Lord—that holy, pure religion which proclaims the nobility of science, inspires the soul to dedicate its powers for the betterment of humanity, and fosters peace, hope, love, charity, and goodwill among all people—will achieve the emancipation of the ignorant. Selfishness will be ashamed, and industry like a giant shall march onward with rapid strides to a glorious future. Woman will take her rightful place in social life, concord will reign in families, equity and justice will prevail in governments, and the pure religion of Christ Jesus will guide us to a glorious hereafter.

I am aware that it has been written that "Edom shall be a desolation" and "Every one that goeth by her shall be astonished." It has also been foretold that "Damascus shall wax feeble, anguish and sorrow shall overtake her" and "the city of price shall not be one of joy—her young men shall fall in her streets, and all the men of war shall be cut off." Concerning Kedar and the kingdoms of Harom, which Nebuchadnezzar King of Babylon shall smite, thus saith the Lord, "Arise ye, go up to Kedar, and spoil the men of the East." The Idomites are indeed dispersed on every side; their women, old men, and children are destroyed! Edom is no more—the shadow of darkness has passed over the land, and not a vestige now remains of all that once was there.

Amid her vast and lonely plains of sand, her barren, sterile mountains, the eye now roams in melancholy sadness—no living object cheers the sight, for there is no life there. Beneath a burning and devouring sun, a parched and sultry sky, where no oasis glads the eye but all is arid and bare, no soft, refreshing breeze from distant glades ever wafts its cool, reviving zephyrs to invigorate the weary pilgrim of the desert. No grass, no flowers—only skeletons and bones blanched 'neath the ardent rays of the hot sun, scattered o'er these regions of Death's empire, alone tell of the past.

Damascus, perhaps the most ancient city of the world, which could send twenty thousand men to the assistance of Hadadezer, the king of Zobah, has been crushed and feeble, according as the holy prophet hath foretold. But the sacred fire of Christian intelligence shall restore it—Damascus shall be made to float o'er the gulf of desolation, as a sure bark on the waves of a calm ocean.

When the Lord shall illumine the bright torches of art and science in Assyria, civilization and liberty will come, flying on angels' wings, and the spirit of Christianity and love, encircled by the halo of righteousness, shall replace the demon of discord and of darkness. Instead of the noise of war and fearful cries of men hurling their fellow mortals to destruction and to death, the groans of warriors and of victims sinking into the yawning grave, there shall be heard the songs of joy and plenty, calling the glad people to civilization and happiness.

The descendants of the sons of Ishmael await but the arrival of the children of the West to restore the riches of their ancient cities, to establish brotherly love and just equality in fair Arabia, which for so many centuries hath been separated from the rest of the world. Arabia, who in former times so gloriously and unaided sustained the conflict of dire war against the Assyrians, Persians, Greeks, and Romans when they poured their hordes of mercenaries o'er the land of thy Arcadian bowers to rob thee of thy liberty and fame, how nobly didst thou act, how faithfully thou hast preserved the purity and sincerity of thy manners, from the most distant date of time when thy merchants sold their incense and their perfumes in the port of Mirza, in the province of Tamer, even until now.

Oh, never forget the mighty power, the wisdom and heroic valor these people have evinced. Think, O ye, whose thousand superb vessels come to the port of Suez, ye who send your thundering cannon on the plains of Egypt, that these Ishmaelites and Kaderini, Nabathians and Hagarini, preceded you a thousand years ago, before Mahomet and his Caliphs revolutionized religion, politics, and despoiled our cities. The Lord of Hosts hath spoken it—the East shall be raised up, yea, soon shall rise high, as the sacred Scriptures have foretold—those holy writings whose sublime grandeur and simplicity surpassed the famed eloquence of Greece and Rome. Yes, the East shall be raised up in all her native majesty and beauty! Soon as the new light of heaven shall rise, its lustrous beams shall sparkle as a thousand fires, and the glorious rays its bright effulgence sheddeth shall dazzle and astonish, while it enlightens. Nathan, whose prophetic spirit saw afar the downfall of proud Nineveh, shall come again and sing of victory and resurrection to a people so long cursed for their sins! And Jeremiah too, whose deep eloquence wept o'er the misfortunes of his people, shall come to chant the praises of the Lord who hath redeemed the fallen.

What an enviable task it would be to restore the spirit of the Orientals to its original brightness! Once they become the children of the Lord, the high intelligence of their nature will assert its rights and lead them back to the pure springs of science and the native source of knowledge. It is well known that Asia in ancient times delved deeper into nature's hidden mysteries than even the learned men of Europe in these modern days.

We must not think that the superstitions of the East have always been. The learned doctors of the West daily discover that what are termed "new sciences and arts" are merely phenomena of nature that have existed since antiquity, known to the wise men of old, but have lain dormant for a time as faith among the masses was wanting. False creeds and errors have slowly entwined themselves around the fount of nature's pure truths, until the fair shrine within was scarcely visible.

Darkness and light each have their reign of power. In every land, day dawns and night succeeds, but the pure flame of heaven still burns unchanged. It is frail man who wavers, who wanders and strays from the light of nature and of God. Oh, what would we be if man could have quenched the holy rays of light forever? But no, God's punishments are tempered by his mercy. We have not valued the glorious gift of light that burst forth in the East—did the Almighty quench it or dim it? No, he merely withdrew it to the western shores, there to enlighten, warm, engender faith, hope, love, charity, and peace, good-will and fellowship unto all the world.

Come then, fair sisters of the West, trim your bright lamps from heaven's own holy source. The light must be refined, ethereal, pure, to illumine the darkness of the East. The voice of inspiration must return to Asia from lips that know no guile, and the halo of consistency and truth must shed their glory round. The Asiatics will then bend the knee before the holy altars of their fathers once more, and become the first men in the world again. Seas, mountains, and oceans shall not divide the sacred bonds of amity and love. Peace shall reign paramount, and the only strife shall be that of kindness.

The children of the Desert must be won; their spirits yield not to constraint or force. Assuage their weary pilgrimage with draughts from the deep wells of truth and knowledge. And what more speaking to the heart, sublime, majestic, and simple than the grand truths contained in Holy Writ? Its mildness is adapted to sympathize with and win their souls. The purity of its moral accords with the unsophisticated simplicity of their habits, and the sublime elevation of its maxims will find a responding chord in the dignified minds of the unconquered sons of the Desert. Unconquered by man, yet will they bend to the pure eloquence of Christian Truths.

That divine eloquence, that moral power, adapted for the happiness of man both here and hereafter—yes, it shall reign triumphant! Hushed be the strife of party, the intrigues of courts, all popular excitements cease. That divine eloquence needs not your aid. You work by passion, exciting the frailties of man's nature to obtain your ends, but Christianity subdues the rising waves of discord, softens the obdurate heart, and leads it on to heaven. Let but the Orientals feel the charm, and they will quickly sacrifice each selfish interest on the altar of their faith. The name of "Mahomet" may linger for a time in the mosques of the land, but Christ will reign in the hearts of her people.

Unfold to them the Holy Spirit of the Scriptures, sow but a grain of that high moral sense which it inspires and which is felt amid each nation of your empire. Let it but take root in the hearts of a few, and the sublime feeling will, like the electricity of heaven, vibrate to the million.

The Eastern peoples are by nature inclined towards melancholy, yet they also possess a bold and daring spirit. Melancholy leads them to reflect on the past, while their daring nature prompts them to look boldly towards the future and strive to elevate humanity to its rightful position. These seemingly contradictory sentiments are intricately blended within the Eastern character, and it is the latter, the daring spirit, that most demands our attention and cultivation.

It is you, the daughters of Europe, who must proclaim and teach the religion of Christ to your suffering sisters in the East. At your approach, pride and ignorance shall bow their heads, and the walls of the harem shall crumble. It is your duty to unveil the boundless treasures of the faith. Who is more worthy or capable than you, the daughters of Albion, who have been nourished since childhood on the sweet bread of mercy and grace, and who have been taught the very parables that Christ himself used to instruct his disciples?

Daughters of Albion, you are imbued with the sacred poetic fervor that fills the holy writings. Yes, you will save them, and they will hear and heed your call, following in the noble and virtuous path that your faith will guide them towards. You must explain the grandeur of the Almighty, who disposes and decrees all things, and how even the direst human malice can be turned to mercy when Heaven wills it. You must also showcase the just and liberal governments of the West, where intellect and reason, guided by moral discipline, work in harmony.

Albion, fair Albion, break the bonds of ignorance and slavery that the sultans have forged to enchain our sex! Our souls are strong, tempered in the furnace of adversity, and our sacred rights are inviolable and eternal, while our oppressors are weighed down by the curse of God, for "they have not known the Lord." The Almighty, who has placed the glorious celestial orb in the heavens, whose golden rays outshine the brilliance of diamonds and sapphires, has entrusted the noble task of emancipation to those who feel the sacred fire within their souls. Do not hesitate to undertake this sublime mission, which will bear the abundant fruits of happiness and virtue.

Before us lie millions of our fellow creatures, living in vile slavery, mere objects of trade and dishonor, who know not the sacred word of Christ. Come, then, and proclaim the equal rights of humanity in a land where man takes a slave as his companion, and where woman is esteemed solely for her beauty. For the very institution of marriage, as it exists in the East, is perhaps the greatest and most serious obstacle to the progressive amelioration of this people. The man who buys a woman reduces her to his slave, his prisoner, with no true sympathy between them. The voluntary principle, the charm that imbues the simplest acts of free affection, is an exotic of the Western shores, and it does not bloom in the East. Can a social state of government truly flourish where the laws are so opposed to nature and justice? Nay, a social state must be based on the equitable rights of all.

When the oppressive reign of brutal force comes to an end and the holy banner of Christianity is hoisted, those people of the Desert will cast off their errors just as the lion of the forest shakes the dew from its mane.

The temple of the Prophet of Mecca already totters, rent on every side. And each effort made to preserve its crumbling structure only seems to hasten its downfall.

Read the signs of heaven and heed the call.

The Chinese have shown more subtlety in their customs

and treatment of women. They have granted them a semblance of liberty, but through the mutilation of their feet, have compelled them to seclusion—a mutilation inflicted voluntarily. Oh, fragile and trusting woman, what arts and flattery have ensnared you, with what ingenious skill has man blinded and bound you!

But the Oriental woman enjoys even fewer social rights than any other. Her reasoning faculties having been left uncultivated for centuries, she is of course of no use in improving and advancing the social order of the community.

Lacking any understanding of laws, liberty or equality, she can feel no rightful resentment at the injustice and corruption to which she has been subjected for so long.

Knowledge and science can only thrive in the soil of liberty and reciprocity. And woman, if she loses her mental powers, is soon despised and degenerates into a mere machine.

Oh, my fair sisters of the East, what power can raise you from the degradation of your wretchedness? Religion answers, truth. Abandon then the paths of darkness and corruption, and enter the bright realms of hope and peace!

Antiquity has bequeathed us many a name exalted by the greatness of the deeds of its noble owner—names that have lived for centuries and will live for ages more, as long as virtue can appreciate and the world endures. But the celestial brightness of Christianity will shine throughout eternity.

Then arm yourselves with courage, and sing unto the Lord. For He will remember His mercy and truth, and all the ends of the earth shall see the salvation of our God.

To the East then! Come, it is the will of heaven.

I need not tell you, fair sisters of the West, that it was one from among us who first proclaimed the words of the Lord amidst the Franks when they established themselves in Gaul.

It was a woman who achieved the destruction of

Mussluman power in Spain—it was a woman who, by her judgment and presence of mind, saved Peter the Great when surrounded by a vast and formidable army on the banks of the Pruth—it was a woman who in former times humbled the pride of the Sublime Porte, and who added the territories of Georgia and Taurida to her empire; who advanced the civilization of rude Russia by her wisdom, and whose mighty name resounded throughout the earth.

When woman does not occupy her rightful place in the social order, it is because the brutal force of despotism has enslaved her. And man, who has thus outraged woman's rights, must answer for it to his Maker.

Alas, my beloved country of Asia has fallen into a state of disarray. Your rulers and soldiers have consumed everything, leaving only destruction and withered land in their wake. There is nothing planted to restore your prosperity.

The people live under the oppressive rule that threatens their very existence, as their homes are pillaged. Corruption surrounds them, and the future looks bleak—their only hope lies in the West, where the bright ray of liberty may dispel the darkness that has fallen over the East.

The persecuted Christian fathers can only look upon their children as victims, doomed to suffer the same fate as their predecessors. They have ceased to feel allegiance to their rulers or country, for the East has been forsaken and all that was righteous has been destroyed.

Yet the moment has come when the Supreme Being, who watches over the suffering and oppressed, will bring solace and comfort to his devoted followers. The task may be difficult, but the mission is grand and glorious. With unwavering zeal and determination, great deeds can be accomplished.

Consider the feats of the women of the Orient—Semiramis, the Queen of Assyria, who followed her husband Ninus, the general of King Ninus, into battle. When the king died, Semiramis succeeded him, setting an example for her son Ninus. Leading her troops, this great woman extended her conquests as far as Ethiopia and India.

During the height of the Assyrian Empire, Semiramis subdued Libya, Media, and Egypt, even engaging in personal combat against King Strabobatus. Upon her return, she built a magnificent tomb in memory of Ninus. She transformed the mountain of Bagestone into statues, lowered hills, and constructed grand roads throughout her empire. Semiramis also tamed the Euphrates River, erecting monumental dykes to prevent devastating floods.

Though some may claim that Semiramis tarnished her legacy, I cannot accept such accusations. How can one with such greatness, magnanimity, and nobility of spirit be capable of cruelty and meanness? She who leveled mountains and conquered nations, surely could not have been driven by base passions. Alas, the deeds of the great are often slandered by the envious.

If Semiramis lived in our time, she would have harnessed the arts and sciences of the world, causing a flourishing of knowledge and prosperity within her empire. Will you, too, not strive to emulate her feats of leadership, conquest, and wise governance? You, who have the divine light to guide you, should not be content to remain inferior to one who shaped the course of nations.

Semiramis lived a remarkable life, marked by her great works and accomplishments. She possessed the power to build, conquer, and create, but lacked the ability to conserve. This weakness in her strength led to the downfall of the greatness of antiquity, which perished under the deadening rule of despotism.

✤

As I sat alone on the broken columns of the Temple of Belus, memories of my youth glided through my mind. I felt the secret, silent voice of wisdom, which filled me with a burning thirst to search for its waters and drink from its fountains, so that my soul might be instructed and expand like the bright flowers of the East. Oh, how many mysteries I might have penetrated and unravelled, had I but known the true value of these ruins! Thought tried to withdraw the veil, but erringly, as I sighed for knowledge and the power to roam, forgetting in that moment that even to think was considered treason against the oppressors of my country, whose victims were not permitted such freedoms.

Alas, the sad remembrance! It recalls the days of my poor martyred father, brothers, and uncles. May peace be upon their honored shades and their blessed remains. Their lovely daughter will not see the land of her nativity and their holy tombs until the blessed day when she shall go there to display the crown of immortality and sing the resurrection of the Lord.

Zenobia, Queen of Palmyra and descendant of the renowned Hassan, King of southern Mesopotamia, governed many of the Oriental provinces of the Roman Empire from the death of Odenath to the day of her captivity. When Palmyra was the capital of the East, from the Euphrates to the Mediterranean and from the Arabian Desert to the center of Asia Minor, Zenobia commanded the admiration of her contemporaries. Emperor Aurelius, when addressing the Senate of Rome, acknowledged the greatness of this woman, who had conquered nations, given battle to the "invincible" heroes of proud Rome, and built a magnificent city on the borders of the Euphrates, whose columns rivaled the grandeur of the monument to the Hero of Trafalgar. Zenobia's life was divided between combating her country's enemies, receiving lessons on civilization, and governing a vast empire, balancing the application of political sciences and the fine arts to advance and beautify the lovely Palmyra, only to have it laid waste and desolate by the wandering Arabs, the Roman legions, the Persians, Armenians, and the devastating Saracens. Yet, Zenobia triumphed through her wisdom, prudence, courage, and the greatness of her genius. Honor and glory to this Eastern woman, beautiful and valorous, respected for her dignity and virtue, without parallel, save that she had been perfect, had she been a Christian.

I might also recount the story of Esther, the daughter of Abehad. Among the fair stars who governed the Roman Empire, she remained spotless despite the vicious and corrupt court that surrounded her. Of all the glorious daughters of the East, why enumerate the proofs of female heroism? If the women of my country have now become machines, it is to despotism that we owe the destruction of our natural energies. For wherever woman is placed high in the ladder of social life, there does she bloom and flourish. There do the pure, devoted feelings of the heart attach themselves, and there do the mental energies expand towards perfection. For nature has given to woman the most delicate and refined organs, and the most pure and brilliant imagination, whereby to organize, arrange, and harmonize the grand whole.

It is true, man has more strength and power to enforce his purpose. But let that power be used in pure accordance with the Messiah's doctrines, and the influence of woman will then be felt and cherished as the best boon of Heaven. Is not the greatest kingdom of the earth, the one that has broken the chains of slavery and will be the first to give liberty to commerce, governed by a Christian queen? An honor to her sex, and the bright crown she wears, shadowing her people's rights beneath the mantle of purity and truth. Her vigorous hand gives strength to the weak, and she never lifts her sword but in a just and righteous cause. Honored, thrice honored, and thrice blessed is the land that owns her sway!

Oh, my beloved sisters of the East, how are ye fallen! How slavery has dimmed the bright gems of Heaven! But Albion's daughters from the Western Isle will come to aid you, wrapped in the glorious robe of Christianity. The valleys of Zion shall again echo the joyful sounds of the harp and tabor, and the imprisoned daughters of the harem, like Albion's fair daughters, happy and free, shall chant again their holy melody, blithe as the birds that pour their morning lay, pure as the dew-drop sparkling on the spray.

✢

The power of Mahomet is melting and passing away before the Sun of Righteousness! The children of the fertile plains of Asia, numerous as the leaves of the forest when summer is in its richest verdure, shall, at the approach of the Christian Aurora, again crowd unto the banks of Jordan—the gazelle shall bound along the little hills of Judah. The turf shall again become green, and flowers shall cover the tombs of our fathers! The day of desolation has passed away, and the day of glory has commenced. The time marked out by the Omnipotent for the holy mission is at length arrived. Come, then, let us unite, and in the fields of the East celebrate the triumph of the Lord! Let us thank God for the privilege and for the liberty which He renders to His people. Glory, joy, and happiness will crown the day when the banner of Christianity is unfurled.

The time approaches when the dew of resurrection shall wet the front of the Arab, who, silently extended on the sand by the side of his tent, shall arise and come forth from the shadow of darkness and of error. And like one who has burst his bonds, shall cry with a loud and joyful voice, "Oh Liberty, Virtue, and true Religion, ye are come to glad the lone Arab of the Desert, and he will become the child of God—yea, of the God of the Christians! Glory—honor—and praise—hallelujah on hallelujah, be unto the Lord for ever and ever."

The End

IN MEMORIAM

A Closer Look at Maria Theresa Asmar

I t is important to understand the context and motivations
behind Maria Theresa Asmar's perspectives, why her writings often took a critical stance towards the Arab world and
Islam. Asmar was an outspoken advocate because at her core
she was a kind-hearted woman driven by a deep passion for
justice and religious freedom. The persecution her family and
fellow Christians faced in the region heavily colored her worldview and the rhetoric she employed.

It is also crucial to recognize that Asmar was a product of
her time—the nineteenth century was an era of heightened religious fervor and zeal across the Western world. Asmar held
an unwavering belief that Christianity, with its promises of
liberation for women, represented the most righteous and enlightened faith. She was sharply critical of practices like veiling
and the confinement of women to harems that she witnessed
in Muslim societies, viewing them as oppressive restrictions
on female autonomy. Her writings reflect the tensions of her
historical moment. Even as she highlighted the very real challenges faced by religious minorities, she, like generations of
Chaldeans, peacefully coexisted with Muslims and people of
other backgrounds, and she was a loyal citizen of whatever
land she lived in.

Maria Theresa Asmar was a courageous, complex, and

deeply passionate individual, driven by a sincere desire to defend the rights and freedoms she held most dear. Her legacy, controversial as it may be, warrants careful examination and contextualization within the social and political currents of nineteenth century Europe and the Middle East. It even warrants that examination in current times.

www.ingramcontent.com/pod-product-compliance
Lightning Source LLC
Chambersburg PA
CBHW030531270626
47155CB00024B/2700